Dear Little Black Dress Reader,

Thanks for picking up this Little Black Dress book, one of the great new titles from our series of fun, page-turning romance novels. Lucky you — you're about to have a fantastic romantic read that we know you won't be able to put down!

Why don't you make your Little Black Dress experience even better by logging on to

www.littleblackdressbooks.com

where you can:

- ♥ Enter our **monthly competitions** to win **gorgeous** prizes
- ♥ Get **hot-off-the-press** news about our latest titles
- ♥ Read **exclusive** preview chapters both from your **favourite** authors and from brilliant new writing talent
- ♥ Buy **up-and-coming** books online
- ♥ Sign up for an essential slice of romance via our **fortnightly email** newsletter

We love nothing more than to curl up and indulge in an addictive romance, and so we're delighted to welcome you into the Little Black Dress club!

With love from,

The *little black dress* team

Five interesting things about Marisa Heath:

1. I often buy second-hand or high-street jackets and cardigans then put different expensive-looking buttons on them to give them a designer look.

2. I am a serious Prince fan and love all of his music and films – if I had the time, didn't have a boyfriend, was a foot shorter and lived in America I could potentially be his stalker.

3. I love my dog and talk to her constantly like some mad old lady. She listens attentively but only if there's food involved.

4. I grew up in Indonesia and had a rather bohemian childhood which I highly recommend, except it has left me with an expensive desire to travel all the time.

5. I used to rescue all sorts of animals and take them home much to my parents' horror when I was young, ranging from a magpie to mice and even spiders which I made little houses for.

Perfect Image

Marisa Heath

little
black
dress

First published in 2009 by
LITTLE BLACK DRESS
An imprint of HEADLINE BOOK PUBLISHING

A LITTLE BLACK DRESS paperback

1

Cataloguing in Publication Data is available from the British Library

ISBN 978 0 7553 5006 3

Typeset in Transit511BT by Avon DataSet Ltd,
Bidford-on-Avon, Warwickshire

Printed and bound in Great Britain by
Clays Ltd, St Ives plc

Headline's policy is to use papers that are natural, renewable and
recyclable products and made from wood grown in sustainable forests.
The logging and manufacturing processes are expected to conform to the
environmental regulations of the country of origin.

HEADLINE PUBLISHING GROUP
An Hachette UK Company
338 Euston Road
London NW1 3BH

www.littleblackdressbooks.com
www.headline.co.uk
www.hachette.co.uk

Acknowledgements

Publishing a book can never be done without a small army of people behind an author. Firstly there needs to be an interest in reading which was developed by my parents, then there is the person who encourages the writer to write in the first place and supports their wild dream of getting published which in my case is my boy-friend David. Then there are those who act as sounding boards which for me were Saskia Heath and Hannah Park. To do anything with that completed manuscript you need a literary agent and that was Sarah Such who believed in me and was willing to spend her time and energy to get a book deal. The final stages of preparing the manuscript, getting a front cover and putting the book on the shelves comes down to the team at Little Black Dress who have been fantastic. To those people I would like to give my sincere thanks.

Paris was a city that was both beautiful and ugly, magnificent architecture stained with fumes and dirt, and pretty cobbled streets where pungent drains gurgled furiously. Patisseries displayed mouth-watering treats, people stared shamelessly, and stylish women smoked endless cigarettes whilst art galleries sat on every corner. It truly was a jungle of culture and sophistication. Each fashion capital was different. Models needed to be able to work them all in order to succeed in a competitive industry where stunning girls came from all over the world. In a proudly ruthless city like Paris, only the fittest survived. The models had to be at the top of their game: thin to the point of invisibility, impossibly beautiful (although the definition of what constituted beauty changed all the time), permanently elevated in heels, and with skin as thick as a rhino's to take the constant rejection.

While the image of an international model's life looked so perfect and glamorous, behind the scenes it was not quite the same, endlessly traipsing across cities on castings and go-sees in the hope of booking a job. Stopping to cross a road, Katrina recalled the woman at French *Vogue* flicking through her book barely even looking at the pictures and not bothering to feign an interest. Then there had been the man for the Japanese catalogue casting who had measured every inch of her and made her try on six equally peculiar outfits before saying that they were actually looking for a blonde. And the go-see for the photographer who was so important that he hadn't even bothered to turn up! Maybe for one in every thousand girls modelling was fun and glamorous. But as Katrina had surveyed the room of waiting models that day, all tall, skinny and striking, she doubted any of them enjoyed tramping round Paris, endlessly being turned down.

The only thing certain was that Katrina had really got to know the city after walking around all day using a useless mini-map and poor GCSE French, which meant eating the same *baguette avec fromage, s'il vous plait* every day. She crossed the road to avoid the advances of a drunken man who was leering at her and let her hair fall over her face. She tried to calm herself down, taking deep breaths in an attempt to suppress tears of self-pity. It was so rare that she let herself get upset; after all, she had loved the idea of being a model and travelling round the world. Living in Paris should have been the most amazing experience ever. Yet the reality was day after day of rejection, still with no job, while her agency account began to run up debt and the money she had earned in London was slowly being depleted by the expensive French capital. It was such a disappointment.

Katrina walked towards her hotel utterly exhausted, with aching feet from her high heels and a sharp pain in her shoulder from lugging her portfolio round all day. She passed by a very glamorous and polished model being dropped off by a chauffeur outside a much smarter hotel. She had on full make-up and styled hair, suggesting she had been on a shoot, and wore extremely fashionable and expensive clothes. Katrina cast an admiring eye over the girl; she doubted *she* had to do the cattle-market castings and the low-paid editorials. A man pulled up in a Ferrari, leapt out and greeted the girl with a kiss before they walked hand in hand through the hotel doors. Katrina carried on her way, feeling the heel of her shoe bending, threatening to snap in retaliation for the punishment it had taken that day.

She reached the familiar entrance to her own hotel. The manager was chasing the phone bill money, so she had to hover outside for ages until he disappeared into his office before sprinting past reception and into the shaky old lift. Her room was quiet and stuffy with the summer heat and had no air conditioning. Katrina was not successful enough to warrant a decent hotel; the Parisian modelling agency put all their girls who weren't top models in cheap hotels whilst charging them exorbitant prices and profiting from their lack of experience. Models had very little control over the money they earned, as expenses were deducted from their agency accounts just as soon as cheques were paid in. With rent, bikes, flights and photo prints taken off, it was always an achievement to be in credit. Katrina dropped her bag amidst the mess covering the bed and went in search of the other girls staying there.

Lydia and Andrea were sitting in their room two doors down moaning about a casting they had gone to for swimwear. Katrina perched on Andrea's bed, painting her toenails with hot-pink MAC polish in a vain attempt to make her angry-looking feet a bit more attractive.

'Honestly, they were so rude! The designer just gave me filthy looks and said my hips were a "leetle too beeg"! Plus the photographer had me strip to my underwear and do poses like I was on a beach! It was so embarrassing!' Lydia exclaimed, trying to pinch fat on her non-existent stomach. 'Will you come to the gym in the morning, Andy?'

'I have a job tomorrow for Deutsche *Elle*,' Andrea announced in her thick German accent. 'I will be very early flying to Berlin and then I go to my family in Frankfurt and eat good food.' She stood up and fanned herself with a magazine, then pulled her top off to reveal an already perfectly toned stomach.

'Damn, that means another new room-mate.' Lydia flicked through a copy of British *Vogue*. 'When are we ever going to feature on these pages and have enough money to stay in a decent place? We don't have long; soon we'll be too old, according to the modelling industry.' She stopped and peered closely at the magazine. 'Oooh! God, he is gorgeous!'

'Who?' Katrina lifted her head from toenail painting. Lydia showed her a picture of a very good-looking man staring intensely into the camera. 'Who is he?'

'Dominic Cayley, the actor. It says here that he's in Paris shooting scenes for a film. Imagine bumping into him!'

Katrina grinned wryly. 'Probably quite unlikely, as I doubt he'll be staying in this hole and frequenting the local patisserie. I have absolutely no doubt that he'd fall instantly in love with you if he was, though, and you'd live happily ever after!'

Lydia threw the magazine at Katrina, yelping as it knocked over a mug of ancient tea. Leaping off the bed to pick it up, she then sent an ashtray of cigarette butts flying and started laughing hysterically. Katrina couldn't help but laugh too and began to feel less miserable.

The prehistorically old telephone rang loudly and Andrea leant over, pulling it off the table with an almighty crash.

''Ello?' She stifled her giggles. 'Yah, she is here. Hold it one moment, right.' Andrea passed the phone to Katrina. 'It is for you. I do not have an idea how this very strange man knew you were in here.'

Andrea made a disgusted expression at Katrina whilst lighting a cigarette. The manager was well known by all the girls for being a bit of a pervert with his habit of bursting into rooms uninvited at random times to do 'safety' checks. He had taken a particular shine to Andrea for the simple reason that she wasn't British.

Katrina grimaced back at her and took the receiver. 'Hello?' she said tentatively.

'Hi, darling it's Rosanna here!' a high-pitched voice trilled. 'How are you, sweetie?' Without waiting for an answer she continued, 'I've flown over for the night and I'm calling to invite you out. I've got Rebecca and Sarah and you must make Lydia come too. An agency night out!'

Rosanna was the owner of Source Model Management, who represented Katrina in London. In her mid-forties, although she had been 'thirty-nine' for the last three years, she was all polish and glamour with fortnightly trimmed shoulder-length caramel hair and lashings of mascara. She continued to pour her remarkably toned body into leather trousers and a variety of brightly coloured silk shirts come winter or summer. Rosanna had a habit of totally ignoring people she knew during the day before becoming their best friend at night after a few drinks and a couple of lines of coke. She was critical, demanding and incredibly bitchy. Katrina's immediate reaction was to decline the invitation, yet that would annoy Rosanna, who liked to make an appearance every so often to take her 'girls' out for a treat. Ultimately if she didn't go she could jeopardise any cash advances from the agency account, or even worse, lose her contract.

'Okay, why not? Great,' she replied resignedly, cursing the manager under her breath for putting Rosanna through to the wrong room. 'I'll tell Lydia about it and we'll be there.'

'Super, darling!' Rosanna's voice gushed down the telephone. 'I have a driver, so I'll pick you both up in an hour. Bye for now!' She ended the call before Katrina had a chance to ask her what an agency get-together would entail.

Katrina informed Lydia of the arrangements then slunk back to her own room to get changed. She pulled on a pair of clean jeans and a strappy black top stolen from a shoot before emptying her purse out on the bed. She had only fifty-four euros left for the entire week, so she hoped the evening wasn't going to cost much. Her whole childhood had been about tight budgets, seeing as it was just her mother's small salary from her charity job and her father's child support to live off. She was good at being careful with money, but the agency allowance of seventy euros a week was difficult to live on when she had to buy skincare, food, travel and any other necessities with it. If she spent that money on a couple of drinks this evening, she would have to call her mother to ask for a loan, and she hated doing that. The whole point of modelling had been for Katrina to make loads of money so she could buy her mother nice things, not beg for emergency handouts.

'Come on, Katkins, it's time to go.' Lydia appeared at her door. 'Surely you're champing at the bit to enjoy a night out with the boss!'

Katrina grinned wryly before pulling her knotty hair back into a ponytail, rubbing the black mascara smudges from under her eyes, and slipping her feet into a pair of pink Miu Miu heels that belonged to her room-mate.

Rosanna was very drunk already, and air-kissed Lydia and Katrina whilst fiercely declaring that she had missed them, which Katrina very much doubted. She sat in the back of the car quietly listening to the others rattling on, and feared that there seemed to be a long night planned, with a variety of different places and people needing to be seen.

The first stop was at the apartment of an owner of a New York model agency who was having a party for no particular reason other than he had a lot of money to throw around. Despite his name being Paulo, Rosanna kept calling him Fabrizio, much to his obvious fury. Paulo was a typical Silverado, with slicked grey hair, fake tan verging on orange, bleached blinding white teeth and the ability to lift one eyebrow in what he considered to be a suave manner. Katrina suspected he drove a convertible Bentley with cream leather seats while wearing tortoise-shell Armani sunglasses. The most surprising thing about him was his silver Gucci jeans, which were so tight Katrina had no idea how he managed to sit down or how he had ever got them on in the first place. There were delicious things to eat, though, and she scoffed four pieces of chocolate cheesecake. Nobody else was eating; they were too busy smoking, taking drugs and staying thin. She supposed that was what she was meant to be doing, but it just seemed so pointless.

After leaving Paulo's apartment, Rosanna led them on to a trendy bar for a designer's birthday celebration. In true fashion-party style, a rich, ancient man with a thin, lizard-like face cornered Katrina. He was wearing a bright green Versace shirt and an eighteen-carat Bulgari watch with so many diamonds it almost blinded her every time he moved his arm.

'I do hate these kinds of parties. I have to come along every so often just to socialise.' The lizard leant close to Katrina in a conspiratorial fashion and pushed a strand of hair away from her face, failing to notice her sickened expression. 'I must say, you're quite a pretty girl. Do you want to come for lunch with me tomorrow? I know a lovely little bistro.'

Katrina leapt about two feet in the air and quickly thought of a plausible excuse. 'I can't: I'm going back to London for work.'

'That's a great pity.' He fixed his predatory eyes on another potential prey and began to slide off. 'Maybe another time . . .'

Katrina breathed a sigh of relief and turned to her left, coming face to face with a very beautiful male model leaning against a wall looking lost in thought. He had an intense frown and a clenched jaw, portraying the perfect picture of man contemplating the meaning of life. Not sure whether to interrupt his concentration, Katrina smiled at him. He was at least better than a million-year-old lizard. Without changing his expression he said, 'Great party. Are you one of Portia's friends?'

'No. I'm more of a friend of Mercedes,' she joked. He looked even more confused.

'Oh, who's that? I haven't met her. Are you a model?' He spoke without moving and continued to clench his lovely jaw determinedly.

'Yes. Are you okay? You seem a little stressed,' Katrina said curiously, catching Lydia's eye across the room and making an exasperated face.

'Well, everyone always tells me I look best when I'm serious; it makes my jaw more defined, and if I clench it then my cheekbones look better too. This is a working party for me. You never know when someone important is going to see you, and I heard that Testino might show up, and maybe Giorgio Armani too.' The male model returned to his pose, leaning against the wall, his eyes narrowed as if he was looking for danger on the South African plains.

Katrina wondered if there were any normal men around. Perhaps she should just give up and forget about finding a boyfriend. Where were the good-looking, vaguely intelligent, not-too-old men that everyone promised existed? They weren't in Paris or London if her attempts to find them were anything to go by. She excused herself from the stupid male model, noticing that Rosanna and her entourage were heading for the exit.

'What a fantastic party!' Rosanna clutched Katrina's arm as she fell off her Jimmy Choos on the way out. She screeched wildly just as a herd of Italian men whizzed by squashed into a Lamborghini.

The next stop was a club called Le Cave, which was dark and packed with sweaty dancing bodies. Female models were allowed in free as it encouraged wealthy men to spend lots of money. Tall, stunning girls of an average age of eighteen sat in clusters like wide-eyed deer with long twig legs, whilst overweight, greying men in suits plied them with alcohol and drugs. Weapons disguised as generosity. There were few conversations, as barely anyone spoke the same language; instead communication was through gestures and the waving of champagne bottles, Cristal and Dom Perignon shouting loudest. Katrina surveyed the seedy scene, watching how the girls behaved like geishas towards the men, seeking admiration, free drinks and hopefully a future date. Money and fame meant everything in a world obsessed with image. Sometimes she wished she could just join in, enjoy it and accept that she was a disposable commodity that needed to get everything she could before being pushed aside for the next one. However, she knew the reality of it was superficial and cruel, and as much as she wanted to be a model, she didn't want the 'extras' that came with it. She declined the glasses of champagne and the suggestions of private parties and sat waiting for the others to be ready to go.

Unfortunately by the time Rosanna was ready to leave the club it was nearly four a.m. Lydia had to be dragged off a dark-eyed Italian whose *'ciao, bella'* and skin-tight T-shirt had certainly paid off that night, judging by his proud smirk. Rosanna dropped them off outside the hotel with lots of shrieks and promises of lunch. The manager unlocked the front door with a murderous expression. When Katrina got to her room, her electronic key wouldn't work, which he refused to believe. A whispered argument commenced that resulted in him swearing in a combination of French and English, waving his arms about wildly and finishing off by throwing an ashtray at her. Oh, the glamour of being an international model, thought Katrina as she finally got into the tiny stuffy room. This was not the luxury suite, gorgeous men and designer dresses that her friends back home joked with her about. If they could see the reality! She crawled into bed, noting that Lauren was not back for the third night in a row. Falling asleep almost instantly, she had a very vivid dream that she was being chased by a giant lizard.

2

Waking to the sound of the next-door room playing loud German techno, Katrina remembered that she didn't have any castings or in fact anything to do that day. No requests by fashion editors, no go-sees for photographers, definitely no job and no money. She slid under the covers to escape the light peeping through the curtain and fell asleep once more.

At about 6.30 p.m. she emerged from the duvet feeling disgustingly lazy and annoyed with herself that she wasn't motivated enough to have gone exploring. It was Paris after all and she was lucky to be living in such an amazing city. She crawled out of bed and put her foot in something squidgy. Leaping up, she found a piece of mouldy pizza stuck to it, and quickly shook it off in disgust. She really was going to have to tidy up, but at this moment that would involve more effort than she could summon up.

After a shower with tepid water, Katrina studied her reflection in the steamy mirror as she tried to comb the knots out of her long auburn hair that fell straight over her shoulder blades. If only it was wavy or curly instead of being so boring. Maybe she would work more if she had sexy Giselle-like hair with sun-kissed streaks or was just more conventionally and obviously beautiful. There were different types of model: incredibly beautiful; pretty with glowing skin and a perfect smile; edgy; cute and fresh; girl-next-door or downright sexy. Katrina fell into the edgy category but she had never thought of herself as a beauty. At school the other girls had laughed at her lanky body, which the uniform drowned, and none of the boys had fancied her; 'Frogface' had been her nickname because of her wide mouth. Her crushes had gone unreciprocated and she hadn't even experienced her first kiss until she was seventeen, shortly after being spotted by Source Model Management while shopping with her mother in Covent Garden. She hadn't quite been able to believe her ears when the agent spoke of her 'modelling potential'; at the time it had sounded so special and exciting, but now she knew it just meant another tall, skinny girl struggling to get work.

Katrina defiantly smeared concealer over her face in an attempt to hide the splatter of freckles across her nose and cheeks. Staring back at her were the strange slanty eyes that photographers said gave her a feline apperance. They were the only part of her appearance that she liked, and yet they had been inherited from her father, whom she barely ever saw. He was too busy with his other family and Katrina had never experienced family life herself. She hardly knew her half-sisters and her father only just about remembered to send her a birthday card, usually a few days late with a cheque for fifty pounds. Whilst lots of the other models were always sobbing into their pillows about being homesick and missing their families, Katrina didn't even know what there was to miss. That was why she never minded being away from home and living out of a suitcase, a very positive trait for a model. It had always been just her and her mother, but she'd always been independent and had looked after herself since leaving home at eighteen for university. Sometimes she felt guilty that her mother was alone whilst her father had his family. She tried to go back home as often as possible, and the plan was that one day she would repay her mother for all her hard work by giving her the money from some huge advertising campaign. Some hope there was of that! Still, she had to give it a go, and maybe something surprising would happen . . .

There was a loud knock at the door.

'Katrina, it's me, I've bloody well forgotten my keys again and the bloke at reception is pretending not to speak any English. Please be in!'

Gingerly holding a towel around her, Katrina stepped over the mass of clothes on the floor and clicked open the latch on the door. Lauren burst into the room, spilling shopping bags all over the place.

'Damn!' she swore as she got her heel stuck in a cup left abandoned on the floor. Lauren always made a dramatic entrance everywhere she went, whether it was a celebrity-filled party or a ladies' toilet. She was everything that people thought a model should be: beautiful, slim, sexy and designer-clad. It was impossible to miss her, all five foot eight of lad-mag fantasy with bouncy blond hair that fell down to the small of her back and evenly tanned skin that every pale girl including Katrina would kill for. Large blue eyes framed by a generous provision of dark lashes and a heart-stopping smile were her not-so-secret survival weapons.

'What have you been doing? I've been banging at the door for ages! That stupid cretin at the desk just would not give me a key! He kept insisting we had already had four and then pretended not to understand what I was saying. This place is a sodding dump. I can't believe the agency have put me in here with all the money I earn them!'

'Sorry, I was in the bathroom. Why don't you ever have a key? What have you been buying?' Katrina eyed the bags jealously. Lauren always came home with beautiful new clothes. She came from a wealthy family and even without money from modelling she had plenty of cash to throw around. Katrina, who had never been able to buy designer clothes, had to admit to coveting Lauren's wardrobe and often tried pieces on when she was alone in the room.

Lauren smirked and picked up a La Perla bag and a Sonia Rykiel one from the selection on the floor.

'I got the sexiest underwear ever. It's pink and tiny and Alex will love it. And I got a wild dress from Rykiel, it's—'

'Wait! Who the hell is Alex? I thought you were still seeing Andrew? And I thought we were going out with him tonight?' Katrina picked the underwear out of the bag. It consisted of a tiny uplift bra and a thong disguised as an elastic band. The price tag said €170. Lauren laughed with the delight of someone superior in wealth.

'Ahh, well actually Alex took me shopping as he wants me to look fabulous tonight. We are going out, just not with boring Andrew. We're going to Alex's bar in the Marais district and it is amazing! Everyone is going to be there and I'm going to be the owner's girlfriend. How cool is that?' Lauren began stripping her clothes off. 'Is there any hot water?' She stopped to check her reflection closely in the mirror, squinting at the symmetry of her plump lips, which she had injected with a touch of collagen, not because they weren't naturally perfect, just because in her opinion a little extra never hurt.

'I doubt it. Who is Alex? And when did you meet him? I can't believe you!' Katrina said incredulously.

'I met him last night at a John Sleaford photographic exhibition thing; they'd booked models to turn up and hang round looking pretty, which is exactly what I did. Alex bought an amazing print and then asked if the model came with it, so naturally I said yes. I spent the night at his huge apartment, which has three floors!' She took a quick gasp of air. 'He owns the bar where the party was held and used to model with Entice so he's totally fit, much hotter than boring Andrew. What are you going to wear, and don't say jeans!'

Lauren was obviously very pleased with herself, but then she generally was. Katrina watched her as she stripped off her clothes and ran round the room maniacally in just her briefs. She had a tiny, narrow body and large breasts that her New York boyfriend had paid for, rather generously Katrina thought, seeing as they benefited many more men than just him.

'I don't think I'll come out tonight. I'm not really in the mood and you'll probably have more fun alone with this Alex guy,' she said dejectedly, wishing that she had a nice man picking her up to whisk her away for the evening. Instead of being a princess rescued from the wicked witch in the tower, she would be rescued from the scumpit hotel with the mad manager. She started to daydream about this nice man, who also happened to be incredibly good looking, and a candlelit dinner where he told her how utterly besotted he was with her.

'No! You have to come out! That's the thing. Alex is out with his friends tonight and I said I would bring some models. I can't turn up alone, I'll look like an idiot, and I even went so far as to invite Nadia, that total bitch that you did the Almond campaign with. Please don't let me down!' Lauren threw herself at Katrina and hugged her tightly.

'Oh thanks, nice to know you only want me to come out as potential bait for his friends, and why the hell did you invite Nadia of all people? She's a nightmare! On top of that I have absolutely nothing to wear.' She disentangled herself from Lauren, aware of the other girl's nudity. Lauren would go round naked all the time if she got the chance; she had the kind of confidence that only comes with the most perfect of bodies.

'You can wear something of mine; just say you're

coming. Nadia is okay really and she can be quite entertaining. It'll be fun!'

Lauren threw open her wardrobe and skipped into the bathroom. Katrina knew that if she didn't go, Lauren would moan for days. She looked through the wardrobe and selected a black top with a high neck, and a pair of jeans. This she teamed with much-loved although slightly knackered Gucci stilettos that had been a bargain in the January sales two years before and a pair of diamante drop earrings. She began to do her make-up using Lauren's hideously expensive foundation as revenge for being dragged out.

Lauren burst out of the bathroom in her new underwear with her chest almost falling out of the tiny bra, and did a twirl.

'What do you think? Sexy or what!' She went into a rendition of 'Do Ya Think I'm Sexy' as she wiggled into the new Sonia Rykiel dress: red, fine-knit micro-mini, and pulled on a pair of butter-soft leather Celine boots. She looked fantastic, although a little overdone.

'What's the time, babe?' she asked as she leant over a compact to do her make-up.

'Eight thirty. So who is going to be there tonight?'

'Yeow! I just got eyeliner in my eye, it really hurts.' Lauren blinked frantically before returning to her make-up. 'Alex knows loads of cool people, so I expect there'll be quite a few celebrities. Dominic Cayley will be there. I can't wait to meet him. He's just starred in a film with Penelope Cruz and is seriously gorgeous, but I bet he'll have a supermodel on his arm. I would kill for just one date with him! There'll be quite a few rich, eligible men, I'm sure, as that's the kind of crowd Alex hangs round with. He's absolutely loaded.'

'Everyone you know is loaded.' Katrina picked up a lipstick and absent-mindedly ran it over her lips before noticing that it was a bright red. She hurriedly rubbed it off.

'True.' Lauren smirked at her own reflection in the mirror. 'You can wear that black Gucci dress if you want. I think it's a bit big for me now as I'm more of a size six, so I don't mind.' She surveyed Katrina's outfit. 'You can't wear jeans. We're going out with millionaires and a film star.'

The phone rang, and Lauren picked it up. 'Oh hi, Christian, yes, I'm fine.' She walked into the bathroom, rolling her eyes at Katrina whilst motioning to the wardrobe and the dress.

Katrina slunk off the bed and reluctantly took the dress out of the wardrobe. Lauren possessed piles of designer clothes and shoes, some purchased with Daddy's pocket money, and some of the most expensive items, such as the Chanel handbags and haute couture pieces, gifts from her wealthy suitors. She also had an extensive jewellery collection, had stayed in a wide variety of luxury hotels across the world, flew in private jets and holidayed on yachts in the south of France, all financed by her good looks and ability to seduce rich and often very unattractive men. There was nothing unusual about that; a lot of girls had found that modelling was not quite as lucrative as they had initially imagined, and used their looks to create wealth in other ways. As she had been reminded the night before, it was not an option Katrina wanted to take, no matter how much she would love to go back home having made enough money to pay for her studies and to buy a flat. Anyway, whilst Lauren felt it was her God-given right to have the best and most expensive things in life, having been influenced by adoring parents, Katrina's parents had been too busy doing their own thing to ever have doted on her so she never had any assumptions about what she should have.

Katrina pulled the dress on and looked in the mirror.

Admittedly it did look much sexier than the previous outfit. It was ridiculously short with leather bands wrapped around it, which suited the faithful old Gucci shoes as they had leather ankle straps.

'Dammit, I shouldn't have suggested that dress; you look a bit too good in it!' Lauren mock-scowled as she came out of the bathroom brushing her teeth. Katrina knew that in reality she didn't see her as any kind of threat. Lauren always seemed to get what she wanted with barely any effort and knew how to hold the attention of whatever guy she chose. Katrina felt quite dull compared to her room-mate and suspected that the kind of flashy men Lauren liked wouldn't look twice at her.

The phone rang again and Lauren answered it. 'Okay, be there in a sec.'

She spat out her toothpaste in the bathroom. 'That was the driver; he's waiting for us downstairs. Can you get my black jacket and the Dior bag out of the drawer and we'll be off.'

As they stepped out of the door, Katrina was about to tell Lauren not to close it as she hadn't got the key. However, she slammed it shut, making the whole building shake and locking them out. An old lady making her way down the corridor scowled at them, muttering something in French. As they went through the reception, the owner screeched, 'I lock at midnight. Don't you think you will be waking me up, silly girls!'

Katrina was rather stunned to find a long black limousine waiting for them outside with a suited driver holding the door open. Some of the other girls talked about their rich boyfriends sending drivers over to collect them or turning up in Bentleys and Ferraris, but a stretch limo was wildly extravagant, especially seeing as it was for just the two of them. Lauren was so used to men sending cars, planes and helicopters for her that she dived in and immediately opened the little fridge, pulling out a bottle of champagne. Katrina slid in, and despite her reservations, a buzz of excitement ran through her at the idea of driving through the bright lights of Paris in such a car. If everyone back home could see her now, they would think she was living the most glamorous life in the world. Pity it was only going to last for one evening, and pity nobody would get to see her.

'Oh my God! I am annoyed! Have you seen this?' Lauren swung the bottle of champagne dangerously close to Katrina's face. 'There's no Cristal! It's bloody Veuve!' She nonetheless downed a glass of the 'inferior' champagne before refilling it. She loved extravagance of course and expected no less than too much from her men.

Katrina couldn't imagine anything more luxurious than sweeping along the Champs Elysées in a limousine, sipping bubbling golden champagne from a crystal glass, and she ignored Lauren's moaning, instead savouring the moment. Lauren would undoubtedly spend the next ten years of her life being driven around and swigging Cristal; it was what she had been born to do.

By the time the car came to a stop they had finished the bottle. Lauren, who never ate, hardly slept and had the constitution of an ox, could down bottles of wine, champagne and spirits and barely get drunk at all. Whilst she looked good, Katrina dreaded to think what her insides were like.

The door opened and a small man with a purple suit on helped them out. Had she been drunker, Katrina might have mistaken him for Prince.

'Hi, I'm Jake, the bar manager. We met briefly last night.' He addressed Lauren in a sing-song voice whilst checking out their outfits with a disdainful pout. 'Alex asked me to greet you and take you inside.' He limply shook Katrina's hand. Lauren had already seen someone she knew standing in the queue and had gone over to boast about how she was the owner's girlfriend.

'Hi, I didn't think you'd come,' a voice behind Katrina said.

Katrina turned around to find Nadia. Nadia was a six-foot Latvian model who was quite successful, as she possessed such a distinctive look. She had feline green eyes, pale skin and a prominent nose, all resulting in a haughty look, which she teamed with an aggressive and pushy manner. She was wearing tight leather jeans and a black vest that made her look even tougher than usual, with her jet-black hair slicked back.

'Are we going in or just standing around gossiping?' Nadia flashed a look of annoyance at Lauren. 'I am going in whether you two are or not.' She turned towards the entrance and stalked past the crowd of people into the bar. Katrina hesitated for a second, wondering whether to wait for Lauren, but when she turned to look for her she had disappeared. She followed Nadia.

The bar was decorated in an ice theme with lots of white and silver and mirrors everywhere. All of the people there were obviously extremely wealthy, as both the men and the women were iced in diamonds, huge rings and drop earrings. Everyone was looking at each other and checking out who was wearing what and who was with whom. Katrina felt conspicuous standing alone and wanted to go to the bar and do something purposeful like buy a drink. But even water would cost at least twenty euros, which would eliminate the chance of a taxi home.

Jake appeared at her side, taking her elbow and leading her to a silver door marked VIP. If Katrina had thought the people in the first section had looked wealthy, it was nothing compared to this room. It was full of men in trendy, expensive designer clothing smoking cigars and talking business deals, and twice the amount of women, many of whom were Russian with heavy make-up, sparkling dresses on perfect bodies, skyscraper heels and enough jewels to keep a Third World country going for years. The rest were models, milling around as usual with their giraffe frames and beautiful vacant expressions, waiting for someone to offer them a drink. They looked at Katrina as she entered, judging whether or not she was competition. She spotted Lauren in a corner with a group of men and made her way over.

'Hi, babe!' Lauren shrieked. 'I was looking for you everywhere! This is my best friend, we live together and when we go back to London we're going to get a place together.'

Lauren always embellished everything and just added details as she saw fit. They had only been living in the same hotel for two weeks, during which time Lauren had barely been there, and Katrina knew she had no intention of getting a place with her in London. Nonetheless she accepted the introduction and smiled at the group of men. She guessed that the one with his arm around Lauren must be Alex. He was good looking in a predictable way, with tousled brown hair and designer stubble, although slightly at risk of going to seed in a few years, with jowls already beginning to form. He leant forward, kissed her on the cheek and ran his hand down her back, his lips curving into an appraising smile. 'Hello, Katrina, it's very nice to meet you. What can I get you to drink?' His accent was strongly American, as were his gleaming white teeth.

She stepped back to remove his hand from her back; she hated men who were too tactile, and Alex's way of greeting her made him seem a little creepy. 'Um, can I just have water, please?'

Alex laughed and replied, 'Absolutely not!' He beckoned a waiter over. 'Bring her a vodka cranberry and a shot of tequila, and get the rest of us top-ups.' He grinned at Katrina, the maniacal grin of someone coked up. 'You look a bit uptight to me; I think you could do with some alcohol to help you loosen up. The night has only just begun.'

'Don't be such a sod, Alex! Just because you can't stop drinking doesn't mean you have to make everyone else alcoholics too,' said an English voice, and Katrina turned to find a man standing behind her. 'Hi, I'm James.' He handed her a bottle of water.

'Katrina,' she replied, taking the water. She noted the creases at the corners of his eyes and the thick dark hair with silver touching the edges. Despite those signs of his age he was very attractive and had a warm, friendly smile. He was dressed casually in blue jeans and a T-shirt and had a tall, muscular frame.

'It's nice to meet you.' He looked genuinely pleased and held out his hand as a means of introduction. Katrina relaxed, hopeful now that the evening wasn't going to be filled with smarmy men like Alex. 'You're a model too then, are you?' She nodded. 'How long have you been in Paris?'

'A couple of weeks,' she replied, grateful that he was being nice enough to talk to her, seeing as Lauren had disappeared. 'I came over from Milan.'

'That's very jet set, Milan to Paris! I've always heard that modelling's a great job for travelling. How long have you been doing it?' James stopped a man crashing into her and gently pushed him away.

'About three years. I did it part time towards the end of university and now I'm seeing if I can get some work here or if I need to go back to London and get a proper job.'

James laughed. 'A proper job, that's something you should avoid for as long as possible! I'm sure you'll do very well in Paris. So what did you study?'

'Philosophy. I want to go back and do a masters or a PhD. That's kind of why I'm modelling, to get some money together to pay the fees,' Katrina told him, noticing he was listening carefully.

'Well, that seems like a good plan. It will let you see a bit of the world and get some money together to do other things. Although I imagine the fashion world must seem rather shallow after Plato and Nietzsche.' James smiled broadly.

Alex laughed out loud, drawing their attention back to him. 'Christ, what a boring conversation! You both look so serious and you're talking about studying. Have a drink and lighten up.' He thrust a shot of tequila into Katrina's hand. 'Girls like you are too lovely to be hidden away in a library and why do you want to bother with that when you have a hot body? Total waste of time if you ask me!' Alex smirked and threw back his shot. 'You should forget about all the studying crap and get down to the important stuff like partying with us. Wouldn't you agree, James?'

James smiled at Katrina and took her tequila, pouring it into Alex's glass. 'I think it's a good thing to look great and to be knowledgeable and I don't see why both can't be done together. Now, if you'll excuse me I must make a quick phone call. My daughter's been unwell and I just want to check with her mother to see if she's feeling any better.'

As he disappeared through the club, Katrina realised that she found him very attractive. She dismissed it immediately; he was much older than her and was probably a businessman, not her usual arty type at all. Plus he had just mentioned a daughter, so she presumed he must be married.

Turning to look for Lauren, she noticed her sitting with a dark-eyed man at a table, chatting and laughing. As Katrina's eyes met his, they fixed on her unblinkingly. When she looked away he continued to stare. Even seated behind a table she could tell that he was tall, around six foot two, with the chiselled face of a male model, which she suspected he probably was. There was something familiar about him that she put down to having seen him on castings or perhaps in an advertising campaign. After a few minutes he got up, revealing that he was indeed tall, with a lean, muscular frame. He excused himself from Lauren, who immediately turned her attention back to Alex and went about removing his nose from Nadia's bosom.

Katrina, feeling conspicuous again, moved towards a corner so as not to look so obviously alone. As she did so, she bumped into someone and on looking up to apologise found herself face to face with the dark-eyed man. He just stared at her intensely without saying anything. As she was thinking that he was most strange, he reached out to touch her arm.

'I've been watching you since you got here. Who are

you with?' He looked her directly in the eye when he spoke and kept his hand on her arm. The physical touch felt like electricity pulsing through her.

Katrina caught her breath in shock that he was actually speaking to her. She had never been the girl the best-looking men approached. At school the pretty girls had been the curvy blondes, not the freckled geek, and even now it was the Lauren types who got the attention, not her. It took her a couple of seconds to find the words to reply, in which time he regarded her with an amused expression. 'With Lauren, the girl you were just talking to. I'm, er, Katrina,' she stammered awkwardly, looking towards Lauren, unable to hold his gaze.

'Hello, Katrina, It is a pleasure to meet you. I'm Dominic Cayley.'

Katrina looked at him and thought that she had never seen anyone, male or female, who was quite as good looking as Dominic Cayley. The picture that Lydia had shown her in the magazine did not do him justice. He possessed a strong, manly jaw and dark eyes hidden by the shadow of his brow. The sharp symmetry of his face almost made him look unreal, such was its perfection; it was as if he had been digitally enhanced. He looked exactly how a movie star should look. All the women were gazing at him, and in fact most of the men in the room were casting envious glances in his direction. Katrina had no idea why he had started talking to her, unless he just chatted to everyone and used the same lines on all the women. She racked her brain, wondering what to say.

Dominic looked her up and down before lifting the bottle of water from her hand.

'Why are you drinking water, have you got to work tomorrow? I presume you're a model, right?'

'No, I mean yes, I am a model, but no, I'm not

working tomorrow, but I, er . . .' Katrina stepped away from him and looked anxiously for Lauren, hoping she would appear to rescue her.

'In that case I'm going to get you a drink myself,' Dominic interrupted, touching her arm to stop her backing into a table. 'Champagne?'

With that he turned for the bar, leaving Katrina just about to say that anything *except* champagne would be great. Lauren appeared almost immediately.

'What were you and Dominic talking about? Did he ask about me? Where's he gone?' she questioned aggressively.

'He just introduced himself and he's gone to the bar to get a drink. Why all the interest?' Katrina knew that was a rather stupid question.

'Because that is Dominic Cayley, the guy I was telling you about, the actor! He is just the most eligible man in the world at the moment!' Lauren grasped Katrina's arm. 'He's famous and rich and gorgeous!'

'Oh, I suppose he is. He seems nice.' Katrina looked over to where Dominic was talking to a blonde girl.

'Nice! That is an understatement. He is more than nice; he's the hottest man on the planet. Imagine the kudos in dating him. If he comes back to talk to you, which I doubt he will, put in a good word for me. I really want him to ask me out tonight. Wow! I'd just die of happiness for one night with him.'

'Okay, although he might not come back to talk to me, and what about Alex?'

'Well, if I had to choose between the two, then Dominic is obviously much the better prospect. Anyway, Alex thinks *you're* really sweet.'

Lauren waltzed off to do a line in the toilet. Katrina glanced over at Alex, who seemed quite content touching up Nadia. She had a feeling that the night wasn't going to go to plan for anyone.

Dominic appeared in front of her holding a bottle of obligatory Cristal and two glasses.

'Shall we sit in that corner? I want to put this on ice,' he told her rather than asked, and taking her arm steered her towards the table. She perched nervously on the edge of the seat and looked at her watch. It was eleven forty, which meant only twenty minutes before the owner locked the front doors to the hotel. If she left now she might just make it, otherwise she'd be locked out and Lauren would go home with Alex. The thought of sleeping rough alone on the streets of Paris was enough to tilt her in favour of cutting short a drink with a Hollywood actor who was probably just passing time anyway.

'I don't mean to be rude, but I'm going to have to go.' She stood up abruptly. 'It was great to meet you, and thanks for the drink.'

Dominic looked shocked at her eagerness to leave. 'Wait, what do you mean, you have to go? It's not even midnight yet, the night's only just started and you haven't touched your drink. Do you have a boyfriend waiting for you somewhere?'

'No, it's not that . . .' Katrina felt a bit ridiculous explaining to him that she lived in a hotel that locked her out.

'Okay, well, that doesn't matter. We'll wake the owner and I'll make him let you in. If he doesn't, then you can stay with me.' Dominic took her hand and pulled her back down. 'You can't possibly disappear like some kind of modern-day Cinderella! Who will I talk to all night?' He gave her a conspiratorial look. 'Look at all these women vying for me to speak to them, all circling like hawks waiting to swoop down. You have to stay and protect me from them.'

'Well, I suppose I can't leave you to fend for yourself.'

Katrina couldn't say no when he had put it like that, and indeed there were lots of female eyes upon him, narrowed and predatory. With a pounding heart she resigned herself to being locked out. She took a sip of the champagne in an attempt to calm herself and then, even though she didn't really want to, said loyally, 'Lauren thinks very highly of you and she's really nice. She's a very successful model.'

'I'm sure she is, but she isn't really my cup of tea, as you English would say.' Dominic looked even more amused. 'She just spent ten minutes telling me what an admirer of my work she was whilst running her hand up my thigh, even though she is here as my friend's date.' He looked intently at her. 'To tell you the truth, I'm a little bored of these beautiful clone models like Lauren. They never seem to have much to say. Stay, talk to me a bit, surprise me.'

Katrina nodded and eyed him with her slanty blue eyes, wondering what he meant by 'surprise me'. He refilled the glass that she had nervously drunk without even realising. Katrina saw James reappear, accompanied by a striking girl with waist-length dark hair. Dominic looked around and also noticed her. The girl saw him and her lips curved into a playful smile before she flicked her hair and nudged James. They made their way over. For some reason Katrina was a little surprised that James knew Dominic. They didn't seem like the type to be friends, but then what did she know about who Dominic might be friends with?

'Hey, Katrina, I see you've met Dominic, and now he's plying you with alcohol.' James laughed and teasingly punched Dominic. He sat down beside Katrina and the dark sultry girl sat down next to Dominic. She was so smouldering that Katrina suspected she might burst into flames at any second.

'Are you okay?' James gave her a concerned look as

she took a gulp of champagne and started coughing. 'I hope Dominic is behaving himself.'

'Sure, of course I am. I am the perfect gentleman,' retorted Dominic indignantly. He turned to the girl. 'How are you, Zora? This is Katrina, she's a model too, so maybe you've seen each other around on castings or whatever it is you girls do.'

Zora turned her dark flashing eyes on Katrina and looked her up and down, pouting very full pink lips petulantly. She picked up her drink and sipped through the straw, enjoying the attention while they waited for her to speak.

'No, I don't think so,' she replied with a strong Russian accent. 'We probably don't go for the same jobs. She looks like one of those cool London-type girls to me and I'm more commercial, pleasing to everyone if you know what I mean.' She laughed lightly as if joking. There was an expression of disdain on her perfect face as she held out a slim brown hand. 'It's nice to meet you.'

Katrina knew that in fact Zora wasn't pleased to meet her at all and would rather she just disappeared. She felt like an ungroomed cob next to a thoroughbred, and Lauren's Gucci dress seemed stupid and overdressed compared to Zora's sexy, tight-fitting jeans. The Russian girl was truly beautiful, with carved cheekbones, thick arched eyebrows and the resilience that Katrina had come to recognise of a girl who would do anything to avoid going back to the poverty she had come from. Zora lit a cigarette and observed Dominic through the smoke. James continued to keep his attention on Katrina.

'Do you want me to get you some more water?' he asked, remembering their earlier conversation.

Zora got up and came around the table. She placed herself elegantly on the edge of James's chair. 'I am sure she is happier with Cristal than water, darling.' She smiled falsely at Katrina before turning back to James. 'I must leave now as I have a shoot in the morning and then I go to Monaco. You will drop me at my apartment?' She ran her hand over James's arm and looked at him under her lashes before slowly sweeping her hair back off her face. Katrina could tell that Zora used her beauty aggressively and would never stop to think that maybe it wasn't quite enough. She knew that she was better looking than James and probably felt that he should fall instantly in love with her.

James shifted in his seat uncomfortably and stood up. 'I'll get you a taxi as you're going the opposite direction to me.' He didn't look at Zora when he spoke and didn't see her face darken. Katrina noticed Dominic making an incredulous face at James. 'It was good to meet you, Katrina, hopefully we'll meet again soon. Dominic, I'll see you in the morning, gym at nine thirty, right?'

Dominic nodded, grimacing at the mention of the gym. Zora went over to him and placing her hands on each side of his face kissed him on the cheek. She glanced over at Katrina.

'Nice to meet you,' she purred again, and taking James's hand she dragged him off just as he was about to lean over and kiss Katrina goodbye.

Dominic raised an eyebrow at Katrina. Any eye contact he made with her caused her to look away nervously. He just continued to stare, unabashed.

'Zora can be a bit rude to other girls, I'm afraid. She seems to be after James. They only met three weeks ago in London and she pursues him relentlessly even though he isn't really interested. God knows why, as she's a seriously hot catch for him. He's a divorcee with two kids, but he's done pretty well for himself on the property scene in London, and girls like Zora are always drawn to a bit of security, I guess.' He laughed and refilled the glasses.

'She's very beautiful,' Katrina said, hoping she didn't sound jealous. Zora had exuded sexuality, and even though Katrina came across beautiful girls every day at castings, this time she did feel a little envious. It was strange that Zora was interested in James when he came with so much baggage, as she could have any man she wanted. She wondered why James hadn't seemed too pleased with Zora's attention. She was also curious about how James had come to be in this circle of wildly glamorous people when he seemed so normal, so British and so grounded. Maybe Dominic was actually quite a normal guy too beneath the ridiculously perfect exterior if he had friends like that.

Whilst Katrina was considering this, Dominic got up and sat down next to her. Suddenly, without saying anything, he pulled her face towards his and kissed her. His strong tongue found its way into her mouth and his arm slipped around the back of her neck to pull her closer. At first Katrina was too dumbstruck to respond, surprised at the suddenness. After a few seconds she began kissing him back, pleased at the sense of urgency behind his kiss like he really wanted her. His hand moved from her neck to the top of her thigh, causing her to jump back as she felt skin on skin. He opened his eyes and studied her, appreciating the effect he was having with just one kiss. Her heart felt like it was going to burst through her skin and she was trembling all over. Everything was happening so quickly and it was quite unbelievable, like a weird dream. She sat in stunned silence as he smiled at her, obviously finding her awkwardness amusing.

'I wanted to do that from the first moment I saw you. Shall we leave now? I've got a car waiting outside.' He drained his glass and stood up expectantly.

Katrina was taken aback and momentarily lost for

words. She had only met him about twenty minutes ago. He *was* incredibly good looking and she still hadn't got her head around the fact that he had wanted to talk to her. She could tell that he was arrogant and sure that she would say yes, and of course she did want to say yes. It would be so easy just to go along with it and to carry on enjoying his attention. But two things stopped her: even if he was a famous movie star, she never went home with random men and slept with them; she also knew that if she did, he would be bored of her after a couple of hours and she would be left feeling used. The only way to keep a guy like Dominic Cayley interested was to play it cool and not fall at his feet. With that in mind she resolutely got up.

'I should find my friends now and see what they want to do. I had a really nice time, and thank you for the drinks and everything. Enjoy the rest of your night.' Katrina smiled, then turned and walked away, her legs feeling strangely weak and shaky. As she left, she wondered if she'd done the right thing, and when he didn't call out her name, as she had hoped, to ask for her number or to arrange to meet, she felt her heart sink. She had just turned down the most perfect man she had ever met.

Having walked around the club twice, Katrina still couldn't find Lauren or Nadia. She spotted Alex leaning against the bar smoking a cigar and surveying the dance floor with narrow, predatory eyes and hesitantly went over to him.

'Hi, have you seen Lauren?' she asked.

He grinned slyly.

'Yes, she's in my office, sweetheart. Go through those doors and tell Marcus that I said you could go in. Hang on, why haven't you got a drink?' He grasped her arm tightly and motioned to the barman. 'We'll be going back to my pad soon, so don't get lost.'

Taking the drink reluctantly, Katrina headed towards the door. A burly doorman, presumably Marcus, opened the office door for her and there she saw Lauren lying asleep on a leather sofa. Katrina fed the drink to a plant before realising that it was fake and actually made out of silk. Giggling, she gently shook Lauren, who awoke, taking a couple of seconds to register her friend. She looked as if she had been crying

'Hey, what you doing in here? Are you okay?' Katrina asked her.

'I think I drank too much and then Alex brought me in here. We had sex but I think I must have passed out during it as I can't really remember anything.' Lauren smiled weakly. 'I guess that's not the way to impress your new boyfriend, is it?'

Katrina noticed a pile of cocaine on the desk next to a thick wad of euro notes and a photograph ripped from a magazine of Alex with Dominic and the Victoria's Secret models. She supposed it would be quite accurate to assume they were the sorts of girls a movie star dated. Lauren had white powder around her nostrils, which Katrina wiped off with the corner of the Gucci dress.

'He shouldn't have taken advantage of you if you'd passed out.' Katrina sat down next to her. 'It's a bit weird of him.'

After a moment's consideration Lauren got to her feet. She stared blankly at Katrina. 'Why? If he wants sex then it's fine by me. He's been pretty generous so far with buying me clothes and sorting out tonight, and he promised to take me to Miami next week for a party.' She raised an eyebrow at Katrina. 'You're so bloody naïve, Katrina. It wouldn't hurt you to loosen up a bit and realise that if you're going to aim high then you have to know how to. How did you get on with Dominic? I saw you getting quite cosy.' Her face hardened. 'Alex told me that once Dom screws someone he totally ignores them. If you sleep with him, don't expect anything to come of it. You're not his type and you won't be able to handle it. The girls Dominic goes out with look like supermodels, they speak three languages, they ski like champions and they dress like *Vogue* editors. You're hardly going to interest him.'

Katrina wondered at that moment why she had given a damn about whether Lauren was okay. After feeling quite good about herself, she now felt stupid for even thinking that Dominic might have come after her.

Lauren checked her reflection in a compact, adding lip gloss before snapping it shut and heading for the door.

'Come on, let's get out of here. I'll find Alex and get his driver to take us home.'

Alex was still standing by the bar alone. Lauren flicked her hair and approached him. She wrapped her body around his and took a sip of his drink. He looked at her, then glanced away with a bored expression. Katrina followed his gaze to where it rested on a young blonde girl dancing with a couple of friends. Lauren tried to kiss him; he moved away.

'What's wrong, darling?' she cooed.' Let's go home now. I want a repeat performance.'

He smirked at her and took a long puff on his cigar. 'You weren't even able to take the first performance, sweetheart. Maybe you should just go home.' He shook her off and with that went towards the young blonde. Within seconds he was sharing his drink with her. Lauren looked furious.

'Bastard!' she spat and pushed Katrina aside before disappearing into the crowd. Katrina groaned and followed but within seconds had lost her and doubted that she would find her again. The only thing to do was to hail a taxi and at least get back to the hotel. Making her way outside, she noticed much to her dismay that there wasn't a taxi to be seen. After standing on the edge of the pavement hopefully for a few minutes, there seemed no alternative but to walk. After about ten minutes her feet started to hurt, so she sat at a bus stop to assess the damage, wincing at the sight of raw skin and blood. She tried to pull together the energy to continue walking but her feet were pure agony and she collapsed back on the plastic seat.

A black Mercedes pulled up next to her. The window was wound down and an American voice drawled, 'Well, fancy bumping into you here. You won't get a bus at this time of night, you know.' It was Dominic, alone in the back of the car and laughing at her, teeth glinting in the dark. 'Get in, crazy English girl, and I'll take you wherever you need to be taken.'

Katrina hobbled towards the car and climbed in gratefully, holding her shoes. Dominic grimaced at her feet.

'Nasty. Where do we drop you off?'

'Thanks, I couldn't get a taxi so I didn't know what else to do. I live at Citidines, Parmentier.' The driver acknowledged her in the rear-view mirror.

'So you turned down my offer of a lift earlier for no apparent reason other than to walk. You would prefer to get bleeding feet than sit in a car with me for twenty minutes; that makes me feel great!' Dominic laughed. 'I certainly must have made an impression on you.'

'I didn't know you would drop me off home. I thought that . . . well, I didn't want to put you out.' Katrina was embarrassed. She had assumed that he wanted her to go back with him. She sat biting her lip, not knowing what to say. He raised an eyebrow.

'I was getting bored of that club. It was too busy, and you said you needed to get back so that you weren't locked out.' He sat back and smiled at her, knowing that he had confused her. 'What happened to your friends?'

'What? Or, er, Lauren had a bit of an argument with, umm, Alex and disappeared, and I don't know where Nadia went. Maybe she left earlier . . .' Katrina stared at his forearms; they were tanned and muscular.

'Ah, Lauren got the office treatment, did she? As for the other girl, I saw her leave ages ago with a guy with a ponytail and a frightening leather suit. You really should do something about her taste.' Dominic reached forward and pressed a button that made a screen appear between them and the driver. He turned towards Katrina and pushed a strand of hair out of her eyes. She jumped, now intimidated by his closeness, despite what had happened earlier.

'What do you mean, the office treatment?' she asked.

Dominic looked at her thoughtfully for a moment before replying. 'Alex always takes his conquests to the office and – excuse me for being crude – he likes to screw them over his very expensive antique desk. Usually it's a different girl every night . . . he likes variety.' He paused and looked out of the window. 'Always models, apparently they're the easiest, and he treats them like shit. His last girlfriend was only seventeen, a Brazilian girl who did the last Chloé campaign, really gorgeous but he cheated on her all the time. Alex always gets his own way with girls; they do whatever he wants. But then all the people in that place have some sort of kink – you get used to it after a while. You seem a bit naïve, which is sweet. Maybe it's that reserved English thing.' He opened the window slightly. 'You have to accept that all sorts of things go on way beyond your and my understanding, English girl.' He smiled sexily.

She didn't really know what to say to that. Maybe she was a bit naïve, and perhaps she was reserved. However, while she knew Lauren could look after herself, it still angered and disgusted her that Alex could behave like that with no thought for the girls he messed around with. She frowned as she tried to think of an answer that wouldn't insult Dominic's friend too much. Dominic laughed.

'I agree that Alex behaves badly, but everyone has a choice. If you don't wanna do something, don't do it. I really wouldn't worry about your friend. She knew what she was getting into and I'm sure she'll get some nice clothes out of it. She seems like the type to make sure she gets something. I don't think Alex will just dump her, as he knows she's a great-looking girl and she'll be good to have on his arm for a while. She'll just have to accept that there will be other girls around too.'

'He is a total arsehole!' Katrina stated angrily, unable to contain herself even if he was Dominic's friend. 'Why does he think he can get away with that? Just because he owns some stupid bar and has money. I am sure she won't see him again after tonight anyway; he went off with another girl right in front of her.'

Dominic gave her a condescending look. 'He gets away with it because he can, because there are loads of pretty girls all looking for someone to buy them a few designer clothes, someone who has a bit of money. It means they can show off to their friends, and on top of that he's a good-looking guy. Alex is twenty-nine and he'll be doing that until he is sixty with girls who are twenty because they let him. Who's gonna stop him?' He didn't pause to let her answer. 'You've been around these people for a while now. They do what they want, when they want, and who the hell can blame them when it's offered on a plate by girls like Lauren?'

'You're saying it's the girls' fault? I don't think that's right. Guys like Alex take advantage of vulnerable girls with no money and no friends in a strange country when some of them are still in their teens.' Katrina felt herself getting very annoyed; after all, from what she had heard from Lauren about Dominic, he was just as bad.

'All I'm saying is that both parties are getting something out of it. Lauren gets some clothes, and she'll be taken out and treated like a princess, and anyway . . .' Dominic leant close to her again, enjoying intimidating her, 'girls do actually get something out of sex too, you know. It isn't all just for the man.'

At the thought of sex with Dominic, Katrina felt her stomach flip over. She went silent. He smirked and picked up her hand, surveying the nails.

'You certainly don't have typical model nails, do you?' Her nails were broken and unpainted.

'I do lots of sport back home.' The truth was she nibbled at them whenever she was nervous or uneasy, a bad habit that led to photographers wincing every time her hands came into shot. 'There's no point doing my nails as they just get broken, and you can't do anything practical with long nails.'

'I quite like long nails, particularly when they are scratching down my back.' Dominic gave a slow, seductive smile that let her know exactly what he was thinking. It made her stop breathing for a moment. He let go of her hand and tapped on the driver's window. 'Stop here.' He turned towards her. 'I guess this is your place, and if I'm not very much mistaken, the door is open so you won't be locked out.' He looked rather disparagingly at the exterior of the hotel. 'I've dropped someone off here before, a Czech girl who from what I remember had just done the Yves Saint Laurent campaign. She passed out in the car from too much coke.' He laughed. 'Here I am defending Alex when actually that was his fault too; he was giving her the stuff. My driver had to carry her in.' He reached over and opened her door. 'Well, it was very nice to meet you, English girl.'

Katrina got out of the car, hesitating on the pavement, hoping that he would ask her for her number. He just looked at her with a slightly mocking expression in his eyes, and feeling like an idiot, she stepped back and smiled weakly.

'Thank you for the lift, and I hope the filming goes well. Maybe I'll see you around,' she said lamely, and shutting the car door made her way despondently towards the hotel, trying not to limp despite the agonising blisters, which was an extremely difficult feat.

'Katrina.' He had opened the window fully. She turned towards him. 'You *have* surprised me.' He grinned. 'How about I pick you up tomorrow evening at seven thirty? I have a party to go to and I want you to come and keep me company.' The window began to shut and the car pulled away. Then his head appeared again. 'Make sure you start growing those nails, okay?' Then he was gone before she had the chance to reply.

She walked into the reception with her head spinning, noticing that the manager and the cleaning lady were asleep together on the sofa with a bottle of whisky beside them. It was rather an odd sight but then the entire evening had been so strange that she barely acknowledged this. If *she* had been kissing Dominic Cayley then it was perfectly acceptable that the manager and the cleaning lady had got together! The door to her room was wide open, and as she entered she found Lauren fast asleep still in her dress and boots. Katrina took her boots off and covered her with a duvet. In her hand Lauren was clutching a little jewellery box, and when Katrina took it from her and opened it, she found a large pair of diamond earrings. She put them on the dressing table and sat down on the other bed, running through the events of the evening.

She noticed a copy of *Arena* on the floor and recognised Dominic's face on the front cover. Flicking through the magazine, Katrina found an interview that described him as the new Brad Pitt and detailed all the top models and actresses he had been linked to. Had Dominic Cayley really asked her out, or rather, told her she was coming out? *How* had she surprised him? She had actually felt rather dull next to him. She had a sick, nervous feeling in the bottom of her stomach, and going to the bathroom mirror, she tried to decide what he had found so attractive. It didn't make any sense when he could have a choice of so many beautiful women. Why her? She took off her make-up, and as she cleaned her teeth vigorously, she remembered him kissing her. He was possibly the best kisser in the world, she decided as she lay on the bed. Tiredness got the better of her, and she fell asleep thinking about attending a film premiere on the arm of Dominic Cayley, the kind of thing that only ever happened in dreams.

5

The noise of someone knocking at the door woke Katrina. Pulling the duvet around her, she opened it and found the manager with a genial smile plastered across his face.

'*Bonjour!*' He bowed his head, which surprised her, having been so used to him being bad-tempered all the time. '*Une lettre pour vous.*' He handed over an envelope.

'Oh right, thanks, I mean *merci*,' she muttered and quickly closed the door in his beaming face. She looked at her watch. 'Damn! I should have set the alarm.' She dropped the envelope on Lauren's sleeping form. 'Something's arrived for you.'

Lauren groaned and pulled the covers over her head. 'What time is it? It's the crack of dawn, isn't it? My freaking head is killing me.'

'Actually, it's twelve fifteen and I'm starving. I'll just pop out to the patisserie. Want anything?' Katrina pulled on jeans and a T-shirt. Getting no answer from Lauren, she picked up her purse and let herself out.

The lady at the patisserie gave her some very strange looks as she bought pains au chocolat, but then she often did, so Katrina ignored her. The street was busy as she stepped out of the shop, and the buzz of cars alongside the heat of the city made her head throb.

She let herself back into the room and found Lauren

still asleep. As she sat down on the edge of her bed, Lauren emerged from her bedclothes.

'Yum, can I have a bite?' Katrina handed over the greasy bag and rescued the envelope, which was about to fall on the floor. Lauren opened it, taking out a sheet of paper. There was a long pause before she looked at Katrina with an annoyed expression. 'Why are you giving me this? Are you trying to brag? Honestly, I really don't care. I'm seeing Alex today and we're going shopping. I have no interest in Dominic Cayley at all. Like I told you, he's just a player, and once he's bored of you, that's it.'

'What are you talking about?' Katrina took the piece of paper and scanned it.

Hi Katrina,
I hope you had a good night's sleep. The plans for today have changed and I will have to pick you up at 1.30 p.m. instead of 7.30 p.m., as the party is starting early. We can't be late. I'll presume this is okay as you said you weren't working today. I look forward to seeing you. Regards,
Dominic.

'Bloody hell!' she howled, leaping off the bed. 'Oh my God! What's the time?' She looked at her watch; it was quarter past one. 'How can he do this? That means he'll be here in fifteen minutes, and he hasn't even told me what sort of party it is! What the hell will I wear?' Katrina looked at Lauren in panic. 'Please help me! I didn't know that envelope was for me; they're always for you, so I just assumed. Please, Lauren. This is a Hollywood actor taking me out. I need fifteen *days* to prepare, not fifteen minutes!' She felt hot with panic. What the hell did you wear out on a date with a man like Dominic? Certainly not jeans and trainers.

Lauren looked calmly back at Katrina, weighing up the benefits of helping.

'Well, I think sorting out your hair would be a good start, so get in the bathroom and I'll find you something to wear.'

Katrina fled to the bathroom and looked in the mirror. She felt slightly nauseous with the fear of seeing him again. She was horrified by the image that gazed back at her. Her hair was one big dreadlock of knots sticking up all over the place, and she had dark circles under her eyes. No wonder the woman in the patisserie had given her funny looks! She picked up a pot with a label that said *Revitalising Cream* and plastered a thick layer over her face, hoping it would do what it claimed. The water was freezing as she showered, but she gritted her teeth and scrubbed vigorously, pouring literally a whole bottle of conditioner on to her hair. Dominic Cayley was coming to pick her up. She couldn't quite believe the reality of it. She hadn't actually thought she would really see him again. One kiss in a dark club would have been enough for her to daydream about for months, let alone an actual date!

When she came out of the bathroom, Lauren handed her a pair of Robert Cavalli jeans and a black top.

'Put this on. These jeans are dressier than normal jeans so you won't look too casual, but at least you won't look overdressed for the day. Wear those heels, and take this.' She took off her own chunky silver bracelet and put it on Katrina's wrist. 'That looks cool. Maybe I should be a stylist.' She eyed her critically. 'I don't think you're ever going to look like a Hollywood actor's kind of girl with those nails and that hair. I suppose you're kind of rock chick.'

The phone rang. Lauren grabbed it. 'Hello . . . Oh, hi, Dominic, how are you? . . . Yes, I'm great. I'm always working so I'm just enjoying a day off today . . . Yes, I am seeing Alex later. It's really sweet of you to take Katrina out today. She gets very lonely here when I'm working all the time and she has nothing to do.' Katrina gritted her teeth as she applied eyeliner, listening to the younger girl being so condescending. 'Yes, I'll tell her, she'll be down in a minute. You look after her, she isn't used to men like you, you know! See you soon. Bye.' Lauren turned to Katrina. 'He's waiting downstairs at reception.' Possibly out of guilt she then added, 'Why don't you use my black Balenciaga bag? It'll look nice with that outfit.'

As she left, with her hair still damp hair and her face only half made up, Katrina remembered that Lauren had said she was seeing Alex that afternoon.

'Lauren, is everything okay with Alex? I didn't think you would see him again after last night.'

'Why ever not? I had a great time last night, and so did you thanks to him. Why wouldn't I see him again?' Lauren snapped aggressively. 'Don't tell me that just because you're going on one date with a film star you think a mere millionaire bar owner's not good enough? He's picking me up and we're going shopping. I'll have just as nice a day as you, and at least he still wants to see me after I've slept with him.' She turned away, and Katrina closed the door behind her, reflecting that Dominic might have been right that Lauren was getting something out of it too, even if it was just a couple of Prada dresses and a handbag or two.

On the way downstairs, a pang of nerves hit Katrina, almost taking her breath away. Her heart was pounding as if she had just run a marathon. She stopped to look at her reflection in a mirror and applied more lip gloss. She did look quite rock chick in the outfit, and although her hair still hadn't calmed down, she hoped it added to the look rather than just being a mess. Maybe he'd think she was quite ordinary in daylight and wish he hadn't asked her out. That was more than likely; after all, she *was* an ordinary girl, who just happened to be tall and photogenic, and that didn't make her movie-star date material. She put on another layer of mascara.

When she reached the reception Dominic was waiting, leaning on the front desk talking to Lydia, who had a couple of other models with her. Katrina smiled, remembering the conversation two days ago, when she had joked with Lydia about bumping into Dominic in Paris. Lydia must have been gobsmacked to have seen him in their hotel! Dominic's back was facing Katrina and her nerves increased as she noted his strong physique. He looked completely out of place standing in the grotty hotel reception, and for a second panic washed over her at the thought of spending an entire day with him. He was wearing jeans, which meant it was obviously going to be a casual party, and she was grateful to Lauren that she hadn't dressed her up. Lydia spotted her and made a wild face, gesturing frantically towards Dominic and mouthing, 'Can you believe it?' Katrina approached the group.

'Hey, Katrina, do you want to come for a coffee?' Lydia squeaked. She smiled what she obviously considered her most enchanting smile at Dominic. 'Would you like to join us, or are you waiting for someone?'

Dominic turned around and saw Katrina.

'I am waiting for someone, and here she is.' He came towards her and kissed her full on the lips. Lydia's mouth dropped open in astonishment. 'You look great, kinda rock chick. Love the jeans.' He took Katrina's hand in a familiar manner.

She looked up at him and could hardly get over how good looking he was. He looked even better in the light, with his dark eyes, which seemed almost midnight blue, and strong, perfect features. He was amazing, and she felt ordinary beside him. He smiled at her, seeming to recognise her awe. 'You ready then? We've got to go or we'll miss the flight.'

'Flight?' she repeated, confused, having been too caught up in noticing how his perfect mouth curled up at the corners like a contented lion.

'Yep, we're flying to Monaco for the party; it's on a friend's boat. It's only a couple of hours away. It was nice to meet you, girls,' he said, turning towards the others with an extremely wide smile, showing off straight whitened teeth. 'Have a great day.' He led Katrina towards the black Mercedes parked outside.

'Bloody hell! Where the hell did you find him? I guess you won't be coming for a coffee then?' Lydia whispered as Katrina went past.

'I guess not,' she replied, feeling both euphoric at their blatant jealousy and worried at the idea of going to Monaco alone with Dominic and his friends. She was totally unprepared for a mini-trip abroad and hadn't brought anything with her, apart from a few make-up essentials. 'I'll see you when I get back.'

As they headed towards the airport, Dominic's phone rang and he answered it, leaving Katrina to flick through a magazine she found on the back shelf of the car. She spotted a picture of herself doing a fashion show in London wearing a leather catsuit. Had he seen it? She hoped so, although she expected most of his dates were girls who did big designer and perfume campaigns. She was glad he was on the phone, as she didn't know what to say to him. Anything she said would sound boring compared to his life. Dominic had a permanent air of boredom about him, having always been surrounded by people who were more interested in him than he was in them. She listened to his conversation.

'Yes, I agree with you totally, Miranda. I'm just not

entirely sure about the role. They want me to play the son, which means that I'm not the main character, and I don't think it's the kind of thing I should do at the moment. I don't want to mess up and get signed up to some mediocre movie when something better might come along. Anyway, they're not offering enough money.' He glanced over at Katrina and rolled his eyes exasperatedly. 'Look, just keep them on ice for now and we'll discuss it over dinner soon. I'm off to Monaco and I've got a lovely girl sitting next to me who's getting bored of me talking on the phone, so I'll speak to you on Monday, okay?'

He cut the call.

'Sorry, that's my agent. She's always on the case and is a very persistent woman, to say the least. She wants me to take a mediocre role because it's a great director. Hey, is that you?' He pointed to the picture and took the magazine off her to get a closer look. 'You look great. Can you sing?'

'No, why do you ask that?' Katrina said.

'You look like a rock chick, so if you could sing then I know some people in the music business who could make you into a *real* rock chick.' He grinned and instantly she felt dizzy at how his attention could be so overpowering. 'Oh well, stick with the modelling. You've got a good look, very unusual. I'm tired of the commercial girl-next-door type of model; they're so boring. You've got a kind of interesting look. James described you at the gym this morning as "an English rose with a twist" when I told him I was taking you out.' He put his hand on the back of her neck and pulled her towards him so he could look closely. It was a bit odd being studied in such detail and she hoped that he would just close his eyes and kiss her. She could feel his breath on her, and his eyes moving across her face. Instead he dropped her hand and moved away without saying anything.

Katrina longed for him to kiss her again and yet he didn't seem interested. Maybe he had decided he didn't like her, had noticed all the imperfections. How could she compete with supermodels and glamorous actresses? What the hell was 'an English rose with a twist' anyway? She tried to run a hand through her hair and push it back seductively, but it seemed to have got even more knotted and her hand got stuck. She was hardly presenting a glamorous, desirable image.

Dominic picked up his mobile, keying in a number.

'Hey, Loretta, how you doing? I'm just ringing to say that I'll be with you in about two hours max. Can you sort me out a lift from the airport to the boat? You're a sweetheart. No, I'm not alone . . . a model.' He started laughing. 'You know me. See you soon.' He ended the call and turned back to Katrina. 'That was the girl whose party it is. She's got a fantastic boat that she got out of her divorce and she has a party every month. She's very glamorous, fake breasts, long blond hair and full make-up all the time; we used to date for a while.' He grinned. 'We're just friends now. I'm sure you'll get on with her.'

Katrina's heart sank at the thought of Loretta: fake tits, glamorous, rich, ex-girlfriend. She sounded like an absolute nightmare! She pictured her as yet another bitchy, competitive woman like Zora, who would be immaculately groomed and would look at Katrina like she had just crawled out of a drain. Of course she understood that these sorts of women could afford boob jobs, thousands of pounds of designer clothing and probably hairdressers and make-up artists on speed-dial, so it was bound to make her feel a bit inadequate. Still, she felt even more painfully aware of her knotted hair and borrowed clothes, which would struggle to complete with any Loretta types.

Dominic was back on his phone again, talking to a friend about a party they were planning.

'I think if you're going to have a decent party you're looking at a few hundred thousand dollars minimum. I mean, you can't mess around and you need to make sure you only invite the very best people, none of that friends-of-friends crap, which brings the tone down. Speak to Imogen at *Vanity Fair* and she'll help you draw up a list. Or Rebecca at *Vogue*. Tell them I told you to call,' he advised before looking up at Katrina and smiling.

Katrina realised she was gawping at him and quickly shut her mouth and pretended to be intensely fascinated by the scenery again. Dominic's friends were the rich and famous who attended parties and were on guest lists organised by *Vanity Fair* and *Vogue*. She suddenly felt wildly out of her depth and had to take a deep breath. She was about to spend the day with those people, maybe even celebrities, and she felt totally out of her depth. Okay, so they were just people who happened to have amazing jobs and earned loads of money, and if they were anything like Alex or Zora or any of those people from the bar, then they were just sycophantic cling-ons that she cared very little for. Nonetheless, it was still intimidating. It also made her wonder for the millionth time why the hell Dominic had chosen her to come with him when he could pick from a long list of much more polished and elegant beauties. Surely it was just a matter of time before he realised how pedestrian and boring she was compared to all of them. She wondered if she could get a photograph of him before the day was up so she could show her friends back home in case they didn't believe she had gone out with him.

The car pulled to a halt and the driver opened the door. There was a helicopter waiting and Dominic was already striding towards it. He turned around, enjoying Katrina's look of amazement.

'Are we going in this?' she asked, looking from the pilot to him. 'I thought we were just getting a normal flight.'

'It wouldn't be a good idea to get a normal flight. It would take much longer, and besides, I don't really want to get recognised and asked for autographs for the next two hours. This is much more fun: we get to be alone instead of surrounded by lots of strangers. I love the way you're shocked by everything still; most girls just act like they've done it all before. You're very sweet.'

He made his way towards the helicopter, stopping to shake hands with the pilot, and Katrina followed, feeling a bit annoyed that he kept making her out to be so naïve. He must think she was a total idiot. She decided that she should sharpen up a bit and act more nonchalant around him, even if her mind was spinning at top speed. She surreptitiously applied another layer of lip gloss and put on her eBay-purchased Gucci sunglasses. Dominic was already in the helicopter.

'So, Katrina, you haven't really told me anything about yourself. I know you're a model. What I don't know is where you come from, how old you are, what you like doing.'

He seemed to move rapidly from being really familiar to being a total stranger. Last night he had kissed her like he meant it, long and hard as if he really liked her, then he'd dropped her off at the hotel as if he was just doing a friend a favour. When he'd picked her up this morning it was like they had known each other for weeks, such was his familiarity, kissing her hello and taking her hand. Now it was like they had only just met, as if she was just a random fan or assistant.

'I'm twenty-four,' she replied. 'I come from a small

town in Hampshire where my mother lives, although I live in London for work. I've finished my degree and I hope to continue studying in the next couple of years when I get the money to do so.'

'Wow, that's great, you must be clever. I never really bothered with school, as I always knew I'd be an actor. I think it's good that you aren't just a typical stupid model with nothing to fall back on except marrying a rich guy. My sister went to college.' He paused and looked at her thoughtfully. 'Now she just looks after her kids.' Katrina detected a sarcastic tone to his voice but dismissed it, thinking she was being paranoid. Dominic looked out of the window as the helicopter began to lift off the ground. 'Twenty-four, that's a good age. I'm thirty-two.' He turned to look at her again. 'So have you got a boyfriend back in England?'

Katrina thought that was a strange thing to ask, seeing as she was here with him. 'Well, no. If I had, I wouldn't be disappearing on helicopters with strange men,' she replied softly, looking directly at him. Did he think she was like Lauren, that she was the kind of girl who dated rich men for fun?

'Why not?' Dominic smirked. 'It's just a bit of fun. All the models do things like this. It's just a day out.' He picked up a sheaf of paper and turned his attention to reading through it. She felt immense disappointment that he obviously did think she was another Lauren, brazen and overly confident, when actually she was just the opposite. It was actually quite insulting and she contemplated telling him that. However, she was already nervous enough about the day ahead without making it worse, plus he was making her feel a bit breathless and faint. She concentrated on looking cool.

The rest of the flight was spent in silence as Dominic read the script and Katrina gazed out of the window, watching the land being eaten up beneath the helicopter. She looked at him out of the corner of her eye, searching for some kind of imperfection to home in on and be put off by. She couldn't find one. It was impossible to find a bad angle to his face; the more she looked, the better looking he became. She herself had lots of imperfections: her nose was like a ski jump, she had freckles, her teeth weren't perfectly straight and she bit her nails. Had he noticed all of that? She wondered how many models he had taken away with him. Most likely loads; after all, what girl would ever say no to him? In the quest for success, recognition and wealth, a movie star was the ultimate catch for any model. It must be impossible to hold his attention for long, and it seemed she had already lost it.

6

A silver Bentley was waiting for them when they landed and the driver took them to the central harbour. Having been told about the glamour of Monaco and how it was a tax haven for the very rich, Katrina looked out of the window curiously at all the tall buildings squashed into such a confined space. The streets were filled with elegant old ladies in fur, despite it being hot, walking small, groomed dogs. The roads were litter free, with police on each corner. There were so many expensive cars parked carelessly on kerbs – Ferraris, Porsches, Lamborghinis, Rolls-Royces – as well as the repetitive hum of highly tuned engines as convertibles sped past driven by men in blazers with women in the passenger seat with long hair flying behind them. Katrina could hardly believe that there could be so much wealth to be seen within the first five minutes of their arriving. As they approached the harbour, she saw lots of gleaming white boats lined up, bobbing gently in the water. Whilst it was not quite beautiful, it was certainly impressive.

The car pulled to a halt beside a huge dark blue boat with *The Lady Loretta* painted in gold on the side. Within seconds Katrina heard a high-pitched voice screech: 'Dominic! I'm so pleased you're here!'

Dominic was halfway up the gangplank when a vision in hot pink appeared and wrapped herself around him, holding on tightly for much too long. As he peeled her off him, Katrina's heart sank. This must be Loretta. She was a tall woman with platinum-blond hair down to her waist, and half-covered breasts almost falling out of her tight satin dress. Katrina felt underdressed. Loretta wrapped herself around Dominic again and whispered in his ear with plump lips dripping in pink gloss, pressing her body firmly against his. When she lifted her head she spotted Katrina and her eyes narrowed as she looked her up and down. She didn't acknowledge her, though, and continued whispering to Dominic. Another voice with a thick Italian accent interrupted them.

'Do put him down, Loretta. Poor boy hasn't even had a chance to get on the boat properly yet.' The voice belonged to a man who was sitting on a chair at the back of the boat. He got up and held his hand out to Dominic to help him aboard. Loretta pouted petulantly and pushed the man out of the way.

'Dominic and I have a lot of catching up to do. Let's get a drink, darling,' she purred, dragging him with her.

The man's eyes rested upon Katrina standing nervously at the bottom of the gangplank.

'*Ciao*, are you with Dominic?' he asked. She nodded. 'Come on board then. What are you waiting for?' He held his hand out to her and helped her along the narrow piece of wood. 'I'm Vincenzo, Loretta's brother, and you are . . . ?'

'Katrina.' She looked up at him, and thankfully he smiled, the skin crinkling around his eyes. At least there might be one friendly person who would acknowledge her existence amongst Dominic's friends. She didn't really know what else to say and simply looked around her in awe. The boat was incredible, with dark wooden floors and chrome fittings. Everything was gleaming and spotless, with the sun highlighting its perfection. It was sheer opulence, like nothing she had ever seen before. She had read about it in glossy magazines like *Vogue* and *Tatler* and had wondered about the sort of people who could enjoy such things. Now it looked like she would be spending the day with them. She laughed to herself at the thought that this one yacht was about four times bigger than her mother's two-bed house, and ten times more luxurious! She desperately wanted to explore it and to sample some of the delicious cakes that had been laid out on a table. For a moment she imagined being a movie star herself and having all that luxury at her fingertips. Would it get boring after a while? Dominic certainly didn't seem remotely impressed; it was his normal life.

Vincenzo interrupted her thoughts.

'Katrina, Loretta is not going to like you very much. She would prefer it if you were not so pretty.' He looked her up and down, as everyone seemed to have been doing over the past couple of days, and nodded admiringly. 'Let's go join the others.' She followed his brown legs and boat shoes up the stairs.

The top deck was the very image of wealth and privilege. Eight topless women were sunbathing on plush white sunloungers whilst the staff bustled around getting drinks and offering them exotic fruit. They were all deeply tanned, with breast implants and hair extensions, and they looked at Katrina expressionlessly through Chanel sunglasses without offering a hello. A couple of them exchanged looks and whispers. One woman with stripy brown and platinum hair went so far as to sit up, take her sunglasses off and stare obviously at her with narrowed, assessing eyes without any embarrassment at doing so. Katrina was reminded of being back at school, where she had tried to make herself invisible when walking into the canteen so that the pretty clique of girls wouldn't start making fun of her. She felt like that awkward, skinny teenager again and skulked past the women with her hair covering her face.

Vincenzo led her towards the table in the centre where the men were playing cards. They were all around the same age as him, with silver hair and dark skin, and they barely looked at her since she wasn't blond and tanned with big breasts. She stuck out like a sore thumb. If she had been Lauren, no doubt she would have whipped her top off by now and would be lying with the other women, pouting like her life depended on it. Instead she pulled her top down over her stomach and took her sunglasses off to say hello.

'This is Katrina,' Vincenzo announced. 'She is here with Dominic.'

The men all looked around to where Dominic was sitting close to Loretta on the edge of the boat. Her hand was on his knee and her pink-glossed mouth was near his ear. Katrina felt rather foolish. They looked back at her in amusement before continuing with their card game, and she sat awkwardly on the edge of a chair. They spoke in Italian so she was unable to understand any of the conversation. Instead she conducted a study of plastic surgery through her sunglasses as she noted that in addition to fake breasts there were also a number of face lifts, nose jobs and collagen lip implants littering the deck.

Someone sat in the chair next to her and she felt a glass pressed into her hand. A boy of about twenty with the typical Italian colouring of caramel skin, dark hair and brown eyes was smiling widely at her.

'We make it ourselves at our home in Tuscany. I promise you will enjoy.' He smiled and lifted his glass in a toast. 'To beautiful wine, beautiful sun and beautiful girl.'

Katrina took a sip of the wine and looked at him over the glass. 'Katrina.' She held out her hand.

'Carlos,' he replied, taking her hand and kissing it instead of shaking it. 'This is my mother's boat and you're very welcome on board.'

'Loretta's your mother?' Katrina spluttered. She'd estimated Loretta to only be around thirty-five.

'*Si*, she is. I'm twenty-two and my mother had me at a young age,' he explained, grinning widely and shaking back carefully cut locks that were falling over his eyes. 'Would you like me to show you around?' He gestured at the boat. Katrina was about to decline, then she looked over to where Dominic was still sitting with Loretta, totally oblivious to her existence, and changed her mind, taking Carlos's hand to help her up. There was no way she was going to hang around like some silly fan while Dominic flirted with his ex-girlfriend. As Carlos led her down the stairs, she saw Loretta remove Dominic's sunglasses and reach over to kiss him. She felt like she had been punched in the stomach and she looked away quickly. She hated Loretta so much and she could not believe Dominic had brought her to Monaco just to get off with his ex, who was a complete bitch. She was angry, but more than that she was hugely disappointed. She wanted to be the one kissing him on that beautiful yacht and she wanted to be the one to whom he gave his attention. Despite telling herself she was out of her depth with him, she had still been hoping he did actually like her.

A deflated Katrina followed Carlos, forgetting to revel in the opulence of the yacht. He led her through the kitchen, where they stopped to say hello to the staff and the chef let them sample various dishes. As they were leaving the kitchen, Carlos took a tub of ice cream from the side, along with a spoon. He then showed Katrina the lounge, with Versace throws and cushions everywhere. She estimated that the decor of the room had probably cost more than most average people in England would spend on an entire house! There were large life-size bronzes of lions and a beautiful Persian carpet that covered the entire floor.

'My mother, she is Versace crazy; bed linens, carpets, cushions, clothes, she loves Versace!' Carlos waved his arm around the room.' He then led her to another flight of stairs going down. 'This is where all the bedrooms are. There are five of them, and this is the master suite.'

He opened the door to a room decorated in Versace animal prints. It was obscenely lavish and not dissimilar to the lounge. A Dior dress that Katrina recognised from the last collection lay on the bed. She picked it up and held it against herself whilst looking in a mirror. It was pale pink and shimmered with opalescent pearls. A ballgown that would be unimaginable for a girl like her to ever wear, she thought. It had a tag hanging off it that said €4,000.

'That would look beautiful on you. I'll ask my mother if you can borrow it. She only ever wears anything once and then she puts it away,' Carlos informed her.

Katrina just smiled and laid the dress back on the bed. She doubted that she would ever have a function where she would wear a floaty pink designer dress worth a few grand. She also doubted that Loretta's generosity matched her son's.

'Can I use the bathroom?' she asked.

'Of course, use this one. I'll wait for you here.' Carlos pointed through the bedroom to a door.

The bathroom was gold and black with Versace tiling. Hanging on a hook were two matching black silk robes with gold tigers on the back. Versace, she guessed, giggling to herself. As she was sitting on the loo, she noticed a photograph of two people at a party. On closer inspection she saw that one of the figures was Loretta and the other was Dominic. It was such a perfect image: handsome man at a glamorous party with a sexy blonde hanging off his arm, with the background showing people laughing and dancing, yet he didn't look like he was having any fun. Loretta was gazing up at him, clinging to his arm in a slightly desperate manner whilst he looked directly into the camera, expressionless.

She let herself out of the bathroom and almost walked directly into Carlos, who was leaning against the wall drinking from a hip flask. He led her out of the room and towards another door.

'This is my room,' he said. She looked in. It was a total mess, with clothes strewn everywhere. The significant feature of the room was a large blown-up picture of Carlos and a stunning blonde girl with a perfect Christy Turlington nose, wide-apart green eyes and huge pouting lips. Her hair was thick and wavy, falling past her shoulders; her skin was lightly tanned and flawless. Her expression told Katrina that she knew exactly how impossibly beautiful she was.

'Who is that?' she asked curiously.

'That is my ex-girlfriend; she is a model. Do you recognise her? She is very famous for modelling.' Carlos walked up to the picture. Katrina studied it for a moment and then realised who it was: Cheryl Hutton, one of the new supermodels. Of course Katrina knew her! She had done a show with her a couple of seasons ago where Cheryl had ignored almost everyone, considering herself far too superior to speak to any average models. She had done lots of the big campaigns over the past year, including the latest Ralph Lauren campaign which featured advertising all over the world. You couldn't go far without seeing her perfect face staring down at you from every billboard and magazine. All the models wanted to be like Cheryl, who seemed to live the most glamorous of lives, always dating rich, eligible men and attending premieres on the arm of the latest rising stars in Hollywood. For a second Katrina imagined living that life, staying on yachts, wearing Dior and having a man like Dominic as a boyfriend.

She turned back to Carlos. 'How long ago did you break up?'

'Three weeks ago. She decided that it was better for her to be single, as she wants to become an actress and it won't be good for her to have a boyfriend. She is a beetch! Come, I will take you to the best room.'

They went back upstairs and he unlocked the door to a room furnished with huge suede sofas. On the walls were black and white photographs of Loretta, Carlos and Vincenzo in all sorts of glamorous locations, including yachts, open-topped sports cars and parties. There were also pictures of Carlos and a handsome older man who, by their resemblance to each other, Katrina guessed to be his father and Loretta's ex-husband. They all summed up a life of wealth, glamour and privilege.

'That is my father,' Carlos confirmed, pointing to the man in the photographs. 'He left my mother five years ago to be with a girl my age.'

With that dramatic statement, Carlos threw himself on one of the sofas, stretching out thin brown legs. He gestured to Katrina to join him, then he opened the tub of ice cream and offered her the spoon. Katrina took it and lay back beside him. Carlos was sweet and she felt comfortable lying next to him. After about ten minutes he fell asleep and Katrina was left eating the ice cream. Having lost out on more sleep than she was used to over the past couple of nights, she felt herself drifting off too.

Suddenly the door burst open and Dominic appeared with a livid expression. He glared at Katrina, then, without saying a word, turned and left. She sat frozen for a moment, wondering why he was so angry. He obviously regretted bringing her with him; maybe he had realised he still had feelings for Loretta and now Katrina was a hindrance. It had been a mistake coming to Monaco and she had been right to think that Dominic had no interest in her. She would excuse herself politely and leave. There had to be an airport or a train nearby, and she would go back to her unexciting life trudging the streets of Paris in the hope of getting a job.

Katrina found Dominic in the main lounge flicking through music channels on Sky. He didn't acknowledge her presence even when she sat next to him. His jaw was set and a muscle in his cheek twitched. Katrina didn't dare say a word.

'What do you want?' he snarled without taking his eyes from the screen.

'Are you okay? You seem angry.' She was stating the obvious as she didn't know what else to say. Dominic remained silent and changed channel again to an interview with Cameron Diaz. Katrina formed the words in her head to tell him that she would leave, yet looking at him she really didn't want to say that out loud.

'She's such a great girl, incredible body,' he commented, then flicked the television off, turning to face Katrina.

'What am I supposed to think?' He jumped straight in, startling her. 'I bring you away with me and within ten minutes you have disappeared! I can't find you and everyone is sniggering at me and then I find you holed up with that Italian wannabe playboy. Kind of rude, don't you think?' He moved to the edge of the sofa.

'Carlos was just showing me around. I've never been on a boat like this before and I saw you with Loretta so thought I'd occupy myself and not bother you. I'm really sorry.' Katrina was shocked that this was the reason he was angry. She secretly felt a rush of pleasure at his obvious jealousy and the fact that he minded that she might have gone off with Carlos. Maybe it had been Loretta kissing him rather than him kissing Loretta.

Dominic furrowed his brow and thought for a moment before the anger melted from his face and a glorious smile took over.

'Oh, I get it! You were jealous of me talking to Loretta.' Katrina's eyes widened as she began to protest that she wasn't at all. However, he mistook her expression for embarrassment and continued, 'Don't worry, there's nothing going on between Loretta and me. We had a lot to talk about as she's investing some money in a joint project. She's a very sexy woman but she's not my type any more. You're my type and that's why I brought you here.' He leant forward to kiss Katrina, leaving her incapable of speech. 'You have to understand that I'm not like ordinary guys you hang out with. I have to be careful about how people see me, as I'm always being watched. If you're going to spend time with me, you need to remember that, if you do something like disappear downstairs with another man, people will talk and then I'll look bad.' He tugged gently at her hair so her face tilted up towards his. 'You'll think before you act next time, right?'

Katrina was too stunned to say anything. Dominic Cayley was saying that he liked her and they were going to spend time together. Whilst she tried to piece this information together, he moved forward and kissed her again. She felt herself melt against him immediately. She had not stopped thinking about kissing him since last night. He pushed his tongue inside her mouth and ran his hand down her body then up again, stopping at her breast. He kissed her neck and then carried on moving downward to her stomach, pushing her top up to run his tongue around her belly button. He stopped again and looked up at her, making her stomach turn somersaults, before pulling her top over her head. He sat up and pulled his own shirt off, staying upright for a few seconds to give her the chance to admire his smooth, muscular upper body, then pressed against her and kissed her with more urgency than before. Pinning her down, he began undoing her jeans, stopping her protests with kisses. In a kind of paralysed state of mind, Katrina recalled what Lauren had told her about him and wriggled out of his grasp. Dominic tried to pull her back.

'Come on, it feels good, doesn't it?' he murmured, gently biting her ear. 'Don't fight it. You want it as much as I do.'

Katrina weakly pushed him away as he tried to undo her bra. 'I hardly know you. I only met you last night. Please stop!' He turned away on his stomach with his face down and was silent. She touched his shoulder tentatively.

'I'm sorry, please don't be mad.'

He groaned and lifted his head. Katrina was relieved to see he was laughing.

'I'm not angry, it's fine. You've left me in a tricky situation. I won't be able to go outside for a minute or two.' He rolled over on to his back, making no effort to hide the large bulge in his jeans. He was not the type to get embarrassed about much; he was confident enough to pull off just about anything without appearing an idiot. He looked at her. 'You can't blame me for trying, can you?' he asked. 'You're so lovely.' He pulled her towards him again so she had to look him in the eye. 'You don't really want to stop, do you? If you're worried that I won't respect you for sleeping with me so soon, then don't be. Honestly, I really like you and I intend to see a lot more of you. Let me, I'll make you feel so good.' He went to kiss her again, determined not to give up, and she felt her resolve weaken. How could anybody say no to Dominic Cayley?

There was a knock at the door.

'Dom? Are you in there?' The door swung open before he had a chance to answer and Loretta came in. She was wearing one of the silk bathrobes with a pair of satin high heels. She glared at Katrina and spoke directly to Dominic. 'Darling, the dinner table is reserved for one hour's time, so make sure you are ready. You will sit next to me so we can discuss business, and darling, please have a word with Carlos. He is devastated by that silly girl dumping him. Tell him how many millions of other models there are out there, all desperate for a rich man!' She gave Katrina a challenging look and with that swept out of the room, leaving the door open.

Dominic burst into laughter. 'Wow, she's such a bitch! She has a hatred of anyone younger and prettier than her, so you'll have to put up with her digs. I'm sure you can handle it.' He got up and reached to pull Katrina on to her feet. 'Come on, we had better go and get ready.'

'Where?' Katrina asked, relieved that Loretta had disturbed them.

'Our room,' he replied nonchalantly. 'I'm sure I told you that we'd probably be staying the night. There's no way we can go out tonight and then fly back to Paris in the dark. Loretta kindly said we could use a room. It'll be fun and it means we have tomorrow to do something.'

Katrina knew that he had not mentioned staying the night, same as he had not mentioned that the party was in Monaco, but she didn't contradict him as she was too excited at the thought that the date was going to continue all weekend. Surely, though, he wasn't so presumptuous as to think that she would share a room with him. But when they went downstairs and he opened the door to one of the rooms and shut it behind them, she realised that they *were* sharing a room and that it only had one bed in it.

'Umm, Dominic?' He turned towards her and looked her directly in the eyes, challenging her to jeopardise the opportunity of spending an entire night with him. Katrina took a deep breath. 'Do I have a different room?'

'Sweetheart, all the other rooms are taken, so no, you don't have a different room. I guess Loretta presumed that we were together, and I was kind of hoping you'd want to be with me tonight.' He paused, obviously suppressing his annoyance. 'If it bothers you that much, I'll sleep upstairs on a sofa, okay?'

'No.' Katrina reacted quickly, thinking of him on the sofa and Loretta prowling around. 'I want you to be with me. I'm sure you won't leap on me in the night.'

'I wouldn't be so sure of that.' He grinned wolfishly. 'You can use the bathroom first to freshen up.' He threw himself on to the bed and turned on the television. Katrina stood staring at him for a moment, amused at the normality of the situation. Just like any ordinary guy, he was lying on the bed flicking channels as if there was nothing odd about it, when for her it felt like her whole world had been turned upside down. She went into the bathroom and looked in the mirror. She decided to use black eyeliner and lots of mascara to emphasise the rock-chick look that he seemed to like. Assessing the finished work in the mirror, she conceded that she had done a good job, but what about the jeans? She looked casual even with an inch of make-up!

There was a tap on the door and she opened it. Dominic handed her a huge bag. 'You might need this,' was all he said before closing the door.

Katrina looked in the bag and pulled out three boxes of various sizes. Lifting the lid of the largest, she was astonished to see a dark blue Lanvin silk dress. In the second box was a pair of Christian Louboutin stilettos also in dark blue with a jewelled turquoise flower on the front, and in the final box was a turquoise suede Christian Dior saddlebag. All three items were absolutely stunning, and for a minute all Katrina could do was gaze at them, running her fingers over the expensive materials. They must have cost a fortune! She put the dress on; it fitted perfectly, although the shoes were slightly too tight. When she put her make-up in the bag, a tiny purse fell out and she found a pair of earrings shaped like little stars with turquoise stones. She beamed at herself in the mirror. This was the sort of thing that happened in her wildest fantasies, and yet here she was in real life wearing Lanvin and Christian Louboutin for a date with the hottest man alive!

When she came out of the bathroom she felt like a film star herself.

'Great, we're ready to go.' Dominic looked her up and down approvingly.

'I don't know how to thank you. The dress is so beautiful. How did you know my size, and when did you get it? It's just perfect. Thank you so much.'

'My PA organised it, I guess she just called a boutique and got them to drop it off. Don't thank me, all I did was pay. It slipped my mind to tell you to bring some stuff, so I had to get you something.' Dominic pushed her hair away from her face before kissing her. 'You look stunning and that's all that matters. Let's go, the car's waiting.'

As they got into the Bentley, it crossed Katrina's mind that actually in this case the reality was turning out even better than the fantasy.

When the car pulled up in front of an ugly concrete building, there were blinding flashes of light and people shouted Dominic's name as photographers snapped away. He grasped Katrina's hand, leading her towards the entrance, stopping a couple of times to smile at the cameras and shake hands with a few of the photographers. They got into an elevator, where they were alone.

'What was all that about? Did you know they would be there?' Katrina asked incredulously.

He laughed. 'There are always photographers somewhere, you should know that. The host tonight is Lawrence Fishbacher and his wife Simone, so press are to be expected.' Dominic studied himself in the elevator's mirrored walls and ran a hand through his hair.

Katrina was even more amazed. Lawrence Fishbacher was a hugely famous director, and his wife Simone was an actress, who, whilst not particularly talented, seemed to get a lot of parts. Katrina wondered who else would be at the table if he had invited people from all the films he had worked on. The elevator stopped and the door opened on to a room with a wooden floor and brown leather sofas and chairs. People were sitting around chatting over the loud music and fashion TV was playing on screens dotted around the place. Dominic led Katrina through the room.

Everyone stopped to look at them and the women gazed admiringly at Dominic. He stopped at the bar and looked around. A girl with blond curly hair wearing a yellow leather miniskirt that revealed long brown legs tapped him on the shoulder.

'Hi, Dominic, long time no see! How are you?' She slid her hand down his arm in a familiar manner.

He looked through her, barely bothering to cover his inability to recognise her. 'Fine, thanks.' He turned away from the girl and Katrina saw her face drop as they walked away. 'That happens a lot,' he remarked. 'People think they know me because they've read an interview or something. I've never seen that girl before in my life. They must all be in the restaurant. We'll go through.'

They went past the bar into another section, filled with people eating at tables and waiters rushing around carrying trays of drinks. The music was as loud in here as in the bar. Again everyone stopped to stare at them as they walked through. People were looking at Katrina with interest and admiration. She felt incredible, like the model she was meant to be in a beautiful designer dress in an exclusive restaurant. Excitement bubbled up within her as she realised that she would be having dinner as the date of a greatly desired film star with other Hollywood actors, producers and directors. She hoped the photographers would get a picture of that so she could show her friends. Dominic stopped suddenly and she collided with his back, apologising profusely. He ignored her, instead flashing his dazzling teeth at the table of people.

'Hi, Lawrence, how are you? Simone, you look as gorgeous as ever. Hi, everyone. This is Katrina. Where do you want us to sit?'

Katrina looked at the faces staring at her, recognisable faces that she had seen on screen. Smiles broke out revealing row upon row of cosmetically perfect teeth as they all greeted Dominic, praising him for his last film and telling him how well he looked. Katrina was ignored and stood feeling awkward until she felt a tap on her shoulder.

'Hi!' James kissed her on the cheek. 'It's nice to see you again. Hi, Dominic. I think Loretta has saved a seat next to her for you.' They exchanged glances. 'Katrina can sit next to me, I'll look after her.'

'Not too well, I hope!' Dominic joked, making his way over to Loretta, who leapt to her feet and kissed him on the lips.

James pulled out a chair for Katrina. 'You look lovely,' he said. 'Did you stay much longer last night? Dominic said you both had fun. He was useless at the gym this morning, couldn't do a thing, so it must have been a late one.'

'I can't remember when we left, although I remember getting home about half one. It was good.' Katrina smiled gratefully at the waiter as he placed a napkin over her knees. She noticed Zora at the end of the table talking to a heavily made-up woman whilst watching her and James. Katrina gave her a weak smile, which was not reciprocated. She turned back to James. It was surprising to see him there. She hadn't realised he was such good friends with Dominic. 'Do you work in films too?' she asked in an attempt to figure it out.

'Well, I owned a property company, which I sold and used some of the money to invest in small productions. That's how I met Dominic; he worked on a film in London for a bit. It was one of his first films, a small-budget thing that never went anywhere but the back of the video shop.' He laughed. 'My finances are a little out of the league of the blockbuster stuff he does now! Anyway, we got on okay and I showed him London, and then after that I got him into a few property investments with all the money he was pulling in. Apart from that, I'm a bit of an outsider. Everyone here is either extremely rich, famous or beautiful, and I am none of those things. The only reason I'm here tonight is because I've been in Monaco for business today and Dominic put me on the list.' He lowered his voice. 'I don't really know any of the people on this table, although Zora who you met last night is here. She was invited by the man she is sitting next to.' They both looked over at the extremely thin man with a sparse arrangement of orange hair and a beaky expression. 'Apparently he owns jewellers' on Bond Street and on the Champs Elysées, which makes him very eligible!' James turned back to Katrina. 'To be honest, I try and avoid this kind of thing if I can, it all tends to be a bit false. Dominic is a lot of fun to be around, though, and there's something about him that's very likeable, as I'm sure you will agree.' Katrina nodded and James refilled his water glass, giving her the chance to look at him. He didn't seem to fit in with the rest of the table, either in appearance or manner. He was wearing black moleskin trousers and a blue shirt while the other men wore suits. His face looked lived-in, with deep lines around his eyes when he smiled.

'Do you still live in London?' she asked curiously.

'God, yes, I couldn't live anywhere else. I'm a Londoner born and bred. Grew up in Harrow, in a rough-as-hell estate, and then moved to Clapham when I got my first flat years ago. Now I live in South Kensington because my offices are there. I hate traffic, so I walk to the office. How about you?'

'I have a room in Oval in a flat that I share with any other models the agency puts in. I kind of live out of a suitcase, though. If I don't get work in Paris then I'll go back to my mother's house in Hampshire for a bit and figure out what to do.'

James raised an eyebrow. 'It's hard to imagine you wouldn't be working all the time, but I suppose there are only a few jobs and a lot of girls. It's such an odd business. Lots of models seem to struggle to earn above an average wage and everyone else takes advantage of that.' He watched as an overweight middle-aged man walked up to a striking young girl who was obviously a model and kissed her. He turned back to Katrina. 'Anyway, how do you like Monaco? Are you staying with Dominic on the boat?'

Katrina didn't know how to answer, as she didn't want him to think that she was sharing a bed with Dominic after having only met him twenty-four hours ago.

'I didn't know we were staying until a couple of hours ago,' she replied carefully. 'I think we're staying on the boat and going back to Paris tomorrow. Dominic has said he'll give up his room and sleep on the sofa so I can stay.'

James raised an eyebrow. 'Has he indeed? That's very kind of him.' He looked across at Dominic. 'I didn't know you were such a gentleman, Dom.'

'What do you mean?' Dominic laughed. 'You know I'm the perfect gentleman.'

'I'm sure.' James turned back to Katrina. 'Just make sure he does behave himself tonight!' Dominic made a face at her. A plate was placed in front of her with a small unidentifiable object on it. Katrina eyed it suspiciously.

'It's a calf's liver pâté,' James said, noticing her expression. He pushed his plate aside. 'Not my sort of food. I can't stand these carefully presented bits of crap that cost a hundred quid. It's a set menu tonight, which is never a good idea.'

'It doesn't look too appetising.' Katrina pushed her own plate away. 'It doesn't matter, as I'm not very hungry anyway.' As she looked around the table, she noticed that no one was really eating; they were lighting cigarettes and topping up glasses. She turned back to James. 'Isn't anyone going to eat?'

'Not if they can help it. They only come to drink and smoke and gossip; the food's irrelevant. This place has got a reputation for having great food but I don't think anyone has actually tried it. If I were you I'd start drinking the wine. It's very good and it helps you forget how hungry you are. Red or white?' He reached for the wine.

'White, please.' Katrina smiled gratefully as James poured her a glass. He leant over to get a piece of bread, looking up as someone's hand touched his shoulder.

'Hi, Zora, you remember Katrina from last night, don't you?'

Zora glanced at Katrina and gave her a fake smile. 'Sure I do, darling. What are you two talking about? I'm getting so bored over there. Stephan keeps trying to touch me up and I can't protect myself for much longer, so I've come over to escape. This is a crappy seating arrangement.' She looked at Katrina as she spoke with a disdainful look in her eye. She was wearing an extremely short black dress and looked just as striking as she had the night before. But there was something about her that made her quite unattractive, perhaps the awareness of how beautiful she was that showed in the way she held herself. She lacked any modesty.

'So, Katherine, how's it going with Dominic? He's a fast worker, no?' Zora perched on the arm of James's chair. 'That's a beautiful dress. Did he buy it for you? He bought a friend of mine a lovely dress a few weeks ago by Gaultier. It cost three thousand euros. She looked amazing in it.' She smirked and ran a hand through her hair. 'James, darling, do you know where the bathroom is?' She stood up and went in the direction he pointed, leaving her questions unanswered.

James retrieved his napkin from where it had fallen under the chair and Katrina suspected he was thinking of what to say in response to Zora's vicious comments.

'Don't listen to her. I expect what happened is Dom needed a date for one of his events and got a stylist to buy the friend a dress. I think it's safe to say you're much nicer than any friend of Zora's, so forget what she said.' James smiled gently. 'She's probably had too much to drink. I'll go and see if she's okay.' He got up and left.

Dominic spotted the empty seat and came over.

'Hey, my crazy English girl, you and James seem to be getting on well. He gets on with everyone.'

'I like him. He was telling me about how you met doing your first film,' Katrina replied.

'Yeah, well, he's a really decent guy, and even though he doesn't fit in with my usual crowd I like him being around. He's always very honest with me. He's one of the only people I trust.' He smiled sexily at her before kissing her very slowly. Then he pulled back and pushed a strand of hair away from her face. 'Oh, by the way, I just got a phone call from Alex and Lauren. She said hello and that she's flying to New York for two days tomorrow so won't be there when you get back, in case you're worried. The food is quite atrocious here, don't you think?' He eyed her untouched starter with disgust and placed a hand on her thigh.

Katrina remembered to breathe again and took a huge gulp of wine.

'Get out of my seat. As soon as I turn my back you're trying to steal my place!' James pretended to tip Dominic out of his chair. 'I am starving. We're going to have to go out for dinner after this. How did you manage to escape Loretta's clutches?'

'She's turned her attentions on another unsuspecting victim.' Dominic rolled his eyes. 'Where's Zora gone this time? She keeps going to the toilet every five minutes. She does far too much coke.'

The woman sitting on Katrina's left, who had not acknowledged her so far, got up and went over to Dominic's seat so she could talk to Loretta. James sat down in her place.

'That's more like it,' he said before clapping his hands sarcastically. 'Oh joy, here comes the main course!' A plate with a thin piece of greyish meat on it and sautéed potatoes was placed in front of each of them. Dominic prodded the meat and then put his fork down.

'I'm not eating this, it's been cooked in butter and I'm trying to keep my body in top shape.'

'My mother always told me not waste food, but this really doesn't look very good,' Katrina said, pushing her plate away. She had no appetite in Dominic's presence anyway.

'I agree,' said James, also pushing his plate to one side. 'I can't believe this place, it's a total rip-off. I'm glad I'm not paying. We'll have to find a Chinese takeaway. Have another drink.' He filled Katrina's glass to the top. 'We may as well get drunk on our empty stomachs.'

'Stop trying to get my date drunk. That's my job.' Dominic reached over for Katrina's glass and took a mouthful of wine. 'I left my glass over there and I'm not drinking out of that woman's. Who knows where she's been?'

'Probably everywhere and more by the look of her.' The three of them looked over at the woman, who had dyed blond hair, massive collagen lips and a very tight face lift that made her look permanently shocked. James laughed. 'Nothing like a bit of collagen to put you off your dinner. Oh great, here comes trouble.' He spotted Zora charging towards them with a furious look on her face.

'I am going to go now! I've got a headache and it's

boring here,' she announced, pouting petulantly at James. 'I do not have anywhere to stay. Can I stay with you?'

Dominic laughed out loud whilst James looked slightly shocked. 'You really haven't got anywhere to stay? What about your date, didn't he sort something out for you?' Zora shook her head. James reached into his pocket and pulled out a key and a twenty-euro note. 'The Bay Hotel, get a taxi.'

'Darling, please, why don't you come with me?' Zora turned her beautiful eyes upon Dominic pleadingly before trying to take James's arm.

'No, just get a taxi and go.' James looked away and filled up his glass. 'So, Dom, what's the plan? Are you going on somewhere?' Zora stamped her foot, then turned and stormed towards the door. 'I don't know how you put up with living and working with girls like that all the time. Always game-playing and manipulating to get their own way; it's all they know.' James spoke quietly to Katrina, obviously trying to curb his annoyance.

'I don't expect Zora is used to being turned down,' commented Dominic, looking with confusion at James. 'Her date's been eyeing me up all evening so he wouldn't have bothered organising a room for her. Are you sure you're not gay too?' He laughed loudly.

'Absolutely positive, and I've got two children to prove it. Zora's beautiful, but she's not my type and I doubt I'm really hers,' James responded drily.

'Anyone with a bit of money and in the right social circle is Zora's type.'

Katrina wondered if that was true. It would make more sense for Zora to be after Dominic. However, she noticed that although the majority of women in the restaurant kept looking over at Dominic, quite a few were also checking James out. He caught her looking at him and smiled. He had nice teeth, not cosmetically whitened like many of the men at the table but straight and even. She looked over at Dominic, who was busy texting someone. His profile was perfect: straight aquiline nose, strong brow. He was biting his lip and looked everything that she expected a film star to be.

'Hey, James, can you take a look at a house in Beverly Hills I'm thinking about buying? I'm going to have to do so much to it and I need to check I can actually do what I want before I get it.'

'Sure, get your PA to send me the details and I'll look into it. How much?' James asked.

'Can't remember ... it's a lot, though. Over ten million, maybe closer to twenty ...' Dominic shrugged and then laughed as James rolled his eyes. 'There's so much going on at the moment. I can't remember stuff like that.'

'Oh, how I would love to be so rich and carefree!' James taunted in good humour.

They were interrupted by Lawrence Fishbacher drifting by.

'Lawrence, why do you always have parties here? The food is dire,' Dominic complained.

Lawrence took a puff of a huge cigar and slowly exhaled. He was fat, with wild white hair floating like a cloud around his head. 'Nothing wrong with the food and I like the atmosphere. Listen, while I've got you for a second, I want you to have a look at a script I'm sending to your agent first thing Monday. Make sure you get it faxed to you wherever you are and read it for once. I take it you *can* read? Everything I send to you, you ignore. For Chrissake read this one, I think you'll like it.' His eyes rested on Katrina. 'Who is this young thing?'

'This is Katrina, she's here with me.' Dominic took a cigar from the box Lawrence held open to him; James declined. 'What is this script, then?'

'I don't really want to get into it right now as Simone wants to leave; she's got a headache as usual. There's already some big names wanting to be involved and it is right for you at this stage in your career. Just pick it up and read it.' He turned his attention back to Katrina. 'So are you an actress, dancer, model?' He squinted through a cloud of smoke. 'You shouldn't hang around with the likes of Mr Cayley; he's nothing but trouble, you know.'

'I'm a model,' Katrina replied, feeling shamefully predictable. 'I met Dominic last night and he invited me here . . .' she added lamely. A look of boredom had crept over Lawrence's face.

'Well, it's a pleasure to meet you, and you look stunning, which is all I would expect from a girlfriend of yours,' Lawrence told Dominic. 'My wife's waving at me from across the room; I'd better go. Don't forget the script. Remind him,' he said to Katrina, winking. He stubbed out his cigar and went towards his wife.

Katrina was quietly thrilled that Lawrence had referred to her as Dominic's girlfriend. She had almost expected Dominic to correct him and inform him that they had only just met. She imagined being featured beside Dominic in magazines and interviews. She pictured her friends seeing her in *Hello!* magazine attending a premiere on his arm. Everyone would be so envious.

Dominic interrupted her visions of fame and glamour by kissing her on the lips. 'You're very sweet, and Lawrence was right: you do look stunning. A good designer dress takes a nice-looking girl and makes her look like the most beautiful girl in the room.' Katrina wasn't sure whether he was complimenting her or Lanvin. She also wasn't sure about the term 'sweet'; surely sexy, stylish or seductive would be better. 'I'm going to order some drinks. Scotch and soda for you, James? Katrina? Do not say water.'

That was exactly what she was about to say and no doubt it would fit with his description of her as 'sweet'. She decided to shock him.

'I'll have a Remy XO, please,' she said. James and Dominic looked at her in astonishment.

'Seriously? You don't really want that, do you?' Dominic asked. 'How about a glass of champagne or a cocktail?'

Katrina shook her head. 'No, I want a proper drink.'

'Okay, whatever you say.' He beckoned the waiter over and ordered. 'Let's go to Electric after these,' he said to James.

'Do we have to? I'd prefer it if we just went out for dinner. Electric is such a poseur's paradise. Have you ever been there?' James addressed Katrina and she shook her head. 'It consists of huge queues of ridiculously glamorous people; most of them get turned away. The drinks are about fifty quid regardless of whether it's water or vodka, there are lots of Zora types everywhere and they have random fashion shows going on in the middle.'

It sounded quite awful to Katrina and she preferred the idea of going somewhere quiet to eat where they would pay her attention, as she was really enjoying the three of them chatting without any other girls distracting them.

'Well, we won't have to queue, will we now? They are hardly going to turn me away. The prices of the drinks is irrelevant, the girls are easy on the eye and Katrina likes fashion shows. Anyway, Zora's got your room, and if you don't feel like her company then you'll have to stay on the boat tonight.' Dominic mock-grimaced at James. 'It's only half past twelve. We'll drink these and then we'll leave.'

The waiter placed their drinks in front of them. Aware of James and Dominic watching her, Katrina lifted her glass and took a large gulp, feeling the Remy burn its way down her throat to her stomach.

'Just what I needed,' she said weakly, hoping her watering eyes didn't give her away.

Dominic laughed. 'Wow, you weren't kidding. You really do drink proper drinks. It's a hundred dollars a shot, that stuff, but I don't mind if you actually drink it. It's better than stupid pink cocktails, which most girls like. I'm just going to have a slash.' He got up and left.

Katrina took a swig of water to calm the fire and looked at the glass of brandy. It was much more than a shot; in fact it looked more like three or four. Just as she was wondering how she was going to finish it, James leant forward, took the glass and downed the lot in one go. He put it back in front of her, wincing as the strong liquid burnt down to his stomach.

'Tell him you drank it. I could see you weren't too keen but I don't think he did.' James winked conspiratorially at her. 'Excuse me whilst I stagger to the loo.'

Katrina was left touched by his gesture. He must have realised that she only ordered the Remy to impress Dominic. If she had drunk it all she would have been horribly drunk and probably sick, which would have gone down really well on Loretta's squillion-pound yacht. She wondered if he had ordered such a large glass purposely to test her or to get her drunk.

Dominic slid back into the chair, jolting her out of her thoughts.

'You drank it all!' he exclaimed, picking up the empty glass. 'I'd be totally pissed on that with all the wine over dinner. My God, you must be a hard case. I thought you said you didn't normally drink?' He tilted Katrina's chin and looked at her. 'You don't look drunk at all. Damn, I was hoping to be able to take advantage.' He kissed her. 'I like kissing you, you taste of cherries.'

'It's my lip balm,' Katrina admitted. He kissed her

again. She noticed his eyes were actually a mixture of blue and green, with long lashes most girls would envy. Her stomach flipped over and she felt incredibly shy as he looked intensely at her. Stubble was starting to form on his upper lip and it scratched her face. She saw James making his way towards them, rebounding off a table and apologising profusely. Dominic got to his feet and helped her up.

'Time to leave before someone suggests going to an apartment for drinks.' He waved goodbye across the table to Loretta, who blew a kiss at him and mouthed 'later' before rearranging her dress so that her hard fake breasts were even more on display.

'God, she's an old tart!' James sniggered in Katrina's ear. 'An absolute man-eater. She'll be sneaking into your room tonight trying to seduce Dom under your nose!'

Katrina made a mental note firstly not to let Dominic sleep in the sofa room and secondly to lock the bedroom door. She would risk her virtue to stop Loretta getting her claws into him.

When they got outside they couldn't see the driver so decided to walk, as the club was only down the road.

'I might be in the States next week on business. When are you going home?' James asked Dominic.

'Mid-week, I reckon. I have a flight on hold for Wednesday. Filming has just about finished which is great because I've kind of had enough of Paris,' Dominic answered.

Katrina's heart sank. He was leaving Paris in a few days and she wouldn't see him again. He obviously hadn't even considered seeing her after the weekend. It was stupid for her to think that it was any more than just a night. He could have anyone he wanted – a Brazilian supermodel, an American actress, a French singer – so why would he be bothered about a mediocre model?

They approached a mass of people all pushing and shouting in various languages.

'What are they doing?' Katrina asked James curiously.

'Queuing, apparently,' he answered, rolling his eyes. The crowd were dressed head to toe in designer, the women all in dresses with skyscraper high heels, yet they were shoving and swearing like the queue for a rave in Croydon.

Dominic caught the eye of a woman with scraped-back hair and a fierce face dominated by the slash of burgundy lipstick on her mouth. She acknowledged him and whispered to one of the many doormen standing next to her. He stepped forward and the queue parted like the Red Sea. Dominic strode through and kissed the fierce woman on both cheeks, with the eyes of the queue upon him in awe. She nodded stiffly at James and Katrina and gestured that the crowd move back. As they walked through into the club, Katrina was stunned by the sight of well-dressed, beautiful women hanging off unattractive men. A particularly stunning girl walked past holding hands with a bald man in his fifties. James and Katrina exchanged glances.

'See what I mean? It's just so sleazy. Where the hell is Dominic going?' They watched him disappear in the crowd. 'I'm just popping to the loo, back in a sec,' said James.

Katrina saw Dominic stop at a table to speak to a man with wild curly blond hair. He caught her eye and beckoned her over.

'I've ordered you a drink,' he said.

The curly haired man looked Katrina up and down before smirking at Dominic, who didn't bother to introduce them. He went on talking, his tone aggressive.

'I just don't think you should have signed without telling me first. I worked with you for six years and then you just go to someone else because you think you're too big for me. That's totally disloyal. I thought we were friends, although you always were an arrogant bastard.'

'Look, Martin, I'm sorry. You couldn't do what Miranda could so I had to make a tough decision. I'm out right now and I just want to relax and have a good time; I've been working really hard. Why don't you just give me a call next week or something.' Dominic dismissed him, waving his hand and turning away.

'Just forget it, like you'll answer your phone anyway. I've been trying for eight months. Twelve years of friendship and then it doesn't suit you any more, doesn't fit into your little world!' Martin looked at Katrina. 'Watch him, sweetheart, guys like him only know how to use people. All that matters is their superficial image!' He slammed his glass on the table and stormed off.

'What was that all about?' Katrina asked timidly. Dominic's face was thunderous for a moment before his expression changed to one of exasperation and he handed her her drink.

'He was my agent when I started out, but as more work came through he didn't have the capacity to handle it; too small-time to deal with the big stuff. I broke the contract and left for another agent. He's a bit sore about it because he reckons that he made me, which is a load of bollocks.' Dominic erased any sign of concern from his face as a tall brunette waved at him. 'That drink's a step up from Remy XO, it's Louis, top stuff. Can you give James his drink and tell him the next one's on him, seeing as that just cost me four hundred euros. I'm just going to say hello to someone I know.' He disappeared again into what seemed to be a mass of hair extensions and fake breasts.

James appeared by Katrina's side.

'What are you drinking?' He sniffed her glass. 'Oh no,' not more, and that's the really good stuff. Louis?' Katrina nodded. 'Christ! That must have cost an absolute fortune in here. You won't be able to drink it, will you?'

'If it cost that much I can't throw it away. I'll have to make myself drink it.' Katrina lifted the glass, wincing at the strong smell.

James took it out of her hand. 'I'll drink it, but please don't let him get another one. It's not really what you want to drink in a club, and especially not after you've just had a mouthful of the other stuff.' He took a long sip of the cognac whilst eyeing Katrina thoughtfully. 'I'll let you in on a little secret. I've seen a number of beautiful, disdainful and often downright stupid girls come and go with Dominic, usually within a night. You're different to the girls he usually hangs around with, and if you like him you should play a bit hard to get, blow him out a few times.' He drained the glass and put it back in her hand just before Dominic got to them.

'You haven't seriously drunk all that, have you?' he asked incredulously. 'My God, you put James and me to shame, and you don't look even vaguely drunk. Is this an English thing because you all grow up in pubs or something? I've never dated an English girl before but they certainly aren't cheap dates like the rumour goes. James, you look awful. You've only had the same as me; you're turning into a lightweight in your old age.'

'It's the lack of bloody food,' James replied, catching Katrina's eye and winking. 'Is there anywhere in Monaco that does a greasy fry-up or fish and chips?' He swayed and held on to her arm.

'Stop thinking about food for five seconds and relax. I've asked for a table over there. They were happy to give us one when I told them one of our party had a taste for Louis at two hundred and fifty euros a shot.' Katrina gulped. That was a week's rent for her!

They went to a tiny table with bony wooden chairs. People were dancing wildly around it to Jay-Z. A sweating man with his shirt undone revealing an expanse of greying chest hair tried to make her dance with him. James pushed him out of the way.

'I think I'm getting quite drunk,' he said, wincing as Katrina stepped back on his toe. She laughed when he went to put his drink on the table and totally missed so it smashed to the floor. 'There goes fifty quid.'

A curvaceous blonde was dancing purposefully in front of Dominic, looking at him as she gyrated around. He didn't notice her; he was engrossed with his mobile. He touched the waiter's arm as he went by and spoke to him briefly. The blonde got a little closer.

'I think Dominic has got an admirer, and so have you, Katrina.' James motioned over her shoulder, where the sweaty man was still hanging around eyeing her. 'Jesus, Dom, why have you ordered more drinks?' The waiter placed yet another round of the same in front of them. Katrina took a gulp of the cognac, worried that James would think he had to drink it again. She started coughing. The blonde leant forward and said something in Dominic's ear, her silicone breast against his shoulder. He laughed and shook his head. She shrugged and carried on dancing in front of him.

'What did she just say to you, Dom?' asked James, raising an eyebrow.

'She asked if I would like to go outside and have some fun.' Dominic laughed. 'It's just so easy being a man nowadays; you don't have to do any legwork.'

'I can't believe she said that.' Katrina was shocked. 'What did you say?'

'That I would love to and I'd meet her out the front in five minutes,' Dominic replied sarcastically. 'You don't mind, do you? She'll charge me a hundred dollars.'

Katrina very much doubted that; the girl looked more like she would pay *him* for the pleasure. She couldn't take her eyes off him. Boldly Katrina moved her chair closer to Dominic and leant over to kiss him. He responded, biting her lip gently and running his tongue around her mouth. The blonde gave her a filthy look and moved off.

'Hello, I'm finally getting a response from you. All that expensive alcohol is beginning to work.' Dominic grinned at James. 'Maybe I won't be sleeping on the sofa after all.'

The way he kissed was so experienced and confident, it made her whole body tingle just being near him. He put a hand on her leg, stroking her thigh as he scanned the room. Katrina felt nervous at the thought of sleeping with him. He would expect someone who knew what they were doing in bed; he might get bored quickly if she didn't make it good for him, and that was if he didn't just cast her aside after he had got what he wanted anyway. Katrina saw so many beautiful girls looking his way, just waiting for the chance to approach him. There were other good-looking men around but Dominic was a star and he could make any girl a star too if they could stay with him long enough. James's advice was good. Dominic was used to girls throwing themselves at him and the only way she could be different was by playing hard to get, never letting him know that she felt slightly out of her depth with him. That, however, was easier said than done.

She felt a tap on her shoulder and looked up. Mark, a male model who was at her London agency Source, was smiling broadly at her. Exactly what she needed to play it cool. Mark would show Dominic that she knew other good-looking men.

'Oh my God, what are you doing here?' She leapt up rather overenthusiastically and kissed him on the cheek.

'I know! The last person I expected to see was you,' he replied, looking her up and down appreciatively. 'I'm here on a job, staying on a boat and doing a fashion show during the day. It's a shite job but good money and I get to come here. How about you?'

'I'm here with Dominic and James; we came over from Paris for a dinner party. This is Mark,' she said. James shook his hand and said hello. Dominic just looked coldly at him and started to talk to James. Katrina felt embarrassed for Mark, who pulled her to one side.

'I'm very impressed that you're with the legendary Dominic Cayley, and you're looking fantastic!' He took her hand. 'Come and dance with me.'

James and Dominic were discussing something intensely so she doubted she would be missed. 'Okay,' she said and followed him towards the dance floor. She noticed Dominic was watching her from the table. As Loretta came in, making a beeline for Dominic, Mark nudged her.

'Talk about mutton dressed as lamb. She'd be arrested in London for dressing like that.'

Katrina giggled. She caught Dominic's eye; he looked stonily at her before walking away with Loretta.

'I'd better go back,' Katrina told Mark. 'Maybe I'll see you again later.'

'Why don't you give me your number and we could meet up tomorrow?'

Before yesterday she would have given him her number right then. 'Just call the agency and they'll give it to you,' she said over her shoulder, leaving Mark pouting sulkily. A male model was no comparison to Dominic Cayley.

Dominic and Loretta weren't at the table. James was resting his head on his hand with his eyes shut.

'Where's Dominic gone?' Katrina asked. James opened his eyes and stood up, swaying slightly.

'They've gone across to a private party in a friend's apartment, someone that Loretta knows and Dominic needs to know, apparently. He said to tell you that he'll see you back at the boat in an hour or so.' James shifted awkwardly as he saw her face drop. 'Trust me, it will do him good to see you aren't going to hang off him. He'll sulk and then he'll come back to find you.'

'Do you really think so?' Katrina wasn't sure if she was up to game-playing with a man who was really out of her league. 'What if he just stays out all night with Loretta?'

'He won't, I promise,' James replied, not looking entirely convincing. They both knew that Dominic always did whatever Dominic wanted to do. 'I'll take you back to the boat. My head is banging from all that alcohol and I just want to lie down.'

When they got back to the boat, the skipper let them in and James opened the door to the sofa room. He threw a cushion on the floor and lay down.

'My head hasn't spun like this for years. I can't believe how much I've drunk. If my liver fails tonight, on your head be it!' He patted the floor next to him. 'Sit down if you like.'

'I'm really sorry about your head. Shall I find you a painkiller or something?' Katrina felt immensely guilty, but he shook his head. 'You've been really nice to me tonight, thank you.'

'No problem.' He moved his cushion so that he could see her. 'You're too good for Dom to mess around with, film star or not. Don't be fooled into thinking he is some kind of god just because of the image he presents to everyone. He's just a guy with a job that happens to be acting.' He pulled his T-shirt off. His stomach was ripped and he had a defined six-pack. Katrina had always thought of forty-year-olds as being middle-aged, yet James looked fitter then most twenty-year-olds. She glanced up and saw him watching her studying him. She averted her gaze quickly.

'Go to bed now, you look tired.' He laughed. 'If you plan to hang out with Dominic, you'll be doing this kind of thing all the time: parties, women like Loretta, people sticking their noses into your business. It's all pretence, and even Dominic must get tired of it. I find it absolutely exhausting!' He leant across and kissed her on the cheek. 'Good luck and good night.'

Katrina was not too sure what he meant. The whole day had been glamorous and exciting, from the helicopter ride to the yacht, the designer clothes, having the best table in an expensive restaurant surrounded by famous people, and best of all being the date of a gorgeous movie star. What was there to get tired of? It was everybody's dream to live like that, and it had been a fabulous day.

Katrina made her way down to the room, marvelling at the beautiful boat. It felt exquisitely luxurious. She kicked off her shoes and unzipped the beautiful dress, carefully laying it in the original box. The T-shirt Dominic had worn all day was thrown on the bed. She put it on rather than be in her underwear when he got back. The clock on the wall said two thirty as she lay back on the bed thinking about the past twenty-four hours and how strange it had been.

She must have fallen asleep, because she was woken by the sound of Dominic closing the door behind him. The clock read three fifteen. Katrina pretended to be asleep and watched through her lashes as he unbuttoned his shirt and came towards her.

'What have I got here? My T-shirt has been stolen by a strange English girl.' He ran his hand down her legs. 'What happens if I need it back? You won't have anything to wear.'

He reached over and began to kiss her neck. Katrina opened her eyes and pulled away from him. He got on the bed and put his weight on her. She couldn't help but kiss him back, and feeling her positive reaction, he put his hands under her top. It was electric for a moment and she pressed against him.

'I think I do need this T-shirt back, you know. I daren't

sleep naked in case you try to ravish me.'

'No,' Katrina protested, backing off.

Dominic laughed before grabbing the shirt at the bottom and pulling it off over her head, laughing at her struggles to keep it on. 'Come on, I know better than that! Models are never shy about being naked.'

Luckily Katrina was wearing the matching pink bra and knickers set her mother had got her for her birthday rather than the usual mismatch. Dominic tried to unclip her bra as she wriggled out of his grasp and leapt off the bed. He went to grab her arm and force her back down but she broke his grasp and fell on to the floor. He looked down at her narrow body with its long limbs and grinned wickedly.

'Come on, I really want to feel your body against mine, and that's what you want too. Just give up.' He went to pull her up.

'Please don't! I didn't know we were staying the night but I don't want to go any further than kissing.' Katrina got to her feet and stepped back.

Dominic's expression switched instantly from amusement to exasperated impatience as he realised she wasn't joking. 'You were happy enough to be all over that guy you were with in the club!' he snarled. 'Either you want to be with me or you don't. I don't have time to mess about. What's it to be?' Despite the fact he was being a total bastard he looked incredible, with his shirt undone and his hair ruffled, clenched jaw covered in stubble. His face was cold, hiding his utter rage. Katrina doubted that any girl had ever rejected him and he was almost daring her to say no as he stood half-naked with his perfect god-like physique. For a moment she contemplated throwing herself at him, doing anything to please him, but she managed to control herself. She had to stick to James's advice no matter what.

'I want to be with you. All I'm saying is that I'm not going to have sex with you,' she replied through gritted teeth, hoping he would accept that and kiss her again. However, he just looked at her with a furious expression before turning without saying a word and walking out of the room, closing the door behind him.

Katrina slumped on the bed miserably; that had totally backfired. All he had ever wanted was sex, nothing more, and now he had probably gone to Loretta. She felt like a total idiot. She would have to spend the day hanging around waiting until he wanted to go home and sit in the helicopter with him or get a flight by herself. She had totally blown it. She would never get another chance with a guy like him. She would have to go back to being a nobody, and return to living in that horrible hotel room. Lauren would laugh her head off.

When Katrina woke up, she immediately felt a pang of nerves at the thought of having to face Dominic. It felt pretty awful pulling on the same clothes from the day before and her face looked pale and dark-eyed. Letting herself out of the room and making her way to the deck, she saw Vincenzo, James and another man with his back to her sitting at a table having breakfast. The sun was glinting off the sea and buildings towered in the distance framed by escalating mountains topped by a brilliant blue sky. She was struck by how fantastically glamorous the scene was and she felt even more depressed that her time in this world was over already.

Vincenzo looked up and saw her.

'*Ciao, bella*, how are you?' He pulled out a chair for her.

Katrina was stunned to see that the third guy at the table was Jon Paul Sullivan, her most favourite actor! He had done some brilliant films, including *Grit* and

Manufacturing Consent. She had watched them both at least ten times and now couldn't stop herself staring at him in amazement.

'This is Katrina,' James said, recognising her awe. Jon Paul reached across to shake her hand. 'Are you feeling okay? Did you sleep well?'

'Yes. I should be asking if you feel okay after all those drinks.' Katrina felt quite shy with the three older men. Vincenzo filled a glass with orange juice and handed it to her. 'Where are the others?' she asked, thinking of Dominic.

'Loretta won't get up for hours yet, Carlos stayed at his girlfriend's place and Dominic is still asleep on the sofa,' James replied, spearing a piece of bacon with his fork.

'Dominic's on the sofa?' Katrina asked sharply.

'Clever girl!' Vincenzo rubbed her shoulders as he passed by her chair.

'Yes, he collapsed on it around half three, not in the best of moods, and fell fast asleep.' James lowered his voice. 'Don't worry, nothing happened between him and Loretta or anyone else. I went back to find him at the party and was with him the whole time.' He smiled at her and turned back to talk to Jon Paul and Vincenzo.

Katrina felt ecstatically happy. He hadn't gone off with Loretta! She felt less sick and took a piece of bread to nibble on while she looked at Jon Paul. Dominic came in looking really tired yet very lovely in just a pair of jeans.

'You managed to get up then, Dom?' Jon Paul said. 'You look rough.'

'Thanks, it's nice to see you too. What's for breakfast?' He stopped by Katrina's chair and looked down before kissing her shoulder. 'Morning, gorgeous, sleep well?' Katrina nodded, happy that he didn't seem to be angry. 'We've got to get the helicopter back in an hour as I've got a meeting for the film.' Her happiness was quickly deflated by this news and disappointment came over her. She had thought they were going to spend the day together. 'What time are you leaving, James?'

'Not until this evening. I've got a six o'clock flight to Heathrow. I'd better go and sort things out at the hotel and turf Zora out.' He got to his feet. Katrina caught his eye and smiled gratefully. 'Great to see you, JP; Vincenzo, thanks for breakfast. Dominic, I'll call you later, and Katrina, I will see you soon, either in Paris or in London.' He kissed her on the cheek and playfully slapped Dominic's shoulder as he went past.

Jon Paul got up too. 'I'd better be off as I'm catching a flight to New York.' He shook Vincenzo's hand. 'I'll speak to you during the week about the house. Nice to see you again, Dominic.' He smiled at Katrina and got off the boat and into a black Range Rover. Dominic drank the orange juice from Katrina's glass. Vincenzo got up.

'I'm going to play tennis so I won't see you go, but come back soon. My apartment in Milan has many spare rooms so you can stay there; you too, Katrina, maybe when you are there for fashion week? I would like you to visit me, so I will see you soon, yes?' He handed her a business card.

Dominic and Katrina were alone.

'We'd better go too,' he stated brusquely. 'Have you got everything? Don't forget your dress, it was a gift.'

'Thank you, it's very generous. Yes, I'm ready.' Katrina watched him rub his eyes and yawn. 'You look tired.'

'What do you expect? I slept on a sofa. I've got backache.' He frowned beautifully.

'I'm sorry. I didn't want you to sleep on the sofa,' she said quietly. Dominic shrugged and they were silent.

Katrina picked up her stuff and followed him to the car. He spent the car journey flicking though a magazine. In the helicopter he fell asleep with his head on his hand.

By the time they were in a car heading back into Paris, the silence still hadn't been broken. The car pulled up outside her hotel. He didn't move.

'Well, thanks, I had a nice time.' Katrina opened the door and got out. 'I'll see you, then.'

'Yeah, see you around.'

The car pulled away. She felt tears prickling behind tired eyelids as she made her way inside, stopping to collect the post and any messages, none of which were for her. Back to reality, she thought as she opened the door to her room and saw the usual mess.

As Dominic got to his hotel, his mobile rang.

'Hey, I've been trying to call you since yesterday afternoon. How was your weekend?' Alex drawled. 'Did you succeed with your latest conquest?'

Dominic ignored the question. 'How's New York? Paris is getting boring; maybe I should fly over there.' He entered the hotel, ignoring the staff fluttering around him, and went straight up to his room while listening to Alex talking about setting up a club in Manhattan. There was a message waiting for him from Karolina Esslin, who was a seriously hot Swedish model turned wannabe actress.

'So, any plans for tonight?' Alex questioned.

'I might see that Karolina girl,' Dominic answered gruffly, only to be met with wild laughter from the other end.

'You didn't succeed, did you? I wondered why you ignored the question. The little Brit was too much for you, was she?' Alex chortled. 'The great Dominic Cayley turned down by a mere model, and not even a successful one!'

Dominic looked at his reflection in the mirror, noting that age seemed to be improving his looks rather than sabotaging them. 'Alex, I'm going to go now, but just for the record, I have not been turned down. It is an action plan still in progress and it's going exactly how I want it to go.'

He ended the call and dialled a different number. Katrina certainly was naïve; she had no idea that what Dominic Cayley wanted, Dominic Cayley got.

Katrina woke up feeling hungry and realised she hadn't really eaten properly all weekend. Her stomach looked flat, which was pleasing. Then an image of Dominic flashed across her mind and she slumped back, pulling the sheets over her head, not wanting to get up. The alarm beeped a reminder and she was forced to swing her legs out and leave the safety of the bed. Six castings, all spread from one side of the city to the other, not the best day when you were feeling depressed. She had a cold shower and used some of Lauren's Chanel body lotion before taking two paracetamol for her headache. Her face was still red from Dominic's stubble, so she covered it as best she could with foundation. Pulling on a pair of jeans and a cream silk shirt, which she had found in a Parisian flea market for one euro, she put her portfolio in a shoulder bag then rushed out via the breakfast room to pick up a stale croissant.

The first appointment was at the agency, so she took the Metro and then walked the familiar route there. It was buzzing as usual with tall, beautiful girls waiting to see the client, and the bookers talking in various different languages on the phones. Neda, the head booker, waved at her as she came in.

'Here she is, the lucky girl!' Neda said, leaping up from her desk and running over. 'You're all over the gossip papers today, what have you been up to this weekend?' She held a copy of a French paper. On the front cover was a picture of Dominic and Katrina getting out of the silver Bentley in Monaco. The other models crowded around to get a look.

'Christ!' Katrina gasped, amazed to see herself looking so glamorous. She felt a strange pang at the thought of what could have been. Dating Dominic Cayley would have changed her life. She could see how impressed everyone was; the bookers and other models were looking at her differently, with a mixture of envy and admiration. She liked the feeling even though she knew it wasn't going to last long, just like Dominic's interest in her hadn't lasted.

'How did you manage to find him?' Neda asked, wiping a mark off her face. 'I must say, you look radiant today – and you look like you've been kissed to death with that stubble rash. Your London agency has been trying to get hold of you. Use the phone in the office to call them back.'

Katrina went into the office and dialled their number. Ben, head booker at Source, picked up.

'Hey, sweetie!' he trilled. Model bookers never just spoke, as it sounded too flat and they were always too busy to speak at normal speed. Instead they trilled and chirped in a tireless effort to convince clients of their success and happiness. 'I'm super-jealous of you! Dominic Cayley, he's so gorgeous!'

'How did you know?' Katrina asked, even more surprised. She heard Rosanna's voice in the background asking if Ben was speaking to Katrina and wondered why Rosanna would care; she never normally did.

'There are pictures of you together on a boat and getting out of a car all over the tabloid gossip columns. They're calling you a stunning mysterious top model! It's hilarious! Bloody good timing for you, as Mr Cayley is just about to be huge! Jesus, that sex scene he did in that *Lion's Walk* film . . . his body is phenomenal! I'd dump my boyfriend for him any day!' Ben cackled with laughter.

'Well, I wouldn't get too excited. It was just one date. I doubt I'll see him again,' Katrina admitted.

'What do you mean? You have to see him again, and be seen seeing him! This could do wonders for your career; you'll earn a fortune if you're the girlfriend of someone like Cayley. We've already had ten phone calls about potential jobs this morning, and it's only nine thirty!'

'That's crap. Suddenly people want to use me because I may have a famous boyfriend, not because they think I have the right look for the job or am a good model?'

'That's the way it works, sweetie. I'd go with it if I were you. It isn't such a hardship dating the world's most eligible man to get some extra work, now is it? I mean—' The sentence ended abruptly as the phone was snatched from him.

'Katrina? It's Rosanna here. I am thrilled, absolutely thrilled that you've managed to snare Dominic Cayley. Do you know what this is going to do for your career? It's all going to change now, darling. As soon as you're back in London, you and I are having lunch so you can tell me everything!' Rosanna went off into tinkling laughter.

Katrina wondered whether to explain to her that she really didn't think it was going to make much difference to her career since she wouldn't be seeing Dominic again, but that would mean ending Rosanna's excitement. There was also the fact that Rosanna was actually taking the time to talk to her, and suggesting lunch.

'Katrina, darling! You must make sure you are seen out with him as much as possible so you can get some more press – just think how the money will be rolling in! I've seen how this makes a girl's career: an ordinary model suddenly becomes famous and all the clients want you to be the face of their company. Only the other night I was questioning whether you should stay in Paris seeing as it hasn't actually been a roaring success, but if the most eligible man in the world thinks you're hot, so will everyone else. You're bound to get work from this. Anyway, I've got to go. Keep us updated and do not let go of him! Byeeee, darling!' The line went dead, leaving Katrina overwhelmed by the fact that one picture of her with Dominic could provoke such a reaction.

She went to join the queue of girls waiting to see the client. Neda came over holding a piece of paper.

'Change of plan for you today. No castings; you've got a short-notice job and it's a good one. American *GQ*. It's excellent exposure for you and exactly what your book needs, sexy pictures rather than edgy. You'd better go now as the client needs you there right away and they said they'd pay for a taxi. I'll show your agency book to the people here, so don't wait around. Do try to keep us updated about what is going on with your new boyfriend!' She dismissed Katrina with a wave of a manicured hand.

Outside, Katrina flagged down a taxi, grateful to be working rather than traipsing the streets all day doing castings. She felt depressed that everyone seemed to think she was actually dating Dominic when he probably wouldn't even remember her name by now. The taxi driver drove fast and screeched to a halt outside a studio. A small girl with dyed pink hair ran out and spoke to him in French, handing him some money in exchange for a receipt.

'Hi, I'm Françoise, the stylist for the day. You must be Katrina, yes? Follow me.' They entered a brightly lit studio where the photographer was setting up a shot. He lifted his head and came towards her.

'Hi, I'm Alan, the photographer, as you can probably tell. I've heard a lot about you. Do you want a drink before you go to make-up?'

'Water would be great,' she replied, wondering what he meant by 'I've heard a lot about you'. She went through to the make-up room and sat on a chair whilst the make-up artist began to work on her face, tweezing her eyebrows aggressively. Katrina watched in the mirror, anxious that her entire eyebrow was going to be removed.

'Do you know what the shoot is about?' she questioned, wincing as the tweezers caught her skin.

'It is all about being glamorous. You will be wearing very sexy outfits and there is a man you are to be photographed with, that is all I know. I'm going to do smoky, seductive eyes and a bold lip to make you look more chic and less wild,' the artist replied, rubbing foundation into the back of her hand and then dabbing it on to Katrina's skin.

Katrina fell silent and began to think about Dominic and the weekend again. It almost felt like it had never happened, just a dream and now back to reality. She doubted he would ever think about her again, but just the thought of him kissing her made her stomach flip.

After forty minutes her reverie was broken as the hairdresser sprayed a cloud of Elnett on to her hair. He worked quietly with pins in his mouth as he scraped her hair tightly back into a chignon. The finished result, together with the darkened eyes and red lips, made Katrina look older and sophisticated. She pictured herself going on a date with Dominic looking sexy and confident rather than her normal scruffy self. Her daydream drifted on, with Dominic telling her how much he adored her and how he thought he was falling for her.

Françoise came in with a black dress that looked as if it was made from wetsuit material. The hairdresser had a little panic attack as they pulled it on over Katrina's hair, loosening a few strands. The Elnett came out again and he used so much, Katrina thought she might pass out. She was beginning to feel quite irritable and just wanted to get the job over and done with. So as not to get annoyed with all the poking and prodding going on, models needed to be able to switch off, something Katrina had never been very good at.

'We're not ready for you yet,' said Françoise, peering around the door. 'You can sit down and relax but be careful not to wrinkle the dress.'

Katrina sat and pulled a book out of her bag. An hour went by and she began to get bored. Françoise came in again, looking flushed.

'He's here and he's as gorgeous as he looks in pictures! I've just given him a suit to put on and then we're ready for the first shot. Is everything done?' she asked the hairdresser and make-up artist, who both nodded. The hairdresser came towards Katrina again with his can of Elnett. She held her breath. As he sprayed furiously she heard a voice and her heart stopped for a moment as she recognised it. Surely it couldn't be, could it?

'You managed to get Katrina, then? I didn't know which agency she's with or her last name so I hope you got the right one. Five foot nine with dark red hair, blue eyes, right? Gorgeous in a kind of goofy way?'

Looking around the corner, Katrina saw Dominic talking to the photographer. He was wearing a dark blue suit and sunglasses. She couldn't believe it; what was he doing here? And how come every time she saw him he looked even better than the last time? Françoise saw her spying.

'Katrina, we're ready for you,' she called out, forcing her to step out into view. Katrina stared at Dominic and he stared back at her without any expression.

'What are you doing here?' She broke the silence first. His face went from blank to his movie-star smile, all gleaming white teeth.

'The magazine's doing a story on me and they needed a model to be in the pictures, so I suggested you for the job. It's a Bond theme, am I right?' he asked Françoise, who was kneeling at his feet rubbing a mark off his shoe. She nodded. The hairdresser sprayed Katrina again.

'So, hello again, English girl. I hope you're pleased to see me.' He looked at her with raised eyebrows. She couldn't answer, as the make-up artist was standing on tiptoe reapplying lipstick, so she nodded slightly. 'Great dress, looks like it's made of rubber.' He came over and touched the material. She jumped and he laughed softly. 'You never gave me your mobile number, so I got the editor to call all the agencies and find you. I sent my driver over to your hotel to give you a lift but you'd already left.' Katrina didn't say anything. 'You look stunning, by the way.' He stared at her a moment before going over to the hairdresser, who carefully applied wax to his hair.

'He told us if we didn't get you for this shoot he wouldn't do the interview,' Françoise explained, raising an eyebrow as she straightened Katrina's dress. 'Dominic is a big star and we need him on the cover.'

'That's true, he is a star and nobody says no to a star. Can you stand on set so I can do a light reading?' Alan instructed, appearing from behind a reflector and making Katrina jump. 'We've got to crack on as time is of the essence, I imagine.'

Dominic strode on to set handing a half-smoked cigarette to Françoise and shading his eyes from the bright lights. 'What's the set-up?'

'Right, I want you to look like a James Bond type standing very square as the pictures are all designer suits.

Katrina, I want you to be like a Bond girl, very strong and sexy yet don't distract from him; stand a bit back or be looking at him, that kind of thing. I'm using different lenses for each shot, so for example the first one will be a fish-eye so it looks like I'm looking down the barrel of a gun.' Alan took another light reading whilst Dominic faced the camera and Katrina stood with her back against his shoulder, leg showing through the split in the dress. Françoise stepped in again and put a holster with a fake gun in it around the exposed thigh.

'Excellent,' said Alan as he began shooting film. 'A bit of a cliché but I love it anyway!'

Katrina felt Dominic's hand touching her bum. 'That rubber is hot,' he whispered so that only she could hear. 'We should take it home.'

'Got it, next shot.' Alan put his camera down.

The next outfit was a leather skirt suit for her and a silver suit for him. While Katrina couldn't imagine that any man could carry off a silver suit, Dominic of course did. In the shot he had her arms behind her back and the gun on the floor as if they had just fought and he had overpowered her. He kissed her neck.

'Brilliant!' Alan said. 'I love it looking tough and sexy. Do more like that.'

Dominic pulled Katrina's head back and kissed her on the lips.

'Perfect, next!'

Françoise handed Katrina a gold catsuit that looked tiny. She squirmed into it and Françoise handed her a pair of breast enhancers that looked like chicken fillets.

'It needs to have lots of cleavage and lots of leg,' she explained, also pushing a pair of size six towering gold heels towards Katrina that she crammed her size seven feet into. 'The Polaroids look hot; have you got something going on with Dominic?'

'No,' she replied. 'I met him in a bar last Friday, but no, nothing going on.'

'Well if there isn't now there will be later. There's a lot of chemistry between you and he must like you to have insisted we book you. We were originally going to get one of the Victoria's Secret girls to do this job, one of the top models, but he insisted it was you . . .' Françoise gave her a pair of huge gold hoop earrings and motioned her back to the set. Dominic whistled when he saw her.

'How the hell did you get that on? I've never seen anything so damn tight!' He was wearing a black suit with a gold tie, simple but effective. In this shot Katrina stood sideways to the camera with Dominic's hand on her bum as he stood directly in front of the camera. 'Great butt,' he commented flippantly. 'I love my job standing round with beautiful girls.'

Alan laughed. 'Yeah, I could imagine worse jobs in life for a guy.' He took the shot quickly.

The final outfit was a white bikini and white heels. Katrina put them on.

'*Merde*, you're way too pale for that,' Françoise muttered. She rooted around in her bag and fished out a pair of jewelled black knickers. 'Put those on.' Katrina did and then looked around for the top half.

'Where's the top?' she asked.

'There isn't one. They are just knickers, not a bikini or anything. They look amazing! I've been waiting for a chance to use them.'

The make-up artist was rubbing a shimmer cream over Katrina's body whilst the hairdresser sprayed her hair again.

'You mean you want me topless?' she asked. Françoise nodded. 'I don't know if I'm happy about that.'

'Oh come on, you're a model, that's what you're here for, to show your body. All the models do – look at Kate

Moss. If you're worried about the boys, well I can tell you Alan is as gay as they come, and the way things are going between you and Dominic, he'll be seeing a lot more of you later. Put the Jimmy Choos on and I'll see you on set.' She swept out of the room, leaving the make-up artist to finish rubbing the cream on.

Katrina had done nudes and worn see-through clothes loads of time, yet it felt weird this time with Dominic there. She wished her boobs were a bit bigger; maybe he only liked big silicone ones.

'Katrina, we're ready for the last shot!' Alan bellowed.

Boldly and with a deep breath she put an arm across her chest and walked out.

Dominic looked up and saw her. He was fully dressed in a tuxedo and was sitting in a leather chair on the set. He didn't say anything, just carried on watching her shamelessly.

'Katrina, you are going to be sitting facing him with your legs over his,' Alan instructed. She wondered if it could get much worse. Dominic grinned at her.

'GQ are making it very easy for me, undressing you and putting you on my lap literally naked,' he remarked. Katrina kept an arm across her chest and sat astride him on the chair as Alan instructed. 'They offered me a supermodel for this job, you know. I'm glad I chose you, and I like your body, it's very . . .' He looked her up and down. 'Fresh.' He ran a finger up her arm. The physical contact felt like electricity fizzing through her and she had a hard time looking him in the eye. He was just so ridiculously confident that it was intimidating, along with the fact that he was the best-looking man she had ever seen, and internationally famous.

'That's wicked. Take your arm away and lean over him. I want you to kind of suck his lower lip while he pulls away a bit and looks at the camera,' Alan instructed her.

She realised that she was going to have to play it out or look like an idiot. She took her arm away and leant forward to kiss him. His hands were on her lower back and she felt Françoise rearranging the knickers on her bum and complaining that the jewels were peeling off.

'Great, that's perfect, don't move! I've just got to load some film,' Alan muttered. Katrina pulled away from the kiss, being careful not to move her body from the position. Dominic's eyes were very close to hers and she couldn't look away without disturbing the shot.

'So, you're having dinner with me tonight?' It was more of a statement than a question. He ran his eyes over her body, aware of her discomfort.

'Are you not getting bored of me?' Katrina asked. 'Friday night, all day Saturday, yesterday and now all day today.'

'No, not at all, and this certainly isn't boring me. I'm having a really hard time trying to control myself. I find you quite sexy in a strange way.' Katrina looked confused. 'I'm just a guy, after all; it's not easy when you've got a beautiful model sitting half-naked on your lap, you know.'

'Really? I would have thought you were quite used to it,' she replied. She wished he would just stop teasing her; it was difficult to tell when he was being serious and when he was joking.

'You know what I mean.' Dominic kissed her, his hand sliding over her back just as the camera started clicking. By the time Katrina pulled away, Alan had got the shot.

'Finished. That was easy. Good choice of model, Dominic, you two worked well together. These images are going to be perfect.' He flicked through the shots on his laptop. 'I'm going straight off to get these to GQ, so I'll say goodbye now.' He began packing up his equipment.

'Dominic, the press office would love it if you kept that suit and perhaps wore it to a premiere or something. You can keep the knickers, Katrina, if you want,' said

Françoise. She had packed up already and was heading to the door. 'I've got to get to an appointment so I must dash. Nice working with you.'

Katrina pulled on her jeans over the knickers, aware of Dominic still watching. She couldn't find the shirt or the bra she had been wearing, and after looking around the studio and the dressing room with her arm over her chest, she realised that Françoise must have accidentally packed them up with her own stuff. She had absolutely nothing else to put on. The make-up and hair artists had gone too. She undid her hair and rubbed the hairspray out of it. Her hair covered her breasts but even so she could hardly go out in the street without a top. She eyed her reflection in the mirror, racking her brain for a solution.

'Oh hell. What will I do?'

'I don't know, what *will* you do?' Dominic entered the dressing room holding a cup of coffee and a sandwich. He sat on the chair and contemplated her whilst eating. 'I've got to stay here and wait for the interview. Why aren't you dressed? The way you've been behaving, I'm surprised you haven't shot out of here as fast as you can.'

'I've lost my top,' Katrina admitted. 'I think the stylist must have packed it up and I don't have anything to put on.' He started laughing. 'It isn't funny!' She looked at him reproachfully. He held out the sandwich.

'Want a bite?' He started laughing again, then got up, taking a couple of steps towards her. 'Oh dear, what will you do? You're going to have to go home topless; that should cause a scene on the Metro. I might take public transport for the first time in my life just to see this.' He pulled a horrified face before smirking and leaning nonchalantly on the wall with his legs crossed. Why the hell did he have to be so perfect, and why did he have to make her feel like she had run a marathon every time he was around? She gulped for air and turned away from him so he couldn't see the red flush that swept over her face.

'Please, can't you lend me your shirt? It's okay for you, you're a man and you've got a car to take you home, so no one will see you. I can't go out like this,' Katrina pleaded.

'Why should I? Firstly I prefer you topless, and secondly I won't get my shirt back. You haven't accepted my invitation for dinner tonight. You seem to reject me at every opportunity you get, so you obviously don't like me very much. You must have a boyfriend tucked away somewhere; why don't you call him and ask him to come here and bring you something to wear? I'd love to meet him.' Dominic finished the sandwich and took a swig of coffee. Katrina slid to the floor, sitting with her back to the wall and her knees in front of her chest, feeling exhausted.

'That's not true. I don't have a boyfriend and I do want to see you again. Of course I like you.' Words spilled from her mouth. 'Everyone warned me that you were just a player.'

'Who exactly is everyone?' he asked, trying to suppress a smile.

'Well, Lauren,' Katrina muttered, feeling stupid.

'Lauren? You know why that is, don't you?' Dominic let out a peal of laughter. 'She is jealous. The night I saw you at that bar she was all over me, begging me to take her out, asking if she could come back to my hotel room. She was offering sexual favours within five minutes of meeting me, for Chrissake! Why are you listening to her? If she was right, I wouldn't be putting this much effort in, taking you away, getting you this job. I'd have given up and pulled someone like Lauren by now if it was just easy sex I wanted. I like you.' He moved away from the wall and went out of the room, returning with another sandwich. He stood over her and they looked at each other until he broke the silence.

'I tell you what, if you wait for me to finish this interview and then promise to have dinner with me tonight, I'll give you my shirt.'

'I don't have much choice, do I?' Katrina said, pretending to be sulky even though she was ecstatic at the thought of dinner with him 'Okay, it's a deal. Give me the shirt then.'

'Not until the interview is over. I don't want to risk you disappearing whilst I'm distracted. No one will mind you being half-naked in here; it is a studio after all.'

A man looked around the door.

'I'm here to interview you,' he said. 'Are you ready now?'

Dominic nodded. 'Sure, we'll go in the room next door.' He handed the half-drunk cup of coffee to Katrina. 'I'll be back in fifteen minutes, sweetie.' The journalist looked at her with interest as Dominic led the way out.

12

When Dominic returned, Katrina was lying on her front on the floor reading her book. He dropped his shirt on her head. Whilst really it was a little late for modesty, she got up with her back to him and pulled it on quickly. It was far too big, so she knotted it eighties-style at the waist.

'It definitely looked better on me,' Dominic said mockingly, tucking in the Zegna label protruding from the collar as they got into his car.

Katrina remembered that she had to check with the agency that she didn't have any castings or jobs tomorrow. Her mobile was back in the hotel; she'd accidentally left it there in her rush to leave this morning.

'Can I borrow your phone for a sec?' she asked Dominic, who was fiddling with the date on his watch. He handed it over to her without saying anything. Katrina dialled the agency number and Neda answered chirpily.

'I am very pleased you've called. I tried to get hold of you at the studio. You have a job in London, you'll need to go back tomorrow. It's a really good job, very exciting . . . Hang on . . .' Neda stopped to speak to someone else, leaving Katrina hanging on the phone curiously. Dominic lit a cigarette and opened the window slightly. Neda came back.

'It's for a sunglasses campaign, a new line by

Moschino. The client saw a picture of you in the paper this morning with Dominic and tracked you down to the agency. I don't know a lot about it apart from it shoots on either Wednesday or Thursday and it's good money, seven thousand English pounds. Call Source tomorrow and they will tell you the details. You have options on your chart for jobs next week in London too, so I don't know if the agency will want you to come back here. We'll speak during the week, okay?'

'Have I got a Eurostar booked?' Katrina was surprised to find she was really annoyed about going home. It was a brilliant job and great money, but if she went tomorrow it would mean never seeing Dominic again, as by the time she came back he would be gone. Ironically it sounded like she had got the job because of him.

'It's all done. You have to get the seven fifteen a.m. train and your ticket is waiting for you. It was the only train with any space left. I have an option for Thursday for French *Marie Claire*, but I don't think it will come off, so enjoy a weekend at home. *Au revoir!*' Neda put the phone down abruptly, as all bookers did. Katrina handed Dominic his phone.

'Everything okay?' he asked, throwing his cigarette out of the window. 'More work?'

'Yes, I'm going home tomorrow for a job and they don't need me for the rest of the week.' Katrina was despondent. 'Today's our last day in Paris together.' She stared out of the window as they sped past the Champs Elysées. Dominic put a hand on her knee.

'I think that means you definitely have to come out with me tonight. It also means that we should have a celebratory going-home dinner at the best restaurant. I shall book the first place I went to when I got here. It's seven thirty now; I'll drop you off to get changed and pick you up in an hour, okay?'

Katrina nodded reluctantly. She wanted to say no, because he obviously didn't care that they wouldn't see each other again after tonight, yet she couldn't, as she wanted to see him again. She couldn't deny the nervous sick feeling she got every time she saw him, and the sexual chemistry was like nothing she had ever felt before. He was everything that any girl would dream of in a man: good looking, successful, rich, adored, famous, a film star who could pick any girl he wanted, go any place he wanted.

The car pulled up outside the hotel and Katrina picked up her bag to leap out. Dominic grabbed her arm and pulled her towards him before she made her escape.

'Why are you always in such a hurry? Kiss me goodbye before you disappear.' Katrina didn't move, so he sighed and reached forward to kiss her slowly, only pulling away as his phone rang. 'Be here about eight thirty, then,' he ordered as he answered it, and Katrina stepped out of the car, heading towards the hotel.

As she got to the room she heard loud music and on opening the door was confronted by a tanned bum going up and down. It belonged to Lauren, but Katrina couldn't see who was beneath her and they didn't notice her as the music drowned everything out. Katrina went back out and hung around the door, wondering whether to knock really loudly pretending she had forgotten her key or just wait outside for a bit longer. She decided on the latter and sat down. The music stopped and she could hear Lauren moaning and a male voice calling her name. After a couple of minutes things went silent. Katrina wanted to start getting ready to look extra fabulous for dinner. She knocked at the door.

'Just a minute!' she heard Lauren call. 'Who is it?'

'It's me, Katrina.' She leant on the door. Bloody Lauren, it was out of order to bring someone to their room when she knew her room-mate would be back. She heard footsteps and the door opened.

'Oh my God, what the hell!' Katrina had walked straight into the arms of a naked Alex. Tanned and worked-out, he was stark naked, with his flaccid cock hanging exhaustedly between his legs. He had a towel slung over his shoulder yet he made no attempt to cover himself with it or move out of the way in the narrow doorway.

'Do you want me to come back in a minute?' Katrina asked, unnerved by his failure to move.

'Not at all, I was just going to leave myself. How are you, Katrina?' He backed her out into the corridor, and she moved back so she was literally pressed against the wall. 'Have you been working today?'

Katrina nodded and decided to make a break for it and get past him. As she moved forward so did he, and he took her shoulders so that she almost fell backwards in an attempt to get away. He had her pinned against the wall.

'Relax, I just wanted to kiss you hello.' He kissed her on each cheek, then let go of her shoulders. Katrina moved into the room, wishing he would put his clothes on and leave. Lauren came out of the bathroom, her eyes narrow and suspicious.

'Hey, I didn't think you would be back. I heard you had a job with Cayley today so I thought you would stay out with him.' She smiled slyly. 'I got an earlier flight from New York.' She glanced over at Alex, who was sitting on the bed, having put the towel over his groin area. 'Do you want a shower?' She addressed him pointedly.

'Only with you in it!' he replied, looking at Katrina. Lauren giggled and pulled him off the bed and towards the bathroom. As they went through the door, Alex turned back. 'Do you want to join us?' Katrina nearly choked.

'Don't be silly, Alex. I told you, Katrina is a good girl,

she doesn't do naughty things!' Lauren purred. 'Come on, I'm more than enough for you.'

The bathroom door closed and Katrina was left feeling horribly uncomfortable. She really didn't like Alex and it seemed strange that he could be such a close friend of Dominic's when his other friend James was so decent and respectful. She heard Alex say her name and Lauren laughing in response. The room reeked of sex and she had to pick up a pair of Lauren's knickers from her bed.

Katrina looked at her face in the mirror and decided that she would just rub off the postbox-red lipstick and leave the rest of the make-up on. The make-up remover was in the bathroom and she was not going to ask for it. She selected a black bra and matching knickers, looking in the mirror to see how she would appear to Dominic. Then she dabbed Chanel No. 5 all over her body, including her cleavage and thighs. She wondered if they would be photographed again that evening, and she also wondered if he would invite her back to his hotel. She wouldn't refuse, as she wanted to know more about him and see what lay behind the movie-star image, and of course there was the tiny detail of wanting him to kiss and touch her like he had in Monaco. With that in mind, she rubbed even more moisturiser in.

Half an hour later, as she pulled on a black lace top and a pair of white jeans, there was a knock at the door. She opened it and found Dominic leaning on the frame wearing a black shirt with black trousers. It was almost like an image from a film scene that she was watching rather than appearing in, this impossibly good-looking man languorously looking her up and down. In fact everything she did with him was like a collection of film clips: receiving the note telling her he was picking her up for a party, the helicopter ride to Monaco, staying on a luxury boat, the beautiful outfit in boxes and then the photoshoot. Nothing had been a disappointment so far.

'Hello, you look lovely.' He kissed her and came into the room, looking a little shocked at the tiny narrow beds and cheap decor. 'Jesus, I knew these places were shitty, but this is terrible.'

Katrina blushed and suddenly wanted to get him out of there as quickly as possible. 'I've just got to put my shoes on and then I'm ready.'

'No rush, the restaurant will hold my table for however long it takes.' A shriek came from the bathroom. 'Who's that?'

'Alex and Lauren,' Katrina replied. 'I really need to brush my teeth.' She put her faithful Gucci shoes on, using spit to rub the faint scuffs on the toes and hoping she looked presentable enough.

Dominic banged on the bathroom door. 'Hey, you two, stop screwing each other and get out! My date needs to clean her teeth and I need to pee.' He grinned at Katrina's horrified expression. The door opened and Alex emerged.

'Hi, how are you? Fancy seeing you in a hotel in Paris with a model!' Alex purred sarcastically. They both cackled with laughter. 'What are you up to?' Alex went to hug Dominic but he stepped back to avoid a wet embrace; he didn't want his shirt to get creased up. Instead he play-punched Alex on the shoulder.

'We're going out for dinner. I don't expect I need to ask what you've been up to.' Dominic rolled his eyes as Lauren emerged unashamedly in see-through underwear and strutted to the wardrobe, where she put on a pair of white jeans and a white top to set off her tan, all the time running her eyes hungrily over Dominic. Katrina could tell she was totally confused by why he was taking Katrina out when she believed it should be her. She went into the bathroom, almost breaking her neck as she slipped on the vast amount of water on the floor from their shower antics. It struck her as quite surreal that Dominic was in her tiny hotel room chatting away to his friend. She hoped the magazine with him on the cover was hidden so he wouldn't think she was some weird stalker type! She brushed her teeth vigorously and gargled with mouthwash.

As she went back into the bedroom, Dominic went into the bathroom. Alex and Lauren were both fully dressed and talking quietly. They looked up as Katrina pulled a jacket out of the wardrobe.

'So, Katrina, this must be, what, the second date now? You're on the way to setting quite a record!' Alex ran his eyes over her body. Lauren noticed and put her arms around him, kissing his neck whilst her eyes were on Katrina.

Katrina nodded and picked up her bag to go.

'Second date and I still don't know if she likes me!' Dominic emerged from the bathroom and walked to the door. 'She's got me running in circles to keep her interested.'

It was obvious he was being slightly sarcastic but both Alex and Lauren's faces darkened visibly and they stared at Katrina in utter bewilderment. She could tell they were thinking that with everyone baying for Dominic's attention, how did this quite ordinary girl manage to command it, particularly in preference to them. She felt incredibly proud.

'We could join you for dinner?' Alex offered hopefully.

'No, the table's for two.' With that, Dominic swept out of the room.

'Maybe another time?' Katrina said apologetically as she went after him. Alex only raised an eyebrow in response.

Katrina caught up with Dominic outside.

'Damn! I've just remembered that I've left my mobile at the hotel. We'll quickly pop back there and get it and then on to dinner.' Dominic led her to a silver Porsche Carrera and opened the door. 'No driver tonight, so I borrowed a buddy's car.' He started the engine with a roar and turned on to the street. Katrina watched his hands changing gear and his muscular arms as he drove confidently. She was most definitely living in some kind of weird dream that was going to end tonight when he dropped her off and she would never see him again. The problem was, she really liked him and she could get used to this life very easily!

T he car jolted to a stop and Dominic leapt out, tossing the keys to the concierge and motioning that Katrina should follow him. The hotel was fantastic, with a grand marble entrance and massive paintings on the walls. Katrina marvelled at the thought of staying somewhere so luxurious. Dominic seemed oblivious to the commotion that he was causing as he strode through the lobby towards the elevator whilst a group of Japanese tourists shrieked in recognition. A man in a suit appeared from nowhere to hold the lift door open for them and stop anyone following them in.

'I haven't bothered having a bodyguard in Paris, but I have one all the time back home,' Dominic commented, absent-mindedly tipping the suited man a hundred-euro bill. 'The Parisians tend to be more aloof than the Americans about hassling me; lucky for you, as we wouldn't get a moment's peace.' He offered her a mint before handing the empty wrapper to the rather surprised man.

They went up to the top floor, where Dominic fumbled for his keycard in his back pocket. Finding it, he stopped before opening the door to kiss Katrina, pushing her against the wall of the narrow corridor. 'You're lovely, really lovely, English girl.'

Inside, a huge four-poster bed stood with pieces of

paper strewn all over it. At the other end of the room was a balcony overlooking Paris, including the most amazing view of the Eiffel Tower.

'This is incredible!' Katrina gasped as Dominic searched for his phone, throwing cushions on the floor and tutting loudly. 'I'd never want to go out if I was staying in a place like this.' She peered into the lounge area, admiring the huge television. Never in her life had she stayed somewhere so magnificent, and she gazed at the paintings and the plates of luxury chocolates scattered around. She was filled with the urge to scoff as many as possible and to leap all over the furniture before collapsing in front of the screen to watch DVDs and order room service. Oh to be rich, she thought, running her fingers over the rows of leather-bound books adorning the walls. Dominic came up behind her, wrapping his arms tightly around her.

'The book girl strikes!' He laughed. 'Help yourself if you want to take one – they can charge me for it – but right now you must give me your attention.' He paused and spun her around, away from the books. 'We don't have to go out, you know. We could stay here and get room service.' He kissed her neck, watching their reflection in a large gold mirror. He let go and went across to the desk, picking up a menu and handing it to her. 'Yes, let's stay here, you're absolutely right. I was getting a bit bored of this place but I reckon you'll make it more exciting. Order some food whilst I make a phone call.'

Katrina selected food and then waited for Dominic to finish his call, which seemed to be going on for ever. When he reappeared, he had changed into a pair of ripped jeans and was bare-chested with a defined six-pack. He stood in the doorway and rubbed his hand through his hair before tossing his phone carelessly on to an armchair. Without saying anything he walked over, took Katrina's shoes off and removed her jacket before taking a mini bottle of Absolut from the minibar and dividing it between two glasses.

'Relax.' He stroked her face. 'This is just like home: make a mess, drink whatever you like from the minibar. You're my guest, a very special guest.' He took a sip of the vodka and stared at her intensely. He didn't need to say what he was thinking and she smiled nervously. He took that as acquiescence and pulled her towards him so that he could kiss her, holding her body hard against his. She didn't try to stop him. Looking up at him, she couldn't believe it was really happening and that she, Katrina Muirhead, was being seduced by a famous actor after only knowing him for three days. She didn't even try to resist when he led her to the bed, where he pushed her down, carelessly throwing the papers out of the way, and lay on top of her, undoing her jeans and easing her top off. He kissed down her body, stopping around her thighs, teasing her with gentle nibbling. Worried that he seemed to be doing all the work, she undid the buttons on his jeans and pushed her hand down between his legs. He was already hard and in response he groaned as he kissed her. She ran her hand up and down and he put his hand over hers, moving it faster before wriggling out of his jeans so he was totally naked. His body was phenomenal: evenly tanned, muscular yet lean, and he had absolutely no shame in being naked. Tentatively Katrina kissed down his body and took him in her mouth. She looked up at him. His eyes were closed and he had his hand on the back of her head, pushing her harder against him. He smelt of shower gel and masculinity and his skin was smooth. For an instant it crossed her mind that he probably had regular waxes and all sorts of skincare sessions to stay looking that good. Then he opened his eyes and pulled her up towards him.

'I felt like I was about to come already. You turn me on so much,' he told her huskily. 'You seem so new, clean . . . I don't know what it is about you, it's just you're so natural and sort of innocent. It's weird, but I adore it.'

He rolled on to her and eased her knickers off, at the same time unclipping her bra expertly. Far too expertly, and for a moment she thought about all the girls he had done this with. Should she stop it now? His mouth covered her nipple and he bit it playfully, causing her to yelp. 'Beautiful,' he muttered, then, grinning, he pinned her arms above her head and pushed her legs apart with his knee. It was too late to stop now, and she didn't want to anyway. He thrust into her hard with his tongue dipping into her mouth before pushing her up against the back of the bed, where he stretched over her, allowing her to view his spectacular body. Katrina felt his lips on her neck, his hands exploring her body; every touch was so confident and practised. It seemed to be occurring in slow motion as she watched their reflection in the mirror as if detached from her own body. It certainly looked like movie sex with his perfect physique. She arched her back whilst he grasped her shoulders to get deeper, his breath quickening before he shuddered to a stop and collapsed on top of her. She felt him slide from her and rest in between her legs.

After a minute he rolled off her and lay on his back. They were silent before he said, 'I forgot to ask, have you got some sort of birth control?'

Katrina was jolted out of her pleasure at being so close to him. Yes, she was on the pill, but it seemed rather awful for him to roll over and say that. She nodded and he lay back thoughtfully. 'Cool, it would be my worst nightmare to get a girl pregnant.'

Katrina immediately felt cheap. The sex had momentarily been amazing, like he was solely into her and wasn't thinking about anything else, but it was over quickly. Now she was just someone else he had screwed, another girl, one of hundreds probably.

'That was an important script.' He motioned towards the papers scattered over the floor, creased and torn. He had gone from being adoring and considerate to being cold and distant. He was making it clear straightaway that all he had wanted was sex, and he was not going to offer any sycophantic adoration to make her feel less used. All the euphoria of being intimate with him was swept away in the realisation that she had just given him what he wanted and he would now move on.

As if to reiterate this fact to himself, Dominic got up and walked to the bathroom, confident in his naked beauty. Katrina watched him, relieved to be left alone. She heard the shower go on and him stepping into it. She knew that it was over now, that he would go through the ritual of dinner, drop her off at the hotel and never see her again. She had thought she could handle it, just sex with a great-looking guy who thousands of women probably fantasised about. In reality she felt like she had been used, and it had all happened so fast that – excusing the pun – it seemed like an anticlimax. After lying numbly on the bed for what felt like ages, contemplating the best and least embarrassing escape route, Katrina got up and went into the bathroom to get a tissue. Dominic opened the shower door.

'Come in here and clean up.' He pulled her in under the pounding hot water and the make-up from the shoot began to run down her face. Dominic laughed and handed her a flannel to wipe it off. He turned the shower off and looked at her thoughtfully. His expression softened and he smiled as he ran a finger over her lips before leaning forward to lick the water off her nipples. He reached up and turned the water on again, letting it run over them as he sucked and licked.

'Wow, I'm getting turned on again.' He pressed her against the tiled wall. 'I don't normally share my shower. I didn't realise how nice it could be.'

He took her weight so her legs were curled around him and slid into her. Katrina was not sure what to do; she wanted to push him away and leave, yet at the same time she wanted to stay with him and enjoy his attention for a little bit longer. She couldn't resist him even though he had been horrible only ten minutes ago. As he slid into her again, she resisted and then relaxed. The water ran over them and their bodies moved together sensually. He pulled her head back by the hair so that the water poured down her face, whilst his lips ran over her throat for what seemed like ages before she felt a warm feeling as he came again, this time with no warning. He didn't release her, holding her body against his. It was an oddly intimate moment, more so than the actual sex, and he pressed his head into her shoulder for ages.

This time it was Katrina who pulled away from him and got out of the shower. He remained in there, and by the time he came out she was dressed and had combed her wet hair into a ponytail. When she went into the room, she found that the food she had ordered was on the table, but she wasn't hungry. Dominic came in with a towel around his waist, his hair slicked back and his body muscular.

'I just realised how late it is. You have to get a Eurostar first thing, don't you?' He didn't look her in the eye. 'I'll take you back to your place.'

'No, it's fine.' Katrina picked up her bag and walked to the door. 'I can get a taxi.' She wanted to get out of there and to have the upper hand of leaving of her own accord rather than him trying to get rid of her. Dominic nodded before he lit a cigarette, looking out of the huge window as the smoke trailed from his mouth and disappeared into the air. He didn't seem to care at all. She felt sick with disappointment. He didn't even bother trying to hide the fact that he had used her and couldn't give a damn about spending time with her now she had submitted to what he wanted. How could she have been so blinded by him being famous and good looking as to have thrown aside her usual caution? So much for playing it cool and being different to all the other girls. She felt like telling him what a bastard he was, but then he would just look at her in that blank way he had perfected and she would feel even more pathetic.

'Are you sure?' She nodded. He came forward to kiss her on the cheek. 'Take care, English girl.'

Katrina let herself out feeling numb. Outside she found a taxi to take her back to her own hotel. Thankfully Alex and Lauren had gone and she set her alarm to catch the train. She lay awake wishing he would call, but of course he didn't. That was the end of that little dream, she thought. She tried to convince herself that it was just sex. Really, in this day and age people had sex all the time with strangers and never saw them again.

However, nothing could get rid of the disappointment she felt. Despite her anger she would probably go running back over to his hotel if he asked her to. She couldn't stop thinking about feeling his hard body against hers and the way his kisses made her go light-headed. If she hadn't given in to her desire for him then maybe he would still have wanted to see her and there would have been more kisses and glamour. Instead there was nothing but a story about how she once slept with a movie star, which nobody would believe anyway.

14

Katrina decided that the best thing to do was go back to her mother's house and stay there for a few days. She could get the train into London to do the sunglasses shoot. She wasn't in the mood to sit in the little flat she rented from the agency in Oval thinking about the past couple of days. It was too depressing. She took a taxi from the train station, stopping to get some credit for her mobile, which had died on her. When she turned it on, it rang immediately. It was her mother.

'Katrina, why haven't you returned my calls? I have left messages on your phone and I even called the agency. What is going on with you and this film guy, this Dominic somebody or other? Everyone at work has been showing me pictures in the newspaper and I didn't know anything about it.'

'Sorry, my mobile ran out of credit and then I couldn't find the battery charger. I should have used a landline but I lost track of time,' Katrina explained sheepishly. She was rather pleased to hear that everybody back home had seen the photographs of her with Dominic. She let her mother lecture her for a few minutes.

'Well I just hope you were sensible and didn't let him use you. You have to be careful. Those sorts of men are only after one thing!' her mother finished off. This piece of late advice made Katrina smile wryly but she didn't comment. 'Anyway, I'm away at the moment.'

This news surprised Katrina. Her mother never went anywhere. 'Away? Where?'

'Scotland, for three days. I thought I deserved a break. Make sure you eat properly, and call your father, please. He rang twice to find out what was going on with you. Ask him for some money if you need some. He's got enough to send the other two to that expensive school.'

'I don't need any money from him,' Katrina retorted. She was actually broke and was going to struggle to pay for the expensive taxi trip to Hampshire, but she wasn't going to tell her mother that.

When the taxi arrived at her mother's house, she paid the driver and retrieved the spare front-door key from the flower pot in the garden.

The house was welcoming, with its worn old Persian carpets and familiar messiness. Bramble, the family pet, was sitting by the pond in the back garden watching the fish hungrily, although Katrina noticed that her bowl by the cat flap was full of biscuits. It was one o'clock, and feeling ravenous she looked through the cupboards and found them bare. Raiding her emergency money, she pulled together twelve pounds and sixty pence, which would pay for the train only. No food, then. Well, at least it would be good for weight loss.

She called the agency and spoke to Theo, the new booker, to get the details for the sunglasses job and was informed that it had been scheduled for Thursday. That really annoyed her as she could have spent an extra day in Paris and perhaps had an extra evening with Dominic. The only bit of good news was that British *Vogue* had an option on her for a feature they were doing on diamonds because the casting director had seen her in the newspaper with Dominic, and film-stars' girlfriends were the ones who wore diamonds, giggled Theo. However, options often fell through as the job came closer, and Dominic would be seen out with a number of models in the next few weeks, so she wasn't going to get too hopeful.

She wanted to talk to someone about him. She could hardly tell her mother she had slept with him and how he had carelessly dismissed her. She called Helen, who had been her closest friend since school, to see if she wanted to meet up. It had been a couple of months since she had seen her, as she never had much time any more with castings and go-sees, but Helen was always loyal and she always gave good advice.

'Kat! I cannot believe you haven't called me for so long! Everyone is going mad after seeing you in the paper with Dominic Cayley! What have you been up to?' Helen screeched down the phone, nearly deafening Katrina. 'Omigod! Are you dating him?'

'No, but I did have sex with him,' Katrina admitted.

'Holy cow! I am so jealous! What was it like? Was it like that film, whatsitcalled, Lion something? Jesus, Kat, that is so mad! You with a film star!'

Katrina immediately felt better; Helen always brought her back to reality. She had had a fun weekend and sex with a movie star and now she was back where she belonged. There was nothing to feel bad about. 'It was good, much better than with Chris, that's for sure . . . ' She paused, watching Bramble chase a butterfly across the garden and recalling the nervous fumbling of Chris, who had been her first serious boyfriend at university. She had ended things with him a few months ago as his incessant whining about her going away for modelling jobs had been so irritating.

'Is that it? It was good? Katrina, I have been your best friend since school. I was there when you had your first kiss! I know that you don't just hop into bed with someone and then say it was good, especially not when it's someone called Dominic Cayley, fittest man alive! By the way, you remember that bitchy Emily from school? She works in that grotty pub near the park and I went in for a drink yesterday. She was all over me, desperate for the gossip on you and Dominic. I told her you were staying with him in Paris and had asked me to keep it confidential. She almost burst with curiosity and I thought, that serves her right for being such a cow all those years! She never even said hello to you and now she's like, "Oh, tell Kat I said hi and we must meet up for a drink." I said you were probably too busy hanging out in Hollywood!' Helen cackled in delight. 'Anyway, you have to tell me *everything*. I'm working late today but what are you doing tomorrow? I could pop over. Please don't tell me you're in Oval. I hate hiking into London.'

'No, I'm at my mum's so we can meet up. Come over after work and please bring food! There's nothing to eat here apart from baked beans and cat food. See you tomorrow then.'

Katrina felt happier knowing that Helen would come over and she would not be rattling around the house by herself all day and night. She smiled at the thought of Emily wanting to be her friend now. At school she had either ignored Katrina or told her she was weird or ugly. There was some justice in the fact that she was working in the village pub looking at pictures of Katrina in Monaco with Dominic.

Katrina unpacked her clothes, paying particular attention to the lovely Lanvin dress, which she placed on a hanger outside her wardrobe so she could admire it. She ran a bath, revelling in the luxury of clean towels and bubble bath. Whilst the house was small and certainly quite humble, it felt like home and it was clean compared to the hotel room. She lay in the bath reading a magazine that her mother had left on the stairs, and as she flicked through it she recognised Dominic's face in a section about the latest film releases. Studying it, she could hardly believe that she had been with him just the night before and knew his body underneath the dark suit in the picture.

Her mobile rang and she saw that the number was Chris, who was always calling on the off chance that she was around and wanted to see him. She didn't answer it; what was the point? No doubt Chris was good looking in a boy band type of way with wide brown eyes and tousled hair, but he was no movie star. The brief encounter with Dominic had made her want someone who made her feel weak with desire and took control. If only Dominic would call her, if it was him wanting to see her, she would be off like a shot. That was not very likely, as he didn't have her number, and why would he anyway? The landline was ringing now but she ignored it, knowing that it would be Chris. After it had finished ringing she turned her mobile off and left the landline off the hook. She fell asleep quickly, comfortable in her familiar bed.

Katrina didn't get out of bed until one o'clock the following day, as she was dreaming about being on a yacht alone with Dominic. The rest of the afternoon she spent lying on the sofa watching trashy chat shows and trying not to think about Dominic, which wasn't easy when every magazine seemed to have a picture of him in it and numerous commercials for his latest film kept flashing up. It was bizarre how she had never noticed him and then all of sudden he was everywhere. When she turned her phone on Chris rang immediately, so she turned it back off.

Helen turned up at six o'clock to find Katrina searching for her mother's car keys in all the usual hiding places. When she located them she turned triumphantly to face her friend.

'Excellent! At least I can drive to the train station tomorrow.'

They hugged and Helen produced a bag. 'Hurray, food!' exclaimed Katrina. 'I'm starving! The only thing I could find here was a tin of cat food.' She put a pizza in the oven and ripped open a packet of crisps, cramming them in her mouth.

'I thought models weren't supposed to eat? You look even skinnier than usual.' Helen surveyed her critically. 'I tried to call you to ask what you wanted to eat but your phone has been off and the landline has been engaged all afternoon. Who were you chatting to for that long?'

'No one. Chris kept ringing,' Katrina explained between mouthfuls of crisps.

Helen sat at the kitchen table, desperate to question Katrina about Dominic Cayley.

'So what happened, then? The girls at work haven't stopped questioning me since they saw your picture in the paper. I Googled him today and found about ten million websites! I know how tall he is, who his favourite designer is, that he likes working out and that he has been linked with the most beautiful actresses and models around. No offence, hon, you know I think you're gorgeous, but I still cannot believe you pulled him. Tell me all about it.'

'There isn't a lot to tell. I met him at a club, we went to Monaco for the weekend and then the night before last I slept with him. Now I'm back here and he's going back to LA, end of story.' Katrina smiled appreciatively at Helen as she found some chocolate in the bag. 'Oh, and he was even better looking in the flesh, and an amazing kisser.'

Helen rolled her eyes. 'Yes, but what was he like in bed and how did you part? Was he nice about it? Will you see him again?'

'He was good in bed, like I said, and it was all very amicable. We said goodbye and he said that if I was ever in LA to call him.' Katrina doubted he would even remember who she was if she did ever go to LA and called him, not that he had given her his number.

'You are unbelievable! You're being all nonchalant about shagging a film star who almost every girl in the world would want! You could sell your story to a tabloid. I can see it now: "My night of 'good' sex with Dominic Cayley."' Suddenly Helen smelt burning and leapt up to retrieve the pizza from the oven. They eyed it sitting on the baking tray, blackened and shrivelled.

'Oops, I guess we're having baked beans,' Katrina joked apologetically. 'Or I could drive to the shop and get something else, only I don't have any cash.'

Helen, who stated she was starving, opted for the second choice and handed Katrina ten quid.

'I can't believe you have no money when you are flitting around Paris with movie stars and millionaires! I'm a customer services rep and you're an international model, but I'm lending you a tenner to get food.'

Katrina could only shrug apologetically before taking her mother's car to replace the pizza and leaving Helen watching *EastEnders*. She ended up buying chips and a bottle of Coke, which, whilst being extremely unhealthy, was exactly what she needed after a weekend of hardly eating. As she pulled up at the house she was surprised to see a silver Mercedes parked on the drive. Odd. Perhaps Helen had a new flash boyfriend that she had not told her about. She went into the house, her fingers greasy from stealing chips out of the bag. Helen was sitting in the kitchen, and sitting opposite her was Dominic Cayley, movie star, the most handsome man she had ever seen, the ultimate fantasy, the man she had slept with only forty-eight hours ago.

Katrina dropped the bag of food in horror. She could not believe what she was seeing, and for a moment all she could think about was how rough she must look after a heavy night's sleep with no make-up on and in baggy tracksuit bottoms. What the hell was he doing at her mother's house in Hampshire, England?

Dominic took in her horrified expression and greasy fingers as she bent to pick up the bag and handed it to Helen. 'Surprise.' He stated the obvious without a great deal of enthusiasm and stood up to kiss her. She backed off, aware that she hadn't cleaned her teeth after scoffing cheese and onion crisps.

'I don't understand. Why are you here?' she questioned, pushing aside the plate that Helen handed to her. 'How did you find me?'

'I changed my mind about going back to the States,' he said simply. 'Instead I got a flight to London. Finding you was a nightmare – I dropped by your agency to get a mobile number from them only it was switched off. Don't you ever use your phone? It's quite ridiculous! Anyway, I got some guy, Ben or Bill or something, to see if you were at your place in London but the flatmate said she hadn't seen you. So eventually I had to take this address and drive all the way over here. That was made worse by the fact my bloody driver has taken the day off ill. I have never done anything like this before!' Dominic looked with disdain at the plate of chips that Helen was offering him and waved it away. 'As for *why* am I here, well, I thought it would be nice to see you.'

'Give me a minute, I have to wash my hands.' Katrina dashed upstairs and into the bathroom, where she brushed her teeth and hair and applied some Touche Eclat under her eyes and lip gloss to her mouth. She used the model trick of Elizabeth Arden Eight Hour Cream dabbed on her skin for a fresh look. She couldn't do a lot about the tracksuit bottoms, as it would be too obvious she had changed for him. Back downstairs, Helen had lost her appetite for once as she gawped at Dominic across the table.

'How long are you here for?' Katrina asked, wondering if he wanted to stay with her. That would be really weird. Her mother would go mad.

'That's a good question. We've wrapped up the Paris film now so I've got to decide what to do next, seeing as I have a gap in my schedule. I've still got all the promotion and advertising stuff to do of course and I have two projects to choose from which are both pretty equal in terms of quality and pay. The only difference is that one is split in location between London and Iraq and the other is in Istanbul. I have to say, I am leaning towards the London one at the moment. It was the script that I pushed off the bed the other night, remember?' Dominic smiled suggestively at Katrina. 'Lawrence Fishbacher told us about it at the dinner in Monaco. I have to go back to LA and sign a contract and attend a premiere beginning of next week, so I can stay here with James and relax until then.'

'That sounds amazing. What will you do with yourself? Have you been to London before?' Helen chipped in, eager to get his attention.

Dominic rudely ignored her. 'I was thinking that maybe you could come and stay at James's too.' He looked around. 'James has got a place in South Kensington; it's rather small compared to what I'm used to, but he offered and I didn't want to say no. Anyway, it's private and James is never around much. He's dating some hotshot lawyer woman.'

Katrina was disappointed to hear that James wouldn't be around. She wasn't entirely sure if it was a good idea going to stay with Dominic after only knowing him for five days. However, she could always go to the flat in Oval, and it wasn't as if she hadn't slept with him already. He had taken the effort to find her and wanted to see her even though he had achieved what he had set out to do. She felt wildly happy. He was looking at her expectantly. The hesitation was gone as soon as she remembered his lips on hers.

'Okay, sure. I mean, I could always just stay one or two nights. I'll get some stuff together.' She skipped up the stairs excitedly. Helen followed her.

'This is surreal! It can't be happening! You have one of the hottest men in the world waiting in your mum's kitchen to whisk you away. I can't believe it! I want your life. He is so, so, so fit! Wait until I tell all the girls at work about this, and I'll go into the pub to let stupid Emily know. Ha!' She watched Katrina throw some clothes into a bag, along with her toothbrush and make-up, and pull on a pair of jeans and vintage cowboy boots. 'You'll be famous for dating him, everyone will know about it.'

'Do I look okay?' Katrina asked, applying mascara without a mirror.

'Well, as okay as you can look when you're going out with a film star. I guess it's better to dress down than get all tarted up.'

They went downstairs to find Bramble and Dominic eyeing each other suspiciously. Katrina picked Bramble up and kissed her on the head before opening the window to let her out. Dominic was looking at some framed photographs of Katrina and she wondered what he was thinking. Perhaps something along the lines of why was he chasing an average unknown model across Europe to her unimpressive house in the middle of nowhere when he could have his pick of so many beautiful girls? Yet he was here and he had gone out of his way to find her.

'Ready? Shall we go?' Dominic asked. He picked up her bag and flicked it over his shoulder. 'Have you actually packed anything? This feels empty.'

As Katrina opened the door, Dominic turned to Helen and kissed her on the cheek. 'Bye, it was nice to meet you,' he said rather insincerely. He was already striding towards the car. Helen was rooted to the spot with her hand touching her cheek. Katrina hugged her, but she was too busy staring at Dominic to respond.

'I'll call you tomorrow and maybe we can all go out.' Katrina got in the passenger side of the Mercedes, failing to notice Dominic's horrified expression. He started the engine with a roar to end the conversation before any plans could be made, and Katrina shut the door.

'See you soon, hopefully,' he said sarcastically and reversed the car at top speed out of the driveway, leaving Helen standing on the same spot still with her hand to her cheek.

15

Dominic drove the Mercedes at top speed, flying round the narrow country lanes expertly. Noticing Katrina gripping the side of her seat as he almost collided with another car coming round a blind corner, he laughed and put a hand on her knee.

'Relax, I've never had a crash. I've been driving faster cars than this since I was sixteen; one of my first cars was a black Dodge Viper. Now I've got a 355 back in LA and a Hummer for a bit of fun, both of which I drive like this. I just bought an Aston Martin too as I drove one on my latest film and thought it was cool.'

He glanced over at her so she tried to look suitably impressed, even though she wasn't entirely sure what a 355 was. 'What's your latest film about?' she asked to sound interested, even though she knew from the magazine articles she'd read.

'I play an action hero who saves the world from a nuclear weapon that has fallen into the hands of Russian villains. It should smash the box office.' He grimaced. 'I spent three months with a personal trainer getting ready for the role, and seriously, if people thought I looked reasonably fit before, they will be blown away in this film. My body is ripped from going to the gym every day, running, swimming and a special diet. There are quite a few scenes where I'm wearing very little, and they say women are made into sex objects!'

Dominic continued to drive at top speed all the way to London, until he slammed the brakes on outside a row of redbrick houses. He reversed to parallel-park, scraping the alloys along the kerb. Katrina winced but Dominic just laughed.

'Damn, that was badly judged. I can't get used to right-hand drive. This is James's car.'

James himself appeared from one of the houses and opened Katrina's door.

'Hey, Katrina, how are you? Jesus, Dom, what the hell have you been doing with my car?' He noticed the scraped alloys and bent to get a closer look. 'I've only had this car for two weeks!'

Dominic ignored him as his mobile rang.

Katrina was pleased to see James again and kissed him on both cheeks. He grinned. 'I guess you were pretty surprised to find Dominic on your doorstep. He was keen to see you.'

Katrina nodded. 'I don't know why he turned up; you know him better than me. I didn't think I would hear from him again, but . . . well, here I am.'

Dominic appeared at her side. 'Have you managed to get your date sorted for tonight yet, James?'

'Of course, she phoned literally as soon as you dropped me off, but I'm not too sure about her now. She doesn't seem to have a sense of humour at all.' James grinned at Katrina.

Dominic rolled his eyes. 'I haven't got a clue what that's got to do with anything. She's not a comedian. I thought you said she was good looking.' He turned to Katrina. 'This is the lawyer that I told you about earlier. James left a message on her phone asking if she would like to join us for dinner tonight and she's agreed. It will save you a fortune on lawyer's fees if you keep on dating her, James.'

'Perhaps, although I think she specialises in divorce, and I am currently clear on that front.' James led them towards his house. 'Welcome to my humble abode, Katrina. It's not as grand as Dominic is used to, I'm afraid, but it does the job for me.'

Katrina thought the house looked lovely. It suited James, as it was impressive and neat without being over-bearing or pretentious. Dominic was better suited to luxury suites and he looked incongruous in the surround-ings of domesticity. She wondered why he hadn't chosen to stay in some lavish hotel suite. Her question was answered as he quickly leapt in through the front door.

'I don't want to be seen. The brilliant thing about staying here is I don't end up with teenage girls howling my name all night, whereas you can bet hotel staff will tell the press and I'll get harassed by all sorts of maniacs.' He pulled the door shut. 'I'll show Katrina the room,' he told James before she had even had a chance to look around properly. He took her bag off James and with the other hand led her up the stairs. As soon as he had shut the door to his room, he undid his zip and leant against the wall invitingly. For a moment Katrina just stared at him in shock. How could anyone have that much confidence? He didn't even feel it was necessary to make small talk to be polite! His mouth curved upwards into a smile as he ran his finger over her lips, and she knew then why he was so confident. She doubted anybody had ever refused him. His hold over her seemed to obliterate any kind of control she had. There was no way she would behave like all the other doting girls, but the truth was she found him completely irresistible. The physical attraction was so intense that she was sure she would never get bored of kissing him and having his hands all over her body. Pleasing him was hardly an awful job, and there were millions of girls who would be quite happy to do it.

*

'That was so needed.' He kissed the tip of her nose. 'I'd better do some work now.'

He lit a cigarette and reclined in a chair with the usual sheaf of papers, undoubtedly a script. Katrina went into the bathroom to take a gulp of water from the tap. He had come all this way to get her, which surely proved his sincerity, but he had a way of making her feel like he was mocking her or testing how long she could keep him interested. He was diabolically handsome, successful, and willing to share his world of fame, wealth and excitement with her: every girl's dream, surely? She was already beginning to understand that his world was his world and that was exactly how it would be staying. People were invited into his life, not the other way around. It was irrelevant to him where she had come from, what she wanted to do, because being his girlfriend was what she would be known as: nothing more, nothing less. If Dominic Cayley wanted to be with her, then she would need to please him by looking great, getting on with his friends (even if she did think they were awful) and satisfying him sexually. She could do that. The one thing she wouldn't do was fall at his feet adoringly like all the other girls, as she knew that then he would treat her badly and get bored within seconds. She applied lip gloss and gave her new, sexier, adventurous self a seductive pout before sauntering back into the bedroom.

Dominic lifted his head and smiled before returning to the script, as if he expected her just to sit quietly until he was ready again. Katrina left the room to have a look around and see if James needed help with anything. The house had three bedrooms, which were all beautiful, with dark walnut floors and high ceilings. The smallest of them had girls' clothing piled up on the floor along with teenage magazines. She presumed they belonged to

James's daughter. Loretta had seemed like a strange mother to have for all the wrong reasons, whilst James seemed like a strange father to have for all the right ones. Katrina imagined he was easy to talk to and good fun to be around. There were framed pictures down the stairs of him skiing, horse-riding, playing tennis, at parties, laughing and looking like he was having a great time. Katrina studied an image of him covered in mud and holding a pint of beer, with a girl who had wrapped her arms around his neck. She was attractive and was laughing with her head pressed against his. Katrina wondered if it was his ex-wife or a girlfriend.

'I'm not quite as photogenic as you and Dominic. I always look best covered in mud or in sunglasses!' James appeared at the bottom of the stairs, grinning up at her. 'Do you want a drink?'

Katrina followed him into the lounge, which was furnished with broken-in leather Chesterfields. On a large red and gold Persian rug a blue cat was teasing a toy mouse.

'Meet Delilah; she rules the house.' Katrina bent down to stroke Delilah. 'Is Dominic on the phone as usual?'

'No, he's looking at a script, I think.' Katrina noticed a book open on the coffee table. 'What are you reading?'

'*The Prize*; it's about the oil industry. Quite interesting but it's taking me ages to get through, as I don't have a lot of time to read.'

'I've read it. It's about the Seven Sisters and the history of the oil conflict. I thought it was really interesting. Quite huge, though . . . does take time to get through,' Katrina admitted.

James looked impressed and gestured for her to sit on a large green velvet chair.

'Do you read a lot, then?'

'All the time. When you're at shoots and there isn't anything else to do, it occupies the mind and passes time. At university we had to get through three or four decent-size books a week.' Katrina ran her eye along the shelves of books above James's head, picking up on titles that she had read as well as a few that she kept meaning to read. It was all mainly factual, books about politics, autobiographies of successful businessmen, travel literature and photographic books. 'It looks like you read a fair amount too.'

'Oh no, that's just for show so people think I'm intellectual and clever. Really I'm not very well read. I would love to be, but things just come up and distract me.' James picked up the huge book and flicked through the pages before giving her a wry grin and putting it on the shelf above him. 'Maybe I shouldn't be so ambitious, picking up such a heavy book, which I stop reading for a week or so and then forget what I have read. Got any suggestions?' He looked genuinely keen to hear her ideas.

'Maybe you should get a fiction book and read just for the pleasure of reading rather than learning. Something that you'll enjoy and that will make you want to read more.' Katrina was struck by a sudden idea. 'Wait there, I'll be back in a second.'

Leaving James looking surprised, she ran up the stairs to Dominic's room.

Dominic looked up and smiled at her. 'What have you been up to?'

'Oh, I was just coming up to get something out of my bag.' She slipped past him into the room to retrieve her book from her battered holdall. When she turned around she went straight into Dominic, who had come up behind her. He put his arms over her shoulders and looked intensely at her, obviously enjoying how nervous she became whenever he touched her. His dark eyes looked even darker in the dim light of the room and his mouth turned up at the corners, making her stomach flip. He kissed her and began to run his hands over her body. He looked surprised when she was the first to break away. She headed for the door.

'Where are you going?' he questioned.

'I just wanted to give this to James to read. Aren't you coming down?' she said as she headed for the stairs. She got no reply, yet instead of turning back to ask again, she continued downwards, assuming that he would follow when he chose to do so.

James was still sitting in the lounge with Delilah on his lap purring happily. Katrina handed her book to him.

'I think you should read this. It's by Martin Amis and is one of my favourite books.' She sat on the floor next to him, leaning over to stroke Delilah's silky blue fur whilst James read the synopsis on the back.

'Okay, I'll do that. I keep meaning to read some Amis so I may as well start with this on your recommendation. Do you mind me borrowing it?' James lifted his head as Dominic entered the room.

'Of course not. I've read it lots of times so I can do without it. It's certainly easier going than an autobiography of John Major!' Katrina giggled, spotting the title on the shelf. James laughed too.

Dominic threw himself on to a sofa to light a cigarette. He looked annoyed, and Katrina recognised it as the same mood he'd been in after he had burst in on her and Carlos. He was a bit like a spoilt child if he felt he wasn't getting all the attention.

'Want a drink, Dom?' James asked, going over to the drinks cabinet.

'Scotch and American,' Dominic replied shortly, pushing a purring Delilah away. James handed him his drink, which he took without a thank-you. 'I've just been chatting to a journalist about this environmental charity I've become a representative for. They're having a huge party next month with all the big names involved. I think it could help with my image change.' He showed James a photograph of himself standing next to people planting trees.

'What image change is that?' asked James, looking amused.

'I keep getting write-ups describing me as an actor who only does action films and a playboy, so I'm looking for more serious roles to take on as well as cutting down on the partying.' Dominic drained his glass. 'Only for a little while, of course, and doing some charity stuff will help get rid of any negative press.'

'What does the charity do exactly?' asked James.

'It's called the Better World Trust and it's environmental stuff; you know, saving rainforests and fighting air pollution, that kind of thing, I guess. It's quite trendy and I can help raise their profile too whilst adding a serious dimension to my image.'

'Shouldn't you know what their actual aim is? Where do they source their funding and how do you know it's better than any other charity you could put your name to?' James queried.

'I presume the aim is to save the world, and I know it's the best charity because they've managed to get some huge stars to sign up.' Dominic looked at James like he was mad. 'You're missing the point anyway. It's about helping a cause whilst managing my publicity, and this will get a lot of publicity.'

'All I'm saying is you should make sure it is a cause you believe in, and not just the most powerful one with the best contacts. There's loads of charity stuff a guy like you could help with. Just because they have managed to create a great image with loads of famous people supporting them doesn't necessarily mean they are doing the most good. You should check them out before you lend them your name.'

Dominic got to his feet. 'Well, all charities are there to do good so I'm sure they are doing what they can to make the world a better place. We'd better get ready for dinner.' He left the room.

Katrina followed Dominic up the stairs, wondering if having a girlfriend was all part of the trying-to-be-more-serious plan. How he was seen was everything to him, and she supposed she should be extremely flattered that he felt she could fit into that. Anyway, who cared! She was spending the night with him, and that meant hours of exploring his perfect body, and in between that finding out more about what lay beneath the movie-star image.

16

Back in Dominic's room, Katrina showered in the en suite and dried her hair straight. The only thing she had to wear was a top she had bought on a modelling job in Egypt that was her favourite: dark blue with heavy pink beads that did up in a halterneck and exposed her wide shoulders. She teamed this with a pair of pale worn jeans, hoping that the restaurant wouldn't be too dressy, and a pair of pink crystal earrings that dropped almost to her shoulders. When she stepped out of the bathroom she found Dominic already dressed in jeans and an extremely well-fitting black shirt with black suede Gucci loafers. His hair was slicked back and he looked perfect sitting on the chair by the window.

'You look beautiful.' He stood up to kiss her, running his hand down the beaded top, feeling her nipples stiffen beneath his fingers. He pushed her against the wall, pressing tightly against her. A knock at the door disturbed them.

'Isabelle is here and we've got a bit of a problem.' James's voice was muffled through the solid oak. Dominic opened the door, causing James to jump in surprise. 'She's got a friend with her who has just spilt up with her husband. Apparently she's too depressed to be left alone and has a stonking crush on you. It would make her year if she came to dinner and I can't really say no now she's here.' James raised an eyebrow. 'Although I don't think she would understand the word no; she's a little bolshy.'

'Oh great, I get saddled with a suicidal mad fan clinging to me all night! I hope you told this Isabelle that I have a girlfriend and that she's coming tonight.' Katrina jumped visibly when he called her his girlfriend.

'Of course I did!' replied James over his shoulder as he went down the stairs.

Katrina was curious to meet Isabelle and followed Dominic into the lounge. As they entered, a tall woman with shoulder-length blond hair stood up. She was very attractive, with fine features, penetrating green eyes and an icy perfection about her. She wore a black knee-length dress with a corseted top, and a black pashmina covered her shoulders. Her appearance couldn't be criticised at all: neat, careful and with clothes tight enough to reveal that she had a fit, toned body. She held out a cold hand to Dominic and then rather unwillingly to Katrina. Her eyes widened very slightly as she took in Dominic.

'Hello, I'm Isabelle. You must be Dominic and Katrina?' She had a clipped, well-educated voice. She didn't seem to suit James's relaxed demeanour at all.

'Correct. It's a pleasure to meet you, Isabelle. You're as beautiful as James said,' Dominic replied charmingly. Katrina smiled politely. Isabelle surveyed her, taking in her jeans and her youthful appearance.

'Oh my God, you must introduce me now before I faint!' screeched a voice behind Isabelle. An overly made-up woman appeared, her face frenzied as she spotted Dominic in his entirety. 'Jesus, I cannot believe this!' She threw herself at him, wrapping her arms around his neck. Dominic looked positively aghast and immediately tried to disentangle himself. Katrina and James exchanged amused glances, knowing how much Dominic hated strange people touching him, unless of course they were extremely beautiful. When the woman finally let go, she would have tripped backwards over a side table had James not had the presence of mind to whisk it away just in time.

'This is Maxine. I hope you don't mind her coming along, but she was feeling a bit lonely tonight.' Isabelle addressed Dominic rather than Katrina. 'She's the life and soul of any party, aren't you, Maxine?'

Maxine had slumped on the sofa and was rooting through her Louis Vuitton. 'Before we all have too much to drink and forget I have to get your autograph.' She thrust a pen and notepad at Dominic, who shot James a deadly look as he signed his name unenthusiastically. Maxine whooped with joy and gave him a lipstick-covered kiss on the cheek. She was short, with a shiny brown bob and huge cartoon-like features. Whilst she wasn't unattractive, her make-up was garish: heavy green eye shadow, spidery eyelashes, too much blusher and solid red lips. She left glitter all over Dominic's face where she had kissed him, and he rubbed at it in the mirror.

They made their way to the front door, where Dominic suddenly remembered he hadn't booked his driver.

'How are we getting to this place?' he snapped.

'Taxi, I guess. It's only down the road but the girls can't walk with heels on.'

Dominic grimaced at the mention of a taxi, but James flagged down a black cab and opened the door to let Isabelle step in first. Maxine followed, strategically sitting in the middle so Dominic had to sit next to her. James and Katrina, used to London cabs, flipped the seats opposite down. The short journey was silent, with Maxine pressing against Dominic's thigh so that he retreated firmly against the door. She gazed at him not caring whether she was offending Katrina, who noticed her hand creeping towards his muscular legs and suspected her mind was going further. At least it wasn't some gorgeous, sexy girl like Zora who was trying to steal Dominic's attention, and with that thought Katrina relaxed a little.

As they piled into the already full restaurant they made a glamorous-looking party, causing everyone to look up from their plates and stare. The maître d', recognising Dominic, asked for a photograph to put on the wall, which he insisted that all the others also be in, and seated them at the best table.

Katrina was placed between Dominic and Isabelle, with Maxine on the other side of Dominic, much to his dismay. Immediately she began to talk about her job in public relations, where apparently she dealt with lots of promising actors and producers. James was discussing property prices with Isabelle, oblivious to Dominic's wild glances in his direction as Maxine touched his arm and moved closer to him so her face was inches from his.

'Katrina came with me to Monaco at the weekend, didn't you, sweetie?' Desperate to fend off Maxine's incessant flirtation, Dominic disturbed Katrina from her observations of the restaurant. He pulled her towards him, kissing her pointedly on the lips.

'Oh, really? So you two have been seeing each other for a while then, have you? I thought you'd just come out tonight.' Maxine failed to suppress the disgust in her voice as she directed her question at Katrina. Dominic leapt in before she had a chance to answer.

'Hell, no! I've been crazy about this girl for ages now. Who wouldn't be? She's beautiful, a very successful model, intelligent, she's got a degree and . . .' Dominic trailed off as he spotted Crystal Douglas, an American actress, enter the restaurant. It had been all over the papers when two years ago they had slept together after a party and he had been caught sneaking out of her hotel suite. Her boyfriend at the time had been totally humiliated when his picture had appeared next to Dominic's in gossip magazines with subtitles like 'Can you blame her for falling for Cayley?' She was still with him, though, and now he trailed behind her to their table. Crystal spotted Dominic and pretended not to have seen him.

'A successful model?' Maxine purred. 'I can't say I've ever seen you in *Vogue* and I read it religiously. I don't think intelligence rates very highly in standing round posing for the camera.'

Katrina, annoyed by Maxine's sarcasm, smiled sweetly. 'Modelling just happened by accident. It earns me money until I decide what I want to do with my degree. I'm shooting a Moschino campaign tomorrow and *Vogue* have got an option on using me for two weeks' time.' It felt great to say that and Maxine didn't need to know it was only because of Dominic. 'By the way, your lipstick has smudged,' she added before turning her attention to the menu. A furious Maxine squeezed out of her seat and gestured that Isabelle follow her to the ladies'.

Dominic ran his hand over Katrina's leg, sliding it upwards and rubbing gently. She glanced at him and he raised his eyes upwards and curled his upper lip. 'I spy with my bored little eye, something beginning with M,' he said drily.

'Madwoman,' James replied, draining his glass and refilling it to the brim.

'Exactly. Hopefully she'll fall down the toilet and not come back. Your lawyer may be easy on the eye but she certainly isn't easy in any other way.' Dominic took

Katrina's hand under the table and directed it to his crotch whilst pushing his glass towards James for a refill with the other hand.

'Hmmm, well we do seem to only talk about the legal profession and her property portfolio. It is slightly exhausting seeing as that is what I do for work.' James grinned at Katrina. 'Sorry that you have to put up with Mad Maxine pawing Dominic all night. I should have said no to Isabelle.'

'It's fine, don't worry about me . . .' Katrina trailed off as Maxine and Isabelle reappeared and sat back down. Isabelle immediately asked James whether he owned any property abroad, to which Dominic pointedly yawned extra loudly.

'So, Dominic, we were thinking about having a party soon at my house in the country. Will you come?' Maxine asked, having decided that it would be the perfect revenge for her husband to open the newspaper and find she was dating Dominic Cayley. That would teach him for running off with his secretary!

'Oh, I'd love to come. In fact I think I'll definitely come.' Dominic smirked at Katrina suggestively.

'Brilliant,' trilled Maxine obliviously, leaning towards Dominic. She slid her hand under the table and leapt about a foot in the air when it met Katrina's. Katrina pulled her hand away in shock whilst Dominic threw his head back and roared with laughter. James and Isabelle looked up in surprise.

'What's so funny?' James asked curiously.

'Nothing. Just a private joke,' Maxine snapped. She had gone bright red.

Katrina couldn't help giggling a bit herself. Maxine shot her a deadly look and composed herself as the starters were placed in front of them. There was silence as everyone ate. Katrina had to admit that it was excellent food and both the men ate ravenously, although Isabelle only had a salad and Maxine barely touched her lobster spaghetti.

'Check your phone,' Dominic hissed in between mouthfuls.

Katrina fished it out of her bag and found there were two text messages, one from Helen asking how it was going and the second from an unfamiliar number. It read: 'I was enjoying that. Perhaps we can continue when we get home. D xx' He was watching her with raised eyebrows. Katrina was surprised at how pleased she was. It felt more intimate than anything he had done before, plus it meant she had his mobile number now, like a proper normal boyfriend. She texted a reply: 'Absolutely, looking forward to it. x' Dominic on receiving it looked up and gave a slow, sexy smile that sent a tremor of excitement down her spine. Her phone bill was going to have a movie-star's number on it and she had a text from him. That almost seemed to prove his existence in her life more than him sitting inches away from her with his hand on her knee.

Following dinner they moved on to a club where James was a member. He led them to the chill-out room, where Isabelle perched on the edge of a chair looking disapprovingly around her. Katrina decided she really didn't like her; she was far too boring for James.

'Does anyone want to go and dance?' she asked, seeing as the conversation was rather stilted. Law, it seemed, had its limits.

'I will!' volunteered James, leaping to his feet looking relieved. The others shook their heads. Katrina followed James through into the next room, where they were playing a salsa beat. He was a much better dancer than her and held her waist to show her the steps. After twenty minutes of laughing, they made their way back to the others feeling exhausted. Dominic was chatting to a tall, dark-haired man wearing a silver shirt. He grabbed Katrina's hand as she went past.

'This is my girlfriend Katrina. This is Ricky.' Ricky kissed her on both cheeks. 'Ricky works for a big publicity magazine in New York,' Dominic explained.

'Wow, that's incredible!' Ricky said. 'I can't believe you've got yourself a girlfriend. That'll put a stop to all the playboy comments. You must really be settling down. What's the plan of action career-wise now?' He looked suitably impressed by Katrina. Dominic put an arm around her shoulder, drawing her towards him.

'Well, there's a project partly based here in London, and now that Katrina's here it seems like a good thing to do. I want to start taking some really meaty roles, you know. Less based around being a hero and getting the girl and more dark – you know, like Brad in *Kalifornia*, stuff that shows I really can act. Katrina's such a great girl and I want to stay in London with her for a bit, so this film might be the one.' Dominic flashed a cosmetically perfect smile at Ricky. Katrina couldn't stop a grin spreading across her own face at his comments. If he really was staying in London because of her then it meant he really liked her and was serious about getting to know her. That was exciting news, and being referred to as his girlfriend in front of a publicist was thrilling.

'So how are you doing? You look well, like you've been working out.' Dominic leant forward and touched Ricky's arm. It was then that Katrina realised Ricky was obviously gay and therefore was lapping up Dominic's slightly flirtatious manner. His face lit up

'Do I? Well, I guess I have been going to the gym a bit more recently. Wow! I tell you, speaking to you is just so refreshing. What I like about you, Dominic, is how you're just so not obsessed with yourself and you always have time for people. No one else I interview ever asks how I am. You are a true star.' Ricky seized Dominic's hand and shook it vigorously.

'Well, you know, I'm just me and I've had a few lucky breaks,' Dominic replied, adequately modest. Ricky was literally pumping his arm off and he looked a little alarmed. 'Just make sure you write some nice stuff, okay?'

'Oh I will do! Absolutely!' Ricky finally let go of Dominic's hand. 'I'm going to write a piece on what you're up to at the moment and just how cool you are. Thanks so much for taking the time to update me!'

'No problem. Keep up the gym. It's working for you.' Dominic flashed his blinding smile and turned away to speak to someone else.

Ricky returned to his date, a pouting young man who wasn't sure who to be jealous of: Dominic for talking to Ricky or Ricky for talking to Dominic. Katrina stood for a moment wondering if she should be impressed that Dominic was so smooth with the publicist or worried that he just said whatever he thought he should say to get a good write-up. Did he mean any of it? Dominic came back and, taking her arm, led her to a dark corner, where he began kissing her and telling her how he couldn't wait to take her back to bed. No matter what he was up to she would be in magazines as Dominic Cayley's girlfriend, and that could be life-changing. She kissed him back, hard.

A camera flashed as someone took a photo of them. Maxine appeared like an apparition in the dark and threw herself down next to them, make-up running and her top almost falling off. Dominic scowled and pointedly carried on kissing Katrina. Maxine tapped him on the shoulder.

'What?' He glared at her.

'I just fink you should know . . .' Maxine slurred, 'that you are the most beautiful man in the world and you could have anyone you want. You don't need to waste your time with a silly girl like that! What can she do for you? I'll show you a good time. I can do things to that hunky body that you never dreamt of!' With that she launched herself at Dominic, who moved out of the way, resulting in Maxine falling off the seat on to the floor, hitting her head on a table on the way down.

Two hours later, Maxine had been discharged from the hospital after being diagnosed with minor concussion. Dominic was signing autographs for excited patients. An exhausted James sidled over to Katrina.

'Can you believe this? Utterly ridiculous! Remind me not to take Dominic with me on a date again. You may as well get used to it, though. You will always have jealous women causing chaos.' As if to prove the point, a group of nurses appeared vying for Dominic's attention. James rolled his eyes. 'See what I mean! You'd think he was some kind of god rather than a man doing a job that just happens to be acting.'

Maxine appeared with a plaster on her forehead, glaring reproachfully at Dominic, who was laughing loudly with a pretty blonde nurse, teeth glinting and shirt undone at the collar, looking like every woman's wildest fantasy.

Having travelled back to the house in silence, with Isabelle patting Maxine sympathetically, Isabelle went straight to her car.

'Don't you want to come in and have a coffee? Maxine looks like she could do with one,' James said.

'No thanks, I have a lot to do tomorrow and it's already two o'clock. Besides, I think Maxine had better get to bed.' Isabelle offered her cheek for James to kiss. 'Thank you for dinner.' She got into the car. Maxine, catching Dominic off guard, managed to kiss him on the lips.

'It was lovely to meet you, and don't forget you promised to come to my party next week. You can get my number off Issie.' She got into the passenger seat and they drove off, leaving James disappointed, Dominic disgusted and Katrina amused.

In Dominic's room Katrina washed her face, remembering she had to be at the studio in the morning. At least it was for sunglasses, she reflected, so any dark circles would be hidden. When she went into the bedroom, Dominic had fallen asleep on the bed with just his jeans on. His face looked gentle and vulnerable compared to its usual haughty arrogance. Katrina lay on the bed next to him and turned the light off. She couldn't sleep; it was too strange in an unknown house with a man who was unfamiliar in every sense of the word, not just because she had only known him for a few days. It was because everything about him was unlike anything she had ever known or imagined. She watched him sleep until light crept in through the curtains.

18

'Oh my God!' Katrina leapt off the bed, pulling on clothes and nearly falling over her shoes. Dominic opened his eyes.

'What's up, sweetie?' he groaned.

'It's nine o'clock and I was supposed to be at work an hour ago. Have you seen my bag?'

Dominic pointed to a heap of clothes on the floor where her bag was hidden and shut his eyes. As she went to leave he called her back.

'Where's my goodbye kiss? I'll get a car sorted today and get the driver to pick you up later, okay?'

That sounded great to Katrina as she ran down the stairs, narrowly missing James holding a cup of coffee.

'Where are you going in such a hurry?'

'Late for work!'

'Grab some fruit from the kitchen and I'll hail a taxi,' he instructed.

Katrina did as he said and he stopped a taxi outside the front door.

'Have a good day.' He grinned as she hopped in.

Katrina sat in the back nibbling an apple and cursing the traffic. She got to the studio two hours late, expecting to see a lot of angry faces.

'I am so sorry. I got stuck in traffic,' she lied, smiling apologetically at the team.

'Hi, I'm Penny, the photographer.' A tall woman stepped forward. 'Don't worry about being late. It's no problem and you've got a good enough excuse. I'd be late if I was in bed with Dominic Cayley.' The team burst out laughing.

'Tell me about it, honey. I'm Dani, I'm doing the make-up today. You must be tired after partying last night. Good job the sunglasses cover your eyes; you can go to sleep,' said another woman brandishing a blusher brush.

Katrina was baffled. Did she look that knackered?

'You're one lucky girl!' said a girl with orangey-red hair who didn't offer her name. 'Whilst we were here at eight sharp, you were probably canoodling with sex-on-legs. God, I should hate you.'

Katrina was even more confused now. How did they know that she had been out partying and spent the night with Dominic?

'Have you seen the papers today?' asked Penny, noticing her bewildered expression. 'You and Dominic are on the front of the *Evening Standard* and the *Daily Mail* and in the *Sun* gossip page. Get yourself a coffee and have a look. The shots shouldn't take too long today, so we're not in a particular rush anyway. We should finish at about three.'

Katrina went over to the coffee machine and on the newspaper rack next to it saw a picture of her and Dominic wrapped around each other in the club. Dominic was looking at the camera, just breaking away from kissing her. The headline on the *Mail* said: 'Cayley and girlfriend in town promoting new film'; another headline stated: 'Dominic Cayley chooses British' and inside was a picture of Katrina from a modelling job and a few lines discussing Dominic's latest films and the fact that he was dating a British model. The *Sun* featured a picture of all of them arriving at the club alongside an article about how they had all got so drunk that one of the group had been taken to casualty. Ridiculously it also stated that Katrina was eighteen and an up-and-coming supermodel! The journalist obviously hadn't been too careful with the facts. She wondered if her parents and friends had seen it yet. It seemed certain that everyone was going to know that she was dating Dominic: people she had gone to university or school with, other models, all the photographers she had worked with and even total strangers. She felt a wave of excitement as she realised that what seemed like it should be a dream was actually real, and she had the proof in front of her. As if to reinforce that her mobile bleeped with a message from Dominic reminding her to send him the address of the studio.

The make-up artist set to work to create the chosen image of a flawless matt base and strong eyebrows. Katrina's lips were a dark pink, carefully outlined, with the cupid's bow emphasised, and the hairdresser curled her hair into big waves like an old-fashioned star. The first set of sunglasses was tortoiseshell, large and round, with the designer emblem emblazoned on the side. Katrina felt a thrill at the thought that she was shooting a proper campaign for such a big designer. If it hadn't been for Dominic she doubted it would have happened, and that thought made her a little annoyed. Nonetheless modelling was all based on luck, so what difference did it make? She had wanted success for so long, and now it was finally happening!

It was easy work and the shots were all close up on the face, meaning she only had to move slightly every couple of minutes. They used a few pairs of glasses before changing the make-up to a caramel lip gloss and hair swept back in a low ponytail. By lunchtime they had done five different shots and Penny was pleased.

'You're easy to work with. We were worried you might be a bit of a prima donna,' she told Katrina. 'Let's break for lunch and you can tell us all about your gorgeous boyfriend. We chose you for this shoot after seeing you in the paper last weekend. You looked stunning with him getting out of that car in Monaco.'

The red-haired girl, who Katrina had worked out was the stylist and called Jenna, took the sunglasses off her. 'So what's the story? How long have you been seeing each other?'

'There's nothing to tell really. We were introduced in a club in Paris. It's all happened so fast, to be honest. When I left Paris I didn't expect to see him again, but then he turned up at my house yesterday.' Katrina looked at their astonished faces.

'What! He just turned up at your place out of the blue?' Dani asked incredulously.

'Yes.' Katrina didn't quite believe it herself. It did sound quite absurd.

'You must think you're dreaming. I would be going mad if I were you. I'd love to meet him,' Dani sighed, biting dreamily into a cheese sandwich. Katrina nibbled on a piece of cake, reflecting that she would probably spend the next few weeks talking to people about Dominic. He fascinated everyone.

As she was thinking this the studio door opened and Dominic himself appeared, cigarette in one hand, mobile in the other. Without putting either down he made his way to Katrina and kissed her on the mouth, acknowledging the others with a smile. Dani had stopped eating to stare open-mouthed and Jenna was smoothing her hair down and rubbing lip gloss on. Dominic finished his phone conversation.

'Hi, gorgeous. I thought I would come and pick you up myself. I'm early, as I was bored without you.' He turned towards the gawping women. 'You don't mind me hanging around, do you?' He held out a hand to Dani. 'I'm Dominic.'

'Yes, I know who you are,' croaked Dani, taking his hand. Dominic gave her his knee-trembling smile and extracted his hand from her grasp to acknowledge Jenna. Within seconds everyone was swarming around him, bombarding him with questions and staring adoringly. The sunglasses were forgotten as they all crowded around, whilst Dominic stood in front of the camera and allowed Penny to take a Polaroid.

'I can't wait to show my sister this picture! She's besotted with you,' cooed Jenna, her moodiness transcended by excitement. 'You wouldn't mind signing the back, would you?' Dominic obliged.

'Hey, can you take a picture of Katrina and me together?' he asked suddenly, grinning at her. 'You guys all get pictures, so it's only fair that I should have one to take home too.' The next thing she knew, Katrina was standing with Dominic's arms around her waist whilst Penny took another Polaroid. Dominic slid the picture into his pocket: a reminder for when she wasn't with him, he told her, although she couldn't tell for certain whether he was being serious or not. Dominic sat down on a sofa and everyone quietened down to get back to work.

Lipstick was reapplied in between constant questioning from Dani.

'What's it like to kiss him? You must think you're dreaming or something; I mean, imagine a girl like you dating him and he seems really into you! He comes all the way here to sit and watch you! I was doing that amazing model's make-up last week, what's her name again? Hutton, is it? Chrissie?'

'Cheryl?' Katrina interjected.

'That's the one. God, she is so beautiful! She's in Hollywood now, trying to break into films. Anyway, she said she had met Dominic and they had a really good time, stayed in a hotel and he did the works. Then she gave him her number and he never called. She was really pissed off; I don't think she's the kind of girl who is used to rejection. The thing is, Dominic Cayley could have anyone and he's here with you. Cheryl Hutton is really beautiful and he dissed her, for God's sake! That must take some getting used to.'

'I guess so.' Katrina was getting a headache from lack of sleep and too much talking. She was shocked that Dominic had been with Cheryl and wondered if Carlos knew. Was it when she had been with him or after?

'It's just so weird. I mean, does he come over to your house, and what do you talk about? How can you have anything in common? I'm not saying that you're boring or anything, but it's just a totally different life. Have you ever even been to Hollywood?'

Katrina shook her head and closed her eyes whilst Dani painted her mouth a dusky pink. The next sunglasses were aviator style, with a pink rim. Penny didn't seem to be concentrating on taking the shot as much as before. Katrina was able to watch Dominic through the shades without him knowing. She had never been a jealous person and was pretty laid back, yet she couldn't stop herself thinking about him and Cheryl Hutton together, imagining him touching her perfect super-slim tanned body and 34C silicone tits that she swore in interviews were natural. She tried to erase the picture from her mind; it was ridiculous getting stressed about girls he had slept with. There were countless women, she was sure, yet Cheryl irritated her the most, as she was obviously such a bitch and also so incredibly beautiful. Still, he hadn't phoned Cheryl, had he? He was here now, watching her not Cheryl.

An hour later and it was all finished. Having kissed everyone goodbye and listened to their praise for ten minutes, Dominic led Katrina to the car.

19

As she sat next to him Katrina thought about how amazing it was to be seen with Dominic. His presence by her side seemed to make people notice her, look up to her. All of a sudden she had gained a desirable, intriguing image that everyone was fascinated by.

'Do you mind if we pop in at the agency?' she asked, imagining the booker's reaction if she walked in with him. 'They have some new tear sheets for my book and I might be working tomorrow so I need to collect the details.'

'Sure,' Dominic replied.

The buzz in the agency dropped when they walked in. Everyone looked up in awe and even Rosanna seemed momentarily lost for words.

'Hey, Ben.' Dominic sauntered over to Katrina's booker, who had given him her details even though it was normally against agency policy. Who would ever say no to a movie star? 'How are you?'

Ben stood up, grinning widely.

'You found her, then? She's nothing but trouble, you know.' Ben winked at Dominic as he kissed Katrina on each cheek.

'Oh, I like a bit of trouble!' Dominic beamed at the bookers. Rosanna stood up, smoothing down her lilac silk shirt and flicking her perfect hair.

'Hello, Mr Cayley, I'm Rosanna D'Orca. I own this agency and so of course Katrina's one of my girls.' She peered up at Dominic through mascara-encrusted eyelashes and smiled sweetly.

'An absolute pleasure to meet you, Rosanna. Call me Dominic.' Dominic's attention was distracted by a stunning blonde model who had just walked into the agency and was bent over the table looking at proofs with an eye lens. She lifted her head, pouting sulkily because none of the bookers were paying her any attention. When her eyes fell on Dominic they widened in surprise and attraction.

Katrina, who normally had to vie for the attention of the bookers amongst all the other girls and was lucky if she got five minutes from any of them, couldn't help feel a little smug about how they were all fawning over her. It was made even better when Dominic wrapped his arms around her to kiss her, telling them all how great it was that he had met a model with a brain. As he perused the wall of model cards, Rosanna dragged Katrina aside.

'This is really unbelievable, Katrina, a guy like that choosing you. You had better work it! We must make sure you're in tiptop shape!' She lowered her voice as she saw Dominic glance over. 'I have had eighteen phone calls about you today regarding jobs in the next few weeks. Everyone's heard that you're seeing him and everyone wants a piece. I just negotiated three thousand quid for a shot of you at London Fashion Week drinking water for some promotion thing. You are first option on a campaign for H&M, and on Friday the *Evening Standard* are doing a little piece on how you are an up-and-coming star, using a shot from *GQ*. This is big stuff and you'd better be ready for a rollercoaster ride, honey! British *Vogue*'s still holding that option on you for the diamond story being shot by Tom Munro, and *ID* magazine have been sniffing around about the possibility of a cover!' Rosanna paused for breath and then continued. 'Everyone wants to know who you are and how long you've been dating. I'm telling them a month. If they think you're Dominic Cayley's girlfriend they're all going to want to use you; girls will be queuing up to know your style and beauty secrets!'

Rosanna reached out to smooth Katrina's hair down and smiled affectionately.

'Dominic has the most perfect image, so we'd better make sure you don't let him down. We need to smarten you up a bit, make you a bit less Katrina-like and more of a gorgeous top model who dates film stars. I've booked you in for teeth-whitening tomorrow afternoon and a haircut with Sorbie afterwards, and I think you should go out and buy some new clothes. I've asked the accountant to put an advance of two thousand pounds into your bank account. Get yourself some expensive designer stuff; dresses with heels work best.' Noticing that Katrina's face was aghast she continued quickly. 'Don't worry, darling, every decent model gets their teeth whitened, it will look fabulous.' She stopped as Dominic and Ben came up behind them.

'What's this? Teeth-whitening? It's worth doing,' Dominic commented, flashing his own super-white teeth as he spoke.

'That's right, you tell her. I guess all you film stars get them done,' Ben gushed enthusiastically.

Dominic gave him a look of disdain. 'I didn't. I'm just fortunate enough to have naturally very white teeth, but most people aren't so lucky and Katrina's teeth could be whiter.'

Katrina didn't know a great deal about dentistry and teeth, yet it was pretty obvious that Dominic's teeth had been whitened – unless he was some sort of genetic freak. They were far too white and perfect not to have been helped along. Paranoid, she ran her tongue over her own teeth. Dominic softened again. 'I've never had any enhancement or surgery; people just assume I have for some reason.'

'That's because you have the most perfect teeth and bone structure. You're very lucky,' said Rosanna. 'If I remember correctly, you used to model yourself, didn't you?' Being practised in dealing with big egos, she had given the answer that Dominic wanted to hear. Katrina noticed him visibly step out of his offended mood.

'I did, just whilst I was at drama school. I did Abercrombie and Fitch, Armani, Versace, that kind of thing. Modelling wasn't for me, although I still get asked to do campaigns as favours for designers.' Dominic peered closely at one of the composites on the wall. 'Hey, you represent Eva Cole? I met her last time I was in London. She's absolutely stunning, phenomenal body.'

Katrina looked at the picture of Eva, who had the all-American look of tanned skin, blue eyes and shoulder-length blond hair. She was the equivalent of Dominic in female form, and Katrina felt another pang of jealousy. Dominic seemed to know every beautiful woman in the world personally.

As they left, Rosanna hissed in her ear, 'Try to keep getting in the papers. The more you're seen with him, the more chance there is of work coming your way, and try to look more like the sort of girl a guy like Dominic would want to be with. For God's sake, Katrina, pull it together. A girl like Eva Cole would jump at the chance to date that man!'

As they stepped outside, Katrina looked at Dominic's immaculate outfit of moleskin Armani trousers, black Interno 8 shirt, Versace leather jacket and Gucci loafers, accessorised with a Rolex Yacht-Master and a Hermès belt. In contrast she was wearing a pair of faded Gap jeans and a white Marks and Spencer vest with scuffed brown boots and no watch or belt. She was out with a man that most women would kill to be with, when he could be with a supermodel or anyone. She sat next to him in the car uncomfortably and noticed that her jeans had a hole in them. Girls like Eva Cole were polished and perfect; she was messy and unstylish. It had never mattered before, but now it seemed like the most important thing in the world. She wanted the polished, perfect image that matched his.

As she tried to untangle her hair with her fingers, the chauffeur pulled up outside Harvey Nichols and Dominic stepped out.

'I need to get some stuff here,' he explained when Katrina questioned him. As they went through the door he led her through the cosmetic counter to the escalator.

'Menswear is downstairs,' she protested as he took the escalator going to the first floor.

'I'm not here for menswear. I'm here for womens-wear.' He grinned at her baffled face. 'No, I haven't decided to cross-dress. We're here to sort you out. I can't have you wearing those jeans with me.'

He had noticed her poor turnout then; she felt even more uncomfortable. 'You don't need to take me shop-ping, and anyway I was going to get some clothes tomorrow, as the agency has said they'll give me an advance. I won't shop here, though.' A zealous-looking sales assistant was bearing down on them with a frighteningly determined expression, causing Katrina to turn towards the down escalator.

'Whoa, you're not going anywhere.' Dominic grabbed the loop on her jeans just in time to prevent her escaping. 'Christ, I've never had problems encouraging girls to shop before. I need you to attend a few functions with me and you have to look a certain way. I really want you to come places with me, so I'm going to get you some clothes whether you want them or not. Either you help me pick them out or I'll have to do it myself.'

A voice interrupted him. 'Excuse me, can I have your autograph?' They turned to find two blonde girls with a pen and paper.

'Sure you can.' Dominic scribbled quickly on the paper and turned back to Katrina.

'So are you going to get some clothes?'

'Omigod, are you Dominic Cayley? You're even more gorgeous in real life than on TV!' Again they looked around to see three teenage girls with heavy make-up and designer handbags gawping at Dominic, who nodded reluctantly. 'Can we get your autograph?' Their loud voices attracted the attention of other shoppers, who began to make their way towards Dominic like a mass of zombies, some not even sure why they were asking him for autographs but just copying the others.

'Why don't you make a start and pick out some clothes? The price tags are irrelevant; just choose what looks good,' he told Katrina over the throng of people. The good thing about everyone being around Dominic was that the rest of the shop was almost empty, meaning that Katrina could look round easily.

Dominic reappeared an hour later just as Katrina emerged from a changing room. She had found loads, including a Diane von Furstenberg dress, suede jeans by Cavalli, a pair of Jimmy Choo black boots and simple black sandals, a pair of Alaia suede flat thigh-length boots that she had always dreamed of possessing to wear with tight jeans or sweater dresses, a pair of Gina stilettos, a studded black belt with a huge clasp, some skin-tight black Joseph trousers, a silk shirt to replace her lost one and a few evening tops. Dominic was holding a leather miniskirt and a pair of heavily jewelled jeans.

'This will be excellent for your rock-chick look.' He

put them with the rest of the clothes. 'Don't bother trying them on. They'll fit and we need to get a move on. Does this stuff all fit?' Katrina nodded. 'Great, we'll take this,' he told a sales assistant.

'Oh, wait, I haven't chosen what to take yet. I only want a couple of things.' Katrina went to stop the assistant. She could hardly afford all that!

'If it fits we'll take it. You can never have too many clothes, so there is no point not getting everything. You'll need it all and I'm paying.' The sales assistant packed quickly without taking her eyes off Dominic. The total was £5,290, and Dominic, despite Katrina's protests, put it on his black Amex without batting an eyelid. She felt light-headed with disbelief that she had five thousand pounds' worth of clothing to take home. Dominic handed her two of the five bags.

'Right, what we need now is a decent bag and some underwear. I like La Perla best. What do you think?' Without waiting for an answer, Dominic strode in the direction of the signs for lingerie.

Once there he flicked through a couple of rails before picking up a black lace bra that tied at the front with matching knickers, a dark purple push-up bra and short knickers and a leopard-print corset-style top with knickers that tied at the side with a silk ribbon. He paid for them at the counter without asking Katrina if she liked them and took the sales assistant's advice, throwing in the smallest emerald-green bra and knickers set that Katrina had ever seen, again without consulting her.

'You'll look fantastic in all of that. I'm looking forward to a private fashion show later.' On the way out he stopped in the bag section and gestured that she look. Remembering the Dior bag from Monaco, Katrina didn't think she needed another bag and fingered the leathers and suedes unenthusiastically.

'You need a bag for the day – the one you're using isn't even designer – and another evening bag. The places we'll be going, everyone has designer bags.' He picked up a heavily beaded Chloé bag that Katrina thought was too fussy and girlie. 'That will do nicely.' She found herself eyeing a Mulberry bag that she had been coveting in magazines. It was less obvious than the Chloé bag and more her style. She picked it up in brown leather. 'Do you like that? I don't think it's right, much too street, although I guess that's why you like it.' Dominic eyed the Mulberry bag with disdain.

Katrina really liked the bag but put it down reluctantly and followed Dominic to pay for the Chloé one, watching it being packed away in tissue paper and wondering how paying eight hundred pounds for a piece of leather could be justified. Suddenly it didn't feel quite as great as it had half an hour ago. Since she had met Dominic he had bought her the outfit in Monaco and now all of this and it came to thousands of pounds. It was great, but he was going a little over the top. She didn't need an entire image makeover; she didn't think she looked that bad, and actually she liked wearing jeans and a vintage leather jacket or something that was a bit quirky. As they left Harvey Nichols, she protested about going on to Chanel.

'I really don't need anything else. You've bought more than enough. Let's go back to the house now.'

Dominic looked at her in surprise. 'You want to stop shopping?' She nodded. 'Well that's a first. I don't think I've ever had a girl say she wants to stop spending my money.' He looked in the bags. 'I guess you've got a few things here, enough for a couple of days anyway and something for this evening.'

'Where are we going?' Katrina asked.

'To a party in a hotel where some friends of mine are

staying. I got a phone call today from her saying I should come along.'

'Who is *her*?' Katrina asked nervously, having now had plenty of experience of women and Dominic in social situations.

'Muciana Zellini and her manager Victor Pink. Do you know them?'

'Not personally, but obviously I know of her.' Katrina recalled Muciana, a tall and curvy brunette with sultry dark Italian looks who had been in a Bond film and a few others in which she always played the temptress. She had round, pouting lips and flashing eyes that made men fantasise about leather and whips. Katrina hadn't heard of Victor Pink but was amused by the name.

In the car she looked at the Harvey Nichols bags. The clothes were so amazing, and they were exactly the kind of things Dominic's girlfriend would be expected to wear. At least she could try to match his perfect image, although she suspected it would be impossible to actually accomplish.

20

Back at the house James greeted them.
'Hello, looks like you two have been busy. Do you want a drink?'

Dominic shook his head. 'I think Katrina had better sort out these clothes and I'm going to shave. Are you going to the Zellini party tonight?'

James laughed. 'I haven't been invited, and seeing as I have no clue what a Zellini party is, the answer is no. I have been asked out by Isabelle, though, so I won't be all alone tonight and with any luck it'll go better than last night.' He grinned at Katrina as he went off towards the lounge. 'See you later.'

Katrina picked up the bags and followed Dominic to their room. As soon as she shut the door she knew from his look what he expected. Wanting to make an effort for him after what he had done for her, she took the bag with the underwear into the bathroom and put on the black lace set, shaking her hair loose. Dominic was lying on the bed when she came out and watched her as she came towards him, his eyes dark with lust.

The sex was quick and only interrupted by him growling in her ear: 'You want me so much, don't you? Just think how many girls would kill to swap places with you.'

Katrina felt a little uneasy about that comment. It was true, of course, but it didn't make it any less arrogant that he was saying it himself. Was she supposed to feel grateful that he was having sex with her rather than all the girls who would kill to swap places? She didn't say anything, though, because there actually were loads of girls who would swap places with her at the drop of a hat. All over the world women were fantasising about having sex with Dominic Cayley, and here she was watching him smoke a post-coital cigarette. What she didn't get was why he needed to make that point. Couldn't he just act like a normal boyfriend for a moment and tell her how great she was and how much he liked being with her?

When she came out of the shower he was shaving. She felt like she was in a Gillette advertisement as he ran the razor over his chiselled jaw. Everything Dominic did looked like a film clip or an advertisement for some exclusive lifestyle that would be obtainable if you just had the right razor or the right shirt or just happened to be in a particular Parisian bar at the right time.

Katrina picked through the bags of clothes, thinking that being looked at all the time must make you start to behave very self-consciously and that perhaps you began acting even in real life. She put on jeans with the new shirt and the Gina heels, mixing a bit of her style with a bit of Dominic's.

'You're wearing jeans again?' Dominic surveyed her critically as he emerged from the bathroom. 'You'll regret not dressing up; the women at this thing will be really glamorous. You should change.' He headed back out of the door. 'By the way, we're going to LA the day after tomorrow. I'm just getting someone to book the flights now.' With that he disappeared, without giving Katrina the chance to ask why, for how long, and most importantly if 'we' actually did mean 'we' and if she was going with him. She put on the leather skirt instead of her jeans, with the Jimmy Choo boots and a beaded vest top.

Heading downstairs, Katrina tripped over Delilah lying on a step and fell into James's arms. Having just got out of the shower, he was shocked to find a girl land on him, pulling his towel off and leaving him totally naked. Dominic appeared to find Katrina, in a tiny skirt, wrapped around a naked James.

'Excuse me! Have I walked in at a bad moment?' he asked sarcastically.

Katrina quickly straightened up, but not before getting an eyeful of James's nude form as he bent to retrieve the towel. It was most definitely aesthetically pleasing to the eye.

'I'm so sorry,' she gasped, blushing magenta.

Dominic surveyed the scene. 'Is my girlfriend molesting you, James?' he asked before breaking into raucous laughter. The look of total mortification on Katrina's face said it all.

'Don't worry about it. I'm the one who's sorry. I should have put some clothes on.' James wrapped the towel around his waist again, pulling it extra tight, and continued his way up the stairs, scooping up the offending cat as he went. Dominic, still amused by Katrina's embarrassment, looked her up and down appreciatively.

'That's much better. You look more like the kind of girl I would date.' He glanced at his watch. 'We have to go in a minute. Before I forget to tell you, Miranda has booked us flights and a hotel. We're not staying at my house, as the interior designers are in and I can't stand mess; it stresses me out.' He bit his lip and narrowed his eyes. 'You'll need to take all the clothes we bought today, plus we need to get you a dress, but I'll get my stylist to sort that out. It's just for a couple of days.'

Katrina felt he was being a bit presumptuous, having not even asked her if she wanted to go to LA. However, what he said next stopped her from protesting.

'We have my premiere to go to, so it's important you have the right look for such a public event. By the way, I bought you something today when you were looking at clothes.' He handed her a bag with a large box inside. She opened the box and found a Cartier Tank watch.

'Wow, is this really for me?' she asked incredulously, her eyes wide in astonishment.

'Obviously,' he said irritably. 'You don't have any decent accessories and a good watch is important. It should be the right size; I got the sales girl to put it on and adapt it to a small wrist.'

Katrina put it on, her heart soaring. The dream she had of attending a premiere with him looked like it was about to come true. Impetuously she flung her arms around him.

'Thank you so much. I love it!'

Dominic disentangled himself.

'I'm pleased you like it. The Cartier Tank is a classic; it looks both elegant and functional on women. I always buy girlfriends them over any other watch,' he said, not noticing Katrina's face drop. 'I'll just put a shirt on and then we'll go.'

As he disappeared up the stairs, Katrina looked at the watch with disappointment. It seemed that Dominic had done everything before; nothing that had happened that day was new to him. He took girls shopping, bought them expensive jewellery, travelled the world, spent time in the best hotels and on fabulous yachts and attended premieres in the same way most people went to the cinema. He had done it all with some girl at some point, and any subject she brought up in conversation he knew more about or didn't care about. He had given her an expensive watch and almost ten thousand pounds' worth of clothes since they'd met, but it was meaningless, because it was something he did all the time. He made her feel like another accessory for his image, and she suddenly feared being thrown aside should she no longer fit in.

Dominic re-emerged from the bedroom wearing jeans with a white Dolce & Gabbana shirt that was simple yet highly effective. As they left, he turned to look her over.

'Good job you're getting your teeth and hair done before we go tomorrow.'

Katrina self-consciously pressed her lips together and pushed her hair away from her face.

21

Outside the bar, people were standing around with cameras trying to peer through the door and push past the security. Dominic's arrival sent them all crazy as they screamed his name and surged forward to touch him. The security guards stepped in and pushed them back. The bar was one of those where lots of people stood in small groups not really talking, just looking around and occasionally swapping bitchy comments. A particularly large group of glamorous-looking people stood by the bar, and Dominic strode purposefully towards them. Katrina recognised Muciana Zellini, who looked a lot smaller in real life, as most famous people seemed to. She was wearing a leather dress with a split up to the thigh and lots of red lipstick. The man standing next to her, presumably Victor Pink, was about half her height, bald, and wearing leather trousers and a white ruffled shirt that was incredibly unflattering. Dominic kissed Muciana on both cheeks before shaking Victor's hand and introducing Katrina.

'Oh, aren't you a lovely thing? Where did you find this one, Dominic?' Muciana offered a cheek for Katrina to kiss whilst winking at Dominic.

'Paris,' Dominic replied, accepting a glass of champagne and passing one to Katrina. 'I'm off to LA for the premiere. You going?'

Muciana looked at Victor, who shrugged and turned to refill his glass.

'Perhaps,' was her answer, causing Dominic to frown. Muciana's attention went back to Katrina. 'I must say, I am surprised that Dominic has gone for someone more discreet than his usual type of girlfriend. Perhaps he is finally settling down. We dated when we were both fresh on the acting scene and he used to drive me mad looking at every pretty girl that walked past. It can't be easy going out with such a man.' She leant over conspiratorially. 'The only way to hold on to him is to keep him excited and be prepared to try new things, you know. I do anything for Victor and so he never has to look elsewhere.' She drained her glass and put her arm around Katrina's waist. 'Perhaps you and Dominic would like to come up to our room later for a nightcap?'

Katrina nodded, surprised at Muciana's friendliness, but she assumed that it was down to the fact that unlike Loretta, Muciana had no reason to feel insecure or threatened by a younger woman as she was so successful and beautiful herself. She couldn't, however, imagine Muciana having to work hard to keep Victor happy, as he was quite hideous compared to her, and she was famous. Surely it was Victor who needed to keep Muciana happy? Katrina sipped her drink and watched Dominic talk to Victor, who was smoking a huge cigar and looked even more repulsive as trails of thick smoke came out of his nostrils. Dominic looked positively god-like compared to him as he lit a cigarette and managed to make the smoke curl beautifully out of his mouth, leaving every woman in the place wishing she were the lucky cigarette. Katrina noticed Muciana point her out to another woman, who stared at her then whispered something to the man at her side. After an hour of standing alone clutching a glass of champagne, Dominic appeared by her side.

'You okay, sweetie? Victor and Muciana are going up to their room now and they've invited us for a couple of drinks. Do you mind?' As usual, he told rather than asked, and was already making his way towards the door behind Victor. As they neared the lifts, Muciana put her arm through Katrina's.

'Everyone in there thought you were very beautiful. Did you know that in America all the magazines are talking about you, saying Dominic has a stunning new girlfriend?'

Katrina shook her head in surprise. The lift doors shut.

'Dominic is America's baby at the moment, they love him! Over there he can barely walk down the street without being mobbed by fans; they see him as their icon so they will naturally want to know all about you. Don't worry, you will please them, a lovely English rose.'

She ran her hand down Katrina's face, pushing her hair back in an overly familiar way. Katrina noticed Victor watching, his eyes sluggish with too much alcohol and coke. Dominic was leaning against the side of the lift, his eyes running over Muciana, a slight smirk lifting the corners of his mouth. Katrina felt uneasy. It was a feeling she was rapidly getting used to.

In the room, Victor filled four heavy crystal glasses with vodka and a splash of tonic before downing his literally in one gulp. They sat on a cream suede sofa with Muciana next to Katrina, who was sipping her drink gingerly out of politeness.

'So, how have you managed what no other woman has managed so far and kept Dominic for more than a night?' Victor addressed Katrina for the first time after the conversation about films and scripts had finished.

'Er, I'm not sure,' she answered nervously, feeling Dominic's mocking eyes upon her.

'Come on, there must be a secret to it. You must be utterly fabulous in the sack and get up to all sorts of kinky things.'

Katrina was stunned by this comment from a man she had hardly exchanged two words with since meeting, and also not entirely sure what he was getting at. Dominic spoke before she had a chance to think of a reply.

'It's still very new at the moment, Victor. I'm sure Katrina will keep me happy and experiment when need be.'

'Really?' Victor pursued the point. 'So if, for example, Dominic wanted to tie you up, you'd let him?' Katrina felt an intense hatred for this repulsive balding man who was lighting up his sixth cigar of the evening. She nodded. 'And how about if he asked you to dress up a certain way for him, say in bondage gear, PVC?' She nodded again. 'Okay, how about if he asked you for some girl-on-girl action? Say for example he asked you to kiss a woman?'

While Katrina wasn't sure how to answer this, the look on Dominic's face said it all. His eyes were wide with interest.

'Well, I guess I would kiss a woman if he asked.'

'Go on then,' said Dominic, giving her a challenging look.

'What do you mean? How?' she asked, confused.

'They mean kiss me.' Muciana had moved even closer to Katrina and now leant forward and pressed her lips against hers. Two things were in Katrina's mind as Muciana kissed her. One, she couldn't believe she was kissing another woman, and secondly, she couldn't believe she was kissing Muciana Zellini. Could her life continue to get any stranger? She felt Muciana run her hand over her leg, moaning softly, and when Katrina pulled away after what seemed like ages despite it only being a few seconds, she saw Victor with his hand down his trousers. Dominic was leaning back in the chair, watching intensely.

'That was lovely,' Muciana purred, leaning forward to be kissed again. Katrina moved away, waiting for Dominic to change the subject or tell them they were leaving. He remained silent. Victor removed his hand from his crotch and stood up.

'I think it's time to take this into the bedroom, don't you?' He took Muciana's hand and led her towards the next room, undoing his ruffled shirt at the same time as unzipping her dress. As they got to the door, Muciana's dress fell to the ground, revealing a scarlet push-up bra and matching knickers encasing the famous voluptuous, sexy body. Katrina tried to catch Dominic's eye, but Muciana, who was standing in the doorway smiling at him, transfixed him. Victor, now wearing only his leather trousers, and possibly the most frightening thing Katrina had ever seen, undid her bra and buried his face in her breasts as she continued gazing at Dominic. Katrina wanted to get up and leave right then and there. However, the sheer horror of it kept her glued to the sofa.

'Join us,' Muciana murmured huskily to Dominic. 'It's been such a long time. We used to have such fun and I like your pretty girlfriend very much.' She laughed as Victor pulled her knickers off and she followed him into the bedroom. Katrina heard Victor moaning, his back to them, as Muciana dropped to her knees in front of him. Dominic got up and came over to Katrina, holding out his hand. Katrina took it and he pulled her up off the sofa. For one terrifying second she thought he was going to lead her into the bedroom; instead he led her to the door.

Once outside the hotel, he burst into laughter and wrapped his arms around her waist, burying his face in her neck.

'The look on your face when Victor took off his shirt was priceless! Sorry, baby, but truly that was funny. Those two are notorious for their foursomes with other couples.' He nibbled her neck gently. 'Victor really gets off on it and I think she'll do anything to please him. You looked absolutely terrified when you saw Victor with his top off. It would have been all right for me, Muciana has got a hot body. If it had just been you and Muciana then I would have stayed. Feel this.' He put her hand on his crotch. 'I got rock hard watching her kiss you.'

Katrina breathed a sigh of relief that they were out of there and alone again. She was meeting some strange people being with Dominic.

On the way home Dominic kissed her all over, and ran his fingers over her face, gazing intensely into her eyes until she had to look away. He continued chuckling to himself. The Mercedes was in the driveway of the house, and on opening the door they found James cleaning up cat sick with Aerosmith on at a deafening volume. He grinned up at them congenially and used the remote to turn it down.

'Hi, you're back early. Any good?'

'Shouldn't we be asking you the same question? I thought you were out for the night? Yuck, I don't know why you insist on keeping that creature.' Delilah peered around the front door, then, spotting that her sick had been discovered, retreated guiltily back out.

'So did I.' James made a resigned expression. 'Half an hour into dinner my daughter rang, having got stranded by a cancelled train, and I had to pick her up. Isabelle didn't seem too enthusiastic about coming with me, so that was the end of that, really. I got a takeaway; the food in the restaurant she chose was bloody nouvelle cuisine: just a bean and half a potato!' They went into the barely used, immaculate kitchen, where James unpacked

Chinese, opening cartons of spring rolls, crispy duck and prawns.

'Too greasy. I'm watching my abs.' Dominic turned up his nose at the sight of the takeaway. He was quite a boring eater, thought Katrina, no cakes, chocolate or takeaway in case it affected his body. She bravely reached for a spring roll, despite a disapproving look from Dominic. James, in contrast, was always looking for food and was now happily shovelling Chinese into his mouth. She understood how some men must feel when they went out with girls on permanent diets who never ate. It was really boring. Dominic pushed the box away from Katrina, stopping her from taking another spring roll.

'You can't eat this kind of thing if you're going to look fabulous in a very expensive dress this weekend,' he told her. 'You look like the type of girl that could put weight on easily around the waist, so you should avoid eating too much. Try a no-carb diet, you'll be surprised at how much weight you'll lose.'

Katrina's mouth dropped open. She had never had complaints about her weight before; in fact, just the opposite. Most men thought she was too thin and encouraged her to eat more. She was a size eight to ten and a model. People described her physique as rangy. She shifted self-consciously and tried to stretch her top over her stomach, which was literally non-existent.

'I don't think Katrina needs to worry about her weight. She looks terrific and she's absolutely tiny. She should eat whatever she wants and enjoy it,' James said firmly.

'She knows I think she's gorgeous or she wouldn't be here, but if she wants a successful modelling career then she has to be more careful.' Dominic turned back to Katrina. 'I think with a bit of weight loss, teeth whitened, hair cut, you'll look fantastic. All the top girls have a little help to ensure perfection; boob jobs are totally normal and you'd look great with them!' He leant over and kissed her. 'Everyone will think you're fabulous anyway because you're with me. I'll have you looking like a supermodel in no time.'

Katrina couldn't help choking on her water. His arrogance was astounding and she could tell from James's face that he thought so too. Dominic just expected everyone to fall at his feet and do what he said. For the first time she looked at him and thought that perhaps he wasn't quite as handsome as she had thought. He looked unreal, like an over-Photoshopped photograph stuck on top of a body, and he expected his girlfriends to be just as perfect. She had never thought there was anything wrong with her weight or her teeth until he had mentioned it. As for a boob job, well of course she would like to be a cup size larger, but his comment now made her feel like they really were too small. Was she supposed to have surgery to reach his levels of perfection?

James gave her a sympathetic look, and when Dominic rose to get a drink he leant over to whisper to her.

'He's just talking rubbish, ignore him. He's been indoctrinated into Hollywood, where nothing is real. You're beautiful and you don't need any help. Eat what you want; all those women he's talking about look like walking skeletons.'

Katrina gave him an appreciative look, but it didn't matter what James thought. It was Dominic that mattered and it would be exhausting trying to match up to his expectations. He wanted her to be like Eva Cole and Cheryl Hutton, drop-dead gorgeous, designer-clad and perfect, whereas Katrina Muirhead was scruffy, low-maintenance, imperfect.

'I think I'll go to bed,' she said quietly, making her way out.

Almost immediately James turned to Dominic. 'That was a bit thoughtless. Are you trying to make her feel terrible? Boob jobs? Teeth whitening? She'll be a nervous wreck by the time you've finished.'

Dominic looked at James like he was mad. 'I'm only helping her. She's with me, so what more of a compliment does she want? She must feel great at the moment.'

'Dominic, I know your conquests have always been a source of amusement for you. Often they are so dim that they'd do anything you say. Katrina's not like that. She's a nice girl and she's intelligent. Suggesting boob jobs and diets is crazy.'

Dominic looked at him for a moment without speaking. Then he got up. 'What are you getting at? It has absolutely nothing to do with you what I say to Katrina, and you've never felt the need before to pick me up on anything I have said to other girls. Stick to advising me on business and keep away from advising me on girlfriends.' He frowned at James, before turning and leaving the kitchen.

Dominic had gone when Katrina woke up in the morning. Her watch said ten and she leapt guiltily out of bed. There was a scrawled note next to the mirror. It read: 'Gone to the gym, back in a couple of hours.'

She got ready to go for her hair and teeth appointments, then packed some clothes for LA. She folded the clothes as carefully as she could into her old rucksack before leaving the house and hailing a black cab. The teeth whitening was not an experience she wanted to repeat, and she was keen to escape from the dentist, who after completing the procedure began to tell her that he could straighten all her teeth too. Katrina was shocked when she bared her teeth in the hairdresser's mirror to get a proper look, and nearly blinded herself.

'Christ, they look really fake! They make me look weird,' she said to the hairdresser, Larry.

'I think they look good. It's just that you're not used to them. My friend had his done and it took a few days for him to get used to it. Now he loves them. The good thing about you is your teeth aren't totally straight and perfect so they don't look too fake. What do you want me to do with your hair?'

'I'm not sure. Something a bit different but not too much off.'

Larry set to work. Checking her phone, Katrina was disappointed to see that Dominic hadn't called or texted to see where she was.

'So, missy, I guess you'll be spending a fair amount of time flouncing around film premieres and celebrity hangouts now that you've snared yourself a Hollywood boyfriend. Dominic Cayley is the hottest catch! Now I'm cutting your hair for free, so you're going to tell me everything from how you met to what he's like in the sack. Don't be coy. Spill it!' Larry chopped off what looked to be too much hair.

'I met him in Paris and now I'm staying with him in London,' Katrina told him, looking worriedly at the hair gathering around her feet.

'No way you're not? Staying with him, like living with him? That is incredible! He's not just famous, he's like premiere-league famous. I mean, that is future Brad Pitt famous! I am seriously impressed. It's so exciting. Tell me more!'

Katrina told him as he worked on her hair. When it was finished she looked at herself in the mirror. It was still past her shoulder blades but Larry had chopped at the long fringe so it melted into the rest of her hair, to which he had added layers. The result was very tousled and natural, exactly how she liked it: low-maintenance yet with more style than before. And with her white teeth, a new outfit of Cavalli jeans and Jimmy Choo boots with the Chloé bag over her shoulder, she looked frighteningly different. Like those rich girls she often saw stalking down Sloane Street rather than her usual broken-in jeans, cowboy boots and old second-hand cashmere jumper. She looked much more suitable for Dominic's arm, that was for sure. Her old friends wouldn't recognise her, and as for all the bitchy girls at school, well they would be green with envy if they saw her. Even now she could recall how upset she used to be when they told her she was ugly and lanky. She had cried on a regular basis into her pillow at night and her mum would tell her it didn't matter because she was just going through an awkward stage and would be beautiful. She still wasn't convinced about the beautiful part, but if Dominic had chosen her then nobody would question his taste and call her ugly again.

'Fantastic! I'm a genius!' Larry praised his own work. 'Right, let's get a picture of you before you become too famous and disappear to live in Hollywood with all the stars!' She posed for him, then said her goodbyes and headed back to the house.

There were three cars parked outside James's house: a Porsche 911, a Bentley GT and James's SL. She knocked on the door and was surprised when a tall, thin blonde girl answered.

'Can I help you?' The blonde spoke with difficulty, having obviously had too much Botox recently.

'Yes, umm, I'm, er, living here with James and Dominic,' Katrina replied.

'Ha ha, that's what they all say. In your dreams!' The blonde slammed the door shut, leaving Katrina on the doorstep with her mouth open. She heard screams of laughter from inside the house. She rang the doorbell again. There was no answer, so she sat on the step, wondering what to do. After about ten minutes she was questioning whether to phone Dominic when James appeared holding Delilah in a cage.

'Hey, what are you doing sitting there?' He placed the cage down and fished his keys out of his pocket. 'I thought it was about time I took Delilah to the vet for jabs and deflea-ing.' Katrina peered into the cage at the disgruntled cat.

'A blonde girl answered the door when I knocked and

then shut it again so I was waiting for Dominic.' She stood up.

'Oh, that will be Annabelle. Was she rude and haughty?' Katrina nodded. 'Yep, it's her. Dominic bumped into her at the gym; old friends apparently. I met her once in St Tropez, bloody rude I thought. Come in.' As the front door opened, more laughter and the sound of glasses clinking could be heard. James knelt down to release Delilah, who, offended by the noise, ran upstairs. 'Wise idea, cat, I might do the same, and you should too,' he told Katrina.

'I can't. I should at least say hello. But don't make me go in there alone.' Katrina pulled James towards the door while he made horrified expressions at her. As they went into the lounge, Katrina saw five women, a man with wild blond hair and Dominic all drinking champagne. There was a pile of cocaine on the coffee table, and one of the women was snorting it through a fifty-pound note. Dominic was sitting next to the haughty blonde, who gave Katrina a filthy look.

'Hello, sweetie, come and sit with me.' Dominic didn't make an effort to get up, instead patting the sofa beside him. Katrina obediently sat down. 'This is Annabelle. She and I used to party in LA,' he explained. 'Her father owns a hotel there and these are her friends.' He gestured at the blank-faced people sitting around. 'Annabelle, this is Katrina. I told her all about you,' he informed Katrina, who tried to ignore Annabelle's snigger. He didn't comment on her improved appearance. 'Where have you been all day, seeing friends?' Without waiting for an answer, he turned back to Annabelle, who was busy talking about why a fur coat was an essential winter item for one's closet. Nobody paid Katrina the slightest bit of attention. James was only slightly better off, as one of the Sloaney companions was fluttering her eyelashes at him. Dominic got up and went to the table, where he shocked Katrina by picking up the rolled note and leaning over to do a thick line of coke. He caught her watching him.

'Want some?' He held the note out to her. She shook her head and he dipped his finger in the powder and came towards her. 'It's okay. I normally don't do this in case the press find out, but I've known this lot for a while and they won't tell anyone.'

James prised the Sloaney woman away from him and came over to the table. 'What are you doing, Dominic? I thought you were on a fitness crusade.' He frowned. 'I'm not sure I want everyone doing drugs in my house.'

'Chill out, it's only a bit of coke. I need it to help me relax. I've been stressed and I just want a bit of fun with some friends.' He rubbed his finger over his gums and sat on the floor in between Katrina's legs. 'Sexy boots. Did someone nice buy them for you?' His sardonic tone made Katrina uneasy. She nodded. Dominic laughed. 'I think you owe me for them. Come with me.' He got up, and taking her hand led her out of the room into the hallway, where he pushed the door shut. The women started laughing loudly, making Katrina feel paranoid and uncomfortable. He began kissing her, his tongue moving rapidly. He was groaning softly and started to undo her jeans. She half-heartedly tried to stop him.

'Shouldn't we go upstairs?' she whispered.

'I'm fine right here.' Katrina felt him pull her knickers aside, seemingly disregarding the fact that someone could walk out of the lounge and catch them. She prayed that no one, particularly James, would come out. She didn't have to worry for long, because Dominic came quickly, his breath hot on her face. He buttoned his fly, kissed her on the forehead and went back into the lounge without saying a word.

Katrina went up to the bedroom. The laughter carried up the stairs. She was angry; she felt like packing her stuff and leaving. The dismissive way he had treated her, like she was totally insignificant, had made her feel like crap. Sometimes he seemed to be a fun-to-be-around nice guy, wildly generous and coming to pick her up from photo-shoots, and then other times he was Dominic Cayley the arrogant, selfish movie star who treated her like a fan. He thought he could get away with anything because he was famous, when actually he was just a good-looking guy who happened to have a job acting. It was hardly like he was a Nobel Peace Prize winner or a president. She picked up her shoulder bag and threw a few items into it. All he really did was act and look good, yet people did whatever he wanted them to and treated him like a god. It was so frustrating; everyone wanted to be with him no matter what he did.

She stopped packing and sat down on the bed. Could she really just leave? He was taking her to a premiere as his girlfriend, and she couldn't forget Rosanna's advice not to blow it. She emptied the bag. Maybe it was the coke that had made him act so badly and he would apologise later. She would at least give him the opportunity to do so before storming off. There was absolutely no way she was going back downstairs to sit with those awful people, though. Apart from James, the people Dominic had introduced her to had been either rude or over-friendly and none had been very likeable.

After taking a shower, she lay on the bed reading. It had gone quiet downstairs, and feeling hungry, she thought it safe to creep down to the kitchen. James was already there cooking bacon and eggs.

'Hi, I've made extra as I thought you might be hungry. I was going to bring it up to you.'

She smiled gratefully at him.

'You would make someone a great boyfriend. Have you spoken to Isabelle today?'

'No. I don't think we'll be seeing each other again, and I'm not so sure about the great boyfriend thing. I certainly didn't make a great husband, that's for sure. This domesticity is purely a one-off. Ask me to make anything other than bacon and eggs and I'm screwed!' He put bread in the toaster.

'Why didn't you make a good husband?' Katrina asked curiously. 'What was being married like?'

James leant on the work surface and looked at her. 'Well, I got bored and lived no differently to how I lived when I was single. I worked very hard, travelled a lot with my friends and partied too much. I was never at home, and after seven years of putting up with it my wife finally got annoyed and wanted me to change. I'm not conventional enough. I got married because my parents expected it and because all my friends were. A lot of the things you do when you're young are because of what you think you should do rather than what you want to do.' He turned the bacon in the pan. 'The problem was, I didn't mentally change for marriage, and whilst she was very patient she wanted different things. The divorce was really hard, particularly because of the children. I felt guilty, but it would have been wrong to stay.'

'How many kids? How old are they?'

'Two. A girl who's fourteen and a boy aged nine.' He passed her a photograph that showed him holding the hands of two children and grinning widely. The boy looked like a miniature version of his father.

'You must have been very much in love to want children, though. Why did that change?'

'It wasn't like that. I was travelling a lot and she talked about having children. It hadn't been agreed, at least I hadn't really thought about it, until one day she just said she was pregnant and that was that. Nothing changed. I carried on working and having fun. She stayed at home, and when Cass my daughter started school she felt a bit abandoned, then out of the blue she was pregnant again and Alex was born. Obviously I love them, but when I look back I am not sure I ever really loved their mother. I don't mean that to sound as awful as it does. Love is a strange thing; it's easy to be fooled into thinking you're in love for lots of different reasons: lust, loneliness, thinking you should be. I guess when you really are in love you know about it.'

'I guess so,' Katrina said. 'I don't think my parents were ever in love and they had me.'

'Or maybe they were in love but it just didn't last for long. These things are very complex and the ideals we start out with don't always work out. Life has a way of taking you by surprise and you realise that it doesn't matter if it isn't perfect.' James handed her a plate of bacon and poached egg on toast. Their eyes locked and there was a long silence until the toaster clicked, making them both jump. 'Anyway, your parents both love you, so something good came out of it.'

'I'm not so sure about that. I barely ever see my father,' Katrina muttered. 'My parents divorced when I was six and he's always been too focused on his other family.'

'Hmm, well maybe he just finds it difficult to know how to be a father to you, and I am sure he had a lot of guilt about not being around.' James shrugged. 'All I know is that things are never as simple as they appear.'

'So haven't you ever been properly in love?' she asked, changing the subject.

'I don't think I have ever been madly, deeply in love

enough to change my ways and feel in danger of someone being able to hurt me. I'm sure it will happen at some point, though. Have you?'

'No, I guess not.' She suddenly became aware of the silence from the lounge. 'Where's Dominic?'

'He went out for dinner with all those awful people.' James rolled his eyes. 'They were all flying on coke. Did you not want to join them?'

Katrina shook her head, not wanting to admit that she hadn't even been invited.

'Let's eat in the lounge, it's more comfortable.' They went through, and James piled the wine glasses and empty bottles out of the way. 'So, are you looking forward to going to LA?'

'Of course. I've never been there, so it will be exciting. I'm not so sure about all the people that Dominic has been telling me about. So far, between Muciana and Annabelle, they all seem a little strange, to say the least.'

James laughed. 'They are! There are lots of strange people hanging on, all after something. I don't know how Dominic deals with it. Personally I'd become a hermit to get away from them all. Imagine, twenty-four hours a day, people desperate to see you, be with you and know everything about you. Everywhere he goes someone recognises him. It would drive me insane.'

'Me too,' Katrina agreed, scoffing the egg and bacon. She had barely eaten since Dominic had told her she needed to lose weight. 'I guess everyone acts differently around him; I mean, I wouldn't normally come to stay with a guy after knowing him for a week and then go off to LA with him.'

'Is that so? Why are you, then?' James queried with a wry smile.

'I don't know really. Dominic seemed like a once-in-a-lifetime experience. I was amazed that he was interested in me and his life seems so exciting. I'm just seeing what it feels like to be part of it for however long it lasts.'

'Well, most of Dominic's flings only usually last one night, so you're doing well. He must like you; the question is, do you really like him? Don't worry, I won't repeat a word of this conversation to him, by the way.'

'I think I do, but . . .' Katrina pictured Dominic in her mind before thinking about how very little they really had in common.

'But what?' James probed.

'But nothing. Yes, I like him.' She dismissed the thought from her head. Lots of couples had nothing in common. If you liked someone it was as simple as that, she told herself adamantly. He was so good looking, it was impossible not to like him even if he did behave so horribly at times. 'Anyway, I'm sure it is just a fling, Dominic can have his choice of girls, so I'm not delusional enough to think I can hold him.'

James remained silent for a moment before getting up and taking her plate. 'Dominic likes you because you aren't fawning over him. I think that is why he is friends with me too, despite the fact that I am rather ordinary compared to his other friends. He likes the challenge. I've seen so many girls fall to pieces around him, constantly touching him, following him, phoning him and basically acting like idiots. You're right, there are loads of stunning women for him to pick from; in fact that is exactly what he's spent the last few years doing, and they've all been beautiful in many different ways. The thing is, beauty gets boring and looks aren't everything. Sooner or later you have to go below the surface, and that's when you find out if you really like someone. Dominic isn't immune to that. The girls he normally picks are either brainless or just not very nice and they do whatever he asks them to do with no questioning as soon as they meet him. They don't hold his attention like you have.'

James went into the kitchen before returning with a huge box of chocolates and also a business card, which he gave her.

'That's got my number on if you need to call for any reason, and better than that I've got some very expensive chocolates. Let's eat the lot!' He sat down on the floor next to her and opened them, offering her first choice.

Two hours later they had almost finished the box as well as a bottle of Rioja. They had chatted about everything from politics to travelling to favourite food and Katrina couldn't remember having so much fun for a long time. At that moment her mobile rang.

'Hey. Are you still at the house?' Dominic's American accent echoed down the phone against the sound of laughter in the background. 'Listen, I'm just getting a lift home so I'll be back in five minutes. I wanted to check you were waiting for me in that nice black underwear set. Or maybe put the green set on and get ready!' The phone call ended abruptly.

'That was Dominic. I think he's a bit drunk,' Katrina explained to James. 'I'd better go upstairs and get ready for bed if we are catching an early flight.' They both stood up at the same time. 'Well, good night.'

She went to kiss him on the cheek, and the next thing she knew their lips met. James held her face in his hands, kissing her deeply and expertly, and Katrina could not help thinking that if she had thought Dominic was a good kisser, nothing compared to this. They heard the front door opening and broke apart, staring at each other dumbstruck, each as shocked as the other.

'I'm so sorry. I didn't mean to do that,' whispered James just as Dominic came through the door. Katrina jumped away.

'Hey, guys, what are you up to?' Dominic slumped on the sofa, unaware of any awkwardness. He pulled Katrina down next to him and before she could say a word placed his lips where James's had been a second earlier. 'Hmm, nice. Let's go to bed.'

Avoiding looking at James, Katrina leapt up, heading for the stairs. She felt quite mortified that she had kissed him and even more mortified that she had enjoyed it. Her whole life since meeting Dominic seemed to have gone quite mad. She took off her make-up before making a face at her reflection in the mirror. It had only been a kiss induced by too much wine and a fun evening; it wasn't as if she had any feelings for James.

Dominic came in. He stood behind her and began kissing her neck. Pressing her against the sink, he watched their reflection as he ran his tongue over her shoulder, his hands cupping her breasts.

'So, did you have a nice time with James whilst I was out?' His voice was gruff and his tone was slightly dangerous, or perhaps she was imagining it.

'It was fine, but I'd have preferred to be with you,' she replied warily.

It was obviously the right thing to say, as his mouth curled upwards at the corners. He pushed her forward over the sink and began kissing her naked back. Whilst he had his eyes shut in lust, Katrina had the chance to watch them together, marvelling at his physicality and the fact that without make-up she looked so ordinary next to him. His forearms were muscular and tanned beside hers as he pressed against her. During the sex, Dominic looked up and caught her eyes in the mirror; his expression was cold and she could not even guess at what he was thinking. Presumably it was the coke he had snorted that was responsible for that. Afterwards he turned on the shower and stepped inside. Having not been invited, Katrina did not follow him; instead she went into the bedroom, where she curled up under the duvet, her heart pounding as she waited for him. It was like living with a total stranger. One minute he was familiar and affectionate, the next cold and arrogant.

The alarm rang loudly in the morning, signalling that it was time to get up in order to catch the flight. Dominic sprang out of bed and disappeared into the bathroom whilst Katrina remained under the bedcovers feeling drained. When he came back into the room he was silent for a moment, then she felt his hand slide under the covers and over her back.

'Lovely and silky. Come on, darling, it's time to get up or we'll miss the flight.' He peeled off the covers and she looked at him, eyes bruised with tiredness. He ran his tongue over her lips thoughtfully before kissing her hard, enjoying her reaction. She pressed her body against his muscular torso. He couldn't resist having sex even if they were running late. 'I like running my hands over your body, it feels so new. There's nothing more annoying than girls who have something to prove in the sack and try to take control.'

Dominic went over to a pile of clothes from which he selected a pair of Armani jeans and a black T-shirt. It was a more casual look than he normally sported, but it suited him and he glanced approvingly at his reflection in the mirror. Katrina selected a more glamorous outfit than usual for flying, which included tight jeans, Jimmy Choo boots and a fitted white shirt with Dominic's Hermès belt. It was LA, after all.

Downstairs in the kitchen she could hear Dominic talking to James. She walked in, avoiding James's eyes, and sat next to Dominic.

'I was just saying to James we should go to St Tropez next week,' he told her. She nodded and gave a glass of orange juice her full attention. Dominic put a hand on her thigh, making her jump about a foot in the air. She was so on edge. 'Christ, what's wrong with you today?'

'Oh, nothing, I'm fine, just a bit tired,' she stuttered, looking up to find that James was pointedly staring down at the floor.

'Well, you had better get untired, as we've got a mad couple of days coming up. There'll be lots of partying and you'll need to look lovely, darling. Dammit! I forgot to tell Miranda to book the facial and massage girl for when we get to the hotel.'

'Oh, don't worry. I don't need a facial or anything special,' Katrina said, nibbling the edge of a piece of cold toast.

'Not for you, for me! I need a facial to get rid of this London pallor and a full body massage to deal with the stress of having people screaming and vying for my attention for the next forty-eight hours.' Dominic gave her a mocking look, making her feel like an idiot for imagining he would book them for her. A snort of laughter escaped from James, causing Dominic to look up in surprise.

'What's so funny?'

'Nothing. I was just picturing you with cold cream all over your face and having your nails manicured when you are playing some tough-guy cop in this movie. It has a certain irony to it,' replied James, pulling on his jacket and picking up his car keys from the table.

Dominic frowned. 'Actually I'm not a cop, I'm a hero who saves America from a terrorist bomb. Aside from that, you clearly have no idea how much work it takes to prepare for a premiere. I have to look my best or else all the fans who go out of their way to be there will be disappointed. As I said, it's very stressful.' He realised that he was ranting a bit and quickly smiled to soften his expression. 'Anyway, just because *you're* past it doesn't mean we all have to give up on looking after ourselves.' He threw his head back in laughter to show that he was joking. However, his underlying tone had an angry edge to it; he was obviously annoyed that James had made him seem a little foolish.

James merely raised an eyebrow in amusement.

'I am sure that is all true, and indeed you look very good in everything you do. I am off now, so have a good trip, and Katrina, enjoy LA.' His eyes met hers very briefly and then he was gone, the front door closing a few seconds later.

Dominic sat huffily eyeing his reflection in the mirror above the table before his phone rang and he slid off to the lounge to talk. Katrina sat very still, feeling quite odd about the look James had given her as he had left. It had seemed almost disappointed, and he had not given her his usual goodbye kiss on the cheek. In fact it had appeared like he couldn't wait to get away from her. There was no doubt he would feel as weird about the kiss as she did, and she felt terrible that she hadn't had a chance to clear the air.

Arriving at the airport was like one of those daydreams Katrina had when she was in a horrendously long queue to check in. For a moment she'd shut her eyes and imagine that she was a star who was rushed past all the normal people straight into a room where a breakfast of champagne and strawberries awaited her. Someone else would sort out her luggage and all the other boring crap you had to do in order to catch a plane. This morning, as soon as the stretch Mercedes pulled up, two men appeared to take their bags, followed by a smartly dressed lady with long red talons holding a clipboard and asking what they would like to eat and drink on the flight. Katrina and Dominic were rushed through the back doors to avoid all the crowds and straight into a room where there *were* strawberries and champagne, as well as delicious Belgian chocolates and, best of all, the possibility of a fry-up! Dominic declined the offerings, and when Katrina made a move to accept a chocolate, he brushed her arm away and gave her a disapproving look.

They boarded the flight after everyone else so as not to draw any attention to Dominic's presence and were seated in chairs that Katrina estimated were probably three times the size of ordinary ones in economy class.

'I loathe flying,' Dominic was complaining. 'They call this first class but it is still a shambles. The only way to do it is to have your own plane. After my next film I'm going to buy one and put a stop to flying in these conditions.'

Katrina, having never flown first class before, couldn't figure out what 'conditions' he was talking about. She was revelling in the extravagance of it all and was particularly excited when the stewardess gave her a bag full of goodies including designer anti-wrinkle creams and a lip gloss that promised it would inflate her pout. After exploring the bag, she looked around the cabin at all the businessmen and wealthy-looking people in first class. She turned back to Dominic, who had his eyes shut and his head tilted back, with the sunlight streaming through the shutter falling on his face. It amazed her that, despite seeing his face every day, he became even more perfect the longer she examined him. The problem was that she could look in a mirror and go away thinking that she looked good and had a nice face, but as soon as she looked at him, her face seemed quite ordinary in comparison, her nose not as perfect, her cheekbones not quite as high and her skin not as clear and flawless. He opened his eyes and yawned like a young lion waking, showing all his gleaming teeth and ruffling his mane of hair. Then he turned towards her and kissed her on the lips before pulling her hair out of the ponytail she had carefully tied it in.

'Looks nicer undone,' he commented and tossed the hair band on the floor before shutting his eyes again. Katrina sighed and took a book out of her bag, not wanting to bother him by asking how the television on the back of the chair worked. Dominic didn't like being disturbed from his own little world and he had turned his shoulder away. Katrina felt a little lonely without anyone to talk to as a way of passing the time, and it struck her that they hadn't actually had a proper conversation about anything other than parties, clothes or their relationship. However, there would be plenty of time for that over late mornings and long lunches in LA.

24

As they landed at LAX, Katrina, conscious that there might be reporters awaiting Dominic's arrival, repaired her face and put on extra make-up in case there were photographers and to compete with all the glamorous women who she had been told wandered around LA's streets. On exiting the airport her suspicions were proved right, as cameras flashed everywhere, momentarily nearly blinding her. Dominic stopped to sign autographs and pose for the cameras while answering the reporters' questions about where he had been. Then came the question that Katrina had been waiting for.

'Who's the girl, Dominic?' a small, plump reporter bellowed.

Dominic paused for a moment before stepping back to put an arm around Katrina and kissing her on the forehead.

'This is my girlfriend, Katrina . . .' He stopped, unable to recall her surname, but covered it quickly. 'She is a very successful English model and as you can see, absolutely gorgeous.' The cameras flashed manically for a moment and Katrina heard her name being called out by reporters wanting her to turn their way. It was quite unbelievable! Before she knew it, she had been bustled into a car with dark windows and they were driving away from the airport. Dominic was on the phone again, talking in a low voice.

'Miranda, I need the stylist over in the next hour. I've just spoken to the reporters at the airport and stated that I have a girlfriend, so it's important that she looks the part tonight. Plus I need a suit. I'm thinking Valentino, I love the cut of his latest collection. And tell the stylist to bring those new satin shirts from Gucci. Oh, and also I want a selection of Oliver Peoples glasses . . . no, not sunglasses, glasses, you know, so that I look a bit more serious. I need to look intellectual so I get cast for some meatier roles.' He stopped to listen to the response before stating, 'Well, I don't think they know what they're talking about! The roles I have played have all been demanding and I think I've proved I can act as well as any of the big stars. Just look at my fan base. It's as big as theirs, if not bigger, and I've got more publicity than any other actor this year. It's a load of crap! Just make sure the stylist is on time.' He cut the call, his face contorted with anger. 'I can't believe that some nobody journalist has written a column about me saying that I've yet to prove myself as an actor; that I have only taken on easy roles with no depth, and on top of that insinuating that I'm nothing more than a pretty face compared with the other top actors at the moment! It's fucking outrageous that some ignorant ass can be allowed to publish such a load of crap!' He gritted his teeth in rage.

'That must be really annoying, having people making judgements all the time. I'm sure nobody believes that. You're a great actor, and like you said, you have a huge fan base to prove it.' Katrina tried to comfort him, but he ignored her and stared out of the window, his brow furrowed with frustration. After a few minutes he spoke again.

'I don't think you understand how important my

image is to my career. Comments like that can make directors think I'm not good enough for the tough roles. They'll all start seeing me as some insubstantial pretty-boy actor and it will take years to change that perception.' He looked at her coldly. 'Models are just blank canvases used to portray whatever image is given to them to sell; nobody cares about the person behind the picture. Being an actor is far more complex, because people are interested in what we do and what is said about us. I've got to be popular and have a great fan base if I'm going to sell movies.'

Katrina remained silent. There wasn't a huge amount she could say in response without insulting him. She thought that he spent too much time considering his image, so that actually there *was* nothing beneath it. He hadn't told her anything about his life in LA, what he liked doing, what he cared about, and they weren't even staying at his house, so she wouldn't get to see the books on his shelves or the photographs on his walls. It would make him more interesting and less one-dimensional if he revealed a weakness or something surprising to make him more likeable as a person, rather than just this image he cultivated.

They pulled up outside a hotel and two men opened the car door to usher them inside. They were led up to their room by a petite brunette who couldn't take her eyes off Dominic. He seemed to be pleased by her admiration, giving her a fifty-dollar tip just for showing them the room. She left smiling widely. A moment later there was a knock at the door and an exceptionally thin woman with waist-length black hair and wild black eye make-up appeared with a small entourage carrying suitcases and bags full of clothes.

'*Ciao*, Dominic,' purred the women in a thick Italian accent. 'I 'ave brought all the most beautiful clothes I could find for you and your girl.' She kissed him on both cheeks before holding out a cool hand for Katrina to shake.

''Allo, I am Maria Carla, the stylist.' She looked Katrina up and down critically. 'I brought the model sizes with me so they should all fit, although you are not as skinny as I thought you would be. Come.' She gestured that Katrina follow her into the bedroom, where she began pulling out dresses and throwing them on to the bed. Katrina stood awkwardly watching her.

'What are you waiting for? Strip, we need to find a dress that looks good!' Maria Carla commanded, noticing her. Obediently Katrina took off her clothes so she was just in her underwear.

An hour and twelve dresses later they had found the outfit that she would be wearing to the premiere: a full-length, crystal-encrusted black Versace dress, totally backless and with a slit to the top of the thigh. Katrina couldn't believe that she was to wear such a dress. Back in jeans, she was taken to a bathroom that was the size of her entire flat in Oval to be manicured and moisturised by a Japanese girl who barely spoke a word of English. Dominic disappeared into the bedroom with Maria Carla to try on suits. As the Japanese girl began to work on her eyebrows, Katrina heard the unmistakable voice of Alex booming through the hotel suite.

'Hi, buddy, how you doing? That is one sharp suit, who's it by?' Katrina didn't hear Dominic's response, but Alex responded by laughing loudly. 'Yes, I got bored so I moved on. I am absolutely shocked, stunned, amazed that you have got yourself into a . . . what are they called? A partnership? A relationship that has lasted more than one night! What's up with that?' Again Katrina couldn't hear Dominic's response, but whatever it was led to Alex laughing even louder.

'I'll order some champagne and room service, then perhaps your stylist can pass me on some of your leftovers for tonight.' Katrina's heart sank at the realisation that Alex was coming with them to the premiere. Dominic hadn't mentioned anything about it.

The daylight was beginning to fade outside the window as Katrina's face was massaged and moisturised, her pores squeezed and tightened, her hair scrubbed and polished. Alex and Dominic had gone quiet, which Katrina guessed was owing to their preparations too. The Japanese lady left, bowing and smiling, making Katrina feel bad as she didn't have any dollars to tip her with. Then, as she began to dig out her make-up bag, a man bowled into the room.

'Honey, what are you doing? That make-up is trash; drop it right now!' He had a very camp voice and was wearing boy-scout-style shorts with a tight black T-shirt emphasising his expanding gut. He minced towards Katrina. 'Lovely skin, honey, nice and pale, not like all these orange bitches that you see round here.' He dropped a huge vanity case on the floor and grinned. 'Let's get started, then.' He opened the case and began to pull out a myriad of bottles and brushes.

'Started?' Katrina asked, baffled. 'On what? Who exactly are you?'

'Oh, sorry, sweetie, I should have introduced myself. My name is Chris and I am your make-up artist, here to make you look very beautiful and lovely. Take a seat.'

'I have a make-up artist?' Katrina asked incredulously. She could not believe that she was considered important enough to merit such a thing.

'Sure you do, honey, everyone has a make-up artist in LA. You didn't think you were just going to plaster a bit of foundation on and then off you go, did you? Especially not that cheap crap. Come on, let's make you look beautiful. Oh, dear God, I have quite a job to do!' He grasped Katrina's chin and began rubbing foundation into her skin, whilst she shut her eyes and tried to imagine what it would be like on the red carpet. She felt a pang of nerves and was grateful that someone else was doing her make-up, as her hands had begun to shake a little. She imagined tripping up and Dominic being embarrassed to be with her, or saying something stupid to someone important.

Chris began to work on her eyes, humming quietly. She appreciated him not talking and asking questions, as it was nice to sit in silence and think about the events of the past few days. She recalled the previous night, sitting with James in the lounge, and how good he made her feel. She wished he was there with them instead of Alex. Even with such a big age gap, and despite him being a successful businessman, he never made her feel uneasy and always seemed interested to hear what she had to say. It was the opposite with Dominic; would she ever be able to relax around him? How could she introduce him to her mother or explain to him the situation with her father or take him out with her friends? He would hate it!

'There you go, you look quite passable.' Chris made her jump by slamming the lid of his case shut. 'Keep hold of this lip colour and take eyeliner to touch up should you need it. I'm just going to try something with your hair. Hold still a minute.' He put some pins in his mouth and twisted her hair back and up, then after a moment's contemplation he redid it with just the top half pinned up. 'Voilà, you are all done. Have a look in the mirror and see what you think.'

Katrina stood up and peered into a mirror, gasping with surprise at her reflection. 'Wow, you are a genius!' Having had her make-up done numerous times for shoots, she was used to seeing herself look different, but it was rare that make-up was done purely to flatter rather than to achieve a specific look. Chris had made her look completely different, not like a normal girl from London, more like the kind of girl you'd expect to see hanging from the arm of a famous man. He had used shading to give the impression of razor-sharp cheekbones and wide, striking eyes, while her lips looked luscious and full. If there was anything to complain about, it could be that close up she looked a touch overdone. She imagined that that would be the case with all the women who wanted to look stunning from a distance and on camera.

Maria Carla burst into the room. 'Very nice, Christopher, you are truly a miracle-worker! Please can you go and do Dominic's hair and face now whilst I dress this one.' Katrina giggled at the thought of Dominic having make-up done. Then she remembered his defensiveness about having facials and his vanity about his hair, and thought it quite likely that he would wear make-up for a premiere.

Maria Carla produced a nude set that consisted of a push-up seamless bra and an absolutely tiny G-string. 'We do not want to see the underwear through the dress,' she said by way of explanation as Katrina took the items between thumb and finger.

She put them on and then was helped into the dress, which was beginning to feel very stiff and uncomfortable to a girl far more used to hanging round in battered jeans than haute couture. Then the jewellery was revealed: a pair of drop diamond earrings and a diamond and jet cuff. Katrina gulped as Maria Carla clipped it on her wrist.

'What if I lose it?'

'Then you will have lost a very expensive piece of jewellery, and I mean *very* expensive.' Maria Carla stepped back to admire her handiwork. 'I am very impressed. You scrub up well. I think you will cause quite a sensation in that dress. Don't forget to mention my name if anyone asks.' She began packing up.

Katrina wasn't sure what to do, whether it was okay to sit down on the bed or go into the sitting room. She felt quite self-conscious about Dominic seeing her, especially with Alex there, who was always so sardonic and smug. The conundrum was answered when Chris poked his head round the door.

'Darling, the boys are waiting for you.' Katrina had a sudden bout of nerves in her stomach that was caused not by the thought of attending a premiere in front of thousands of people, but by the thought of having to step into the room in front of Dominic and Alex and have them look her up and down to assess whether she was acceptable or not. It was one thing getting ready for a date, putting on your own make-up and all that. It was quite another being shut in a room having people massage, manicure, make you up, dress you and everything else possible to make you look beautiful. She looked like a stranger in the mirror, and having finally achieved the perfect image, she wasn't sure if she liked it.

She took the tiny bag that Maria Carla had left for her and looked inside, finding nothing more than the lip gloss and eyeliner. Where was her wallet so she could take a credit card, just in case, along with her mobile? Her heart crashed when she realised that she had left them in the Cholé bag from the day before and hadn't remembered to transfer them to the bag that she had taken that morning.

'I am a total idiot,' she told her reflection. 'There is nothing I can do but front out this night and try to have a good time.' She added some extra lip gloss, feeling pity for all the women who had to do this kind of thing regularly. As she stepped into the other room, Dominic, who was leaning on the mantelpiece drinking champagne, watched her silently. Alex got to his feet, knocking his champagne over.

'Well, hello.' He kissed her on each cheek, a bit close to the mouth for her liking. 'Don't you look beautiful? I am impressed.' He poured another glass of champagne and handed it to her. 'It looks like I picked the wrong girl in Paris. Silly me, always go for what's bright and often miss what's valuable.' He put his arm around Katrina, his fingers meeting the nakedness of her back and running down to the base of her spine. Fortunately Dominic stepped forward.

'Hands off, Alex, it's too late to change your mind. Luckily I am able to spot potential.' He kissed Katrina. 'You haven't disappointed me; you do look beautiful, really stunning. How do I look?' He stepped back showing her the well-fitting suit. Dark graphite grey, it had a satin sheen to it, and the jacket, unlike the current fashion of wide fit, was instead really tailored, narrow at the waist and with wide lapels making his shoulders look broader than they actually were. It complemented his dark skin tone so that he looked every inch the movie star. He could not be criticised for his appearance in any way, no matter how hard Katrina tried to find fault. There was the slight sneer that tilted his upper lip, but most would just say that added to his godlike stature in Hollywood. He knew he looked great and didn't wait for an answer. Instead he pulled a pair of glasses from his pocket. 'I think I look good in glasses.' He put them on. 'What do you think? Do I look like I could play a highly intelligent role in these?'

'Are they Oliver Peoples?' asked Alex, lighting a cigarette and watching his reflection in the mirror. 'They look good. We had better make a move. We need to pick up my date on the way and it's getting late. That suit is killer, man. If I was a girl I'd fancy you.'

Personally, Katrina thought that the glasses looked a bit strange. After all, why would a rich actor wear glasses to a premiere? If he really did have a sight problem it would be easy to sort out laser treatment or at worst contact lenses. It would be obvious that he was only wearing them to make a point after all the criticism about his intelligence, and that would lead to more mockery by the press. She debated whether or not to tell him that, but catching sight of him trying out serious poses in the mirror, she thought better of it. Besides, if anyone was going to make glasses look good, it was him.

25

In the car, Alex opened another bottle of champagne and filled three glasses.

'Easy, Alex, that's the third bottle you've drunk,' warned Dominic, putting his arm around Katrina, which encouraged her to move closer. 'Careful, I don't want to get creased up before we arrive.' She moved away again.

They pulled up outside a huge apartment block and a girl climbed into the car. Katrina was surprised to see that it was Zora. She kissed both men hello and nodded a vague acknowledgement to Katrina before downing a glass of champagne. Recalling her exceptional beauty when she had first seen her in Paris, Katrina was shocked to see that Zora was not looking so good. Her face was drawn and there were dark circles under her eyes. Katrina wondered what had happened to her in such a short time to make her look so knackered. It didn't take long to find the answer, as Alex produced a roll of coke and began cutting it on a magazine. He and Zora then consumed it through a fifty-dollar note. Zora couldn't seem to get enough of it, and rubbed it vigorously into her gums before catching Katrina watching her. She smiled and held out her hand.

'My name's Zora, you are . . . ?'

Katrina was confused and wondered for a moment whether Zora was mocking her. Nonetheless she took her hand. 'Katrina. We did meet in Paris recently.'

'Really, on a job? My memory is not good, I meet so many people.' She bowed her head to do another line.

'No, it was at a club with Dominic and then a restaurant in Monaco. You were with James,' Katrina said, catching Alex's eye and looking away quickly.

Zora looked up instantly. 'You know James? Is he in LA?' she asked, her eyes brightening.

'Just through Dominic. No, he's not in LA,' answered Katrina, slightly shocked at Zora's response to James's name. Alex rolled his eyes and grimaced at Dominic.

'Zora has a little obsession with our friend James,' he purred. 'In fact, I am quite sure the only reason she's seeing me is to try to get at him. It won't work, sweetheart, he won't touch you with a bargepole now that you're screwing me.' Turning to Katrina he said, 'Zora isn't such a clever girl but she makes up for it in bed.' Dominic roared with laughter.

'Fuck off, Alex!' hissed Zora, rooting in her bag for a lipstick. 'It's a pity I can't say the same for you.' Alex's face changed instantly from mirth to fury. Katrina wriggled uncomfortably. Dominic sighed loudly and lit a cigarette, opening the window to let the smoke trail out. The rest of the journey was spent in silence, with Katrina stealing glances at Zora, who was gazing into space looking very unhappy.

They pulled up alongside crowds of screaming people. Security milled around, camera lights flashed, helicopters buzzed overhead and Katrina saw the red carpet stretching out, with familiar faces doing interviews along it. She pulled herself together, realising that they were here; her first premiere as Dominic Cayley's girlfriend was about to begin.

The car doors were opened by suited men and the cheers became nearly deafening as they got out of the car.

Alex went first, followed by Zora, then Katrina and finally Dominic. As he straightened himself out and the crowd recognised him, they went into a frenzy, screaming his name. Katrina saw girls of all ages in tears, fighting to get as close to him as possible, yelling as loudly as they could to get his attention. He was waving and grinning, signing autographs without acknowledging the adoring people in front of him, almost seeming bored with it all. Alex, Zora and Katrina made their way to the stairs and waited while Dominic continued posing for the press photographers and for pictures with fans. He cringed when a middle-aged woman grabbed his hand, and pushed her off. He ignored the pads of paper shoved under his nose when the cameras weren't upon him. A reasonably pretty blonde screamed his name and he stopped to allow her to take a picture before making his way up to Alex and the girls. He approached Katrina and kissed her deeply on the lips, which made the cheers increase. Taking her hand, he led her up the stairs, then gave a final wave and disappeared through the entrance doors.

Katrina was shaking slightly, such was her amazement at the whole scene. It had lasted all of ten minutes and had been absolutely crazy. The crowds had gone mad for Dominic and he had kissed her in front of them all, showing the whole world that she was with him. He must really like her to want all the press and fans to accept her as his girlfriend. She would be in *Hello!* and *Now* magazines. Never had she imagined that her life would turn out like this: skinny, geeky Katrina Muirhead dating the best-looking man in the world, who any woman would kill just to touch! The best part about it was the fact that everybody would open up the newspapers and magazines and see her image staring back at them. She stood up extra tall in the dress, vowing to stop fidgeting and just concentrate on looking elegant on his arm.

Once inside, Dominic released her hand and disappeared to talk to a grey-haired man, taking Alex with him. Katrina found herself standing next to Zora. They silently took in the melee of people buzzing round them. Katrina wondered whether to risk getting her head bitten off by saying something to Zora, when the decision was taken out of her hands by Zora speaking first.

'Alex said that you and Dominic stayed with James in London this week. How is he?'

'Fine, he seemed to be working hard,' Katrina answered, not sure what else to say.

'Did he mention me at all?' Zora avoided looking Katrina in the eye.

'No, although I didn't speak to him that much. Maybe he said something to Dominic,' Katrina lied, not very convincingly. 'Are you dating Alex?'

'I just thought it would be nice to come to a premiere,' answered Zora. 'Alex is good looking and rich, no?' She glared at Katrina. 'Maybe he is not Dominic and I have not been as lucky as you. I date many men who are very handsome and many who have more money than Dominic.'

'Okay, that's good.' Katrina had no doubt that Zora would be able to have her pick of any guy, and she seemed to suit the flashiness of Alex. Her questions about James were slightly odd, though.

Dominic and Alex reappeared and Zora assumed her usual haughty pose, as if the conversation had not taken place. Alex put an arm around Katrina, an arrogant smirk contorting his even features. He failed to either notice or react to her cringing.

'So how are you enjoying your first premiere? Bet you're excited.' He pulled her along, leaving Dominic and Zora to follow. 'That is one sexy dress and you have a surprising body. You shouldn't hide it in jeans so much. Guys like me can't see what you've got to offer and you're missing out on a lot of fun. Take a leaf out of Lauren's book: put it out there. Although it cannot be denied that she's one crazy girl. I just couldn't deal with her mental instability.' He took two glasses of champagne from a waiter and handed one to her.

'What do you mean, mental instability?' queried Katrina, curious at what might have happened between him and Lauren in the end.

'She was crazy, clingy, annoying, telling me after a couple of days that she loved me and thought we should move in together, not to mention how much coke she got through. That, with the clothes shopping, almost bankrupted me. You should know, you lived with the girl.' He turned back to Dominic, nudging his arm. 'You thought she was nuts, didn't you, Dom?'

'Who did I think was nuts? If it was a woman, then yes, I did. I think most women are crazy,' said Dominic, surveying the people milling around and stopping to shake the hand of a man with long hair and too much jewellery.

'That Lauren girl, you know the one that Katrina lived with.' Alex spotted an Amazonian blonde wearing a skin-tight leather dress. Putting his glass down, he said, 'I've just seen someone I need to talk to, back in a minute.'

Dominic turned his attention to the girls and ran his eyes approvingly over Katrina. 'I think you should come and meet a few of my work colleagues, darling. Will you be okay for a moment, Zora?' Zora glared at him and stomped off in the direction of the toilets.

Taking Katrina's hand again, Dominic led her up to a group of fabulously glamorous people whom Katrina was sure she would recognise if she took more of an interest in celebrity gossip magazines. They didn't speak to her, although everyone did stare a great deal. They were discussing the film and the money that had been spent on it, which was an unbelievable sum. Katrina, despite being a little light-headed from the champagne, thought that it was utterly ridiculous that one stupid film that would be out for a month could have cost that amount of money, when there were people starving and wars going on. They were talking about one of the actors being paid eighteen million dollars, which caused Katrina to choke on her drink. That led her on to thinking about how much Dominic was worth, not in a fortune-hunter kind of way, more out of curiosity, as she hadn't really considered before that he must be a millionaire a few times over.

'Dominic! How are you?' boomed a voice behind them, and turning round they saw Lawrence Fishbacher emerging through the smoke of the largest cigar Katrina had ever seen. She was pleased to see a familiar face, particularly after he had been quite pleasant to her the previous week in Monaco. Lawrence slapped Dominic on the back. 'I am very happy to hear you are considering the role in my next film and that you read the script. Miranda was just telling me how keen she is for you to get it and prove your ability as a serious actor.'

'It's a good script and I'm pleased that the role you want me for is quite intense, so I guess we'll be working together again soon, depending on the deal. I still have other options to consider . . .' Lawrence was eyeing up Katrina quite obviously, so that Dominic was forced to break off and draw her forward. 'This is Katrina.'

'Hi, we've met before,' she said, wishing he wouldn't keep looking her up and down.

'At a casting? I think I would remember such a pretty face.' He held out his hand. 'It's an absolute pleasure.'

'No, at the dinner in Monaco,' she replied weakly, trying to withdraw her hand from his sweaty grasp as politely as possible.

'Are you sure? Who were you with? It's a pity I didn't

have a chance to get to know you then.' Lawrence finally let go of her hand, turning back to Dominic with a smirk. 'Oh Mr Cayley, you certainly do find them. It's a different one each week and all so lovely. I could truly envy you.' Katrina was outraged that Lawrence couldn't remember her. He had been nice when she had last met him and now she felt like an idiot. Not only did he not remember her, he was now treating her like a piece of meat to stare at and talk about as if she wasn't there. If this was the film industry, it was hardly glamorous. With all the fake, pretentious people milling around, it was as bad as, if not worse than the fashion industry.

She excused herself to go to the toilet, where she found Zora sitting on the side of the basin staring off into space. Katrina applied more lip gloss and savagely darkened the black round her eyes.

'You don't look too happy,' purred Zora, picking up the lip gloss and running it over her mouth without asking. 'Are you starting to realise what an arrogant arsehole Dominic is?' She started laughing loudly, irritating Katrina immensely.

'No, I'm fine. I've just got a headache,' Katrina snapped, taking the gloss out of Zora's hand. 'You must be having a great time sitting in the toilets while your boyfriend chats up every other woman in sight.'

Zora was silent for a while. Katrina went to leave.

'Alex is not my boyfriend. I don't care who he chats up and I don't care who he screws. My agent says it is good to go to these parties if you can get invited, and if it earns me money then I'll go.'

Although Zora spat out the words, Katrina saw a flash of vulnerability and in that instant felt almost sorry for the beautiful girl, who was looking almost with hatred at her own reflection in the mirror. It was as if she was resigned to being used by men like Alex and had given up on the idea of a normal relationship with someone who cared about more than her beauty. All she seemed to be concerned about was money, status and her appearance, and yet Katrina suspected that behind the image was just a girl in her twenties trying to survive in a pretty ruthless industry.

'Shall we get a proper drink?' Katrina offered in an attempt to be nice. 'I'm sick of champagne and it's giving me a headache.'

Zora looked up and after a moment's hesitation replied. 'Why not, there's not a lot else to do, until we have to watch what I am sure will be a terrible movie.'

Two vodkas later, Zora had thawed and was actually being reasonably friendly.

'I do not like Alex very much!' she spat. 'I only go out with him because he takes me to nice places and buys me clothes. I would not give him any of my feelings, I have seen what he is like in the past to girls like your room-mate—'

'Why? What did you hear about my room-mate?' interrupted Katrina.

'That he treated her so badly that she had to go home to London. He made her have sex with one of his friends, and when she did he told her that she was a whore and that he didn't want to see her again. He gets off on humiliating girls, but not me! I started seeing him before I found out about what he did to some of his past girlfriends. Men like that should be used as much as they use other people, and so I am just using him.'

They both looked over to where Alex was talking to a girl with short brown hair cropped in a savage fashion and a low-cut dress showing off huge breast implants. She couldn't take her eyes off Alex and kept leaning over to give him a better view. Not far from him was Dominic with his co-star Naomi Esker, who was dressed in a flesh-coloured dress that made her look nude. Katrina was pleased to see that Dominic seemed quite uninterested in her and kept looking around the room. Naomi was petite, about five foot one, with the Spanish look of dark curly hair, dark eyes and dark skin, and always came high up in the top ten sexiest women polls. Katrina suspected that men would be blind sided by her curvy body, revealing cleavage and the sultry pout that played about her affected mouth.

Dominic was actually looking for Katrina and getting very annoyed that she had disappeared for so long. Naomi was prattling on about how great his suit looked. Dominic drained his glass for what seemed like the millionth time and looked at his watch. It was nearly time for the movie to be screened. Alex came over pocketing a card.

'Got her number for lunch tomorrow.' He grinned. 'How about you with Naomi? She was looking very nude.'

'Naomi would jump at the chance to sleep with me again but I'm not interested. She was irritating me by insisting we be seen together for publicity for the film. Have you lost your date?'

'No, she's over there with yours, conspiring to kill us no doubt.' Alex pointed to where Zora and Katrina were now drinking cocktails.

Dominic frowned and went over to the girls. 'I don't suppose it is the done thing in England to actually stay with your date rather than go off drinking? This seems to happen over and over again with you. The point of tonight is that you come with me and stay with me.' He kept his voice lowered, noticing a couple of well-known producers nearby.

'I'm sorry. I just thought you needed to circulate and chat to a few people so I should make myself scarce,' replied Katrina, putting down her drink.

'Don't be so moody, Dominic, someone might overhear you and realise what a control freak you are.' Zora jumped off her bar stool and kissed Alex on the cheek. 'Alex loves it when I disappear, don't you, darling.' She took his hand and dragged him off, winking at Katrina as she went. A nerve in Dominic's jaw twitched as he clenched it but he merely offered her his hand.

'It's time to watch the movie now. Are you ready?' he asked sarcastically.

The movie was a typical Hollywood action flick in which there were goodies who won and baddies who were either savagely killed or thrown in gaol. Dominic played the hero, all muscle-bound and beautiful with a myriad of heroines to rescue. Katrina noticed a number of women in the screening room stealing glances at him when he stripped for a love scene. His body was unbelievable, and it had to be said that although the role he played was rather clichéd, his ability to look good on camera was undeniable and he lit up the screen. Katrina felt a bit uneasy during the scenes where Dominic simulated sex with Naomi Esker. They looked so beautiful together, it was almost like it was actually happening. One thing she always tried to block out of her mind was the thought of Dominic with other girls, as she knew it would open a floodgate to his seemingly huge history and her insecurity would increase. He was hardly the type of guy who had had two steady girlfriends before her, and he was also very unlikely to put up with questioning about all the beautiful women he had been with. She watched him kissing Naomi, the camera zooming in on his fingers running tenderly over her face. It was very odd knowing that he kissed her exactly the same way. It made her wonder whether he ever stopped acting; was everything just a façade with him?

26

Everyone approached Dominic to congratulate him on the film, and then he was whisked off to do some publicity interviews. A women with cropped bright red hair appeared beside Katrina.

'Katrina? I'm Miranda, Dominic's agent. Are you having a good time?' She was wearing bright red lipstick to match her hair; it was drawn heavily over her natural lipline to give the appearance of a full pout, but it actually made her look oddly like a child who had stolen her mother's make-up. Inches of mascara were flaking off her lashes and the hand held out to Katrina by way of introduction had bright red talons. She smiled falsely, revealing perfect cosmetic teeth that bore the red traces of her lipstick.

'Hi,' replied Katrina. 'Pleased to meet you.' Actually she was quite terrified of her.

'No time for chit-chat, sweetie. I need to know a bit about you. Dominic is going to be on the front pages of every newspaper and magazine in the next few weeks as this movie hits the screens, so he's got to be on top form. You won't be able to stay anonymous either, as they'll want to know who you are if he continues to be seen with you.' She made a rather disparaging face at this thought. 'I'm sure that's what you want, sweetie, so we don't need you to mess up and annoy him, do we now?'

'I suppose not.' Katrina disliked the way she was being spoken to like a small child. She even went so far as to make eye contact with Alex in the hope that he would come over and rescue her from this strange, condescending woman. He just smiled and raised his glass.

'Let's get a few things straight then, shall we? Never, ever comment to anyone, whether it be a journalist or your closest friend, on anything personal about Dominic. Nothing he tells you should be shared and nothing you do together should be spoken about unless he does so first. That means, sweetie, that what you get up to in the bedroom remains that way, no matter what. Girls like you get all excited and caught up in the fun of being in this environment. The next thing we know you've told some journalist all about it and it's headline news. I wish Dominic would just date another actress who knows how to deal with this kind of stuff, but, well, he seems to quite like you, so it's my job to make sure you don't step out of line. I protect his image and I won't have you damaging it, sweetie.' Her mobile began to trill loudly in her pocket. 'Dammit! Why do people always call at inconvenient times?' She looked at the caller ID. 'I must take this. Stay there and I'll be back in one tick.'

Katrina took that as the ideal opportunity to get away, and fled in the direction of the toilets. Alex grabbed her by the elbow as she went past.

'Where you off to in such a hurry?' He pulled her towards him.

'I was looking for Dominic. Where's Zora?' she asked him, pulling away.

'Gone home; got the driver to take her back as she wasn't feeling too great,' he answered before adding, 'If you want to go, I'm sure that will be fine with Dominic. He'll probably be here for a while doing interviews and chatting to people. I could tell him you went back to the hotel as you had a headache.'

Katrina was slightly surprised that Alex was trying to be nice for a change. 'That would be great. Do you think he'll mind?'

'Ask him yourself, he's coming over.'

Dominic had taken off his tie and undone the first couple of buttons on his shirt, making him look dishevelled and sexy. He had a cigarette hanging from the corner of his mouth and his mobile pressed against his ear. When he reached them he ended the call and dropped the cigarette into a glass of champagne belonging to a woman standing nearby. She looked excited rather than offended.

'I'm about ready to move on now,' he told them. 'There's an after party at the Pelius Bar.'

'Actually, Katrina isn't feeling too great. I suggested that she take the car and go back to the hotel. You don't mind, do you, Dom?' Alex smiled at Katrina.

'I suppose not,' said Dominic. 'I'm not planning to be too long at this party anyway. We can go in Lawrence Fishbacher's car and Katrina can take ours back to the hotel.' Turning to Katrina he leant forward to kiss her. 'I won't be long. The driver will be waiting outside, so tell him to take you back and I'll see you in a bit.' He made to leave with Alex, but not before turning back and saying with a melting grin that made her instantly forget his moodiness and arrogance, 'By the way, you look beautiful tonight, every inch of you.' He disappeared into the crowd.

Katrina found the car waiting at the bottom of the red carpet. The driver opened the door for her.

'Early night for you, miss? I just dropped the other young lady off at a bar downtown. Was it not a good evening?' he asked. Katrina was amused to hear that Zora had gone off to another bar after telling Alex she was going home. She was a girl who knew how to match Alex for manipulation and lying. Feeling ridiculously opulent in a stretch limo all to herself, Katrina looked inside a little cupboard and found a fridge filled with drinks and chocolate. She opened a bar and devoured the whole lot, having barely eaten all day. She noticed she had dropped some on the dress and it had melted into the gems. Horrified, she rubbed anxiously away at it. Two of the gems fell off, leaving a really obvious bare patch.

'Damn!' she swore and scrabbled around to find them. The dress was probably worth more than a year's earnings for her, and she couldn't risk Maria Carla refusing to take it back. She found the jewels and figured that if she got some glue she might be able to fix it. Tapping on the driver's screen, she asked if they could quickly stop at a convenience store. On arriving, she realised she had no money nor did she have her credit card. This was the kind of situation when her mother's advice never to go anywhere without a card and some cash came into force. Knocking on the driver's window again, she asked him if he would mind lending her five dollars, which she would pay back the next day. He gave her ten.

Katrina couldn't help laughing to herself as she entered the shop to find two spotty adolescents behind the counter gawping at her in the glittering dress and full make-up. Back to the land of reality, she thought as she sped down the aisle marked Household Goods. It could only be her who went to a premiere in thousands of pounds' worth of diamonds and then turned up at a 7–11 in a limousine, having borrowed the money to buy Super Glue. It was truly the best part of the evening so far in terms of amusement, she giggled, although she was sure Dominic wouldn't be so impressed by her hanging round in a store in diamonds that weren't even hers and that could be stolen at any moment, With that in mind, she went to the till to pay, handing over the note and putting the glue in her bag.

'Can I have your autograph?' asked one of the spotty youths, revealing missing front teeth.

'Why do you want my autograph?' she asked, confused. 'Who am I?'

'You're the chick that actor guy's dating, that one all the girls think is really hot. My sister's got a poster of him over her bed. She thinks he could do better than you but I reckon she's just pissed that it's not her,' he answered, holding up a magazine that featured a picture of Dominic with Katrina standing next to him. Katrina laughed out loud. How bizarre to be in an American magazine, and to be autographing it. She signed it and left the shop just in time, as a group of rough-looking men pulled up and started yelling.

Outside the hotel she thanked the driver, promising she would get the ten dollars back to him, and headed up to the room, fishing her keycard out of her bag. She opened the door and smiled to herself at the thought of having the lovely suite to herself for a couple of hours. First thing she was going to do was ring Helen, and the second thing would be to have a huge bubble bath. Then she would order room service. Perhaps she would do them all at the same time! She dropped the bag on to the floor and walked into the lounge, trying to undo the zip on her dress.

'Do you want some help with that?' a voice asked. Katrina jumped about a foot in the air and turned round to find Alex leaning on the door frame to the main bedroom with brandy in a crystal glass and his shirt undone to the waist. He looked his usual arrogant self, with his hair purposefully dishevelled to match the stubble on his face.

'What are you doing here? Is Dominic back?' She looked into the bedroom to see if he was there. It was too quiet and her worst suspicions were confirmed. 'Why are you here?' she repeated. Alex sipped the drink and came towards her with a strange smirk. 'Why aren't you with Dominic?'

'I wanted to spend some time with you, sexy. I left

Dominic to go to the party and got a taxi here. I thought you'd be pleased that one of his best friends likes you enough to want your company. If you want me to go . . .' He made no effort to leave, instead sitting on the arm of a plush suede sofa and running his hand over the fabric.

'I'm really tired and just want to go to sleep, so maybe another time, Alex,' she replied, walking towards the bedroom. The next thing she knew, Alex had leapt up to grab her by the shoulder and was kissing her roughly, forcing his tongue into her mouth. He stank of alcohol. She pushed him away violently.

'What the hell do you think you're doing? Get off me!' As she went to get away from him, he held on to the strap of the dress so that it tore down the seam at the back. He let go instantly, standing with his hands in the air in mock innocence. There was a long silence as Katrina looked at him in horror.

'Oops, that's going to take some explaining,' he said calmly, wiping lip gloss from his mouth without taking his eyes off her. 'How will you tell Dominic that you just cost him a few grand by ruining your dress?'

'I'll tell him *you* ruined it trying to attack his girlfriend!' spat Katrina, furious at his lack of remorse and trying to maintain her dignity by not letting the fabric fall.

Alex started laughing and then sauntered back into the lounge before returning with his drink.

'Girlfriend? Is that what you think you are? Honey, get real! He's just using you to help with his new image. Anyway, he won't give a damn, especially when I tell him it was you who came on to me. Who do you think he'll believe? His friend for over twenty years or some girl he has known a few weeks who he can easily replace? He'll be bored of you soon anyway. All of Dom's girlfriends, if that is what I should be calling them, turn to me in the end. You can either play ball now and I won't say a word, or I'll tell Dom you have anyway and you'll be on the first flight in the morning. It all depends on how long you want this little fantasy of yours to last.'

'Fuck you!' was Katrina's retort as she struggled to hold up her dress.

'That's right, fuck me.' Alex approached her again. 'I've seen the way you look at me. You'll enjoy it as much as I will. You come across all sweet and shy, but I know what you're really like. I know that Dominic wouldn't keep seeing someone like you unless they had a hidden talent, so why don't you show me what it is? Come on, it'll be fun.' He casually dropped his glass on the floor, watching the dark liquid soak into the carpet. 'It doesn't matter, they'll just charge a new carpet to Dominic's account, and the dress doesn't matter either.' He grasped her shoulder and put his mouth to her ear, making her step backwards as he whispered: 'All that matters is that you want to be with me, not him. I'm just as good as him, just as rich and just as good looking!' He stepped forward, making her retreat into the bedroom, and then with a violent shove sent her sprawling on the bed. He grabbed her arms to pin her down, trying to keep her still so he could push her dress up.

'You're insane!' she yelped, trying to free an arm. 'You're jealous of Dominic and desperately trying to compete, but you can't! It's just not possible, is it? Let me go! I swear if you don't get off me I'll call the police! You won't get away with this!' Whilst he used one hand to hold her arms, the other slid down to unzip his trousers. She tried to twist away, but the force of his weight prevented her from moving.

'Your word against mine, baby. Anyway, I know you want it too!' She felt his hand pressing down hard on her waist and as a last attempt she screamed as loudly as she could whilst struggling to free herself.

Someone entered the room and Alex was pulled off her. Katrina, pulling the torn dress back down, saw that it was Dominic. He had Alex pinned against the wall by the collar of his shirt.

'What the fuck are you doing, Alex? You've gone fucking crazy!' Dominic looked round at Katrina before pushing Alex even harder against the wall. 'I don't give a shit what you do with all those other girls; I turn a blind eye to you bringing them into my hotel rooms and getting them to do all your sordid stuff, but this is crossing the line. What is your problem? I do everything for you and this is the way you repay me?' He let go of Alex and stared at him. 'You need to get help; you're taking it too far.'

Alex straightened himself, glaring at Katrina. 'I'm sorry, Dom. She threw herself at me and I just couldn't resist. She asked me to meet her here; that's why she told you she wasn't feeling well. Normally you're okay about me with any of your girls.'

Dominic whirled around and slammed his fist into Alex's face, knocking him to the floor.

'You stupid fuck! Firstly, they are just girls who hang around, not a girl I have made it clear I am with. Secondly, I am going to give Katrina the benefit of the doubt and presume that because she was screaming and fighting you, she was most definitely not throwing herself at you. Why would I believe that she would want you when she's got me? You are so fucked up! All the drugs and shit are scrambling your brains!' Dominic turned away, rubbing his hand over her head, then turned back to Alex. 'I don't want it happening again, got it?' Alex nodded pathetically, trying to stop the blood from his split lip dripping on his suit. To Katrina's surprise, Dominic held out his hand to help him up. 'Now go home and take it out on someone else. I'll see you tomorrow when you're sober. Apologise to Katrina before you go.'

Alex looked at Katrina, who was sitting absolutely stunned, and offered a mumbled apology before slinking out of the room. Dominic went into the bathroom and she heard him peeing before he came back out and went into the lounge. She wondered if he was upset and needed some time to compose himself. However, after a few minutes he came back in with the bottle of brandy and the room service menu.

'Have a sip of this to calm down, and order some food. I'm starving.' He sat on the bed, undoing his shirt. His calmness unnerved her and she felt uncomfortable. Alex had just attacked her and he was talking about ordering food? It was as if that sort of event was a typical occurrence in his life. Surely he should be going mad, and surely he would never talk to Alex again?

'I didn't know he was going to come back here,' she said finally, breaking the silence. 'I was shocked to find him waiting.'

'How did he get here before you?' Dominic asked sharply. 'You just said he was here waiting for you.' He looked at her with narrowed eyes.

'I stopped at a store to get some stuff,' she answered lamely, then, feeling the need to elaborate, 'I needed some glue to stick the gems back on my dress, but that's a bit pointless now, I guess.' She held up the torn strap.

'You're a very strange girl. So what if sequins or gems or whatever fall off a dress? It's only a dress. Were you really going to sit here trying to stick them back on? Why?'

'It's an expensive dress and I didn't want you to get charged for it being damaged.' Katrina looked woefully down at the stain on the carpet from the spilt drink.

'Why would I get charged? The dress is already bought and paid for. The stylist couldn't borrow a dress from a designer at such short notice, particularly as your name isn't known, so I just paid for one. All of what you're wearing is yours now. It really doesn't matter to me. Throw it away, it's ruined anyway. What do you want to eat?' He picked up the phone, flicking through the menu. Katrina looked at the diamond cuff, wondering if that was included too. 'Yes, the diamonds are yours as well. You might need them for another event anyway. I think I'll have a club sandwich. Why don't you have a salad?' Without waiting for her response, he ordered it over the phone.

Katrina fell back on the bed in shock. What the hell was going on? In less than twenty minutes she had been attacked by Dominic's best friend, and then, as if nothing had happened, he had just told her she owned thousands of pounds' worth of diamonds. For a brief moment she allowed herself to feel excited that she, Katrina Muirhead, was the proud possessor of diamonds, and not just little ones. Big, expensive diamonds bought by a fantastic film star who was unbelievably good looking! It was like a fairy tale come true. Yet the excitement was doused by the thought of Alex and how he had just walked away like it was quite ordinary for Dominic to come home and find him trying to force a girl – in this case not just any girl, but his girlfriend – to have sex with him. She recalled what Zora had told her about Lauren earlier and felt uneasy. Was she taking the diamonds in exchange for her acceptance of this awful behaviour? All night she had been treated like she was either invisible or just an accessory on Dominic's arm. Was that the price you paid for all the wealth and designer clothes? It certainly didn't look like Dominic had any intention of ending his friendship with Alex; after all, hadn't he said he would see him tomorrow? Surely if Dominic really liked her he would be so angry with Alex he would never want to see him again. Katrina touched the bruises already forming on her arm and felt resentment rising up within her. Maybe Dominic didn't give a damn about her at all.

She watched him strip down to his black trousers, displaying his broad tanned back. As he walked past, his eyes drifted to the cuff on her wrist and the corner of his mouth lifted. She wanted to thank him but it felt a bit odd, as the diamonds had hardly been given in a romantic fashion. He had just told her matter-of-factly that they were hers because he had had to buy them for the premiere, rather than choosing them because he thought she would really like them. Although she didn't know a huge amount about their value, she realised that they were probably worth more than she could earn in a year or two, or perhaps even ten! It was amazingly generous of him and she wondered if she was overreacting a little. Maybe Dominic would deal with Alex and he just didn't want to ruin the special evening by going mad. What did she expect him to do? Beat Alex to a pulp and throw him out of the window? He had acknowledged Alex's drug and alcohol problem, so maybe he would get him into rehab or something. Katrina lifted up her wrist so the diamonds glinted. Lighten up, she told herself, and just appreciate all the amazing experiences Dominic keeps giving you. Resolutely she leapt off the bed and took off the ripped dress, folding it carefully in the bottom of her bag. No way would she throw it away; a needle and thread would fix it.

In the lounge, Dominic was lying on the sofa drinking whisky and watching the television. His eyes were darker than usual and his expression was cold. Katrina, noticing this, went to return to the bedroom.

'Where are you going? Come back,' he demanded, shifting his legs so there was room on the sofa for her to sit beside him. She did as he requested and they sat in silence for a few minutes, Katrina looking at the television screen and trying to ignore the fact that he was staring at her.

'Strange girl. I thought you were all quiet and demure when really you're quite the little seductress.' He leant forward and grasped her chin roughly so that she was looking at him. 'I wonder if you are as innocent as you seem. How many boyfriends have you had?'

'Only one before you. I mean, I have been on a few dates but I have only had one proper boyfriend.'

'Okay, let me put it differently then: how many men have you had sex with?'

'Why are you asking me that?' she replied shortly, wondering what he was getting at. He just stared back at her until she backed down. 'Two.'

'Crap, I don't believe that for a second. You don't have to lie to me. I don't care if you've slept with one hundred men. I am just curious, that's all. What's the true number?' He emptied his drink before pouring himself another.

'That is the true number,' Katrina replied.

'Christ, if that is so you're literally a virgin compared to the girls I know! What I don't understand, then, is how you have managed to seduce me and two of my closest friends. How have you done it?' He reclined back on the sofa, his eyes glinting dangerously, eyebrows raised questioningly.

'I don't understand what you mean. I haven't seduced anyone.' Katrina was confused and did not know how to react to him. He was doing a good job of intimidating her but she was not going to just take his accusations lying down. 'What do you mean, I have seduced two of your closest friends? Alex just attacked me, not the other way around, and I did nothing to provoke it! In fact I have gone out of my way to avoid him, so I don't get how you can say that. And who is the other friend? I told you nothing happened with Carlos, if that's what you mean.

You're the one with girls everywhere and countless stories of who you've slept with!'

He laughed arrogantly. 'Don't be upset. I don't even know most of the girls I am supposed to have slept with. Although I'll admit that I have been with a lot of models. I like beautiful girls and there are plenty out there to choose from.' He ran his tongue over his teeth, alerting Katrina to the fact that he had been doing coke again, which would also explain his dark eyes and strange mood. She got up to go to the bedroom. He grabbed her wrist, pulling her back down. 'Don't leave! I want to find out more about you. After all, if this is a relationship it is important that we understand each other, don't you agree?' He didn't wait for an answer. 'I didn't mean Carlos, I meant James. I think you know why.'

Katrina's heart stopped for a moment as she realised that James must have told him about the kiss.

'James and I just have a lot to talk about, that's all,' she said slowly. 'I didn't mean to lead him on in any way—'

Dominic interrupted her. 'Yes, well I don't see James as a threat and I know that you wouldn't do anything with him. I just wonder why he has such an interest in you when he hasn't given a shit about any of the girls I've been seeing before. As for Alex, he would never betray me without reason, so I think that you did have a part to play in what happened tonight. He must have got some signal from you to encourage him to come back here, to wait for you. I think you're playing me, sweetheart, and I must say I'm very impressed. You're not the most beautiful girl I have ever been with but you've sure got my attention with your games!'

Katrina was astounded by this comment. There was absolutely no way she was going to be spoken to like that, no matter who he was. She pulled away from him, getting up off the sofa and going into the bedroom, where she grabbed her bag to throw her clothes into, hastily pulling on her jeans at the same time. He followed her, watching as she put on shoes.

'What are you doing?'

'If you really think that is the truth, then I may as well leave. I can't believe that you would say that. I just don't understand why you are being like this. I guess it's your way of saying that you are bored and want me to leave, so I'll go.'

'Very clever, darling! I think the reason you're so good at getting men to do what you want is because you take more risks than most girls.' He laughed. 'You walked away from me the very first night I met you in that club. You walked away from me after we had sex in Paris, and went home quietly, and now you're doing it again. If you walk away this time, I'm not coming after you. I've had what I wanted, so leave if that's really what you want to do. Just remember, nobody forced you.'

Katrina picked up the bag. He didn't move out of the way, so she pushed past him and out of the door, slamming it behind her. She paused for a moment in the hope that he would come after her, but the door didn't open.

K atrina stopped in the lobby, unsure of where to go and what to do, seeing as it was one o'clock in the morning. She still had on a full face of make-up that contrasted sharply with the tatty jeans and rucksack. She put her hand in her pocket to look for a hairband and instead discovered a folded card. Opening it she found James's number that he had given to her in case of emergencies. Without so much as a second thought she went to reception.

'Can I use the phone, please? You can charge it to the penthouse. I'm with Mr Cayley,' she told the snooty-looking man behind the counter. He pushed the phone towards her and she dialled the number. It rang ten times before James answered, his voice muffled by sleep and distance.

'James, it's Katrina. I'm really sorry to wake you.'

'What? Katrina, what's up? You didn't really wake me. It's late morning here, I've overslept. Are you okay?'

'No, I need your help.' Katrina briefly told him about the evening's occurrences.

'Right, get a taxi to the airport and I'll make sure you have a flight as soon as possible to Heathrow.'

'How much will it cost?' she asked, wondering how the hell she would pay for it all.

'Don't worry about the flight. I'll take care of that. Just

make sure you have enough money to get a taxi, then phone me when you get to the airport and I'll give you the flight details. I'll pick you up from Heathrow.'

She thanked him a hundred times before he stopped her so that he could phone around for a flight. On the street the concierge helped her into a car, with the instruction to the driver that they charge the fare to the hotel suite.

On the plane at last, the adrenaline gradually ebbed away and Katrina felt empty and alone. She couldn't stop the tears that trickled down her face. Dominic had thought she was just like all the other girls, happy to hang off his arm so she could mingle with important people, receive expensive gifts and enjoy holidays and dinners that she didn't have to pay for. She had had all of that, a bag full of clothes worth a fortune, diamonds, and it all felt cheap. The whole Muciana and Victor thing, Annabelle, Loretta, Dominic's reaction to Alex attacking her, the list went on, and it had all happened in such a short space of time! She knew that she was best off out of it. But another part of her knew that if Dominic had stopped her she would have stayed and forgiven him for everything that he had said. Who was she to think she could hold him? It had been a ridiculous fantasy destined to end before long. She felt an intense hatred for Alex, although she couldn't blame him for Dominic's nasty mood.

James met her at the airport as he had promised, taking her bag and giving her a sympathetic look. It was raining heavily and they drove back to his house in silence.

'I'll just get my stuff together and then I'll go,' she said as he opened the front door. 'Is it okay if I give you a cheque for the flight?'

'Don't be silly. You stay as long as you like, and don't worry about the money, it doesn't matter.'

'No, I must pay you for the flight, it wouldn't be right not to. How much was it?'

'Six hundred and eighty. Expensive, I know, but it was so last minute. Really, I don't want you to pay me back.'

Delilah ran towards Katrina, meowing for strokes.

'I absolutely will pay you back. It was hardly your fault it was expensive.' She stroked Delilah's silky fur coat before standing up.

'Do you want to tell me exactly what went on in LA?' James asked gently. 'I'll get us something to eat, you must be starving. Let's order a takeaway. How about Thai?'

Katrina nodded glumly, not really caring what they ordered. She seemed to have lost her appetite. As he picked up the phone, she went upstairs to pack up the clothes that she hadn't taken to LA. Most of them she had to put into their original carrier bags because her rucksack was too small for them all. Then she went downstairs to the kitchen, where James was looking into a box of food with a confused look on his face.

'That takeaway is so odd. I never get what I ask for. I think they just take your call for the hell of it, then send out whatever they have going in the kitchen irrespective of the order. Never mind, I'm sure we will salvage something.' He took plates out of the cupboard and arranged the food on the table. 'Sit and eat! You look like you've lost weight, far too skinny.'

'Not according to Dominic,' Katrina muttered to herself. She found after the first mouthful that she actually was really hungry.

'So tell me, what made Dominic behave that way? Too much coke, I imagine,' James said drily.

'I think so. There was also a bit of an issue with Alex that may have had something to do with it. I left the premiere early, and when I got back to the hotel Alex was already there, waiting for me. He threatened me and said that if I didn't do what he wanted he would tell Dominic that I had come on to him. I told him to go and he attacked me. Dominic walked in just in time and threw Alex out. Then he started saying that I was the one who had provoked the attack and that I must have led Alex on.' Katrina started to get upset and stopped to take a gulp of wine.

'This is unbelievable! I am going to kill Alex when I see him. Jesus Christ! Let me get this right, Alex attacks you but you get the blame?' James looked furious.

'That's what Dominic was implying. I don't think he really meant it. It was more the coke and that he was angry.' Katrina tried to excuse Dominic's behaviour, scared that James would call him, which would lead to Dominic hating her even more. 'Please just forget about it, it doesn't matter. It wasn't exactly going to last anyway. Dominic was probably just bored and pleased to find an excuse to get rid of me.'

'No, I don't agree. Dominic really does like you, from what he told me. He has never followed a girl to England before and tracked her down, let alone invited her to stay with him. He just keeps bad company with guys like Alex and takes too much coke. It's so typical of Alex, and so typical of Dominic to forgive him and not just beat the crap out of the little bastard.' James handed her a box of spring rolls. 'Dominic's also got this thing about testing people and pushing them to their limits to see how much they'll take. Most girls just sit there agreeing with whatever he says and then apologising for things they haven't even done. Don't think you did the wrong thing; you were absolutely right to walk out.'

'I didn't really have much choice.' Katrina stood up. 'Well, I guess I should go.'

'I'll drive you home. Are you going back to Hampshire or to Oval?' He picked up his keys from the table.

'To Oval, but really you don't have to drive me. I'll be quite fine on the tube.' She picked up the numerous bags, surprised at how heavy they were.

'Absolutely not, I'll give you a lift. I would never let a woman get on a tube when I can drive her.' He took her rucksack from her and once outside put it in the back of his car. Then he opened the passenger door, indicating that she get in.

When they pulled up outside her flat, there was an awkward silence as Katrina struggled to think what to say. Would he want to stay in touch? Probably not; why would he? It was a pity, as he was such a nice guy and they had got on well. Should she suggest it? What if he thought she was trying to flirt with him now that she was not with Dominic? Then he might think she was just desperate for any guy and exactly what Dominic had accused her of. Before she had time to decide what to say, James had slid out of the car and opened the door on her side.

'Let me help you with your bags.' He reached across and took them out.

'No, really, I'm fine,' she insisted, thinking how weird it would be if she let him carry them up to the flat. 'Honestly, I'm quite happy to take them.' She grabbed them from him and began making her way to the front door before turning back. She fished around in one of the bags and pulled out a dog-eared cheque book and a pen. She filled out a cheque and, leaving the bags on the floor, went to hand it to him. 'This is for the flight. I owe you for helping me out.' He did not take it.

'I don't want you to pay me back. I can put the flight on my expenses or something. Use the money towards tuition fees.'

Katrina leant forward and put the cheque in his shirt pocket. 'Please take it. You shouldn't have to pay for my stupidity. You barely know me and it would be wrong to accept over six hundred quid from you.' She turned back to the flat.

'Katrina, let me know how you get on with the studying. You've got my number, so stay in touch and forget about Dominic. He lives in a different world to you and me. Don't take it personally, he did really like you. I just don't think he'll ever have a normal relationship. We'll meet up for a coffee soon, okay?'

Katrina nodded and smiled weakly. She felt worse than she had when she had left LA. It seemed more final now saying goodbye to James. She let herself in and watched James drive away. Back to reality, she thought, as she turned the lights on and surveyed the bleak, colourless flat.

The following morning Katrina unpacked the clothes and hung them up in the wardrobe. They made a sharp contrast to her usual high-street items. She put the diamond cuff and earrings in a box under her bed, but not before sitting and looking at them for ages. It seemed like an odd dream that only twenty-four hours ago she had been wearing them at a film premiere, and that her movie-star boyfriend had bought them for her. She wondered how much they were worth and if it would be possible to sell them, although she knew she wouldn't. They were a memory of her moment in a perfect world: being with an incredibly handsome film-star boyfriend, wearing an amazing dress, being given diamonds. The reality of course had been somewhat different. Nonetheless, it was every girl's dream, wasn't it?

Katrina spoke to the agency, who informed her that she had been confirmed for in-store posters for Gap.

'You must be going down well with the Americans. We should get you over to New York soon and then back to Paris or maybe Milan. To think only a few weeks ago I was going to call you in and have a chat about whether you should continue modelling or not. I have an option on a Dior perfume advertisement for you; if that comes off you'll be a star!' purred Rosanna. 'You won't be spending much time in London over the next few months, although obviously I understand you need to go where Dominic goes. How are things going there? You must hold on to him, darling. If you lose him now, before you've established yourself, then you'll lose all this interest, so no silly tantrums, just behave like the perfect girlfriend. Call me tomorrow, darling.'

Katrina put the phone down wondering why she wasn't swinging from the ceiling at the news that she had a job for Gap and the chance of getting a perfume campaign. There was a gentle knock and Claire, the latest flatmate, peered around the door.

'Hey, I thought I heard you turn up last night. How you doing? Can I come in?' she asked in her thick Welsh accent. Katrina nodded and Claire stepped into the room, her eyes widening at the sight of all the clothes lying around. 'Wow, that dress is gorgeous!' She was looking at the dress that Katrina had worn in Monaco.

'Yeah,' she replied, putting it on a hanger. 'It's Lanvin, I've always loved their stuff.'

Claire sat on the edge of the bed. 'Who was that who dropped you off last night?' she asked. 'I looked out of the window and saw you talking to a guy but it wasn't the film star, was it? Everyone's talking about you at the agency; Rosanna loves you just because you've got a famous boyfriend.' Claire was not the sort of girl who would get starstruck for anyone; in fact she rarely watched television or films and had a strong hatred of celebrity magazines and gossip. Despite being stunning – six foot, with an elfin face and cropped blond hair – she had fallen into modelling by accident after being spotted in a Cardiff shopping centre with her boyfriend, whom she had been with since she was fourteen. The only reason she had agreed to spend the summer in London was to get the money together so that they could put a deposit down on a house in Wales. She made a welcome change from all the sycophantic people Katrina had been around for the past few days.

'That was James, a friend of Dominic's,' Katrina replied, cramming the rest of the clothes into a drawer that was already too full.

'He looked nice. I liked the way he opened the car door for you and then waited until you were in the flat before he drove off. My mother always told me you can tell a lot by the little things a man does. I figured he wasn't the film-star guy by that.' Claire looked questioningly at Katrina. 'So why was the friend dropping you home and not the main man?'

'It's over with Dominic,' muttered Katrina. 'James helped me bring my stuff back but I'm not seeing either of them again.'

'Pity,' was Claire's muffled reply as she pulled a moth-eaten jumper over her head. 'He looked really nice, and good looking too.'

'He was the best-looking man I've ever seen; not so sure about him being nice, though. Sexy, dangerous, fun maybe, but not nice. I don't suppose famous actors have to bother with being nice,' Katrina said wryly.

'I wasn't talking about the actor guy. I meant the other one, James. What's the story there? I am an expert in body language, and he likes you!' Claire laughed. 'If the film one has gone, you may as well try him.'

'No, I couldn't, it would be too weird. Anyhow, he comes with too many complications. There's the whole Dominic thing, and then he has an ex-wife and a couple of kids, and on top of that he's older,' Katrina protested. 'I couldn't possibly phone him and ask him out. It would be ridiculous. He would think I was a right cling-on nutter; now that Dominic has dumped me, I am after his friend! No way, absolutely no way would I even consider the possibility of going out with him, even if he does look nice to you from the second-floor window of a block of flats at one in the morning!'

'Whoa, chill, I was only joking. One doth protest too much!' Claire laughed.

Katrina slumped despondently on the bed, staring up at the Lanvin dress and remembering how much fun it had been in the restaurant with Dominic and James.

'Whatcha doin' tonight?' asked Claire in a mock American accent. 'I've been invited to a party, wanna come? There ain't gonna be no movie stars, just ordinary folk like li'l ole me, and maybe there'll be a nice boy for you.'

'Not in the mood,' replied Katrina, wondering how a date with any 'ordinary' guy would ever compare to the excitement of Dominic.

'Tough! You are coming if I have to drag you out, and you have lots of clothes to wear now, so no excuses.' With that, Claire bounded out of the room to go shopping, leaving Katrina alone for the rest of the day.

Later that evening, Katrina pulled on her old jeans and a vest to go to the party. She couldn't face putting on any of the new clothes after Dominic's comment about her gaining thousands of pounds of jewellery and clothes off him. A tiny part of her felt a bit guilty as she realised that, like so many other girls, the fact that Dominic could bring so much glamour to her life had been one of the reasons why she had been so drawn to him, and indeed was still drawn to him.

They got the tube and then walked in the pouring rain to a badly decorated bar in Hoxton. Katrina sat in the corner whilst Claire chatted to arty types about music. How quickly life returned to normal, she thought. One day you are at a Hollywood premiere with the most eligible man in the world and the next you are in a smoky bar in Hoxton drinking beer. She wondered what Dominic was doing.

For the millionth time that day she checked her phone to see if he had called. This time there was a text message from an unknown number that read: 'If you had just said yes to me you'd still be here with us today enjoying LA. Instead I am here with Dominic and two very pretty girls. It was such a pity we were interrupted as I could have shown you some fun! Feel free to call me to continue where we left off any time. Alex xxx' Katrina deleted the text immediately. How the hell had he got her number? Another text came through. 'Just in case you deleted that message here is my number again because I know you're going to need it.' Furious, Katrina deleted it again. A moment later her phone bleeped for the third time. 'You needn't worry about Dominic, he is fine and has just left for his hotel room with a hot blonde. Let me know when you want to hook up – looking forward to finding out what is so special about you.' This time Katrina did not delete it straight away, instead reading it over and over. That was that, then: Dominic was over her in less than twenty-four hours and on to the next conquest. She felt like a total idiot. Everyone would just see her as another stupid model that Dominic Cayley had screwed. A tiny part of her had hoped that he might call, but the truth was he wouldn't be thinking of her any more, while she could think of nothing else. On impulse she tapped out a text to him: 'I am sorry I left you in LA. I really want to see you again. Maybe if you come back to London we could meet up and I could give you back the jewellery.' She stopped momentarily to consider whether she should send it, but she had absolutely nothing to lose, not even her pride, so she did.

*

Dominic was lying on his bed in his hotel room, bored, while the pretty blonde stripped. He sipped vodka as she removed her bra to expose her surgically enhanced breasts and came forward to push them towards him. His phone beeped loudly and he shoved her aside to reach for it. The message flashed up from Katrina and he read it silently, a smile playing on his lips. The blonde presumed that she was pleasing him and slid her hand down his trousers to find him soft and unexcited.

'Sorry, sweetie, you really aren't doing anything for me,' Dominic said, pushing her away. He reached over to a drawer, pulled out three hundred dollars and chucked it on the bed. 'That should cover a taxi. Get dressed and get out!' Then he disappeared into the bathroom, ignoring her pleas. He didn't send Katrina a reply; he wanted to make her sweat a bit. He was undeniably pleased that she had backed down, as he had been thinking about her. Alex said that she had flirted non-stop with him and that was why he had leapt on her, but Alex was a notorious liar. Anyway, why would she would mess with Alex when Dominic was around, and as for James, well, it was laughable to think she would have any interest in him when she had been spending time with what American *Vogue* in their latest edition had described as 'the most eligible man in the world'.

Katrina checked her phone approximately every five minutes, in the way of all the annoying, paranoid women that she had always laughed about, until it was approaching midnight and she realised that she was not going to get a reply that evening. Dominic would have fallen asleep after the blonde had done her job. A friend of Claire's called Simon, who was the guitarist in the band playing that night, asked if he could take her out sometime, and under Claire's glare she gave him her number. He was attractive and Claire told her that the band had just signed a record deal and that Simon had a masters degree in politics. He was still a league away from Dominic.

As she lay in bed trying to fall asleep, her phone bleeped and her heart leapt in the hope that it was Dominic replying at last. Instead it was Simon, saying that he had enjoyed meeting her and asking when he could take her for a drink.

When her phone rang loudly the next day, waking her from her deep sleep, she was slow to answer it, presuming it would either be her mother, the agency with castings or Helen, as they were the only people who called her as a rule. She didn't look at the caller ID, instead answering with an annoyed, 'Yes?'

'That's not a very nice way to greet your favourite person, now is it?' said the voice and Katrina sat up in surprise. It was a deep male voice.

'Hi?' she replied tentatively.

'I hope you don't mind me calling so soon. I really wanted to know if I can take you out tonight.' At that point she realised it wasn't an American accent and she was so disappointed she forgot to reply. 'You do remember me, don't you? You didn't reply to my text so I thought I would give you a buzz,' explained Simon.

'No, I didn't,' she said. 'I'm not sure about tonight . . .' She couldn't think of a plausible excuse so merely trailed off.

'Oh please don't give me some feeble excuse about washing your hair.' He laughed. 'How about we go for something to eat near where you live and then if you hate me you can just walk home. How does eight o'clock suit you?'

Katrina just wanted to get him off the phone. 'Okay, sure, you know where the flat is, right? Well, press the buzzer for number four and I'll come down,' she told him reluctantly. All she really wanted to do was stay in bed alone and think about Dominic.

'Excellent stuff! See you at eight.'

She was annoyed that he had managed to bully her into seeing him that evening and considered texting him to say that something had come up. She got the feeling that he would not take no for an answer. Lauren would have advised her to go, as she believed that you could never have too many men, and it was always wise to have a few hanging around. Thinking of Lauren, Katrina had a sudden urge to speak to her. She wasn't sure if Lauren would still be in Paris but nonetheless she found and dialled the old hotel number. Eventually the switchboard picked up the phone and confirmed she was there. The call was transferred to her room and a thick Italian voice answered. After a few seconds of muffled whispering Lauren came to the phone.

'Hello?'

'Hi, Lauren, it's me, Katrina.' There was a brief silence as Lauren racked her brain to remember Katrina, before it came to her.

'Hey, Katrina the cunning little seductress!' Lauren laughed. 'Hey, Carlos, you know Katrina, don't you?' Katrina heard the Italian voice muttering a reply. 'Yes, he remembers you, said that you and him had some fun together. I never imagined that I would be in your shadow, Kat!'

'What do you mean, in my shadow?'

'From what I've heard, you're screwing your way around the world. From Paris to London to LA you've managed to fit in how many men? Let's see, Alex called me yesterday to tell me all about you and him, and of course I was there when you whisked Dominic away from me, and there's darling Carlos, who I am sure you'll agree is the kind of yummy boy who should be shared. I am impressed by the innocent act, Katrina. It really seems to work. I am going to try it myself from now on.'

'But I haven't been doing any sort of act, and nothing happened between Alex and me apart from him trying it on and me fighting him off. If you just ask Carlos he'll tell you nothing happened between me and him either. The only one I've been with is Dominic, and I didn't steal him off anyone!' Katrina stated.

'Crap, I've seen you in the papers, all over Dominic. No girl would have been able to hang on to him like that unless they were extremely good at something. Dominic Cayley can have any girl he wants; what would he want with you? So you not only seduce him, you dig your nails into all his friends too so you can have your pick when he dumps you. I can't believe how you've done that.' With that, Lauren slammed the phone down.

How could one man cause so much damage? Ever since she had met Dominic, her reasonably quiet life had suddenly become filled with jealousy and attention-seeking. Alex had attacked her because of his jealousy of Dominic and everything he had; Lauren was happy to believe any negative stuff, as she hated the fact that Dominic had chosen Katrina over her. A relationship with Dominic came with a heavy price tag: the interference of all the people who wanted to be part of his life and all the negative feelings that came with one man's success. It was impossible for him to have a one-on-one relationship.

Katrina threw her phone across the floor in frustration. She lay back on the bed, part of her wishing desperately that she could see Dominic again, the other part wishing she had never met him in the first place. How could an ordinary guy like Simon compete against film premieres, celebrity-filled dinners and designer shopping trips? Dominic could be a bastard, but being with him was exciting and fun, whereas going for a drink in the local pub seemed like the dullest thing in the world now, even if the man was nice looking and decent. She wasn't ready to let go of the potential of being a movie-star's girlfriend, with all the perks that came with it, and she wanted to be back in that world rather than one based in a damp flat and involving drinking beer in grotty pubs.

A t four o'clock, the silence of the flat was broken once more by her mobile ringing shrilly. She found it wedged behind a chest of drawers and answered it quickly without looking at the caller ID.

'Hello, gorgeous, where are you? I've just landed at Heathrow,' drawled Dominic. 'Tell me where you're hiding and I'll have my driver bring me over.'

Katrina dropped the phone on her foot and retrieving it fell backwards on the bed with joy. 'In my flat in Oval, 26 Kennington Park Road!' she squeaked.

'See you soon then,' he replied and the phone went dead. Katrina felt like howling with happiness. He wanted to see her again despite everything and it was all back on! She danced around the room before catching sight of herself in the mirror and panicking. If he saw her like that then it would all be over again in seconds.

'Omigod, I look hideous! Help!' Katrina flew into the bathroom, sending a surprised Claire reeling, and began throwing off her clothes.

An hour later the buzzer went and a perfectly made-up Katrina, wearing La Perla underwear and a tight black dress, answered the door. Dominic didn't say anything, just picked her up so that her legs were around his waist, and kissed her long and hard. He carried her towards

Claire's room. 'Wrong room!' she yelped. Once inside Katrina's room, he kicked the door shut. Still having said nothing, he pulled off his T-shirt, making her stomach do its usual flip, and undid her dress so that it fell to the ground. Then he proceeded to kiss her entire body until she was squirming with delight. He had never spent so much time on her before, and when they finally had sex it was the best Katrina had ever had. Afterwards he lay without saying anything, smoking a cigarette on the little bed in her messy room.

'I missed you, which is strange. I mean, we hardly know each other and I never miss anyone,' he said finally, as he finished his cigarette and ground it out on a bottle top. Katrina was sitting on the edge of the bed with her back to him. He pulled her down and kissed her softly. She couldn't believe how nice he was being, and her only reasoning was that he must really have missed her.

She wanted just to stay there with him and talk all night, without any interruptions from the rest of the world. She barely knew anything about him apart from what she had read in interviews, and she wanted to know things that no one else knew.

He interrupted her thoughts. 'I've got a party to go to. Want to come with me?' With that he swung his legs off the bed and looked round for his jeans. Katrina collapsed flat on the bed with a sigh, causing him to look at her questioningly. 'What's up with you?'

'Nothing. It just would have been nice to spend some time alone with you.'

'But we've been together non-stop for a while now; in fact we are always together. What does it matter if other people are around, we're still together. Personally I like lots of people around me as I get bored easily. I mean, if we just stayed here, what would we do? We'd just lie around wasting time when we could be out being seen and having fun.' Dominic pulled on his T-shirt and stopped to admire his reflection in the mirror before ruffling his hair. 'As long as you're with me you're happy, aren't you?' He did not look for an answer to his question, instead pulling the jewel-encrusted Cavalli jeans that he had bought her off a shelf and handing them over. 'Put them on with a tight vest and we're ready to go.'

'Where are we going?' she asked, obediently putting on the jeans.

'Graham Hunt is having a party to celebrate his album release in a club in the West End. Everyone is going and loads of people have come over from LA just for the night.'

That seemed ridiculous to Katrina. Imagine paying a fortune for a flight for just one party, and all the hassle of getting there. Only people with too much time and money would be able to consider such a thing. She applied make-up again and followed him out of the bedroom. Claire was standing awkwardly in the hallway.

'Katrina, can I have a quick word before you go,' she said, ignoring Dominic and pulling Katrina into her room. 'You are a nightmare!' she hissed. 'Simon is downstairs waiting for you. He just buzzed and said you were going out for a meal with him. I told him you weren't here, but he said he would wait downstairs as that was what you had arranged. What are you like? You're going to saunter out with Dominic and he'll feel like a right dick, and then he'll blame me as supposedly you're my mate!'

'Oh no, I totally forgot. Shit!' Katrina grimaced. 'What the hell am I going to do?' Claire glared at her. 'Look, I'm sorry. He forced me to say I'd go out with him even though I tried to say no, so it is his own fault technically. What the hell am I going to do? It will look so bad to Dominic if I have a date waiting outside.' Katrina thought for a moment. 'You go down first and get Simon to go somewhere. I'll quickly sneak out with Dominic and then they won't see each other and I can text Simon saying I've got stuck at work or something.'

Claire shook her head fervently. 'Do not try to drag me into your mess! How am I supposed to get him away?'

'Katrina? Are you ready to go?' Dominic called through the door. 'I'm getting bored standing here.' Katrina went to leave.

'If you ask me he's an arrogant prick anyway,' hissed Claire. 'Just because he's some hotshot actor does not mean you have to do whatever he tells you do to. I'll go down and try to get Simon to leave, but you owe me big-time. Tell Mr Hotshot that you have to get something from the bedroom and hold him up while I go downstairs.' She pulled on her trainers, opened the door and left the flat.

'What was that all about?' queried Dominic, although he was not really interested.

'Nothing. Listen, I've just got to get a lip gloss from my room and then we'll go,' she muttered. In the room she timed three minutes before Dominic put his head round the door.

'Let's go,' he insisted. Worried that it had not been long enough, she tried another tactic.

'Wait, we're not in so much of a rush, are we?' She attempted to purr sexily. He just gave her a strange look in return. She did what she thought was a slink towards him and wrapped her arms around his neck, pulling him down for a kiss. He reciprocated momentarily before pulling away.

'What is up with you? Plenty of time for all that later. Let's go!' He grabbed her hand and dragged her out of the door and down the stairs. Outside, Simon and Claire were nowhere to be seen. Neither was the car. 'Fucking driver!' raged Dominic. 'I told him to wait. We'll have to get a taxi.' There were none in sight, so he began to stride down the street looking for one.

'We could go back inside and call a cab,' offered Katrina hopefully. She heard her name being called, and turning round saw Simon approaching. 'Oh no,' she groaned. Dominic stopped walking and turned to look at Simon.

'There you are. Did you get held up?' Simon failed to notice the look of horror on Katrina's face and kissed her on the cheek. 'You look great. I thought we were just getting a bite to eat?' Katrina saw Dominic bearing down on them.

'I'm really sorry but I've got other plans tonight,' she muttered feebly.

'What's going on now?' Dominic asked, looking Simon up and down with a disdainful expression. Despite being nice looking, Simon dressed like a wannabe rock star, and to Dominic that was pathetic. Katrina stared at both of them in horror.

'Hi, I'm Simon, a friend of Katrina and Claire's.' He held his hand out by way of introduction. Dominic ignored it.

'Come on, Katrina, let's go.'

'What do you mean? Where are you going? I thought we were doing something tonight?' Simon asked Katrina. 'I've been waiting outside for twenty minutes. Claire tried to make me go to a pub, but I knew you would turn up.'

'I'm really sorry, I should have told you earlier. I can't have dinner with you. I'm going to a party with Dominic. He came back from LA and I didn't think he would. I didn't mean to give you the wrong idea,' Katrina gabbled, looking at Dominic as she spoke. His face was blank.

'You're cancelling on me? What the fuck? So I'm being

blown out and you're just going to leave me standing here like an idiot? Why the hell did you arrange to go out with me if you had no intention of coming?'

Katrina felt very uncomfortable. In a normal world she would have been quite excited going out with a guy like Simon, and would have spent ages getting ready for the date. She had not wanted to make him think she was a total bitch, and by the look on his face that was exactly what he did think. It was not helping that Dominic was watching her with a dark expression beginning to form, as well as a few passers-by eavesdropping.

'I'm really sorry, honestly. It was just a mistake, Simon, and I feel really bad.'

'It seems like Katrina has been setting herself up with a few alternatives in case she gets bored of me,' drawled Dominic. Simon glared at him. 'I'd just go home if I were you. She's coming with me tonight.' Dominic reached across to take Katrina's hand and drag her away. Simon was left standing on the street with his mouth agape.

'You're an absolute bitch!' he yelled after her. 'Have a shit night!'

In the cab, Dominic stared at her with an amused expression, not saying anything until she was shifting uncomfortably under his gaze.

'Alex was right about you. You know exactly what you're doing,' he commented finally. 'Lining up men so you are never alone, making them all think you're un-attainable. It's a bit cruel, don't you think? Poor boy got all dressed up in his best rock-star gear to take you out and you saunter off with me.' He started laughing. 'Christ, Katrina, I thought I was good but you are bloody brilliant!'

His comment about Alex stung, and Katrina was shocked that he obviously still believed Alex's lies after

everything that had happened. For a moment back in the
flat it had felt like he really cared about her and she had
thought that maybe he was remorseful about LA, even
though he hadn't mentioned it. Now she was confused
again. If he really believed she was like that, why had he
come back for her? Even worse was the realisation that if
he did see her as the manipulative and provocative type,
then he really didn't know her at all.

'I didn't do it on purpose,' she insisted in a quiet voice,
not wanting to start an argument again. 'I only met him
last night and he wouldn't take no for an answer. I didn't
think you wanted to see me again.'

'Doesn't matter, forget it.' Dominic's phone rang and
he answered it, leaving Katrina feeling as if they had gone
back to square one. It was so complicated being with him
and she never knew where she stood. At times he softened and she felt like he might actually like her, and then
something would happen to make her think the exact
opposite. For some reason James popped into her head.
He would have found the whole thing funny, and it would
probably have ended with him, Claire, Simon and her
getting drunk together and laughing their heads off.

They pulled up outside a bar and Dominic tossed a
fifty-pound note at the driver. Without waiting for any
change he went in, not bothering to see if Katrina was
following him. The driver sped off and Katrina had no
choice but to go into the bar. Once inside, she saw
Dominic already holding a glass of champagne in one
hand and Annabelle in the other; she had added long hair
extensions and collagen lips to her appearance since they
had last seen her. Feeling incredibly awkward, Katrina
made her way towards them and stopped next to
Dominic.

'Champagne?' He handed her a glass. 'Annabelle, you
remember Katrina?'

Annabelle looked her up and down frostily. 'No, why should I?' she replied, taking the cigarette from Dominic's lips and inhaling, while studying Katrina through the haze of smoke.

'You met briefly the other week at James's place, the night before I went to LA.' Dominic took the cigarette back in a way that was a bit too familiar for Katrina's liking; something almost post-coital about it. Annabelle suddenly brightened up.

'Oh my God, yes, I remember who you are! Alex was talking about you on the phone to me this morning!' She grinned slyly. Dominic had turned away to talk to a guy in a brown leather jacket. 'Yes, I've heard a lot of stuff about you. You must be having fun hanging around with Dominic and Alex.'

'It's been interesting,' Katrina replied guardedly, wondering what Alex had told her.

'Well sure, I imagine it has. I mean, from what I've heard you're from a little house in the country and you haven't really made it as a model, so I expect you are enjoying all the freebies. Dominic must have bought you a few nice things, no?' Annabelle looked at the Cartier watch on Katrina's wrist. 'I doubt you had even heard of Cartier before Dominic. That's so sweet.'

Katrina was lost for words and just stood with her mouth open.

'Please, don't let me keep you from mingling with your friends,' Annabelle purred, raising her eyebrows as she watched Dominic disappear into the VIP section with a group of people. 'Delightful as your company is, I must not keep it all to myself.' With a tinkle of sarcastic laughter she disappeared into the crowd, leaving Katrina standing alone.

Everyone was in small, hostile groups, offering no opportunities for her to join in any conversations, and she did not want to annoy Dominic by hanging off him, so she was at a loss. She contemplated going home and texting him to say that she did not feel well. That would mean he would be in the hands of Annabelle and the other predatory women who were watching from a myriad of dark corners with sharpened eyes and wistful mouths. Katrina found a chair by the wall and sat down. Her mobile bleeped and there was a text from Simon calling her a user and a time-waster. She contemplated texting an apology. Instead she just deleted his message. If it had happened to her, no apology would make up for it; in fact she would probably take it as condescending and even more embarrassing. She was doing a great job of annoying people since meeting Dominic.

After an hour, Dominic reappeared and, spotting her, sauntered over. His eyes had a dangerous glint in them and there was a lipstick mark on his cheek. He sat on the edge of the chair and offered his drink.

'I'm really bored,' he said, after sitting in silence for a few minutes. 'These kinds of parties can be so dull, don't you think?' He lit a cigarette and eyed Katrina through the smoke. 'You aren't really a party girl, are you, baby?' She shook her head. 'Sometimes it helps to do a bit of coke or something just to liven things up, although tonight nothing is going to get me in the mood for a dark noisy bar. Let's go.' He got up and pulled her off the chair before leading her to the door.

In the car he seemed really angry and lit yet another cigarette, ignoring the No Smoking sign. The driver just gawped at him in the rear-view mirror.

'I am so sick of people clinging on to me.' He pulled a wad of cards out of his back pocket and threw them on the car floor. 'Look at all the contact cards that people give me, as if I'm ever going to call any of them!'

Katrina didn't know what to say to that. 'Where are we

going?' she asked quietly, noticing that he was watching her in a strangely predatory manner.

'Where do you think? To James's house via a quick detour, of course; yet another of your admirers!' He smiled sarcastically. Katrina remained silent and shifted awkwardly at the thought of seeing James. Dominic picked up her hand to look at the nails she had been trying to grow. They only just reached her fingertips. He made no comment and turned to gaze out of the window. They did not exchange another word until the car suddenly pulled up outside her flat.

Katrina turned to Dominic in confusion as he leant across her and opened the door for her to step out. 'Be quick.'

'What do you mean?' Was he telling her to go, that he regretted coming back for her?

'Clothes. If you think you're coming back without any clothes again you're mistaken. Go and get the stuff I got you as we're bound to have events to go to and I can't have you trailing around in the same things all the time.'

Katrina hadn't even considered her wardrobe, as usual, and rather sheepishly she slunk out into the flat and packed a bag for what seemed like the millionth time. Trust Dominic to think about her appearance.

Back in the car Dominic pushed an envelope towards her. Peering in she found a little diamond heart necklace.

'Chopard sent me this as a gift so you may as well make use of it.' He yawned and turned away.

Another meaningless trinket to add to the collection, thought Katrina, dropping it into her bag like it was a piece of costume jewellery. The car sped towards James' house and Dominic did not speak again.

31

To Katrina's great surprise, Zora opened the front door wearing only a man's shirt under which her slender brown legs seemed to be endless. The buttons were open low enough to reveal the curve of her enticing cleavage and she looked stunning. Dominic did not seem surprised to see her and kissed her on each cheek as he went through the door. Gone was the friendly disposition that Zora had shown Katrina at the premiere; instead she seemed cold and hostile again.

'Hi,' Katrina muttered as she passed her. In the lounge she heard Dominic and James talking loudly and paused as a sudden pang of nerves hit her at the thought of seeing James. Zora pushed past and she was forced to follow her in.

James immediately stopped talking and gave her a hug, during which he whispered in her ear, 'I knew he'd come back for you.' He smiled widely and Katrina felt at ease instantly. James was able to make anyone feel good about themselves, and in his company tension seemed to disperse. Even Zora had softened as she sat on the sofa, legs curled beneath her, never taking her eyes from James. Katrina noticed Dominic admiring Zora's amazing body and wished she would put something on other than a see-through shirt. She presumed that the fact that Zora was there wearing one of James's shirts meant they were together. She was surprised at the wave of sadness that swept over her at the thought of Zora and James laughing, joking and having fun as a couple. She quickly put it down to the fact that she liked James as a person and did not want to see him getting hurt.

Over a takeaway, Dominic told them about the Lawrence Fishbacher film he now looked certain to be signed up to. It was set in Iraq and London and was the story of a love affair between an English businessman and a Muslim housewife married to a man who eventually killed her when he discovered her infidelity.

'I think this could be my ticket to an Oscar and I am so pleased Lawrence pressed me to look at the script. He was going on about it in Monaco and I didn't think much of it at the time. In truth I hate the work Lawrence does, his films are so gritty and realistic with everyone dying in the end. Miranda's the one pushing me to do it as she reckons it will take something like this to catch the eye of the critics, who love these depressing dark films.'

Zora smiled sweetly. 'You're such a brilliant actor that you will make any film amazing, Dominic. I would love to do what you do; it's so special to be able to take on any role and make it your own. Yesterday I was reading that you have the biggest fan base of any actor.'

She was such a sycophant that Katrina was sure Dominic would see through her flattery. However, he turned his full attention on her, refilling her wine glass.

'Maybe I can get you a part in the film, Zora,' he said. 'I bet you'd look fantastic on screen, and your accent would sound so sexy.'

Zora's eyes lit up. 'Really? Would you really be able to do that? That would be amazing! Did you say Simon Cartilage was directing it? I absolutely love his films, they're so powerful, and the imagery is stunning. Morocco is amazing too.'

Dominic smiled, pleased that he had got her attention, and glanced briefly over at Katrina. 'Yes, of course. I mean, you have dark colouring so you'd fit in nicely. I think that when I go to Morocco I have a girlfriend before I fall in love with the main female role, so perhaps I could mention you for that role. You have had some acting experience, haven't you?'

'Oh yes, I have an agent. I had roles in two small films and I've done lots of television commercials. I would love to be in a film with you! Who's up for the main female role?' Zora had become surprisingly animated and enthusiastic. Katrina looked at James. He did not seem to be interested in the conversation; instead he was looking at his mobile.

'Excuse me a minute, guys, my daughter has just texted me. She's got herself stranded with no money so I'll have to pick her up. I'll be back in an hour.' He picked up his car keys and left.

'Kelsa Sherpa is playing that role,' Dominic continued, and then added, 'I've never seen such a beautiful woman. I usually prefer tanned blondes myself, but she is quite incredible, with that dark skin and those huge brown eyes and incredible lips. And she has a killer body, so I guess I won't have any objections to doing sex scenes with her!' He laughed loudly and filled up his glass again.

Katrina felt depressed and took a large gulp of wine. She contemplated asking if she could go up to bed. But she had not actually been invited to stay the night, so that might seem a little presumptuous. Instead she remained quiet and hoped that James would be quick. Zora and Dominic continued to talk about films until they heard the front door open and James appeared with two teenage girls. One had light brown hair that fell long and straight to the small of her back, and the same blue eyes as James. She was very pretty and wore tight jeans with a red T-shirt. The other had short black hair and a lot of make-up on. She wore a denim miniskirt with knee-high boots, and although she was not as pretty as the first girl, she looked older and far too sexy with her defiant air.

'My God, you are getting them young now!' Dominic said to James as the two teenagers stared at him in absolute fascination.

'Don't be ridiculous!' snapped James, looking annoyed. 'This is my daughter Cassie and her best friend Edwina.'

'I prefer Eddie,' interrupted the defiant-looking one. 'Can I have your autograph?' She handed a receipt to Dominic along with an eyeliner pencil to write with, which he took looking surprised.

'Cassie and Edwina – sorry, I mean Eddie – are going to stay the night, as Cassie's mother is not too pleased that she sneaked out this evening without asking.' Everyone looked at Cassie, who stared sheepishly at the floor before peering up at Dominic under her eyelashes. He grinned at her and she went bright red. James frowned.

'Off to bed, you two, and don't make too much noise,' he ordered.

'Oh Dad, can't we just watch TV for a bit and hang out? We're starving!' Cassie put her arms around James and he rubbed her head affectionately. She grinned mischievously at Edwina. It was odd seeing him as a dad with a daughter only ten years younger than herself and Zora. James reached into a cupboard, pulled out some crisps and chocolate, placed them in Cassie's arms, kissed her on the cheek and pushed her towards the door.

'Off you go, both of you, and tomorrow if I'm feeling nice I'll give you some money to go shopping.' The girls went to leave. Just as she got to the door, Eddie turned to retrieve her receipt that Dominic had scribbled on, and planted a kiss on his cheek before both girls scuttled out giggling. Dominic roared with laughter too.

'She'll be a handful when she's a bit older,' he commented.

'Already is. Both of them are always up to no good,' replied James, looking slightly downcast. Zora got off her stool and stood next to him, her hand on his arm. He quickly moved away and busied himself tidying up. Zora glared at Katrina and sat back down.

'I'm going to bed,' said James. 'I've got a cracking headache and lots to do tomorrow.' He left the kitchen, and after a moment's hesitation Dominic went after him. Katrina and Zora were left alone in silence.

'So you and James are together? That's great,' Katrina said, hoping to soften Zora and bring out the slightly friendlier girl who had emerged at the premiere.

Zora's eyes flashed angrily. 'There's nothing great about it. James has let me stay because I have no money and I need to sleep somewhere. For once I like a guy who is decent, yet he does not want to be with me. He says just friends!' Zora snarled. 'I heard about you and Alex and I see the way you look at James. Alex tells me you are a tease and that you threw yourself on him. Stay away from James or I'll play with Dominic. You have too much to lose, all the fame and jobs because you are with him. He will dump you and then you will be after his friends.' She got up abruptly and left the kitchen.

Katrina was getting used to being accused of all sorts of strange things, but it was starting to get a bit ridiculous. She rested her head on the table and closed her eyes.

'Are you okay?' asked a male voice. It was James, wearing only a pair of jeans and looking concerned. Remembering Zora's warning, Katrina felt uncomfortable alone with him half-dressed and pulled herself together.

'Yes, just a bit tired,' she replied, getting up from the

table and heading towards the door. She could not help asking, 'How about you? You seem a little stressed.'

James leant against the sink. 'I am stressed. Cassie keeps misbehaving and my ex-wife is threatening to move abroad with the kids, and work's a bit tough. It's nothing that won't sort itself out, though.' He smiled gently. 'Thank you for asking. I sense that Zora's not being too welcoming to you. She's only staying for a few days until she sorts things out, so just ignore her. You're very welcome in my house.'

James straightened up and left before she had a chance to tell him that she was grateful for all that he had done to help her and how much she appreciated it. Her heart sank and she had the oddest feeling of being alone and isolated, although she had been surrounded by people ever since she had met Dominic. She could see him through the window in the back garden talking on his mobile, and for the first time her stomach did not flip at the thought of being with him. Dominic was not caring or thoughtful; he did what he wanted to do and she followed because she liked the idea of it all. But the reality of going out with him – well, that was something very different. It was full of hateful men like Alex, angry women like Loretta, jealous girls like Zora, spiteful people like Annabelle, and feeling out of place. Katrina had lost confidence, which was odd. She thought she should be brimming with it seeing as she was getting more modelling jobs and everyone was telling her how great she was. She just never felt right for the places Dominic took her and the people he introduced her to. Yet she still wanted to be with him and still wanted his attention. He was like a drug.

She got up and went up the stairs, looking at the pattern on the carpet as she walked until she bumped into James, who was standing on the landing. She tried to hide her tears but he saw them. He wrapped his arms around her and hugged her against his naked torso without saying a word. Katrina felt immense relief that James understood the loneliness she had been feeling. He was so manly and protective towards her. They heard Dominic come in, and James released her, kissed her on the forehead and went back to his room.

The following morning over breakfast, Dominic surprised everyone by announcing that he had booked all four of them into a hotel in St Tropez for the weekend and that they would be flying by private plane that day, paid for by him. Katrina felt exhausted at the thought of glamorous parties and women in bikinis everywhere, while James looked immensely annoyed.

'I've got work to do and the kids are meant to be staying over,' he stated, throwing dishes into the sink. 'I can't possibly go away. Take someone else instead. How about Alex?' He glared at Dominic challengingly. Katrina had not seen James in such a bad mood before. Zora winced and stared at the floor.

'Yes you are going! It'll be fun. You can take your mobile and make work calls there. I've booked one of those huge suites with three bedrooms, a lounge and a balcony, so it will be great fun. Everybody is going to be in St Trop this weekend for the big parties, and Alex has a house right near the centre so I guess he'll be there already.'

James saw Katrina look up with a fearful expression on her face. 'Oh brilliant!' he said sarcastically. 'All the more reason not to go.'

Katrina sat silently, hoping that James would agree to go with them. Alex would be a bastard, that was for sure, and she doubted Dominic would look out for her. He was reading the newspaper with an expression of intense concentration and not really paying any attention to James.

'Ha, it says in here that Katrina is a well-known model who I met on a *GQ* photoshoot and fell instantly in love with!' He laughed, showing the article to Katrina. 'It says that you're from an ordinary background and I've whisked you off your feet!' He dropped the paper on the table and got up. 'Right then, I take it you are coming, James, so I'll get everything organised.'

Reluctantly James agreed and began to make the necessary work calls to absent himself from meetings that day. Katrina read the newspaper article, shocked to find that the writer had obviously done some research on her. He knew where she had gone to school and how she had got into modelling. What made her laugh out loud was a quote from a girl she had never even spoken to saying how they had been great friends since childhood. There was also a picture from the *GQ* shoot of Dominic and her. It was odd to have people talking about her like she was famous. Zora looked over her shoulder.

'You'll be thinking you're famous too. Just wait until he finds some other girl and you're a nobody again,' she muttered. 'I'm going to pack.' Katrina followed her.

At the top of the stairs Zora turned around.

'Maybe you can make yourself useful this weekend and keep Alex occupied so he leaves me and James alone.' She turned away, stripping off her clothes as she went, exposing her perfect bum and smooth tanned back. As she got to her room she turned back to Katrina. 'I have any man I like, and maybe I will like James or maybe Dominic.' She flashed her a challenging look.

'Wow, nice body.' Dominic appeared at the top of the stairs and leant against the wall, gazing at Zora. He did not look at Katrina, instead narrowing his eyes as he admired the other girl. She was unbelievably beautiful, and Dominic said, 'I must congratulate James for being able to resist you, Zora. You're way out of his league.'

Zora smirked at Katrina, allowing Dominic to absorb the whole of her body and Katrina to see the lust in his eyes, before she turned, disappearing into the bedroom.

Katrina was angry, furious even. Zora was taking it too far with this stupid accusation, and now even threatening her. She had just had to watch Zora flaunting herself in front of Dominic, and even worse, Dominic had fallen for it. She threw clothes into her bag, deliberately choosing the sexiest items. If Zora wanted a war, then she had one. No more soft make-up, jeans and ponytails; she was going to take a leaf out of Zora's book and do the whole tousled hair and pouting lips thing, if that was what it took. She applied dark eyeliner and lashings of mascara before painting her lips pink. Then she pulled on a short black skirt with a push-up bra, a blue vest and a pair of high heels. The trainers could stay at home, she decided, before changing her mind and shoving them in her bag.

From the top of the stairs she saw Zora and Dominic sitting together in the lounge rather too close for comfort and she paused to check her own reflection in a mirror. She wanted to put her jeans back on.

'Dad, can't we please stay here while you're away? Please, pleasssssssse,' Cassie asked James. Katrina stepped back up the stairs out of sight. 'We'll be good, and Mum doesn't have to know. Purlease.'

'I have said no, Cassie, and that is that. Please do stop going on. I've ordered you a taxi to take you back to Mum's, and I'll give you some pocket money. Are you ready to go?'

Cassie's face dropped in disappointment. 'You're so horrible! What difference does it make to you if we stay for the weekend? You're bloody well off on holiday again and you don't care about me. I hate you! I hope Mum does move miles away so I never have to see you again!'

She made to push past James but he grabbed her shoulder. 'Don't use that kind of language, Cassie, and don't be so rude.' He forced her to look up at him. 'I'm only going away for a couple of days and I don't want to have to worry about you, darling. Please be good and go home. I will dedicate next weekend to you, I promise.'

Cassie looked up at him furiously before stomping out of the front door towards the waiting car.

'I love you. I'll ring you later,' James called after her. She did not answer and the car pulled away, disappearing into the traffic. James stood at the door for a while staring after it, looking sad.

Katrina remembered that she hadn't called her own father despite her mother telling her to. She wondered if maybe she should make more of an effort with him and try to understand his position. After all, relationships and people's feelings weren't always as clear-cut as she had once thought they were, and perhaps she had made things rather difficult for her father with her lack of communication and her resentfulness. She would call him when she got back from St Tropez and arrange to meet up.

She walked down the stairs and James turned at the sound. He looked a little surprised at her make-up and hair. When they entered the lounge, Zora looked furious, as she too was wearing heels and a skirt. She had obviously been expecting Katrina to be in her usual jeans. Dominic whistled.

'Hello, you! Did someone kidnap Katrina and replace her with this sex goddess?' He got to his feet and walked around her admiringly. 'Perhaps I should postpone the flight and take you upstairs.'

Zora glared at Katrina, who merely raised her eyebrows challengingly. She was getting sick of being nice and soft. It didn't work in Dominic's world, which seemed characterised by jealousy and nastiness.

In the plane, Dominic kept whispering in Katrina's ear about how much he fancied her, and what he was going to do to her when they got to the hotel. He was being incredibly charming and looked exceptionally handsome, eyes cobalt blue as the sun glinted off his face. Katrina bathed in the warmth of his attention, knowing it wouldn't last long when other people were around.

Zora told James about the many times she had been to St Tropez and he listened politely. It was obvious he was not interested. Katrina thought that Zora had been stupid, because if she had kept her on side instead of threatening her, then she would have helped by telling Zora how to interest James, and it was not by talking about all her trips with other rich men.

James told Katrina that August was the fashionable time to go to St Tropez to party, at which point he rolled his eyes, making her laugh. Zora's eyes grew dark and she sat silently until they landed, when she pulled out a compact and repaired her make-up.

A dark-haired Frenchman was waiting for them with the keys to a four-seater Ferrari. He smiled admiringly at Zora before handing the keys to Dominic.

'Sir, this is your hire car.' He stepped back to let Dominic look at the Ferrari.

'I asked for black, not red. So crass!' was all Dominic

said as he handed his bag to the man. He got in the driver's seat and turned on the engine with a roar. Zora too gave her bag to the man, who seemed a little taken aback.

'Excuse me, I don't know what you expect me to do with the bags,' he said. 'I do not work for a travel company, I just drop off the car.'

Dominic glared at him. 'Well, I'm hardly going to fit them in the boot, am I now? Just make sure they're dropped off at my hotel right away.' He waved irritably at Katrina to get in next to Zora, and James was left apologising to the man before getting in too. Dominic spun the car around and sped off.

By the time they reached the hotel, after Dominic had insisted on driving around the town with the roof down and music blaring, the man had already dropped off their bags. Whilst Dominic and James went to look around, Zora emptied her bags in the middle of the lounge and began sorting through an expanse of outfits. Katrina went into the room she was sharing with Dominic and put her stuff in the corner. When she came back out Zora was reading a piece of paper and laughing.

'What's so funny?' she asked curiously.

'The car man has left me a note in my bag saying that my boyfriend is an arsehole and I should call him.' She showed Katrina the hand-written note with a telephone number on it. 'I think he thought I was with Dominic. The way things are going with James, I may well call him. He was very good looking, no?' She looked up questioningly at Katrina, who was surprised that Zora was being friendly.

'Yes, he was good looking. Maybe you *should* call him,' she replied tentatively.

'Beetch,' came the response, though strangely without any venom. 'You would do anything to get rid of me, have me go out with some other man so you can have James and Dominic to yourself, but it won't work.' She pulled a tiny black dress out of her bag and hung it up. 'This is what I will wear tonight,' she announced dramatically, and went out on to the balcony overlooking the pool.

All the glamorous people by the pool looked up at her, and as if giving them a show, she pulled off her top and then let her skirt fall to the ground, revealing only a tiny red G-string. Still in heels, she sat on a chair with her legs dangling over the railings, staring back at all the envious female eyes and smiling at the admiring men. Katrina laughed quietly to herself. Zora was certainly entertaining, and she couldn't help admiring her brutal honesty and lack of shame.

Dominic and James came in.

'Nice show, Zora!' Dominic called. 'Very hot!' Zora leaned back on her chair to smile at him and he blew her a kiss.

Katrina bit her lip. If Dominic wanted overly sexy and confident, then she was quite capable of that. She went into the bedroom to consider her options. She really wasn't up for stripping naked on the balcony and sitting next to the perfectly tanned Zora. She rummaged through her bag and picked out her bikini, which looked plain and boring. It just wouldn't do. Dominic peered around the door.

'I'm going with James and Zora to sit by the pool, have a drink and see who is staying here. Come and join us when you are ready.' Katrina nodded in response. He left without asking if she wanted him to wait for her. She felt so lonely, and picked up the phone to call Helen, telling her all that happened over the last week.

'Christ, you have got yourself into a fine scrape! This is so crazy,' Helen spluttered through the gasps of shock and hysterical laughter. 'I so wish I was there.'

'Me too,' said Katrina. 'I feel awful and I need help. What shall I do?'

Helen was a loyal friend and a good thinker. After a moment she announced, 'What you are going to do is be the old Katrina who wasn't intimidated by anyone, who is clever and fun and beautiful. Stop feeling inadequate because you are there with a famous actor. Just remember, he has taken you away with him, his best mate fancies you and all the other women are jealous of you. Play up to it. Don't let them win by scaring you away; make them jealous, have all the men looking at you and enjoy it! You can compete with all those empty-headed bimbos because you've got a brain. Now bloody well use it and play the conniving seductress, if that is what they all think you are. Go find a shop, buy a fab bikini and prance on down eighties style in a pair of heels to the pool, looking like a goddess, sunglasses on and hair big! You're my best mate and I don't want you letting me down. Go work it!'

After talking to Helen, Katrina felt very positive. She pulled on her jeans and sprinted in her trainers to the hotel shop, which unlike most hotel shops was full of designer clothes for all the rich women who stayed there. She found a bright blue bikini for a horrifying two hundred euros and slunk back to the room with it. She put it on and padded the cups with foam fillers, then slapped on extra make-up and a pair of heels. Glancing in the mirror, she thought she looked as if she was about to step on set for a photoshoot, which was ridiculous given that she was just going to sit by the pool. It wasn't her, and what was the point of pretending to be something she wasn't? She quickly took off the majority of the make-up.

It was scorching hot, yet Katrina noticed that no one was in the pool. All the women stayed on loungers, protecting their make-up and hair. It struck her as absurd, and in defiance she kicked off the stupid heels and got on the diving board, not caring that everyone was watching her. It was like being in some sort of competition; there was silence as everyone stared at her, almost in horror that someone was actually going to get wet. She felt a bubble of laughter rise in her throat and began to make a performance out of it, shaking back her long hair and tying it up off her neck, removing her sunglasses and tossing them carelessly on the floor. She dived perfectly, all that training for the school swimming team finally paying off, breaking the surface of the water and not caring about her hair or make-up or about looking poised.

As she surfaced at the far end of the pool, she looked up to find a sandy-haired man smiling down at her.

'Beautiful,' he said, not making it clear whether he was complimenting her, the dive or the pool. He bent down. 'Casper.'

Just as she was about to introduce herself, an arm slipped around her waist and she was pulled into a kiss. Dominic stopped momentarily to look up at the man.

'Fuck off, she's with me,' he said gruffly, and returned to kissing her. When he had finished, she looked up at him in surprise. 'You looked gorgeous on that board. Everyone was watching you, wondering who you were. What an entrance! I thought Zora had surpassed all entrances today.' He kissed her again, running his hand over a padded boob.

They got out of the pool watched by a hundred pairs of eyes hidden by designer glasses. Dominic led her to the loungers, where James and Zora were lying, much to her horror, alongside Loretta and a young man who was introduced as her boyfriend. If looks could kill, Katrina would have crumpled under Zora's furious glare, particularly when James commented on her performance.

'Very nice, where did you learn to dive like that?' He was reading a book, and looking up was unable to hide his admiration of Katrina's athletic body in the blue bikini. Almost immediately Zora stood up topless and did a pretend stretch so that all eyes were drawn to her chest. She went to walk towards the pool, then stopped, limping.

'I think I have a thorn in my foot,' she complained, sitting on the edge of Dominic's lounger, her tanned skin touching him and her breast near his arm. 'Have a look,' she purred, leaning even closer to him so that she was pressing her near naked body into his. Dominic examined her foot and unsurprisingly found nothing. 'Oh well, thank you for looking.' She got up, deliberately brushing her breasts against his chest as she turned to smile up at him. It was impossible for him to hide the bulge in his tight Armani swimming trunks. With a glance so brief that Katrina only just saw it, Zora looked down at his crotch and then up again pointedly with a suggestive raise of her eyebrow. Dominic watched her slide into the pool before sitting back down. Loretta stared at Dominic, James was looking at Katrina and Katrina looked at her feet.

There was a very long silence before a waiter approached them to take a drinks order. Katrina felt like she was losing control again. She recalled Helen's words and undid her ponytail, shaking her hair loose, then applied lip gloss. She couldn't go topless as her boobs weren't as big and magnificent as Zora's, so she was at a loss as to what to do. Dominic was still watching Zora swimming lengths. Katrina was sick of all the game-playing and preening; it was utterly exhausting and it was pointless.

'Where are you going, baby?' drawled Dominic lazily as she walked by.

'For a walk,' was all she offered as she strode by, aware of eyes upon her. Dominic hesitated for a moment, then leapt off the lounger and caught up with her. As they got around the corner he took her hand and rubbed it on his crotch.

'Look what you've done to me.'

'I think you have me confused with Zora, don't you?' She pulled her hand away.

Dominic laughed. 'Oh, someone's jealous, are they? You don't need to be. Okay, I get a hard-on because some girl rubs her breasts on me. I'm a man. I'm hardly going to just ignore that, especially when they are fantastic breasts. That doesn't mean I fancy her.' They got to the door of the room, which Katrina opened. 'Come on, don't be a bitch!' Dominic pulled the strings on the bikini so that the pads fell out of the top. He looked at them, confused, before grasping her wrist, forcing her to drop her sunglasses. He tried to kiss her but she moved her head away. He was silent for a moment, just staring at her, before he dropped her wrist and turned away. He went on to the balcony and slumped down on a chair, lighting a cigarette. Looking over his shoulder, he noticed that Katrina was pulling on a pair of jeans, and then a moment later the door shut behind her.

'Stupid bitch!' he told himself. He felt more annoyed than usual. He leaned over the railing and saw Zora looking up at him. James had gone and she waved him down. He ignored her and turned to light another cigarette, inhaling the smoke deep into his lungs.

'God, I wish you would just get off my mind,' he said aloud, thinking about Katrina.

'I'll get off your mind if you'll just let me get on something else,' came the reply, and turning round he found Zora, still only wearing her bikini bottoms, her skin shiny from sun cream and her eyes dark with smudged mascara. She walked slowly towards him. 'Your girlfriend has just gone for a nice long walk with James and left us all alone. What shall we do with ourselves?' She undid the string on the bikini bottoms so that they fell to the ground.

Dominic got up and went towards her. 'Your being naked all the time is beginning to bore me, Zora.' She pouted sulkily. 'What do you mean, they've gone for a walk?'

'I think you've noticed as much as I have how well they get on together; all those secret glances and chats about books. Katrina seems more interested in your friend than in you. They suit each other, both boring and serious.' Zora curled her naked body around him, pressing her mouth to his ear. 'Come on, Dominic, we both know how much you want to screw me. You've wanted to since the moment you saw me.' She ran her hand down the front of his trunks.

'What the hell!' He pushed her away and she fell back on the sofa. He ran his hand through his hair, confused. 'Why would Katrina have any interest in James? It makes no sense!' Zora got up and approached him again. This time he allowed her to press against him, her lips touching his until he stopped caring and let his body take over. He kissed her hard and pushed her against the wall. Just as she reached to remove his trunks, he stopped and walked into the bedroom. She followed.

'I was quite happy to be against the wall, but if you prefer the bed ...' She dropped on to it, looking ravishing, with a sly smile. 'If we take long enough they'll walk in on us and that will save us having to tell them.' He was pulling on a T-shirt and jeans. 'Why are you getting dressed?' Zora leapt up indignantly. 'I am lying here waiting for you and you're getting dressed! What's your fucking problem?'

Dominic pushed past her out of the door. She followed him outside, still completely naked. 'Where the hell are you going? Come back!' she screamed, causing passers-by to stare at her. Dominic ignored her and began walking down the driveway away from the hotel. He pulled his phone from his pocket, flicking through to find Katrina's number. As he was about to call it, he saw her sitting on the grass with her back to him. He made his way over and sat down next to her without saying a word. It was not his style at all to sit on grass for no reason, and he fidgeted for a while before she lifted her head to look at him.

'Where's James?' he asked. 'Zora said you'd gone walking together.'

Katrina shook her head. 'I haven't seen him,' she replied, wondering why Zora would have said such a thing. Then the realisation hit her. She wondered if Zora's plan had worked. She had only been gone for about twenty minutes, so it must have been quick sex for Dominic to have got dressed and come to find her. Katrina glanced up at him.

'Zora just threw all her clothes off, not that she was wearing much in the first place, and leapt on me, so I guess she is not as obsessed with James as she had us think,' Dominic commented. 'I hope you don't count her as a friend, darling, as she literally tried to rape me in there.' He leant over to touch Katrina's face. She flinched. 'What? Oh, don't be stupid, I didn't do anything. I pushed her away.'

Katrina had to admit she was surprised. She had thought that if Zora offered it up to Dominic he would have just taken it and then cast her aside. She got the impression he was trying to say that it was because of her that he had pushed Zora away, and that that was why he was here now.

'I like you being around, English girl,' he said. She looked at his ridiculously perfect face and traced his lips with her finger. He smiled, revealing his dazzling teeth, and they lay down next to each other looking up at the sky. It had to be the most normal five minutes Katrina had spent with him.

'Let's go out, just you and me tonight.' Dominic kissed her wrist and then circled her finger with his tongue. 'I'll book a restaurant and we can have some privacy.' He got to his feet and helped her up. Katrina realised that it would actually be their first proper date, just the two of them face to face with no distractions. Maybe she would finally get to find out a bit about him and what lay beneath that perfect image.

34

They headed back to the suite, where they found Zora watching Fashion TV with a thunderous expression and James making work calls on the balcony. They both looked disappointed when Dominic said that he was taking Katrina out alone.

Katrina showered and washed her hair in the lovely mosaic-tiled bathroom, then looked at the array of clothes she had brought: the Von Furstenberg wrap dress, the leather skirt, the beaded jeans. Instead she chose her old denim skirt and vest, and added skyscraper Jimmy Choos to please Dominic.

Dominic was lying on the bed totally naked when she came out, bronzed already from one day in the sun. He got up and ran his hands over her legs as if she were a racehorse.

'You know what? The more I see you, the sexier you become, which is odd, as you weren't at all sexy when I met you.' He pulled off her vest and gazed at her before lifting her up so her legs were around his waist. He kissed her so hard his stubble hurt and she pulled away. Lying on the bed together, he ran his tongue over her entire body until she was squirming with delight.

The sex was slow and surprisingly gentle. Dominic took the time to explore her body, and afterwards he traced his fingers over her back.

'You're mine, barely touched, unlike the Zoras and Laurens. Who would have thought it? I saw through the cheap clothes and the awkwardness to how lovely you could be.' He leant over to get his cigarettes and lit one before leaning back and inhaling the smoke deeply. 'I bet you never imagined something like this happening to you. This must be beyond your wildest dreams. How do you feel when you're with me?' He didn't wait for an answer, instead kissing her and running his thumb over her lower lip.

Although Katrina was slightly annoyed by his comments, she couldn't be bothered to react. Dominic was Dominic and his insensitivity was nothing personal; he just wasn't a very considerate person. Nobody ever pulled him up on anything; they were all too busy fawning and adoring him for their own selfish reasons. People like Alex, Miranda and Annabelle were just out for what they could get from him, and Katrina guessed that the actual reason Dominic liked her was because she didn't have the pretentiousness, falsity or bitterness that dominated his world. That was the same reason he was friends with James when actually they didn't have a great deal in common.

Dominic got dressed and she put her clothes back on. They arrived late at the restaurant and were shown to a table in the centre of the room. The waiter was hopeful that Dominic's presence would make other people want to be there. Katrina was surprised when Dominic refused to take it, asking for a table in the corner.

'I actually just want to talk to you tonight, so let's hide. Maybe no one will recognise me.' Dominic ordered vintage Dom Perignon. The restaurant was intimate, with flickering candles, shadows and mellow music. It was romantic, full of couples who had been gazing across at one another. But they were now looking over at Dominic and whispering animatedly. A camera flash went off.

Dominic leant back in his chair and looked amusedly at Katrina. 'So here we are,' he commented. 'What do you think?'

'Well, it's nice, a bit dark but nice.' Katrina sipped from her glass of Dom Perignon.

'No, silly, I don't mean the restaurant. I mean, what do you think about all of this: St Tropez, me, the past few weeks? You never really say much. By the way, the spinach salad is good; you should have that.' He beckoned the waiter and ordered for both of them, then nodded at someone he knew across the room before turning his attention back to Katrina. 'Is this how you dreamt it would be? The whole thing of dating a movie star, going to premieres, staying in flash hotels?' His face was intense before it cracked into laughter. 'Seriously, let's talk about something that interests you. Fashion, perhaps? Who's your favourite designer?'

'I've got a few, but I guess John Galliano and Alexander McQueen,' replied Katrina, nibbling on a piece of bread, nervous that he might tell her not to eat it in case she put on weight.

'I know John, he made me an amazing suit.' With that Dominic launched into a story about designers he knew and fashion parties he had attended. Katrina half listened while her mind was elsewhere. She watched his mouth as he spoke; it was so perfect, and his teeth gleamed when he laughed. His tanned skin contrasted with his white Gucci shirt, making him even more physically irresistible. He was too handsome, and almost too unreal. A flaw would have made him more interesting and given his looks some depth. She might as well have been having dinner with a stranger, because she still knew very little about him. What he told her was stuff that she could have found out on fan sites. She wanted him to talk about things that mattered to him, that would make him more likeable, yet he didn't. He only spoke about films, parties and other famous people, the world that so many seemed desperate to be a part of. The word shallow came to mind. Katrina dismissed it and tried to concentrate on what he was saying.

Dominic moved from designers to talking about top hotels as he ate. Katrina nibbled on the rather tasteless spinach salad. It was the only time they had gone out alone and the conversation was very one-sided, with a number of long pauses as they ate. As he finished his main course, Dominic was asked to have his photograph taken with an Australian couple, who told him gleefully that they were on their honeymoon. He was extra nice to them and asked the waiter to take a picture of all of them together.

'Oh, wow! He is even better looking in the flesh!' gushed the woman, clutching Katrina's arm. 'I've never seen such a handsome man! What a lucky girl you are, although my Luke isn't too hard on the eye!' She turned to Dominic. 'I saw you two looking so great in my *Hot Gossip* mag and I said then you made a lovely couple, didn't I, Luke? Are you going to get married?'

Dominic laughed and handed them his autograph. 'You never know what might happen.' He drew Katrina towards him. 'Anyway, it was nice meeting you. Have a great holiday.'

The couple continued to linger, however, ordering another drink and waving at Dominic and Katrina if they looked up. Another couple began to prowl, building up the nerve to approach.

'Bill, please,' ordered Dominic as the waiter passed. 'It's looking like the end of our peaceful night.' His mood seemed to lift, though, as a couple of girls walked by whispering and pointing.

Katrina realised then that he lived for the attention and drama that his fame brought. If he wasn't at some party or event then he had to talk about that kind of stuff. She felt disappointed, slightly hollow at the thought that Dominic's whole image was just that, an image, and the real person was absent. She really liked him during the times when he softened and did something unexpected, like hug her or give a private grin. The bit that bothered her was knowing that part of the reason she was with him was because of who he was. She was drawn to the whole excitement of having a famous boyfriend and having people think it was amazing. If it ended, all her friends and the agencies would be so disappointed, Rosanna would be furious; perhaps she would lose her modelling contract. Then she would go back to being just Katrina. And not to forget the fact that he was just so damn good looking!

'Katrina.' Dominic disturbed her reverie. 'I've been thinking about things. You know, the new film isn't going to start shooting for at least two months whilst Lawrence sorts out the crew, so I'll be heading back to LA for a while. There are a few things I need to do over there and that means I'm not gonna be in London for much longer.' He leant forward and smiled gently.

Katrina's heart stopped beating for a second. He was going to tell her it was all over; any doubts she had were irrelevant, as he was making the decision.

'So anyway, what I thought was that you should come with me.' Katrina looked confused, so Dominic elaborated. 'You should come to LA and live at my place for a few weeks. You can do some modelling over there; you're bound to get some work as you're my girlfriend. You'll love it!'

Katrina sat in stunned silence. Going to stay in LA with Dominic? She had gone from thinking that meeting him was just a wild dream to moving into his house! He was probably right that she'd get some work out there too. She batted the negative thoughts from her mind. There was absolutely no reason not to go.

'Okay, if you're sure you want me to,' Katrina replied.

Dominic grinned. 'Of course I'm sure. It'll be great. I've got people milling round my pad all the time: cleaners, stylists, PRs and friends popping in. You won't disturb me and you're not a diva who's going to annoy me with outbursts and drama all the time.' He glanced up and noticed that a friend of his had walked in. 'Marcus!'

Katrina saw an extremely tall man with shoulder-length blond hair and an angular face look round and smile in recognition. Within seconds Dominic and Marcus had sat down and ordered drinks. Katrina was next to Gina, Marcus's girlfriend, who immediately started prattling on about the beauty treatments at the hotel she was staying at.

'So I wanted to get a facial but they don't do the ones I want, which is an ultra-rich moisturising treatment. And I desperately need to get my nails done and my eyelashes tinted but they're booked up until Monday! Can you believe that?' Gina flicked her blond hair over her shoulder and revealed her cosmetically perfect teeth as she grimaced. 'In LA I have a facial every other day, and I've gone for fours days now without one. It's crazy!'

Katrina smiled sympathetically.

'I'm so bored, too. I have bought just about everything there is to buy and read every magazine there is to read and there is absolutely nothing else to do. Marcus loves it out here, with all the parties. For us girlies, well, it's so exhausting having to find different outfits.' Gina pouted and fluttered her eyelashes at Marcus. 'You just don't understand, do you?' Marcus ignored her and continued talking to Dominic.

'There must be some nice places to visit just outside of St Tropez? A friend told me about a really beautiful monastery on top of a mountain which is only an hour or so away,' Katrina said.

Gina looked at her as if she was mad. 'Why would anyone want to look at a monastery? I reckon maybe getting the helicopter to Monaco for lunch or something would be fun. Hey! Why don't we all do that on Sunday or something? Marcus, don't you think that's a good idea?'

Marcus, who wasn't really listening, waved his hand at her to shut up. Katrina eavesdropped on the men's conversation as Gina told her about a dress she had bought. Dominic was talking to Marcus about setting up a production company and having a meeting with financiers when they got to LA. It was quite obvious that they thought business shouldn't be discussed with the girls, who would just talk about clothes and make-up. But Katrina would have preferred to learn a bit about how production companies worked rather than listen to Gina going on about the latest Dior collection.

After an hour of Katrina being bored to near death, Dominic turned his attention back to her.

'Ready to go?' he asked, standing up. He turned back to Marcus. 'Let's get together and start working on a business plan. The girls can go shopping or something next week and we'll meet up.' Plans were made for the meeting.

'If you don't know LA very well, I'll book you in to get your nails and hair done where I get mine done. We can have a lovely day being pampered while the boys talk about how to make even more money.' Gina giggled. 'She'll love that place we went for lunch last week, won't she, Marcus?' He looked at her blankly. She was quite sweet, harmless, but Marcus was dismissive of her, ignoring everything she said. They left with air kisses and promises of dinner.

'Sorry to have bored you with business talk back there. I had to speak to Marcus about it before next week,' Dominic said on the way back to the hotel, as he expertly manoeuvred the Ferrari through the narrow streets.

'I like hearing about business, it's interesting,' Katrina replied.

Dominic laughed. 'Thank you for being so sweet, but I am sure you're not really interested. Setting up companies worth millions of dollars is a long way from walking down a catwalk.' With that he turned up the music and concentrated on driving.

When they got back to the hotel, James was sitting watching Sky News, with Zora doing sit-ups on the floor in hotpants and a bra.

'Good time?' he asked.

Katrina nodded. 'Yes, it was a nice restaurant. What did you do?'

'We just popped out to a little place round the corner. Zora wasn't very impressed, were you?' Zora screwed her nose up. 'Cheap and cheerful, no champagne or caviar for us. Have you seen this, Dominic? That Better World Trust charity has been exposed for fraud; apparently most of the money donated went to making a better world for the director, Atnam Fuller, who now has a luxury mansion and a private jet.' James tossed the *New York Times* over to Dominic, who looked at it, his face darkening as he read. 'According to that article, Atnam went out of his way to befriend celebrities, as he knew that if they lent their image to the organisation, everyone would think it was credible and it would become trendy to sign up. Quite clever, really. He's run off with about thirty-five million dollars.'

Dominic threw down the paper and picked up his mobile. 'Miranda, I take it you know about Better World? Well, it says here that because of the celebrities endorsing the charity, millions of ordinary people gave money to it and the celebrities are to blame for not checking it properly and seeing where the money was going. So much for charity work when it was all fake. You need to find a way of getting my name out of it; say that they didn't have my consent or something.' Dominic left the room to stand outside on the balcony.

'I thought it sounded a bit suspicious at the time. It just goes to show that as long as you package something well and make it sound good, people will fall for it without looking beyond the surface.' James yawned. 'Katrina, there's a documentary on in a minute that you might find interesting. Sit down. I'll enjoy the intelligent company.'

As usual, Dominic was on his mobile on the balcony, and Zora went to wash her hair. Katrina and James were so deep in conversation, it wasn't until Dominic interrupted them that she realised they had been sitting on the sofa for two hours.

35

The next day was spent beside the pool once more. Dominic had invited a number of friends to join them and they all drank champagne, ate exotic fruit from platters and talked loudly about people they knew. Nobody spoke to Katrina, and James was not around. Zora was pointedly wearing one of Dominic's T-shirts over her bikini, which struck Katrina as odd.

'We've got to be at the Rhol villa at ten-ish for a party,' Dominic said to James, who finally appeared after lunch looking fraught. Dominic looked briefly at Zora. 'Why are you wearing my fucking T-shirt? Take it off!' Zora dropped her cigarette in a glass of champagne, leapt to her feet and stormed off. Dominic laughed.

'Oh my God, that girl! She could be a fabulous actress. I really don't know why she is wasting her talents on us.'

'You can be such a bastard, Dominic!' James got up, throwing down his newspaper, and went after Zora. Katrina felt a pang of jealousy at the thought of him taking Zora in his arms like he'd done with her the other night. She wished he had stayed to chat to her. Instead she sat silently with all the sunglassed, designer-bikinied, perfect-looking people who surrounded Dominic.

Later on, Katrina showered and got ready, pulling on skinny jeans and a white vest. She didn't want to compete with Zora that night, and if it was a party in the grounds of a villa she couldn't see everyone getting too dressed up. Dominic was wearing jeans too and a designer T-shirt that despite being brand new had been ripped and torn purposefully to look retro. He was drinking straight vodka and talking on his mobile about a new car he had ordered back in LA. She watched him prowling the balcony holding the glass, looking like some sort of mythological god.

A knock at the door broke her reverie, and she opened it to find Alex with a small curvy girl who appeared to have dyed her head bright red. He pushed past her.

'Hello, everyone!' he boomed. James came out of his room. 'James, how you doing?' Alex went forward to hug him. James pushed him away.

'Fuck off, Alex. I'm not a friend, so don't kid yourself I am.'

'Whoa! What's that all about?' Alex stood with his arms held out in a gesture of confusion, to which James did not react. After a moment he dropped them. 'Chill out!' He grinned widely.

'Katrina was forced to fly home from LA alone in the middle of the night because you attacked her. I am not going to chill out about something like that.' James looked furious, his fists clenched.

'Hang on a minute. Is that what she told you? Let me put the record straight. I'm sure Katrina meant no harm and just got a bit confused. The truth is we both got a bit drunk and ended up alone together. One thing led to another and then Dom walked in and was pissed off at Katrina, so kicked her out. Just a misunderstanding, and if Dom can forgive and forget, I'm sure you can.'

James was clearly restraining himself and his voice was low and dangerous. 'I am sick of your shit. I don't know why Dominic lets you hang off him, but I'm warning you, don't annoy me again, because I swear I will make you sorry. Leave Katrina alone and keep your lies to yourself!'

Alex stood without saying a word until he saw that Katrina was still standing by the door, staring at James. A slow smile came across his face. 'Oh, I see what's going on. Katrina's playing her games with you too, James. I understand. Okay, I'll back off, but Dominic wants me around tonight. He needs someone looking out for him.'

At that moment Dominic walked in.

'Hey.' He hugged Alex. 'How's it been going?'

James went to the drinks cabinet, where he poured himself a large Scotch, not bothering to ask anyone else if they wanted a drink. Katrina slunk into her bedroom and sat on the bed, trying to work out if she should be annoyed or not that Dominic behaved as if nothing had happened with Alex. For some reason she didn't really care. She was more touched that James had seemed so angry with him. She heard Zora's voice in the lounge sounding strained, and peering round the corner saw her sitting on the edge of a chair opposite Alex, who was on the sofa with his arm around the redhead.

'I heard that was the new thing,' he said, pointing to the dyed hair. 'Redheads are in so I thought I'd better get myself one. The only problem is, I could only find blondes in LA; real redheads seem to be a rare commodity.'

Dominic shook his head in an amused fashion at Alex and handed him a glass of champagne.

'I dyed my hair just for Al,' cooed the girl, applying lip gloss and fluttering her eyelashes at Dominic. 'By the way, I'm Paisley.' She held out a limp hand, which Dominic looked at blankly while lighting a cigarette in a slow, meticulous manner, eyes narrowed against the smoke.

'Paisley? Like the pattern?' he drawled. 'Alex, where

do you get these girls from?' Paisley giggled, mistaking it for a compliment. Alex frowned momentarily before smirking as he turned his attention to Zora.

'So, Zora, how's it going with James? Managed to get into Mr Righteous's pants? Not really sure why you're bothering; he isn't nearly as rich as you normally like them.'

Zora looked stonily at the glass of champagne that Dominic handed her before taking a large gulp. 'Things are just fine,' she snapped.

Alex raised an eyebrow and looked up at Dominic. 'Is that true?' he asked.

'Yeah, everything's great, particularly the bit where Zora threw off all her clothes and begged me to screw her. There is also the little fact that James has no interest in her whatsoever.' Dominic mocked Zora's voice perfectly. 'Fuck me, Dominic, I've always wanted you and I know you want me.' He returned to his own voice. 'Poor Zora is running out of people to screw.' Alex and Paisley laughed loudly. Katrina saw Zora struggle to maintain her composure for a moment before sipping her champagne slowly and studying her nails.

'What did Katrina have to say about that?' asked Alex. 'She won't be happy to know she has serious competition in the attention stakes.'

Dominic didn't answer. Katrina backed into the bedroom. She was feeling utterly exhausted, and the night had not even really begun yet. She applied more make-up, sprayed on perfume and cleaned her teeth again, trying to waste time before having to step into the hostile lounge with Zora sulking, James angry, Alex smug and the stupid Paisley giggling.

'Katrina, we're going,' Dominic called, and she was forced to come out. Alex winked at her as they walked out and got into the car that was taking them to the party. He slid in next to her. Katrina moved away against the door but he pushed himself closer to her.

'You haven't told me how you are.' He looked at her closely. 'Still having fun with Dominic?' Katrina ignored him, and irritated, he slumped back in the seat, taking a vial of coke from his breast pocket and snorting deeply. Paisley did the same then passed it to Zora, who after a moment's hesitation also snorted it and passed it over to Dominic. James looked across at Katrina with a blank expression. They sat in silence for the entire car journey, with Dominic texting and Paisley sniffing intermittently.

B y the time the car pulled to a halt outside an impressive stone villa, everyone seemed to have brightened up, either because they had arrived at a party or more likely because of the coke. Alex, taking Paisley's hand, disappeared almost immediately through the opened door, where people spilled out holding glasses of champagne and talking in loud, obnoxious voices. Katrina saw Zora reach across for James's hand, and to her surprise he did not pull away; instead he put his arm around her and they walked slowly in, with her gazing adoringly up at him.

'Looks like Zora's succeeded in her mission.' Dominic smirked. 'Poor James! If only he knew that it was because I rejected her.'

That was that, then, Katrina thought, James was succumbing to Zora. She hadn't expected it from him. She told herself that she only felt bad because James was too nice for her. Dominic walked ahead, and when he got to the door everyone turned to acknowledge him, stopping him to say hello, desperate to get his attention.

The centre of the villa consisted of a gigantic stone staircase curving around into a large balcony. Women in expensive designer dresses and men more casually dressed in designer jeans and shirts overlooked more people on the ground level drinking and dancing. Music boomed through sets of speakers in the corners and laughter rang through the building. A man of about fifty, wearing a bright Cavalli kaftan and tight black swimming trunks, was dancing wildly in the middle of a crowd of young girls, who were screaming in delight. Waiters holding trays of drinks dodged flailing arms, stepping neatly in and out of groups, offering cocktails and champagne in heavy crystal glasses. The room opened up into a spacious lounge that in turn led out to a patio, upon which fire-eaters and jugglers performed a show that nobody watched. They were too busy looking at each other, sizing up wealth and beauty.

Katrina was captivated by the fire-eaters and stood alone watching while Dominic disappeared into a crowd of females. He was gone for ages and Katrina had to fend off several middle-aged, overweight men who lurched over to offer champagne or cocaine. She saw Zora and James walking past into the garden together, James still with his arm around her. He looked muscular and manly in a plain black T-shirt and jeans, compared to all the unfit men in their designer shirts with trendy hair and fake tans. Zora kept looking up at him, her face gentle with happiness. It struck Katrina that Dominic never made her feel happy; excited maybe, intimidated yes, but not happy. She was quite stunned by this sudden revelation, as she had never thought about something as simple as happiness. After all, being with Dominic was everything any girl could want, wasn't it? It was the dream that she had coveted, the perfect image.

James and Zora disappeared around a corner and Katrina turned away.

Dominic was standing next to her, silent and watchful. She jumped.

'Hi, I didn't hear you come up.'

'I guessed that,' he replied. 'Why are you standing here alone looking at James and Zora?' His eyes were like dark shadows and she couldn't see his expression. He sounded angry.

'I was watching the fire-eaters and then I just looked round and saw them. I was wondering where they were going,' she replied feebly.

He stepped forward into the light and she saw that actually he didn't look angry; instead he seemed a little confused.

'Katrina, I don't know how I find myself asking this, but I'm going to.' Dominic paused, resting his dark eyes on her for a moment. 'Do you like James? I mean, I keep finding you chatting with him, you called him when you walked out on me in LA, and I always see you looking at him.'

Shocked, Katrina looked up at him and found that she was unable to answer. She hadn't really thought about it. How could she like James when she was with Dominic? What girl would be distracted by any other guy when she was with someone like him? Dominic shook his head in amazement.

'I'll take that as a yes. Zora and Alex did warn me. What I don't understand is why. I'm offering you everything that any girl could ever dream of. I've taken you away with me, bought you clothes, jewellery, taken you to a premiere as my date, the best parties. I even went so far as to turn up on your doorstep. Before I met you, I had whoever I wanted and I didn't have to do a thing. I've known far more beautiful girls than you, girls who are better in bed, girls who entertain me more.' He paused to look at her thoughtfully. 'The most annoying thing about all of this is that I still actually really like you and I just don't understand why you would prefer James. I mean, he's a nice guy and everything, but . . . he's so ordinary and I'm so . . .' He lapsed into a dramatic silence and together they watched the fire-eaters perform. He spoke again. 'I like you, really like you, and I have never been in a position of questioning whether a girl likes me or not. It's crazy.' He kicked the ground in frustration with his suede Gucci loafer.

Katrina knew that for the first time she was in the position of power, and what a position it was. Dominic Cayley was telling her that he had feelings for her, that she meant something to him, and all she had to do was say she felt the same. Then she would truly be in the most perfect relationship in the world, a proper relationship, and who knows, he might really fall in love with her. It would be happily ever after, just like the dream.

'Katrina, I think you're just a bit confused, and I guess this whole situation must have been pretty weird for you. I don't really think you actually have feelings for James; it's just he is the only normal, unintimidating one out of all of us. I should have understood how difficult bringing you into my world was going to be. I know you feel that I'm going to get bored of you and move on. What you need to understand is that I want you with me and I think it's a really good time for me to be a bit more settled, for my career and image. Come to LA with me next week, and not just for a few weeks. I want you to move in with me and you can come wherever I'm shooting the film too. Don't worry about studying and that crap. It doesn't matter; you'll never have to work.' He spoke without looking away from the fire-eaters.

There, he had said it! He had offered her the chance of a lifetime: live with him and join his world, become as famous as him. She could tell by the expression on his face that he knew she would say yes. He pulled her towards him to hug her.

Over Katrina's shoulder, Dominic saw Cheryl Hutton,

the supermodel he had screwed earlier that year, staring at him. She winked and smiled seductively. His mouth curved up at the corners as he watched her playing with the diamond necklace he had given her, before he had stopped returning her increasingly frantic phone calls. She beckoned him over, but he shook his head and mouthed, 'I'll come and find you later.'

Over Dominic's shoulder, Katrina saw James walking alone through the patio doors. Zora was nowhere to be seen. She looked at the coke-fuelled people, all dancing wildly. Alex raised a glass when he caught her eye; his girlfriend was sniffing coke from a mirror balanced on her knee. It wasn't what Katrina had expected from being in such a supposedly A-list world. Maybe the dream had changed somewhere along the line, or maybe the image had been rubbed away to reveal a life that wasn't as perfect as it seemed. She hadn't been at all comfortable with Dominic, nor with the people who were part of his life; it felt like she was the one acting the whole time, pretending to be someone she wasn't. She pulled away from Dominic and noticed Cheryl Hutton walking by, giving her a filthy look. Instantly Katrina made a decision that she hadn't ever thought she would make; she had always assumed it would be Dominic who would decide when he was finished with her.

'I'm sorry, Dominic. I don't want to go to LA. I really have had fun with you, but I think it's probably best that this ends now. I'm going to get a flight home; I'll be gone by the time you get back to the hotel. Thank you for everything. Take care.' She kissed him on the cheek, took a deep breath and walked away. Out of the villa, out of this strange and uncomfortable life, and out of the dream.

Dominic stood with his mouth open, stunned, quite unable to comprehend what had happened. Had Katrina just finished with him? It was unbelievable! He had never expected that to happen. How could she have turned him down? Surely it couldn't really be anything to do with James. He felt like going after her and demanding to know why she didn't want to be with him. He had chosen her because he liked her, really liked her. When he had first seen her she didn't measure up to the stunning women he had been with and he only invited her out as she seemed a bit of a challenge, but oddly, the more he got to know her, the more beautiful and intriguing she had become, whereas he usually got bored once he had scratched beneath the perfect images that the others presented him with. As he had watched her standing on the steps looking at James, he had suddenly realised just how special she was. Dominic rubbed his hand over his face and went to go after her.

Then he stopped to think about it and realised he was actually quite humiliated. He had been dumped! Dominic Cayley didn't get dumped! What kind of an idiot was she? He had just offered her the chance of a lifetime and she had walked away. Was she crazy? Imagine if the press got hold of it. All his friends, including Alex, would laugh their heads off and he'd never live it down. He walked slowly down to the garden, trying to light a cigarette, until he realised that he had put it in his mouth the wrong way round. He sat down on the edge of a little wall and managed to light it before coughing on the smoke when he inhaled too heavily.

He became aware that he was not alone, and looking up, he found Zora watching him.

'What?' he asked gruffly. 'Why are you just standing there?'

'I was here before you got here!' she retorted indignantly. He took a drag of his cigarette and offered it to her. 'Katrina's gone, then?' He nodded, frowning. She came forward and took the cigarette from him before dropping to her knees and unzipping his jeans, burying her face in his lap.

Dominic momentarily thought about stopping her. Then he moaned in pleasure and leant back. There was no better way of forgetting than moving on, and he could always tell everyone that he had finished with Katrina because of Zora.

37

Katrina opened the door to the suite and went straight to her room, where she threw her clothes into a bag. As she tidied up Dominic's T-shirt and jeans that he had been wearing that day, something fell out of the back pocket. Picking it up, she saw the Polaroid that he had insisted on the photographer taking the day he picked her up from the studio. In it, Katrina was looking up at him and he was smiling charmingly into the lens. But his expression was slightly bored, and she was looking adoringly at him, rather like the picture she had seen on the wall in Loretta's bathroom. She knew now that she had made the right choice. Whilst it had been an amazing few weeks, if she had gone to LA with him she would have lost who she was. She slipped the photo into her bag as a reminder and left the room.

At the airport, she managed to book a flight for six a.m. It was already one, so she settled on an uncomfortable chair and spent the next few hours trying to sleep, but failing. By the time her flight was announced she felt awful and did not dare look in a mirror. Instead she put on sunglasses and queued up to board. She began to feel quite miserable, picturing James and Zora, Dominic and probably some girl he had picked up at the party returning to the hotel to find her gone and not being bothered. She would just be known as that English girl

Dominic had once screwed, and she knew he would tell everyone that it was he who had got rid of her. What did it matter? Who cared what other people thought, as long as she had made her decision and it was the right one, which she knew it was.

The aeroplane was half empty, and as soon as she got to her seat she shut her eyes and tried to sleep. It was impossible, though, as her head was spinning. She flicked through a discarded magazine and saw a picture of the two of them at the premiere, her looking uncomfortable as Dominic waved to the crowd. She felt immense relief that she would not be doing that again. The magazine slid to the floor and she shut her eyes. She felt sad, but not about Dominic.

'Excuse me, is this seat taken?' a familiar male voice asked.

Her eyes opened immediately. He was looking down at her, his expression serious. Katrina nodded incredulously and he sat down.

'What are you doing on this flight?' she whispered. 'I thought you'd be at the hotel with Zora.'

'Why would I be with Zora?'

'But I thought you liked her.'

He smiled widely so the laughter lines around his eyes deepened. 'I do like Zora. Despite all her craziness and silly games she is a survivor, and she's not a bad person, just a little screwy. I certainly never saw her in that way, though. I left the party early and went for a drink with a business friend who I knew was in town. When I got back to the party I found Dominic, who told me that you'd gone.' He did not say any more. He didn't tell Katrina that he had found Zora all over Dominic, and that Dominic had told him angrily that he was responsible for Katrina leaving, and that they no longer had a friendship. He had already known, or rather hoped that to be the case.

Katrina rested her head on James's shoulder and sighed. While it might not be her original dream coming true, it was certainly perfect for her. Dominic was every girl's fantasy, but James had been her hero, rescuing her from the very beginning.

'Personally, I am glad it's all over,' James said, looking out of the window as the plane took off. 'How about we go for a bloody decent meal when we get back? I'm starving, and you look far too skinny.' He leant over and removed her sunglasses. 'By the way, has anyone ever told you that you look best wearing jeans and no make-up?'

little black dress

**brings you fantastic new books like these
every month - find out more at
www.littleblackdressbooks.com**

Why not link up with other devoted Little Black
Dress fans on our Facebook group? Simply type
Little Black Dress Books into Facebook to join up.

And if you want to be the first
to hear the latest news on all things
Little Black Dress, just send the details below to
littleblackdressmarketing@headline.co.uk
and we'll sign you up to our lovely email
newsletter (and we promise that we won't share
your information with anybody else!).*

Name: _____

Email Address: _____

Date of Birth: _____

Region/Country: _____

What's your favourite Little Black Dress book?

_____

How many Little Black Dress books have you read?_____

*You can be removed from the mailing list at any time

You can buy any of these other
Little Black Dress titles from your
bookshop or *direct from the publisher*.

FREE P&P AND UK DELIVERY
(Overseas and Ireland £3.50 per book)

Girl From Mars	Julie Cohen	£5.99
True Love and Other Disasters	Rachel Gibson	£5.99
The Hen Night Prophecies: The One That Got Away	Jessica Fox	£5.99
The Fidelity Project	Susan Conley	£5.99
Leopard Rock	Tarras Wilding	£5.99
Smart Casual	Niamh Shaw	£5.99
Animal Instincts	Nell Dixon	£5.99
It Should Have Been Me	Phillipa Ashley	£5.99
Dogs and Goddesses	Jennifer Crusie, Anne Stuart, Lani Diane Rich	£5.99
Sugar and Spice	Jules Stanbridge	£5.99
Italian for Beginners	Kristin Harmel	£5.99
The Girl Most Likely To . . .	Susan Donovan	£5.99
The Farmer Needs a Wife	Janet Gover	£5.99
Hide Your Eyes	Alison Gaylin	£5.99
Living Next Door to Alice	Marisa Mackle	£4.99
Today's Special	A.M. Goldsher	£4.99
Risky Business	Suzanne Macpherson	£4.99
Truly Madly Yours	Rachel Gibson	£4.99
Right Before Your Eyes	Ellen Shanman	£4.99
The Trophy Girl	Kate Lace	£4.99

TO ORDER SIMPLY CALL THIS NUMBER

01235 400 414

or visit our website: www.headline.co.uk

Prices and availability subject to change without notice.